EVERYMAN,

I WILL GO WITH THEE,

AND BE THY GUIDE,

IN THY MOST NEED

TO GO BY THY SIDE

EVERYMAN'S POCKET CLASSICS

STORIES OF SOUTHERN ITALY

EDITED BY ELLA CARR

EVERYMAN'S POCKET CLASSICS
Alfred A. Knopf New York London Toronto

THIS IS A BORZOI BOOK
PUBLISHED BY ALFRED A. KNOPF

This selection by Ella Carr first published in
Everyman's Library, 2022
Copyright © 2022 by Everyman's Library

A list of acknowledgments to copyright owners appears at
the back of this volume.

All rights reserved. Published in the United States by Alfred A. Knopf,
a division of Penguin Random House LLC, New York, and in
Canada by Penguin Random House Canada Limited, Toronto.
Distributed by Penguin Random House LLC, New York. Published
in the United Kingdom by Everyman's Library, 50 Albemarle Street,
London W1S 4BD and distributed by Penguin Random House UK,
20 Vauxhall Bridge Road, London SW1V 2SA.

everymanslibrary.com
www.everymanslibrary.co.uk

ISBN 978-0-593-53551-6 (US)
978-1-84159-633-4 (UK)

A CIP catalogue reference for this book is available from the
British Library

Typography by Peter B. Willberg

Typeset in the UK by Input Data Services Ltd, Isle Abbotts, Somerset

Printed and bound in Germany by GGP Media GmbH, Pössneck

Contents

CALABRIA

BASILICATA

APULIA

CAMPANIA

8

PREFACE

The story of Southern Italy, and perhaps the rest of Europe, begins in Sicily. It is, as Goethe put it, 'the clue to everything'. Famed for its extreme natural beauty and proverbial fertility, no part of Europe has been dominated by a greater number of races – the Phoenicians, Greeks, Romans, Goths, Byzantines, Arabs, Normans and Spanish among them – each of whom have left their traces in the island's cultural DNA. As one of its greatest writers, Leonardo Sciascia, observed, the palimpsestic culture of Sicily can be seen as 'a metaphor for the entire world'.

In his novel *The Skin*, Curzio Malaparte attaches similar primordial significance to the ancient city of Naples: 'that terrible, wonderful prototype of an unknown Europe, situated outside the realm of Cartesian logic – that *other* Europe of whose existence he [the American protagonist, Colonel Jack] had until that day had only a vague suspicion, and whose mysteries and secrets . . . filled him with a wondrous terror.' This 'wondrous terror', I would argue, speaks to the baroque sensibility of the whole of Southern Italy. If Florence and Rome represent the light and reason of Italy's Renaissance, the *Mezzogiorno* is its primeval underbelly, both more beautiful and more terrible.

Southern Italy is characterized by extremes of light and dark, the unutterable beauty of its landscape sitting side by side with its legacy of violence and suffering. After Italian unification in 1871, the Southern economy suffered greatly;

brigandage, poverty and organized crime, already longstanding issues, became entrenched, with economic difficulties persisting throughout the twentieth century.

These poles of light and dark are reflected in the literature from this region. Like a Dutch *vanitas* portrait, Peter Robb's almost indecently voluptuous description of Palermo's food market captures Sicily in all its unbridled vitality, while simultaneously auguring death and decay – a metaphor for the ever-present threat of the mafia. This double-edged sword of beauty and horror haunts many of the stories in this anthology, of Sciascia, Somerset Maugham, Dacia Maraini and Elena Ferrante among others, as do the themes of corruption, hardship and injustice.

Exile and return is another running theme. Vito Teti's 'Clouds and Back Streets', based on his hometown in Calabria, explores the experience of being left behind following the mass emigration to *la merica* and Canada in the latter half of the twentieth century, which decimated much of the region and contributed to what Teti calls 'the restless and precarious state of mind of the Calabrese, of being "here and elsewhere"'. Elio Vittorini's *Conversations in Sicily*, which follows the narrator's return home after eighteen years away, is equally suffused with Proustian longing for a vanished world, and with the sounds and smells of Sicily.

The classical Greek inheritance of the *Mezzogiorno* is evident in the stories of Malaparte, Lampedusa and Elsa Morante among others. In its earliest times, Southern Italy was said to be populated by gods and demi-gods, monsters and heroes, some of whom feature in the stories of Theocritus, Virgil and Ovid: the giant Typhoeus, for example, on whose shoulders the island of Sicily creaks, the Cyclopes who inhabit the caves of Etna, as well as the infamous sea monsters Scylla and Charybdis located at the Strait of Messina.

While the travel writing Southern Italy has inspired could have filled this anthology many times over, my focus was on native Southern Italian authors, with a sprinkling of notable exceptions. The literary centres of Sicily and Campania are inevitably over-represented, but the stories from Calabria, Basilicata and Apulia should give at least a taste of the literary character of these regions. By necessity, this anthology can only skim the surface of what Southern Italy has to offer, but I hope it will set the reader on course for an odyssey of discovery that endures well beyond the final page.

Ella Carr

MYTHOGRAPHY

THEOCRITUS

THE CYCLOPS
(IDYLL XI)

Translated by R. C. Trevelyan

The race of giants known as the Cyclopes have always been linked to Mount Etna in Greek and Roman mythology. Unlike the savage cannibal famously represented in Homer's Odyssey, *the Sicilian-Greek poet Theocritus writes Polyphemus in the character of a simple-minded Sicilian shepherd, tormented by his love for the sea-nymph Galateia.*

THERE IS NO other medicine, Nikias,* against Love,
Neither by way of ointment nor of plaster, take my word,
Save the Pierian Muses. A gentle remedy
And sweet is that for men to use, yet very hard to find.
Well indeed must you know this, physician as you are,
And dearly loved beyond all others by the Muses nine.
'Twas thus at least our countryman the Cyclops eased his
        pain,
That Polyphemus of old time, when he loved Galateia,
And upon cheek and lips as yet his beard was scarce grown.
Not with apples nor roses did he woo, nor locks of hair,
But with sheer frenzies; all things else he reckoned as mere
        trifling.
Often from the green pastures would his sheep unshepherded
Wander back to the fold, while he, singing his Galateia,
There on the weed-strewn sea-beach all day from early dawn

* Theocritus addresses the poem to his lovesick friend, the physician
Miletus.

17

Would sit and pine, nursing within his breast a cruel wound,
Dealt him by mighty Cypris, whose shaft had pierced his
heart.
Nevertheless that cure he found; and seated on the crest
Of a tall rock, and gazing towards the sea, thus would
he sing:
  'O white Galateia, wherefore thus cast off the man who
  loves you?
Whiter to look upon than curds, more delicate than a lamb,
Than a young calf more skittish, plumper than ripening
grape!
Wherefore do you keep coming thus, whene'er sweet
slumber takes me,
Only to vanish straight, whene'er sweet slumber lets me go,
Fleeing me swifter than a ewe, when the gray wolf she spies?
  I fell in love with you, dear maid, that very day when
  first
You came here with my mother,* to gather iris flowers
Upon the mountain, and 'twas I went with you as your
guide.
Thenceforth, once having seen you, I could not cease to love,
Nor can I yet. But naught you care, no by Zeus, naught
at all.
  I know, beautiful maiden, why it is you shun me thus.
It is because from one ear to the other, right across
The whole width of my forehead, one long shaggy eyebrow
runs,
With but one eye beneath; and broad is the nose above my
lip.
Nevertheless, though I be such, a thousand sheep I feed,

---

* The parents of Polyphemus were Poseidon and the sea-nymph
Thoösa.

And from these do I draw and drink milk of the very best.
And cheese neither in summer nor in autumn do I lack,
Nor in winter's depth, but always overladen are my crates.
Then I am skilled in piping as no other Cyclops here,
And of thee, my dear sweet apple, and of myself I sing
Many a time at dead of night. Moreover eleven fawns
I am rearing for you, all with brows crescent-marked, and
    four bear-cubs.
  Nay, come to me, and nothing, that is yours now, shall
    you lack.
Leave the blue breakers of the sea to gasp against the land.
More sweetly will you pass the night beside me in my cave.
There do laurels grow, and there the slender cypress trees,
There the dark ivy, there the vine with its sweet clustering
    grapes;
There are cool streams of water, that from her white snows
    drawn
Forest-girt Etna sends me hither, an ambrosial drink.
To such delights who would prefer the sea-waves for a
    home?
  But if my body seem too rough and shaggy for your
    taste,
Well, neath the ashes on my hearth oak-logs are ever
    smouldering,
And gladly would I suffer you to singe my very soul,
And this one eye of mine, the dearest treasure I possess.
Ah me, would that my mother at my birth had given
    me gills,
That so I might have dived down to your side and kissed
    your hand,
If your lips you would not let me: and I had brought
    you then
Either white snowdrops, or the soft, scarlet-petalled poppy.

Nay, but these blow in summer, those in the winter months.
So I could never bring you both these kinds at the same
        time.
But now, my darling maiden, now I'll learn at least to swim
(If hither sailing on a ship some stranger chance to come),
And so discover why you love to dwell thus in the deep.
    Oh come forth, Galateia, and coming straight forget,
Even as I now sitting here, to go back to your home.
Be content to go shepherding and milk the flocks with me,
And learn to set the cheeses, pouring tart rennet in.
It is my mother alone who wrongs me; yes, 'tis her I blame.
Never once has she spoken to you one kind word for me,
And that although day after day she saw me wasting
        thinner.
I'll tell her that my head and both my feet with pain are
        throbbing.
Thus will I make her suffer, since I am suffering too.
    O Cyclops, Cyclops, whither are your wits gone
        wandering?
Nay go and weave your baskets, and gather tender shoots
To feed your lambs. If you did that, far wiser would you be.
Milk the ewe that's beneath your hand. Why pursue one
        who shuns you?
You'll find perchance another and a fairer Galateia.
Many are the girls that call to me to play with them by
        night,
And each of them laughs softly, if I deign to give ear.
It's plain enough, I too on land seem to be somebody.'
    Well, thus it was that Polyphemus shepherded his love
With song, and found ease better so than if he had spent
        gold.

20

VIRGIL

HELENUS' WARNING

From

THE AENEID (BOOK III)

Translated by Robert Fitzgerald

*Aeneas and his Trojan fleet arrive in Buthrotum where they are
welcomed by the warrior and seer Helenus, a fellow countryman
and son of Priam. In this passage Helenus advises Aeneas on how
best to avoid the perils along the coast of Sicily in his journey to
consult the famous sibyl of Cumae, near modern-day Naples.*

Helenus cut down bullocks at his altar
With ceremony, begged the gods for peace,
Unbound the sacred ribbons from his head,
And took me by the hand, leading me in
A-tingle at the overshadowing power—
O Phoebus! in thy shrine;
Then with oracular voice the priest addressed me:

'Born of the goddess, highest auspices
Are clearly to be seen for your sea faring,
The Lord God deals out destiny so
And turns the wheel of change; so turns the world.
A few things, out of many, shall I tell you,
So you may cross the welcoming seas
More safely, to find harbor in Ausonia;
Other details of time to come the Parcae
Keep from Helenus, and Saturn's daughter,
Juno, will not allow him speech of these.

23

That Italy you think so near, with ports
You think to enter, ignorant as you are,
Lies far, past far lands, by untraveled ways.
You are to make the oar bend off Trinacria,
To pass Ausonian water, lakes of the underworld,
The island home of Circe the Aeaean,
Before your walls can rise in a safe country.
Here are signs for you to keep in mind:
When in anxiety by a stream apart
Beneath shore oaks you find a giant sow,
Snow white, reclining there, suckling a litter
Of thirty snow-white young: that place will be
Your haven after toil, site of your town.
And have no fear of table-biting times;
The fates will find a way for you; Apollo
Will be at hand when called.

       But now avoid
The shoreline to the west, a part of Italy
Lapped by the tide of our own sea: the towns
Are all inhabited by evil Greeks.
Here the Locrians founded a colony
And Lyctian Idomeneus with soldiers
Took the Sallentine Plain; here is that town
Of Philoctetes, captain of Meliboea,
Little Petelia, buttressed by her wall.
Another thing: when you have crossed and moored
Your ships ashore, there to put up your altars
For offerings, veil your head in a red robe
Against intrusions on your holy fires,
Omen-unsettling sights amid your prayers.
You and your company retain this ritual
Veiling in the future, let your progeny
Hold to religious purity thereby.

24

Now then: at sea again, as the wind takes you
Toward the Sicilian shore, and headlands northward
Dwindle up the Narrows of Pelorus,
Steer for the coast to port, the seas to port,
A long sail round, away from shores to starboard.
These land-masses in the past, they say,
Though one unbroken mainland long ago,
In cataclysm leaped apart: a change
That the long ages of the past could bring—
The sea rushed in between, to cut away
Hesperia's flank from Sicily, and washed
With narrow tide the sundered shores and towns.
Now Scylla haunts the starboard side, Charybdis,
Never appeased, the side to port—and deep
In her whirlpool gulps down the great sea waves
Three times a day and spews them up again,
Sending the whiplash of her spray to heaven.
Scylla lies immured in a rocky cave
In clefts of inky darkness, darting out
Her faces, pulling ships on to the reef.
First she looks human—a fair-breasted girl
Down to the groin; but then, below, a monster
Creature of the sea, a wolvish belly
Merging in dolphins' tails. Better to round
The seamark of Pachynus, and stand out
To sea, taking the long route west, than sight
Weird Scylla in her overhanging gloom
And froth of rocks where sea-green hounds give tongue.
Further, if Helenus can look ahead,
If you can trust a seer, and if Apollo
Fills his mind with truth, I have one thing
To tell you, over and over again, one thing
To warn you of, son of the goddess: make

Your prayer first of all to Juno's godhead,
Chant with a will your vows to her: secure
With humble gifts the power of that lady,
So in the end in triumph, with Trinacria
Left behind, you will be sent to Italy.
Ashore there, when you reach the town of Cumae,
Avernus' murmuring forests, haunted lakes,
You'll see a spellbound prophetess, who sings
In her deep cave of destinies, confiding
Symbols and words to leaves. Whatever verse
She writes, the virgin puts each leaf in order
Back in the cave; unshuffled they remain;
But when a faint breeze through a door ajar
Comes in to stir and scatter the light leaves,
She never cares to catch them as they flutter
Or to restore them, or to join the verses;
Visitors, unenlightened, turn away
And hate the Sibyl's shrine.
                              But here no thought
Of time spent in delay should count with you—
Though crews reproach you, though the course you set
Call seaward now, and you can fill your sails
With wind in the right quarter, even so
Pray to the prophetess that she herself
Consent to utter and chant her oracles.
She will inform you of the Italian tribes,
The wars to come, the way you should avoid
Each difficulty, or face it. Do her reverence
And she will bring you through, by sea and land.
These are the matters I may warn you of.
Go, and exalt the might of Troy in action.'

OVID

THE RAPE OF PROSERPINA

From

THE METAMORPHOSES

(BOOK V)

Translated by Allen Mandelbaum

' "THE ISLAND MASS of Sicily is heaped
upon a giant's body: underneath
its soil and stones Typhoeus lies – the one
who dared to hope for heaven as his kingdom.
He writhes; he often tries to rise again.
But Mount Pelorus (closest to the land
of the Italians) crushes his right hand;
his left is in Pachynus' grip, just as
his legs are in Mount Lilybaeum's grasp;
his head is pressed – vast Etna holds it fast.
Beneath this mountain, on his back, in rage,
Typhoeus' mouth spits ashes, vomits flames.
He often strives to heave aside the ground –
the towns and heavy peaks that pin him down.
Then earth quakes. As it trembles, even he
who rules the kingdom of the silent dead
is anxious, for the crust of Sicily
may split and a wide crack reveal things secret:
daylight might penetrate so deep that it
would terrify the trembling Shades. His fear
of such disaster led that lord of darkness
to leave his sunless kingdom. Mounted on
his chariot – it was drawn by two black stallions –
he carefully assessed the island mass.
When he was sure that there were no vast cracks,
that Sicily was everywhere intact,

his fears were ended. Then, as Pluto rode
from site to site, down from her mountain slopes
of Eryx, Venus saw him. As she clasped
her winged son, Cupid, this is what she asked:

' " 'O you, my son, my weapon and my armor,
dear Cupid – you, my power – take those shafts
to which both gods and mortals must submit;
with one of your swift arrows pierce the chest
of Pluto – god who, when the lots were cast,
assigning the three realms, received the last.
You conquer and command sky-deities –
not even Jove is free from your decrees;
sea-gods are governed by your rule – and he
who is the god of gods who rule the sea.
And why should Tartarus elude our laws?
Why not extend your mother's power – and yours?
One-third of all the world is still not ours.
We have been slow to act, but indecision
has earned us nothing more than scorn in heaven.
And – son – if my authority should weaken,
then yours would suffer, too. Do you not see
how both Athena and the hunting goddess,
Diana, would defy me? And the daughter
of Ceres, if we let her choose, will be
like them: she is so bent on chastity.
But for the sake of all I share with you,
please join that goddess-girl, Proserpina,
to her great uncle, Pluto.' This, she asked.
Love, opening his quiver – he respects
his mother – from his thousand shafts selects
the sharpest, surest shaft – the arrow most
responsive to the pressure of his bow.

Across his knee, the pliant bow is bent;
Love's hooked barb pierces Pluto through the chest.
*

' "Not far from Enna's walls there are deep waters.
That lake – called Pergus – hears a music richer,
more songs of swans, than even the Cayster
hears as its current courses. Tall hills circle
that lake. Woods crown the slopes – and like a veil,
the forest boughs abate the flames of Phoebus.
Beneath those leaves, the air is cool, the soil
is damp – with many flowers, many colors.
There spring is never-ending. In that grove
Proserpina was playing, gathering
violets and white lilies. She had filled
her basket and, within her tunic's folds,
had tucked fresh flowers, vying with her friends
to see which girl could gather more of them.
There Pluto – almost in one instant – saw,
was struck with longing, carried that girl off –
so quick – unhesitating – was his love.

' "The goddess-girl was terrified. She called –
in grief – upon her mother and companions,
but more upon her mother. She had ripped
her tunic at its upper edge, and since
the folds were loosened now, the flowers fell.
So simple is the heart of a young girl
that, at that loss, new grief is what she felt.
Her captor urged his chariot, incited
his horses, calling each by name and shaking
the dark-rust reins upon their necks and manes.
He galloped over the deep lake and through
the pools of the Palici, where the soil

spews fumes of sulfur and the waters boil.
He reached that place where the Bacchiadae –
a race that came from Corinth, which is bathed
by seas upon two sides – had built their city
between two harbors of unequal size.

' "Between the spring of Cyane and the spring
of Arethusa (which had flowed from Greece),
there is a stretch of sea that is hemmed in,
confined between two narrow horns of land.
Among those waves lived Cyane, Sicily's
most celebrated nymph, and she had given
her name to that lagoon. Above the eddies,
just at the center, Cyane rose, waist-high.
She recognized Proserpina and cried:
'Pluto, you cannot pass. You cannot be
the son-in-law of Ceres unless she
gives her consent. To ask is not to rape.
And if I may compare small things to great,
I, too, was wooed – by Anapis – but I
wed him in answer to his prayers and pleas –
he never used the terror you abuse.'
That said, she stretched her arms upon both sides
to block his chariot. But Saturn's son
could not contain his anger any longer:
he spurred his terrifying stallions, whirled
his royal scepter with his sturdy arm.
He struck the very depths of Cyane's pool.
The blow was such that, down to Tartarus,
earth opened up a crater: on that path
he plunged to darkness in his chariot.

' "But Cyane nursed an inconsolable –
a silent – wound that was incurable:
a sadness for the rape of Ceres' daughter
and for the violation of the waters
of her own pool – for Pluto's scorn and anger.
She gave herself to tears and then dissolved
into the very pool of which she had –
till now – been the presiding deity.
You could have seen the softening of her limbs,
the bones and nails that lost solidity.
Her slender hairs, her fingers, legs, and feet –
these were the first to join the waves. In fact,
the slenderest parts can sooner turn into
cool waters. Shoulders, back, and sides, and breasts
were next to vanish in thin streams. At last,
clear water flows through Cyane's weakened veins,
and there is nothing left that one can grasp.
*

' "Meanwhile, the heartsick Ceres seeks her daughter:
she searches every land, all waves and waters.
No one – not Dawn with her dew-laden hair,
nor Hesperus – saw Ceres pause. She kindled
two pinewood torches in the flames of Etna.
Through nights of frost, a torch in either hand,
she wandered. Ceres never rested. When
the gracious day had dimmed the stars, again
the goddess searched from west to east, from where
the sun would set to where the sun ascends . . .

' "To tell the lands and seas that Ceres crossed
would take too long: the world was not enough
to satisfy the searching mother. She
returned to Sicily, explored again

each part. She reached the pool of Cyane.
If Cyane had not been changed, she now
would have told Ceres all she knew; but while
she longs to speak, she lacks a tongue to tell.

' "Yet Cyane transmitted one sure clue:
upon the surface of her waters floats
the girdle that Proserpina had worn;
that girdle – one that Ceres knew so well –
had chanced to fall into the sacred pool.
No sooner had she recognized that sign,
than Ceres – as if now, for the first time,
she knew her daughter had been stolen – tore
her unkempt hair; her hands beat at her breast
again, again. She did not know as yet
just where her daughter was, but she condemned
all lands. She said they were ungrateful and
unworthy of the gift of harvests she
had given them – above all, Sicily,
the place that showed the trace of the misdeed.
And there, in Sicily, she – without pity –
shattered the plows that turned the soil; her fury
brought death to both the farmers and their cattle.
She spoiled the seeds; she ordered the plowed fields
to fail; she foiled the hope and trust of mortals.
Now Sicily's fertility – renowned
throughout the world – appears to be a lie:
as soon as grass is in the blade, it dies,
undone by too much rain or too much sun.
The stars and winds bring blight; the greedy birds
devour the seed as soon as it is sown;
the crop is blocked by chokeweeds, tares, and thorns.
Then Arethusa, whom Alpheus loved,

lifted her head above her waters – these
had flowed to Sicily from Grecian Elis.
She brushed her dripping hair back from her brow
and said: 'O Ceres, mother of the girl
you seek throughout the world, you, mother of
earth's fruits and grain, forgo your fury, end
your devastating violence. This land
does not deserve your scourging: it was forced
to yield before the bandit's brutal course.
And I do not beseech you on behalf
of my own homeland. I was not born here:
I come from Pisa, in the land of Elis.
My origins were there – yet Sicily
is dearer to me than all other countries.
I, Arethusa, have a newfound home:
sweet Sicily is now my country – and,
kind Ceres, may your mercy save this island.

' " 'Why I have left my homeland, why I crossed
so vast a stretch of sea until I touched
Ortygia – there will yet be time enough
to speak of that, a time when you are free
of cares, a moment of tranquillity.
But I can tell you now my journey's path:
earth, opening a chasm, let me pass.
I flowed through caverns deep below the surface,
then – here – I lifted up my head again,
again I saw the stars I had forgotten.
But in my passage underneath the earth
among the eddies of the Styx, I saw
Proserpina with my own eyes: she was
downcast, still somewhat touched by fear – and yet
she was a queen within that world of darkness,

the powerful companion – mighty mistress –
of Pluto, tyrant of the underworld.'

' "Hearing these things, the mother, Ceres, stood
as motionless as stone. Long moments passed:
her mind seemed lost. When that paralysis
of fear had given way to grief no less
oppressive, Ceres, on her chariot,
rode toward the upper air. With shadowed eyes,
her hair disheveled, hate-inflamed, she cried:
'For one who is of both your blood and mine,
o Jupiter, I come to plead with you.
Though I, her mother, do not matter, you
at least can care to save your daughter – I
should hope your care will not be any less
because she owes her birth to me. Our daughter,
after so long a search, is found – if one
can speak of finding when it just confirms
the loss more certainly, when finding means
no more than merely knowing where she is.
As for his theft of her – that I can bear –
he only has to give her back! My daughter
is mine no longer, but you cannot let
a robber win her as his wife – through theft.'

' "Then Jupiter replied: 'We share the care
and tenderness we owe to our dear daughter.
But if we would have things named properly,
then we must speak of love, not injury
or robbery. We should not be ashamed
of Pluto as a son-in-law – if only
you, goddess, would consent to that. Were he
to lack all else, it is no meager thing

to be the brother of a Jupiter!
But he, in fact, has many other splendors:
the portion of the world assigned to him
is, after all, a kingdom, only less
than what my portion is – and only chance
assigned this part to me and that to him.
In any case, if you are so intent
on separating them, Proserpina
can see the sky again – on one condition:
that in the world below, she has not taken
food to her lips. This is the Fates' edict.'

' "These were his words. And yet, though Ceres wanted
to bring her daughter back, the Fates prevented
Proserpina's return, for she had broken
her fast: the girl, in all her innocence,
while she was wandering through a well-kept garden
within the underworld, from a bent branch
had plucked a pomegranate. She had taken –
peeling away its pale rind – seven seeds
and pressed them to her lips. No one had seen
that act of hers – except Ascalaphus
(the son, they say, that Orphne – not the least
famous among Avernus' nymphs – conceived
out of her love for Acheron, and bore
within the dark groves of the underworld).
He saw her taste those seeds: denouncing her,
he thwarted her return to earth. She moaned –
the queen of Erebus. Then, in revenge,
she changed that witness. He was made a bird
of evil omen: on his head she poured
waters of Phlegethon. Enormous eyes
and beak and feathers now are his. Deprived

of what he was, he now wears tawny wings;
his head is swollen, and his nails grow long
and hook back, forming claws; and it is hard
for him to move the feathers that now sprout
upon his sluggish arms. He has become
the bird that men detest – that would announce
calamities. He is the lazy screech-owl,
bringer of bitter auguries to mortals.

' "Ascalaphus indeed seems to have earned
his punishment – his tongue was indiscreet.
But, Achelous' daughters, why do you,
as Sirens, have birds' feathers and birds' feet –
and features like a girl's? Is it because
you, Sirens skilled in song, had been among
the band of friends who joined Proserpina
when she was gathering spring flowers near Enna?
For after you – in vain – had searched all lands
for her, so that the waves might also witness
that search for one you loved, you voiced a plea
to be allowed to glide above the sea,
using your arms as oars to beat the air.
You found the gods were well disposed to answer:
your limbs were wrapped – at once – in golden feathers.
But you were mesmerizing, suasive singers,
born to entrance the ears; and that your lips
not lose that gift, each one of you was left
with young girl's features and a human voice.
*

' "And what did Jupiter do then? Between
his brother Pluto and his grieving sister,
he has to strike a balance: he divides
the turning year into two equal portions.

Proserpina is shared by the two kingdoms:
the goddess is to spend six months beside
her husband, and six months beside her mother.
At once, the goddess' face and spirit alter:
her brow, which until then seemed overcast
even to somber Pluto, now is glad,
just as, when it defeats the dark rainclouds,
the sun appears – victorious and proud.

SICILY

GIOVANNI VERGA

HIS REVERENCE
(1883)

Translated by D. H. Lawrence

HE DIDN'T HAVE his monk's long beard any more, nor his poor friar's hood, now that he got himself shaved every Sunday, and went out walking in his grand cassock of fine cloth, with his silk-lined cloak over his arm. And on those occasions when he was looking at his own fields, and his own vineyards, and his own flocks, and his own labourers, with his hands in his pockets and his little pipe in his mouth, if he ever did chance to recall the days when he washed up dishes for the Capucin monks and they out of charity put on him a lay-brother's long frock, he would make the sign of the cross with his left hand.

Yet if they hadn't taught him to say mass and to read and write, all out of charity, he would never have succeeded in wedging himself in among the first families of the place, nor in nailing down in his account books the names of all those half-profits peasants who laboured and prayed to God and good fortune for him, and then swore like Turks when it came to reckoning day. 'Mind what I am, not what I was once,' says the proverb. Who he was, everybody knew, for his mother still did his house-cleaning. His Reverence had no family pride, no; and when he went to the baroness's to play at piquet with her, he had his brother to wait in the anteroom for him, holding the lantern.

His charity began at home, as God Himself enjoins; so he's taken one of his nieces into his house, not bad-looking, but without a rag to her back, so that she'd never have found

45

the ghost of a husband; and he kept her and maintained her, what's more he put her in the fine room with glass in the windows, and the bed with bed-curtains, and he wasn't going to have her work, to ruin her hands with rough jobs. So that everybody thought it a real God's penalty when the poor creature was seized with scruples, such as will happen to women who have nothing else to do and pass their days in church beating their breasts because they're in mortal sin – though not when her uncle was there, for he wasn't one of those priests who like to show themselves on the altar in pomp and splendour before their inamoratas. As for other women, outside their homes it was enough for him to give them a little caress with two fingers on their cheek, paternally, or through the little window of the confession box to give them the benediction after they had rinsed out their consciences and emptied the sack of their own and other people's sins, by which means he always learned something useful, being a man who speculated in country produce.

Blessed Lord, he didn't pretend to be a holy man, not he! Holy men died of hunger, like the vicar who celebrated mass even when he wasn't paid for it, and went round the beggarly houses in a cassock so tattered that it was a scandal to Religion. His Reverence wanted to get on, and he got on, with the wind full-sail, at first a little bit scuttling, because of that blessed frock which bothered him, so much so that for pitching it into the vegetable garden he had been had up before the Monastic Tribunal, and the confraternity had helped him to get the better of it, so as to be rid of him, because so long as he was in the monastery there were stools and dishes flying at every election of provincials; Father Battistino, a servant of God sturdy as a muleteer, had been half slaughtered, and Father Giammaria, the superior, had

46

lost all his teeth in the fray. His Reverence, himself, kept mum in his cell, after he'd stirred up the fire, and in that way he'd managed to become a reverend, with all his teeth, which were of good use to him; and everybody said to Father Giammaria, who had been the one to take this scorpion into their sleeve, 'Good for him!'

But Father Giammaria, good soul, chewing his lips with his bare gums, replied:

'Well, what do you want! He was never cut out for a Capucin friar. He's like Pope Sixtus, who started by being a swineherd and then became what he was. Didn't you see what promise he gave as a boy?'

And so Father Giammaria remained superior of the Capucin friars, without a shirt on his back or a cent in his pocket, hearing confession for the love of God, and cooking vegetable soup for the poor.

His Reverence, as a boy, when he saw his brother – the one with the lantern – breaking his back hoeing in the fields, and his sisters unable to find a husband even if they'd give themselves away for nothing, and his mother spinning worsted yarn in the dark so as to save the floating-wick lamp, had said: 'I want to be a priest!'

They had sold the mule and the scrap of land in order to send him to school, in the hope that if they got so far as to have a priest in the house, it would be better than the patch of land and the mule. But it took more than that to keep him at the seminary. And so the boy began to buzz round the monastery for them to take him as a novice; and one day when they were expecting the provincial, and there was a lot to do in the kitchen, they called him in to lend a hand. Father Giammaria, who had a good heart, said to him: 'You like it here? Then you stop with us.'

And Brother Carmelo, the porter, in the long hours when

he had nothing to do, wearying of sitting on the low wall of the cloister knocking his sandals one against the other, put together a bit of a frock for him out of the rags of cassocks that they'd flung on to the fig tree to scare away the sparrows. His mother, his brother, and his sister protested that if he became a friar it was all over with them, and they gave up the money that had gone for his schooling as lost, for they'd never get another halfpenny out of him. But he, who had it in his blood to be a friar, shrugged his shoulders and answered, 'You mean to tell me a fellow can't follow the vocation God has called him to?'

Father Giammaria had taken a fancy to him because he was as light as a cat in the kitchen, and the same at all the menial jobs, even in serving at mass, as if he'd never done anything else all his life long, with his eyes lowered and his lips sewed together like a seraph. Now that he no longer served at mass he still kept his lowered eyes and his sewed-up lips, when it was a question of some shady business with the gentry, or when there was occasion for him to bid in the auction of the communal lands, or to take his oath before the magistrate.

He had to take a fat oath, indeed, in 1854, at the altar, in front of the ark that holds the Sacrament, while he was saying holy mass, and people were accusing him of spreading the cholera, and wanting to make him dance for it.

'By this consecrated host that I have in my hand,' said he to the faithful who were kneeling, crouching low on to their heels, 'I am innocent, my children! Moreover I promise you the scourge shall cease within a week. Have patience!'

Yes, they had patience; perforce they had patience! Since he was well in with the judge and the force captain, and King Bomba sent him fat chickens at Easter and at Christmas, because he was so much obliged to him, they said; and

Bomba had sent him also the counterpoison, in case there did come a serious accident.

An old aunt of his whom he'd had to take under his roof so as to prevent folks talking, and who was no good for anything anymore except to eat the bread of a traitor, had uncorked the bottle for somebody else, and so had caught the cholera out and out; but her own nephew, for fear of raising people's suspicions, hadn't been able to administer the counterpoison to her.

'Give me the counterpoison; give me the counterpoison!' pleaded the old woman, who was already as black as coal, without any regard for the doctor and the lawyer who were both there, looking one another in the face embarrassed. His Reverence, with his brazen face, as if it wasn't his affair, muttered, shrugging his shoulders, 'Take no notice of her, she is delirious.'

The counterpoison, if he really had got it, had been sent to him by the king under seal of confession, and he couldn't give it to anybody. The judge himself had gone to beg it of him on his knees, for his wife who was dying, and he'd got nothing for answer from his Reverence except this:

'You may command me in life and death, dear friend; but in this business, really, I can do nothing for you.'

This was the story as everybody knew it, and since they knew that by dint of intrigues and cleverness he had managed to become the intimate friend of the king, of the judge, and of the force captain, and had managed to get a handle over the police, like the intendant himself, so that his reports arrived at Naples without ever passing through the hands of the lieutenant, nobody dared to fall out with him, and when he cast his eye upon an olive garden or piece of tilled land that was for sale, or on a lot of the communal lands that was to be leased out by auction, even the big somebodies of the place, if they dared to bid against him, did it with smooth words and smarmy phrases, offering him a pinch of snuff. Once, with the baron himself, they kept on for half a day haffling and chaffling. The baron played the sugary, and his Reverence, seated in front of him with his gown gathered between his legs, at every higher bid offered him his silver snuff-box, sighing:

'Why, whatever are you thinking of, Baron, my dear sir? Now the donkey's fallen down, we've got to get him up again.'

And so until the lot was knocked down, and the baron gave in, green with bile.

Which the peasants quite approved of, because big dogs always quarrel among themselves over a good bone, and there's never anything left for poor devils to gnaw. But what made them murmur again was that that servant of God squeezed them worse than the antichrist. Whenever they had to share with him, he had no scruple about laying hold of his neighbour's property, since he had all the implements of confession in his own hands, and if he fell into mortal sin he could give himself absolution.

'Everything depends on having a priest in the house,' they sighed. And the most well-to-do among them denied themselves the bread out of their mouths to send their son to the seminary.

'When a man works the land, he has to give himself to it completely,' said his Reverence as an excuse for himself when he had no regard for anybody. Even mass itself he wouldn't celebrate save on Sunday, when there was nothing else to do, for he wasn't one of those little priests who'd run round after the small change for the mass. He wasn't in want. So that Monsignor the Bishop, in his pastoral visit, arriving in his house and finding his breviary covered with dust, wrote on it with his finger: '*Deo gratias!*' But his Reverence had something else to do but waste his time reading his breviary, and he laughed at the monsignor's reproof. If his breviary was covered with dust, his oxen were glossy, his sheep had deep fleeces, and his wheat stood as high as a man, so that his half-profits labourers enjoyed at least the sight of it, and could build fine castles in the air on it, before they came to reckon with the master. The poor devils opened their hearts like anything. Wheat standing like magic! The Lord must have passed by it in the night! You can see it belongs to a servant of God; and that it's good to work for him who's got the mass and the benediction in his hands!

In May, in the season when they looked up into the sky to conjure away any cloud that was passing, they knew that their master was saying mass for the harvest, which was worth more than the images of saints, or the blessed seeds to drive away the evil eye or ill fortune. So it was, his Reverence didn't want them to scatter the blessed seed loaves among the wheat, because it does no good except to attract sparrows and other mischievous birds. Of images of the saints however he had pocketfuls, since he took as many as he liked from the sacristy, good ones too, and gave them to his peasants.

But at harvesttime he came on horseback, along with his brother, who served him as estate keeper, with his gun on his shoulder, and then he never stirred, but slept there, in the malaria, to look after his own interests, without bothering even about Christ. Those poor devils, who had forgotten the hard days of winter in that fine weather, stood open-mouthed when they heard the litany of their debts being recited to them. So many measures of beans that your wife came for in the time of the snow – so many bundles of kindling given to your boy – so many measures of corn advanced for seed, with interest at so much a month. – Add it up for yourself!

A swindling account! In the year of famine, after Uncle Carmenio had left his sweat and his health in his Reverence's fields, he had to leave his ass as well, come harvesttime, to pay off the debt, and went away himself empty-handed, swearing with awful words that made heaven and earth shudder. His Reverence, who wasn't there to confess him, let him say his say, and led the ass into the stable.

Since he had become rich he had discovered that his family, who had never even had bread to eat, possessed a benefice as fat as a canonry, and at the time of the abolishing of the mortmains, he had applied for the release and had definitely laid hands on the farm. Only he was annoyed at the money he had to pay for the release, and called the government a thief for not letting the property of the benefices go gratis to those whom it belonged to.

On this score of the government he had had to swallow a fair amount of bile, until 1860, when they had made the revolution, and he'd had to hide in a hole like a rat, because the peasants, all those who had had trouble with him, wanted to do him in. After that, had come the litany of the taxes, which there was no end to paying, and the very thought of it turned his wine at table into poison. Now they were setting on the Holy Father, and wanting to take away from him the temporal power. But when the pope sent out the excommunication against all those who profited by the mortmains, his Reverence felt the fly settle on his own nose, and he grumbled:

'What's the pope got to do with my property? He's got nothing to do with the temporal power.' And he went on saying mass better than ever.

The peasants went to hear his mass, but without wishing it they thought of all the robberies of the celebrant, and were distracted. Their women, while they were confessing their sins to him, couldn't help letting out to his face:

'Father, I accuse myself of having spoken ill of you who are a servant of God, because we've been without beans and without grain this winter, because of you.'

'Because of me? Do I make good weather or bad luck? Or am I to own the land so that you lot can sow it and use it to your own advantage? Have you no conscience, and no fear of God? Why have you come here to confess yourself? This is the devil tempting you, to make you lose the sacrament of penitence. When you go and get all those children of yours you never think that they're so many mouths to feed? And what fault is it of mine if then there isn't enough bread for you? Did I make you get all those children? I became a priest so as not to have any.'

However, he absolved them, because he was obliged to; but nevertheless in the heads of those rough people there still remained some confusion between the priest who raised his hand to bless in the name of God, and the master who falsified the accounts, and sent them away from the farm with their sack empty and their sickle under their arm.

'We can't do anything, we can't do anything,' muttered the poor creatures resignedly. 'The pitcher doesn't win against the stone, and we can't go to law with his Reverence, because it's he who knows the law.'

He did know it too! When they were before the judge, with a lawyer, he stopped everybody's mouth with his saying: 'The law is like this and like that.' And it was always as it suited him. In the good days gone by he laughed at his enemies and his enviers. They had bedevilled him, they had gone to the bishop, they had thrown his niece in his face, Farmer Carmenio and the ill-gotten gains, they had had mass and confession taken away from him. Very well! What then? He had no need either of the bishop or anybody. He had his own possessions, and was respected like those who lead the band in the village; he was at home with the baroness, and the more row they made about him, the worse was the scandal. The big people are never touched, not even by the bishop, and you take your hat off to them, out of prudence and love of peace.

But after heresy had triumphed, with the revolution, what good was all that to him? The peasants were learning to read and write, and could reckon up accounts better than you could yourself; the political parties were wrangling for the local government, and dividing the spoil without regard to the rest of the world; the first beggar that came along could find a gratuitous counsel, if he had a lawsuit with you, and he made you pay all the costs of the case yourself! A priest didn't count any more, neither with the judge, nor with the force captain; nowadays he couldn't even get a man put into prison on a mere hint, if they were wanting in respect to him, and he was no good any more except to say mass, and hear confession, like a public servant. The judge feared the newspapers, and public opinion, what so and so might say, and he dispensed justice like Solomon! And then even the property he'd got together with the sweat of his own brow, they envied it him, they'd thrown the evil eye on him and black magic; that bit of nourishment he ate at table gave him a great to-do in the night; while his brother, who led a hard life, and ate bread and onion, digested better than an ostrich, knowing that within a hundred years' time, when he himself was dead, he'd be his heir, and would find himself rich without lifting a finger. The mother, poor thing, was good for nothing any more, and only lived on to suffer and make others suffer, nailed down in bed with paralysis, so that she had to be waited on herself now; and his niece herself, fat, well-clad, provided with everything she could want, with nothing to do but go into church, tormented him when she took it into her head to be in mortal sin, as if he was one of those excommunicated scoundrels who had dispossessed the pope, and she had made the bishop take away mass from him.

'There's neither religion, nor justice, nor anything left!' grumbled his Reverence as he grew to be old. 'Now everybody wants to have his say. Those that have got nothing want to take what you've got from you. – "You get up, so that I can take your place!" Those that have got nothing else to do come looking for fleas in your house! They wanted to make a priest no better than a sexton, say mass and sweep the church. They don't want to do the will of God any more, that's where it is!'

LUIGI PIRANDELLO

CITRONS FROM SICILY (1900)

Translated by Stanley Appelbaum

'IS TERESINA HERE?'

The servant – still in his shirt sleeves, but with his neck already squeezed into an extremely high collar and with his sparse hair carefully dressed and arranged on his cranium – raised his thick, joined eyebrows, which resembled a displaced mustache that had been shaved off his lips and pasted up there so he wouldn't lose it, and examined from head to foot the young man standing in front of him on the staircase landing: a rustic from the look of him, with the collar of his rough overcoat raised up to his ears and his hands – purple, numbed with cold – holding a dirty little sack on one side and a small old suitcase on the other, as a counterweight.

'Who is Teresina?'

The young man first shook his head to get rid of a little water drop on the tip of his nose, then replied:

'Teresina, the singer.'

'Ah!' exclaimed the servant with a smile of ironic amazement: 'That's her name, just plain Teresina? And who are you?'

'Is she here or isn't she?' asked the young man, knitting his brows and sniffling. 'Tell her that Micuccio is here, and let me in.'

'But there's no one here,' continued the servant with his smile congealed on his lips. 'Madame Sina Marnis is still at the theater and . . .'

'Aunt Marta, too?' Micuccio interrupted him.

'Ah, you're a relative, sir? In that case, step right in, step right in . . . No one's at home. She's at the theater, too, your aunt. They won't be back before one. This is the benefit night* of your . . . what is she to you, the lady? Your cousin, perhaps?'

Micuccio stood there embarrassed for a moment.

'I'm not a relative . . . I'm Micuccio Bonavino, she knows . . . I've come on purpose from our hometown.'

Upon receiving this reply, the servant deemed it suitable above all else to take back the polite *lei* form of address and go back to the ordinary *voi*; he led Micuccio into a small unlighted room near the kitchen, where someone was snoring noisily, and said to him:

'Sit here. I'll go and get a lamp.'

Micuccio first looked in the direction from which the snoring was coming, but couldn't make out anything; then he looked into the kitchen, where the cook, aided by a scullery boy, was preparing a supper. The mingled aromas of the dishes being prepared overpowered him; their effect on him was like a heady intoxication; he had hardly eaten a thing since that morning; he had traveled from Reggio di Calabria: a night and a full day on the train.

The servant brought the lamp, and the person who was snoring in the room, behind a curtain hung from a cord between two walls, muttered sleepily:

'Who is it?'

'Hey, Dorina, get up!' the servant called. 'Look, Mr. Bonvicino is here . . .'

* The night, contractually set aside, on which a member of a dramatic or operatic troupe would perform his or her specialties and share in the box-office take.

'Bonavino,' Micuccio corrected him, as he blew on his fingers.

'Bonavino, Bonavino . . . an acquaintance of the mistress. You really sleep soundly: they ring at the door and you don't hear it . . . I have to set the table; I can't do everything myself, understand – keep an eye on the cook, who doesn't know the ropes; watch for people who come to call . . .'

A big, loud yawn from the maid, prolonged while she stretched and ending in a whinny caused by a sudden shiver, was her reply to the complaint of the manservant, who walked away exclaiming:

'All right!'

Micuccio smiled and watched him depart across another room in semidarkness until he reached the vast, well-lit salon at the far end, where the splendid supper table towered; he kept on gazing in amazement until the snoring made him turn once more and look at the curtain.

The servant, with his napkin under his arm, passed back and forth, muttering now about Dorina, who went on sleeping, now about the cook, who was most likely a new man, called in for that evening's event, and who was annoying him by constantly asking for explanations. Micuccio, to avoid annoying him further, deemed it prudent to repress all the questions that he thought of asking him. He really ought to have told him or given him to understand that he was Teresina's fiancé, but he didn't want to, though he himself didn't know why, unless perhaps it was because the servant would then have had to treat him, Micuccio, as his master; and he, seeing him so jaunty and elegant, although still without his tailcoat, couldn't manage to overcome the embarrassment he felt at the very thought of it. At a certain point, however, seeing him pass by again, he couldn't refrain from asking him:

'Excuse me . . . whose house is this?'

'Ours, as long as we're in it,' the servant answered hurriedly.

And Micuccio sat there shaking his head.

By heaven, so it was true! Opportunity seized by the forelock. Good business. That servant who resembled a great nobleman, the cook and the scullery boy, that Dorina snoring over there: all servants at Teresina's beck and call . . . Who would ever have thought so?

In his mind he saw once again the dreary garret, way down in Messina, where Teresa used to live with her mother . . . Five years earlier, in that faraway garret, if it hadn't been for him, mother and daughter would have died of hunger. And *he*, *he* had discovered that treasure in Teresa's throat! She was always singing, then, like a sparrow on the rooftops, unaware of her own treasure: she would sing to annoy, she would sing to keep from thinking of her poverty, which he would try to alleviate as best he could, in spite of the war his parents waged with him at home, his mother especially. But could he abandon Teresina in those circumstances, after her father's death? – abandon her because she had nothing, while he, for better or worse, did have a modest employment, as flute player in the local orchestra? Fine reasoning! – and what about his heart?

Ah, it had been a true inspiration from heaven, a prompting of fortune, when he had paid attention to that voice of hers, when no one was giving it heed, on that very beautiful April day, near the garret window that framed the vivid blue of the sky. Teresina was singing softly an impassioned Sicilian arietta, the tender words of which Micuccio still remembered. Teresina was sad, that day, over the recent death of her father and over his family's stubborn opposition; and he too – he recalled – was sad, so much so that tears had come to his eyes

62

when he heard her sing. And yet he had heard that arietta many other times; but sung that way, never. He had been so struck by it that the following day, without informing her or her mother, he had brought with him his friend, the orchestra conductor, up to the garret. And in that way the first singing lessons had begun; and for two years running he had spent almost all of his small salary on her; he had rented a piano for her, had purchased her sheet music and had also given the teacher some friendly remuneration. Beautiful faraway days! Teresa burned intensely with the desire to take flight, to hurl herself into the future that her teacher promised her would be a brilliant one; and, in the meantime, what impassioned caresses for him to prove to him all her gratitude, and what dreams of happiness together!

Aunt Marta, on the other hand, would shake her head bitterly: she had seen so many ups and downs in her life, poor old lady, that by now she had no more trust left in the future; she feared for her daughter and didn't want her even to think about the possibility of escaping that poverty to which they were resigned; and, besides, she knew, she knew how much the madness of that dangerous dream was costing him.

But neither he nor Teresina would listen to her, and she protested in vain when a young composer, having heard Teresina at a concert, declared that it would be a real crime not to give her better teachers and thorough artistic instruction: in Naples, it was essential to send her to the Naples conservatory, cost what it might.

And then he, Micuccio, breaking off with his parents altogether, had sold a little farm of his that had been bequeathed to him by his uncle the priest, and in that way Teresina had gone to Naples to perfect her studies.

He hadn't seen her again since then; but he had received

her letters from the conservatory and afterwards those of Aunt Marta, when Teresina was already launched on her artistic life, eagerly sought by the major theaters after her sensational debut at the San Carlo. At the foot of those shaky and hesitant letters, which the poor old lady scratched onto the paper, as best she could, there were always a few words from *her*, from Teresina, who never had time to write: 'Dear Micuccio, I go along with everything Mother is telling you. Stay healthy and keep caring for me.' They had agreed that he would leave her five or six years' time to pursue her career without impediment: they were both young and could wait. And in the five years that had already elapsed, he had always shown those letters to anyone who wanted to see them, to combat the slanderous remarks his family would hurl at Teresina and her mother. Then he had fallen sick; he had been on the point of dying; and on that occasion, without his knowledge, Aunt Marta and Teresina had sent to his address a large sum of money; part had been spent during his illness, but the rest he had violently torn out of his family's hands and now, precisely, he was coming to return it to Teresina. Because money – no! He didn't want any. Not because it seemed like a handout, seeing that he had already spent so much on her; but . . . no! He himself was unable to say why, and now more than ever, there, in that house . . . money, no! Just as he had waited all those years, he could wait some more . . . Because if Teresina actually had money to spare, it was a sign that the future was now open to her, and therefore it was time for the old promise to be kept, in spite of anyone who refused to believe it.

Micuccio stood up with his brows knitted, as if to reassure himself about that conclusion; once again he blew on his ice-cold hands and stamped on the floor.

'Cold?' the servant said to him passing by. 'It won't be

long now. Come here into the kitchen. You'll be more comfortable.'

Micuccio didn't want to follow the advice of the servant, who confused and irritated him with that lordly air. He sat down again and resumed thinking in dismay. Shortly afterward a loud ring roused him.

'Dorina, the mistress!' screamed the servant, hurriedly slipping on his tailcoat as he ran to open the door; but seeing that Micuccio was about to follow him, he stopped short and issued an order:

'You stay there; let me notify her first.'

'Ohi, ohi, ohi . . .,' lamented a sleepy voice behind the curtain; and after a moment there appeared a large, stocky, carelessly dressed woman who trailed one leg on the ground and was still unable to keep her eyes open; she had a woolen shawl pulled up over her nose and her hair was dyed gold.

Micuccio kept looking at her foolishly. She too, in her surprise, opened her eyes wide when confronted by the outsider.

'The mistress,' Micuccio repeated.

Then Dorina suddenly returned to consciousness:

'Here I am, here I am . . .,' she said, taking off the shawl and flinging it behind the curtain, and exerting her whole heavy body to run toward the entrance.

The apparition of that dyed witch, and the order given by the servant, suddenly gave Micuccio, in his dejection, an anguished presentiment. He heard Aunt Marta's shrill voice:

'Over there, into the salon, into the salon, Dorina!'

And the servant and Dorina passed by him carrying magnificent baskets of flowers. He leaned his head forward so he could observe the illuminated room at the far end, and he saw a great number of gentlemen in tailcoats talking confusedly. His sight grew dim; his amazement and agitation were so great that he himself didn't realize that his eyes had filled with tears; he closed them, and he shut himself up completely in that darkness, as if to resist the torment that a long, ringing laugh was causing him. It was Teresina laughing like that, in the other room.

A muffled cry made him open his eyes again, and he saw before him – unrecognizable – Aunt Marta, with her hat on her head, poor thing! and laden down by a costly and splendid velvet mantilla.

'What! Micuccio . . . you here?'

'Aunt Marta . . .,' exclaimed Micuccio, almost frightened, pausing to examine her closely.

'Whatever for?' continued the old lady, who was upset. 'Without letting us know? What happened? When did you get here? . . . Tonight of all nights . . . Oh, God, God . . .'

'I've come to . . .,' Micuccio stammered, not knowing what more to say.

'Wait!' Aunt Marta interrupted him. 'What's to be done? What's to be done? See all those people, son? It's Teresina's celebration . . . her night . . . Wait, wait here for a bit . . .'

'If you,' Micuccio attempted to say, as anxiety tightened his throat, 'if you think I ought to go . . .'

'No, wait a bit, I say,' the kind old lady hastened to reply, all embarrassed.

'But,' Micuccio responded, 'I have no idea where to go in this town . . . at this hour . . .'

Aunt Marta left him, signaling to him with one of her gloved hands to wait, and entered the salon, in which a moment later Micuccio thought an abyss had opened; silence had suddenly fallen there. Then he heard, clear and distinct, these words of Teresina:

'One moment, gentlemen.'

Again his sight grew dim with the imminence of her

66

appearance. But Teresina did not come, and the conversation resumed in the salon. Instead, after a few minutes, which seemed an eternity to him, Aunt Marta came back, without her hat, without her mantilla, without her gloves, and less embarrassed.

'Let's wait here for a while, would that be all right?' she said to him. 'I'll stay with you . . . Now they're having supper . . . We'll remain here. Dorina will set this little table for us, and we'll have supper together, here; we'll reminisce about the good old days, all right? . . . I can't believe it's true that I'm here with you, son, here, here, all by ourselves . . . In that room, you understand, all those gentlemen . . . She, poor girl, can't avoid them . . . Her career, you get my meaning? Ah, what can you do! . . . Have you seen the newspapers? Big doings, son! As for me, I'm all at sea, all the time . . . I can't believe I can really be here with you, tonight.'

And the kind old lady, who had gone on talking, instinctively, to keep Micuccio from having time to think, finally smiled and rubbed her hands together, looking at him compassionately.

Dorina came to set the table hastily, because there, in the salon, the meal had already begun.

'Will she come?' Micuccio asked gloomily, with a troubled voice. 'I mean, at least to see her.'

'Of course she'll come,' the old lady immediately replied, making an effort to get out of her awkward situation. 'Just as soon as she has a minute free: she's already told me so.'

They looked at each other and smiled at each other, as if they had finally recognized each other. Despite the embarrassment and the excitement, their souls had found the way to greet each other with that smile. 'You're Aunt Marta,' Micuccio's eyes said. 'And you're Micuccio, my dear, good son, still the same, poor boy!' said Aunt Marta's. But suddenly the kind old lady lowered her own eyes, so that Micuccio might not read anything else in them. Again she rubbed her hands together and said:

'Let's eat, all right?'

'I'm good and hungry!' exclaimed Micuccio, quite happy and reassured.

'Let's cross ourselves first: here, in front of you, I can do it,' added the old lady in a mischievous manner, winking an eye, and she made the sign of the cross.

The manservant came, bringing their first course. Micuccio observed with close attention the way that Aunt Marta transferred her helping from the serving platter. But when his turn came, as he raised his hands, it occurred to him that they were dirty from the long trip; he blushed, he got confused, he raised his eyes to steal a glance at the servant, who, now the height of good manners, nodded slightly to him and smiled, as if inviting him to serve himself. Fortunately Aunt Marta helped him out of his predicament.

'Here, here, Micuccio, I'll serve you.'

He could have kissed her out of gratitude! Once he received his helping, as soon as the servant had withdrawn, he too crossed himself hurriedly.

'Good boy!' Aunt Marta said to him.

And he felt carefree, contented, and started eating as he had never eaten in his life, no longer thinking about his hands or the servant.

Nevertheless, each and every time the latter, entering or leaving the salon, opened the glass double door, and a sort of wave of mingled words or some burst of laughter came from that direction, he turned around uneasily and then looked at the old lady's sorrowful, loving eyes, as if to read an explanation there. But what he read there instead was an urgent request to ask no more for the moment, to put off explanations till a later time. And again they both smiled at each other and resumed eating and talking about their far-off hometown, friends and acquaintances, concerning whom Aunt Marta asked him for news endlessly.

'Aren't you drinking?'

Micuccio put out his hand to take the bottle; but, just at that moment, the double door to the ballroom opened again; a rustle of silk, amid hurried steps: a flash, as if the little room had all at once been violently illuminated, in order to blind him.

'Teresina . . .'

And his voice died away on his lips, out of amazement. Ah, what a queen!

With face flushed, eyes bulging and mouth open, he stopped to gaze at her, dumbfounded. How could she ever . . . like that! Her bosom bare, her shoulders bare, her arms bare . . . all ablaze with jewels and rich fabrics . . . He didn't see her, he no longer saw her as a living, real person in front of him . . . What was she saying to him? . . . Not her voice, nor her eyes, nor her laugh: nothing, nothing of hers did he recognize any more in that dream apparition.

'How are things? Are you getting along all right now, Micuccio? Good, good . . . You were sick if I'm not mistaken . . . We'll get together again in a little while. In the meantime, you have Mother with you here . . . Is that a deal? . . .'

And Teresina ran off again into the salon, all a-rustle.

'You're not eating any more?' Aunt Marta asked timorously, after a brief pause, to cut short Micuccio's silent astonishment.

He looked at her in bewilderment.

'Eat,' the old lady insisted, showing him his plate.

Micuccio raised two fingers to his smoke-blackened,

crumpled collar and tugged at it, trying to draw a deep breath.

'Eat?'

And several times he wiggled his fingers near his chin as if waving goodbye, to indicate: I don't feel like it any more, I can't. For another while he remained silent, dejected, absorbed in the vision he had just seen, then he murmured:

'How she's turned out . . .'

And he saw that Aunt Marta was shaking her head bitterly and that she too had stopped eating, as if in expectation.

'It's not even to be thought of . . .,' he then added, as if to himself, closing his eyes.

Now he saw, in that darkness of his, the gulf that had opened between the two of them. No, she – that woman – was no longer his Teresina. It was all over . . . for some time, for some time, and he, the fool, he, the imbecile, was realizing it only now. They had told him so back home, and he had stubbornly refused to believe it . . . And now, how would he look staying on in that house? If all those gentlemen, if even that servant had known that he, Micuccio Bonavino, had worn himself out coming such a distance, thirty-six hours by train, seriously believing he was still the fiancé of that queen, what laughs they would raise, those gentlemen and that servant and the cook and the scullery boy and Dorina! What laughs, if Teresina had dragged him into their presence, in the salon there, saying: 'Look, this pauper, this flute player, says he wants to become my husband!' She, yes, she had promised him this; but how could she herself suppose at that time that one day she would become what she now was? And it was also true, yes, that he had opened that path for her and had given her the means to travel it; but, there! by this time she had come so very far, how could he, who had stayed where he was, always the same, playing the flute on Sundays in the town square, catch up to her any more? It wasn't even to be thought of! And, then, what were those few paltry cents spent on her back then, now that she had become a great lady? He was ashamed merely to think that someone might suspect that he, with his coming, wanted to assert some rights in exchange for those few miserable pennies . . . – But at that moment he remembered that he had in his pocket the money sent him by Teresina during his illness. He blushed: he felt a twinge of shame, and he plunged one hand into the breast pocket of his jacket, where his wallet was.

'I've come, Aunt Marta,' he said hastily, 'also to return to you this money you sent me. Is it meant as a payment? As repayment of a loan? What would that have to do with anything? I see that Teresina has become a . . . she looks like a queen to me! I see that . . . never mind! It's not even to be thought of any longer! But as for this money, no: I didn't deserve such treatment from her . . . Where does that come in? It's all over, and we won't talk about it any more . . . but money, no way! I'm only sorry that it's not all here . . .'

'What are you saying, son?' Aunt Marta tried to interrupt him, trembling, pained and with tears in her eyes.

Micuccio signaled to her to be silent.

'It wasn't I who spent it: my family spent it, during my illness, without my knowledge. But let's say it makes up for that trifle I spent back then . . . you remember? It doesn't matter . . . Let's think no more about it. Here is the difference. And I'm leaving.'

'What! Like that, all of a sudden?' exclaimed Aunt Marta, trying to hold him back. 'At least wait until I tell Teresina. Didn't you hear that she wanted to see you again? I'm going over to tell her . . .'

'No, it's no use,' Micuccio replied, with determination. 'Let her stay there with those gentlemen; it suits her there, she belongs there. I, poor fool . . . I got to see her; that was enough for me . . . No, now that I think of it, do go over there . . . you go there, too . . . Do you hear how they're laughing? I don't want the laugh to be on me . . . I'm leaving.'

Aunt Marta interpreted that sudden determination of Micuccio's in the worst possible light: as an act of anger, a jealous reaction. By now it seemed to her, the poor woman, as if everybody – seeing her daughter – ought immediately to conceive the meanest of suspicions, that very one which caused her to weep inconsolably as, without a moment's rest, she bore the burden of her secret heartbreak amid the hubbub of that life of detestable luxury which ignominiously dishonored her old age.

'But I,' the words escaped her, 'by this time there's no way for me to stand guard over her, son . . .'

'Why?' asked Micuccio, suddenly reading in her eyes the suspicion he had not yet formulated; and his face turned dark.

The old lady became bewildered in her sorrow and hid her face in her trembling hands, but failed to check the onrush of the tears that now gushed forth.

'Yes, yes, go, son, go . . .,' she said, strangled by sobs. 'She's not for you any more, you're right . . . If the two of you had listened to me . . .'

'And so,' Micuccio burst out, bending over her and violently pulling one hand away from her face. But so afflicted and wretched was the look with which she begged him for mercy, as she put a finger to her lips, that he restrained himself and added in a different tone of voice, making an effort to speak softly; 'And so she, she . . . she is no longer worthy of me. Enough, enough, I'm leaving just the same . . . in fact, all the more, now . . . What a dumbbell, Aunt Marta: I hadn't understood! Don't cry . . . Anyway, what does it matter? Fate . . . fate . . .'

He took his little suitcase and little sack from under the table and was on his way out when he recalled that there, in the sack, were the beautiful citrons he had brought for Teresina from their hometown.

'Oh, look, Aunt Marta,' he continued. He opened the top of the sack and, creating a barrier with one arm, he emptied that fresh, aromatic fruit onto the table. 'And what if I started tossing all these citrons I brought for her at the heads of those honorable gentlemen?'

'For mercy's sake,' the old lady groaned amid her tears, once more making a beseeching sign to him to be silent.

'No, of course I won't,' added Micuccio, smiling sourly and putting the empty sack in his pocket. 'I'm leaving them for you alone, Aunt Marta. And to think that I even paid duty on them . . . Enough. For you alone, mind me now. As for her, tell her "Good luck!" from me.'

He picked up the valise again and left. But on the stairs, a sense of anguished bewilderment overpowered him: alone, deserted, at night, in a big city he didn't know, far from his home; disappointed, dejected, put to shame. He made it to the street door, saw that there was a downpour of rain. He didn't have the courage to venture onto those unfamiliar streets in a rain like that. He went back in very quietly, walked back up one flight of stairs, then sat down on the first step and, leaning his elbows on his knees and his head on his hands, began to weep silently.

When the supper was finished, Sina Marnis made another appearance in the little room; but she found her mother alone crying, while back there the gentlemen were clamoring and laughing.

73

'He left?' she asked in surprise.

Aunt Marta nodded affirmatively, without looking at her. Sina stared into space, lost in thoughts, then sighed:

'Poor guy . . .'

'Look,' her mother said to her, no longer stemming her tears with the tablecloth. 'He had brought citrons for you . . .'

'Oh, what beauties!' exclaimed Sina, cheering up. She clutched one arm to her waist and with the other hand gathered up as many as she could carry.

'No, not in there!' her mother vigorously protested.

But Sina shrugged her bare shoulders and ran into the salon shouting:

'Citrons from Sicily! Citrons from Sicily!'

VITALIANO BRANCATI

MY GRANDFATHER
(1934)

Translated by Gregory Conti

DURING THE EUROPEAN WAR, my grandfather came down with an attack of appendicitis that brought him almost to death's door. He had frequent bouts of delirium in those days, and he said something that he had never said to anyone: that his father hadn't died of natural causes, but had poisoned himself over the pain of losing his wife. On several occasions, he called out to his daughter and asked her to stand between him and the doorway because looking toward that corner of the room scared him.

He had always been a brave man, forthright, full of spirit, and he had loved me more even than his own eyes. From his meager salary as a town employee – which he had to hand over, penny by penny, to my grandmother – he managed to make disappear, with the ingenuous tricks of a student, a few silver lira coins that he kept squirreled away in a little purse. The purse would sit there for months at a time until my family made the trip back to our home town; would wait for me to step down off the stagecoach that brought me from Spaccaforno to Pachino and, after a three hour nap, go out with its owner into the main piazza of the town, surrounded by stores lit by oil lamps, with no signs, no shop windows, each with maybe twenty items to sell and just barely distinguishable from the houses of the local farmers. I emptied out my grandfather's purse in those stores and filled my arms with old, simple toys, threadbare stuffed animals, dented toy guns, and puppets made of sugar with their noses and ears already broken off.

I was three years old and rather domineering in my own lethargic way. From inside a bundle of white clothes and coveralls, I would stick my right hand out to point to some little piece of the world that I would have preferred belonged to me or that should be treated in some particular way. One afternoon with my grandfather, I pointed to a drowsy, fat horse in a team of six, whose owner, an important personage in the town, had often been the object of caricature in the dialect rhymes that my grandfather used to invent at banquets. I wanted my grandfather furtively to separate the horse from its companions and mount it together with me. Naturally, he said no, that wasn't possible. But I'll never forget the pained look in his eye, the disheartened gaze he cast on a world so poorly arranged as not to permit, without fear and shame, untying a horse from a team of six and making a present of it to a little boy. I didn't say a word to my grandfather for the rest of the evening, but during the night I was overcome with remorse and soaked my pillow with tears. All in all, that was the bitterest episode of my friendship with my grandfather, and it brought to an end, once and for all, my first five years of life. A year later, I was already less domineering and more serious. Something like the shade of a world-weary man had entered my body. I loved leaning on little walking sticks, smoking chocolate cigarettes, and listening to people while holding a hand up to my ear. My grandfather was the only man in the world who respected these new habits of mine with which I was preparing to make my way slowly to my first venerable age: ten.

He would take me on long walks that ended at the gates to the city, on a cracked and flaking terrace called 'the round,' where we could see the water off Marzamemi and the minuscule, clouded skyline of Noto.

Pachino sits on a hilltop, pelted by the wind of two seas:

the Ionian and the Mediterranean. This wind sweeps the town continuously and makes the cobblestones shine like diamonds.

The streets are wide and white and all come together in the large central piazza that, being the highest point in the town, is visible from everywhere and has that smooth aspect and red hue of places that are constantly battered by the wind.

That wind is tied, in a very intimate way, to my childhood. I can still see my grandfather's goatee brought to life and yanked to the right or left by that wonderful wind that so often took my breath away.

In the piazza was the mother church, and on the mother church the clock and the only lightning rod in town. The church, with its high, blank wall like the side of a ship, flanked a wide avenue that was considered the main street. This was the site of the local market and home to an exorbitant number of aunts and uncles, cousins, great uncles, great cousins, witnesses at my father's wedding, doctors who had treated my grandmother, midwives who had helped bring into the world my father, my brother, and me; all people who knew a heap of things about me that I didn't know, and who irritated me with their all-knowing air and that gaze that slid down over my head and rushed off into the past, as if I was nothing more to them than a pretext for resting their chins in their hands and remembering. My grandfather, no less than I, was offended by the demeanor of our relatives. I was more important to him than all of that past; though doubtless that past had some small value for him in so far as in the end it had deigned to produce the ten kilos of living being that were me. So, in total agreement with each other, we avoided the main street and made our way to the round via side streets full of children, of wagon wheels leaning against walls, and groups of people, each of whom was holding onto a horse so it could be shoed.

But in the evening, when the street was deserted, and the houses and the shops were all closed up, except for the pharmacy run by my grandfather's brother, Uncle Carlo, who stood next to the counter and, holding a guitar in his left hand, added a few hendecasyllable verses to one of his tragedies with his right; when the last lamps went out in the marketplace and it was no longer possible to tell whether what was moving around in the shadows was a watchman, a dog, or a calf; when the wind finally calmed down for a while, my grandfather and I, after having done twenty laps around the piazza, would head down the main street. Near the church, there was always someone sleeping. Up above, the stars amazed me with the way they look, on cloudless nights, over a smooth, blank wall. My grandfather used to smoke cigars and every now and again the breeze would snatch a spark and carry it off into the distance. The smell of that cigar is something I'll never be able to forget, and it's one of the three or four elemental sensations that I always draw upon when, after some unusual incident that has upset me, I start to get hold of myself. On winter nights, he would hold my little hand inside the pocket of his overcoat. On summer nights, he would give me, so I could use it to fan myself, his gray panama hat. The stories that I asked him to tell on those occasions were always of a musical nature. He would tell me, slightly out of order so I could always ask for some further explanation, about the performances of a certain *Lucia* and a certain *Norma* given in the theaters of Catania.

These stories were mixed with others of army life, but these too were sprinkled with songs. My grandfather would sing for me the tunes of his regiment, especially the one where the soldiers berated the 'corporal of the week' for having woken them too early.

L'è suonata la sveglia L'è ancora schiur, Caporal di settimana . . .

The alarm has sounded And it's still dark Corporal of the week . . .

Then there were stories of more intimate episodes, from which I learned two things: that once my father, incredibly, had been really small, even smaller than me, and that, beyond the clouds in the northern sky, there existed a city called Napoli, where my grandfather had bested an overly vain tenor in a singing contest.

Then the talk turned again to my father, and it was said that, if he had been there with us at that moment, we would have been two sons, one grandfather, two fathers and a grandson, and that my grandfather would have had to be in the middle because he was the most important of the three.

But actually, my grandfather and I felt the same affection for my father and the same respect; his gaze instilled in both of us the same apprehension, and his presence disturbed, in equal measure for my grandfather and myself, our lively spontaneity. By this time, my grandfather and I had developed a taste for life that no one, not even my father, could share. We were ready to judge anything in a way all our own and in which we were never in disagreement. Exactly how this single taste had come about, I don't remember, but I think little by little, with our holding hands, with the trust that his gray goatee inspired in me, with the ten things that he chose among the many in his long life, figuring that they were the only really important ones, worthy of being told to me. I sensed immediately that he was happy with that choice, and I was flattered and enamored of the way he recounted those ten things to me. It was truly noble, worthy of a grand gentleman, of a man of true heart, as if all the rest, everything about his life that he didn't tell me, he thought not only was unsuitable to be heard by my little ears, but that it was stupid for him too, and useless, and had been lived for no reason at all.

This perfect accord, that I had the great good fortune to reach with an elderly gentleman whose yellowed photographs of when he was a child strangely resembled me, had a great power over me. I matured quickly, without the perils and pitiful frailties of a precocious child. I matured, because I was happy and because I knew how to appreciate my happiness. With the blessed confusion of someone who has had a good long sleep and now the sun is beating down on his face, I could feel the stirring, in my brain and in my eyes, of the man of tomorrow. During the periods I lived with my grandfather I was serene, never afraid at night, and I gave to the prospect of things bigger than me the order that a budding snake charmer is able to give to a group of lizards. When one is living in a world like that one does not need, in order to fill up his life, either poetry or riches, or even – I hesitate a little to say it – religion.

But, during the war, my grandfather came down with appendicitis. At the time, I was in Pozzallo, in a house with huge balconies whose windows were filled with water and boats. I spent hours and hours reproducing in my little diary the freighters that struggled in vain to move out of sight, rather like an ant on which one has let fall a drop of ink. I heard that my grandfather was delirious, and this worried me. I was afraid that he would let slip his army stories, the songs, the episode of the tenor, and that our intimacy would be lost. For fifteen days, I let the freighters go by without reproducing them in my diary; and for me that renunciation was filled with the melancholy of a hunter of flies who keeps his hand open while two of those insects are playing on his palm. In the end, I heard that my grandfather was feeling better, that he was no longer delirious and had started a diet. Less than two months went by and around our dinner table the rigor with which grandma imposed the new diet on granddad was already famous. There were tales of how meticulous and precise he had become, and how he had developed certain habits from which he never deviated for any reason at all.

When I saw him again, in '16, he was a lot thinner and his eyes shone with a brightness that was almost gleeful. I couldn't understand if he was changed or not. His ways were those of before and the words with which he greeted me were the same. His gaze, however, didn't quite convince me. Yes, it was still affectionate, it kept coming back to rest on my shirt, on my shoes, on my belt and on my cheeks, but it lacked that special stare with which it distinguished me from others.

The first day of our meeting went as it was supposed to. He told me the story of the tenor, described the war just as I wanted, and as no one else had ever described it: a group of regiments that, upon awaking in the trenches at dawn, would break out singing, *L'è suonata la sveglia, l'è ancora schiur. . . .* But that night he didn't smoke his cigar anymore, because it had been forbidden him, and the next day he had to endure in silence a harangue from my grandmother, reprimanding him because, for the first time after months of dieting, he had changed his dinner time by an hour. I was secretly very pleased. As I had predicted, the famous diet, which it appeared my grandfather had sworn to uphold, went up in smoke as soon as I appeared on the scene. But that night, I came in for a bitter disappointment. As we were out walking together, he singing and I listening, my grandfather looked at the clock in the piazza with an expression that I had never seen on his face. It seemed to me that the clock, red against the deep sky, provoked in him the dread and delight that a feared island might provoke in a tired old sea dog. (I learned, several years later, that my grandfather's father had also been reduced, in his last years of life, to following a diet, and he too had regulated his meal times according to the spheres of that big clock.) Three times, my grandfather shifted his gaze from the red clock face to my hair. Then he smiled weakly, accompanied me to my father and, without saying a word, left me there, for the first time in my life in such a brusque way, and went to drink his milk. I remember his stooped shoulders, the rapid gesture he made when, upon reaching the church, he looked up at the clock again, and the vast piazza where he walked off into the distance, making himself as small and insignificant as a stranger. From the storefronts came the light of oil lamps, spreading over the ground and leaving the air completely dark. The only parts of their bodies that were illuminated were the men's shoes, while the rest of them remained blurry and indistinct, like animals in the woods. The sky was strangely high and full of stars that I couldn't separate from a subtle smell of meadow and a sweet bewilderment that was a prelude to sleep. There was a great confusion in my heart as there must be in a house that has never held a party and the order suddenly arrives to give a reception on the spot. I didn't know where to begin, and what thoughts to select and what others to reject in order to suffer the profound pain that my grandfather had given me. In my confusion, that pain hung there in front of me without my being able to take full possession of it. Finally, tiredness got the better of me and I fell asleep on a chair. I think it was my father who carried me home. Between sleeping in the chair and sleeping on the bed there wasn't but a moment in which I saw the Milky Way and heard two words: 'It's late!'

The next day, things were already different. I felt myself disposed to observing granddad attentively, to staying slightly behind him on our walks in order to see his shoulders, to acting distracted when we walked past the front of the church, observing out of the corner of my eye whether he really did make a fleeting sign of the cross. That day I saw in my grandfather a man I had never seen before, a man with slightly stooped shoulders, big shoes, and a moist forehead. He was a sort of stranger who had been following me around since I was born, or rather who had been following us around, my grandfather and me, and whom I had only now become aware of. But I had no sense of hostility toward him. I thought he was nice, honest, and worthy of being loved. Only there was something about him that was weak and too entertaining. And perhaps I must attribute to these two qualities, which became more marked with time, the extraordinary fact that my grandfather should have slipped imperceptibly out of my life and, fifteen years later, when I was twenty-four, he barely existed for me. Or better, in Pachino there was an old man who had my name and to whom I sent hugs at the end of letters I wrote to my aunt. There was a little man whom I sought out with my eyes every time I went back to the house where my father was born. But he was reduced to saying three or four phrases; to sitting alone in a room as big as a drawing room, leafing through for the thousandth time some illustrated magazines; to mistaking me for my brother; to being afraid of having his picture taken; to displaying visible annoyance when I sat down on one of the two chairs that, in a little while, he would use to hang his jacket and pants on, and that always had to be the same ones. When they came to rest on me, his eyes would shine weakly and immediately refuse to make the effort to look at me in any special way. There were times when it even seemed he hardly recognized me as someone he knew. I wasn't hurt by all this because we had come to this point gradually, from year to year, and I would have almost been amazed if each new visit of mine to Pachino had not found my grandfather still more distant from me. My life, full of work, strange friendships, and foolish plans, had gotten pleasantly used to this poison of detachment, taken in ever stronger doses. By now, nothing in him reminded me of the old gentleman who had filled the early years of my life with his friendship. His handsome gray goatee had vanished. His eyes seemed distant and indifferent like the eyes in portraits, and his whole person increasingly fled from the memories and the love of others. At times, a question would come out of his mouth that alarmed us, as though he were about to recover the affection he once had for us. But it turned out to be a question enunciated by chance, like certain resemblances to persons we hold dear, that we see for a moment in a stranger and that make our hearts beat faster. A minute later, he would go back to his little furtive gestures and to expressing his desire for food and sleep with the violence of a child, immediately betrayed by the fact that he didn't digest well and suffered from insomnia.

By now, nothing of him came to me from Pachino: no greetings, no good wishes, not even an answer to my picture postcards. It was extraordinarily easy to forget him completely, and for months on end his image didn't come back to my memory even for a second. In April of '33, when I was in Catania for a short visit with my family, he died suddenly.

It happened on Wednesday of Holy Week. The news was communicated to us by telephone during the night. The next day at dawn, my father and I left for Pachino. I recall that, as I was getting in the car, I saw a man down at the end of the street, dressed in gray and acting very strangely, as though he were trying to hit, with the cane that he passed rapidly back and forth from his right hand to his left, a short figure that appeared first behind him and then to the side and then immediately disappeared. I couldn't understand if the man was a drunk or a cripple or just a swinger of canes. In any event, I was thoroughly disgusted by him. What he was, finally, was the opening episode of the time when my grandfather would no longer be alive. My grandfather had died of old age, which is to say, he died to make room for the things that were supposed to come after him. And these things were inane and useless to the point of absurdity. They were that man swinging his cane around in the air, staggering around like an old blind dog. . . .

When the car started moving, my father pressed himself up against his side window and kept his eyes fixed straight in front of him, off in the distance. His hand, resting on the seat between us, looked a lot like my grandfather's hand. At dawn, meanwhile, the sky lit up with the aurora; the front steps outside the closed front doors gleamed softly; the old door of a church opened little by little; a wagon pulled by a donkey creaked its way toward a fountain; and I felt, as though for the first time, all the happiness one feels on a morning in a closed bedroom when you're next to the bed of a loved one and you see them open their eyes again and smile. . . . My grandfather, on the other hand, for the first time in seventy years, would not be opening his eyes that morning.

Not until we were on the train did I realize that granddad, whom I saw dead, was not the insignificant little old man that had been eluding my affection for ten years. Instead he was the gentleman with the gray goatee, the friend of my early years, my companion on long walks, the one who bounced me on his knee, telling me about the most beautiful and important things that had happened before I was born. He was the old gentleman who adored me and whom I loved infinitely. . . .

On clear days, the mountains in the province of Siracusa shine all the way to the sea near Catania. But even close up those mountains have a mysterious splendor, as though the sun had ceded them to a blue star and its strange satellites. At sunrise and sunset especially, those majestic peaks appear to be the flimsiest and most delicate part of the earth. In summer, when the wild *simun* blows up from Africa, the mountains of Siracusa, seen from afar in the brilliant light and vibrant air, look as though they won't be able to hold up against the wind and that they'll be ripped to shreds like a veil. Those mountains were upon us in an instant, as I was remembering and snoozing. Suddenly they surrounded the train; a rich, mild light settled onto the velvet seats and the pictures in the compartment. My mind went into a fog and my heart felt a painful, profound sweetness, as if all of a sudden, after so many years, I had re-entered the enchanted grotto of childhood.

An old, dust-covered automobile was waiting for us and immediately set off toward Noto. It was still morning, and we felt ourselves heading into the sea as we sped along this last, ever narrowing strip of Sicily. All around us by now, waves were shimmering and the saline wind was blowing. This was where I had launched my little boy's cry; this was the dust that had filled my shoes. The sensations and thoughts of my boyhood had remained so alive in me that I was ready to have them again, and not as memories, but as proper thoughts and sensations. I was right on the edge of letting go. That sky that stretched out on all sides and was sliding along the small, rounded hump of the maritime plain, like a giant trying to climb up onto a minuscule piece of floating ice; that sky looked again as it had long ago. What it had said to me then, it was saying to me again with great simplicity. So that, for the trees whitened with sand, the dogs that for a long stretch came running behind the car, the children sleeping together with the chickens in large baskets strapped to the backs of donkeys, I easily felt again the mysterious pity I had felt back then, and the fear that I'd once had of those who suffered and of things that appeared to be suffering, because I saw in them something of the chastised and therefore of the wicked. Sitting in the car, I also felt a strange satisfaction; and this too was tied to the idea I had of the road in my early years, when I was afraid of horses because they reared up at passing cars, and I admired the cars because they made the horses rear up and then kept right on going, fast as the wind. Actually, my life was still under the dominion of my boyhood. The splendor of that age was following me as, at the start of a dark hallway, the light of the drawing room one has just come out of. I would always have to turn back to it, to my boyhood, if I wanted to be spontaneous and true. But had I always been spontaneous and true? And hadn't I instead shown my bones, like a scrawny horse pulling its wagon from a ditch, in the sad endeavor to be different from what I am?

At the foot of the hill where Noto rises up, I rediscovered intact an old impression of mine which had always made me realize when I had arrived in the vicinity of Pachino. It was a blend of the smell of bunches of grapes fallen to the ground and burnt by the sun and a profound respect for everything that had been living for a long time and that I had never seen. Along the road, the return of these old impressions kept getting more vivid and numerous. What I noticed in them was a great seriousness.

Back then, I had notions of death and life that were very simple and clear, but above all serious. Then I wouldn't have said, not even in my stupidest and strangest dreams, a phrase like the one which, later on, I had even written: 'I believe in life!' That phrase sounded fake, like something from a circus or a fair, compared to the clear and simple feeling that I nourished for life in my early years. Nor would I have said: 'We must be happy and strong!' What meaning could they have had, at that time, words such as those? What meaning could they have had in a way of living so full and natural as mine was during my boyhood? None! But what had happened inside me in the last fifteen years? Was it my grandfather who had vanished from my life, or I that had become so clouded that I was no longer able to see the friend of my first years, the man who had been so clear when my life was clear?

In the room, big as a drawing room, where he used to spend his afternoons, going back to leaf through for the thousandth time some illustrated magazines from fifty years ago, I found a small stranger, stretched out on a sort of altar. This one didn't even look like the insignificant old man into which my boyhood grandfather had slowly transformed himself. He was a short little man, dressed in black, who had closed his eyes the night before and retained no other signs of humanity on his face except for one, infantile, that could have been the pain caused by lack of food. No sign of the seventy years of life that, according to the testimony of the living, were to be attributed to that little man. That little man contained to the point of absurdity the stranger that had broken off, some fifteen years ago, from my grandfather, and brought him to his grave. I couldn't bring myself to cry for him. But suddenly, when I realized that my boyhood granddad, the beautiful man with the gray goatee, would never come back to me, could never exist again, for the fact that the little unknown man had closed his eyes after having said he felt fine in order to induce my aunt to give him some raisins, the whole thing seemed so brutal, violent, and unfair that my heart squeezed shut as though it would never beat again.

I accepted the chair that someone offered me and sat down in the darkest corner of the room. I cried like a baby, but without desperation. My grandfather wasn't dead, but just mysteriously forced not to show himself to be more than that minuscule old man lying on the catafalque. It was as though he had gone away or gone into hiding forever. Death could never touch the beautiful and vital gentleman with the gray goatee who had given me, with his smile and his love such a calm, natural, and full sense of living. No, he had vanished, like a magician, like the most beautiful of my dreams. All that was fabulous about him remained intact forever. I may sometimes doubt that he ever really existed, but I'll always have the hope that, from behind the curtain near which I'll be sitting in a moment of ennui, he'll stretch out his strong, warm hand and touch my head, smiling.

The room was dark, and the door across from me that led into a room that opened onto the street was lit up like the mouth of a tunnel. The doorway framed a continuous passing of women wrapped in shawls, their hands thrusting out to send kisses and make the sign of the cross. One of them, very old, cried more than the others and collapsed against the doorframe. 'Beautiful! Beautiful!' were the words that were heard cried out most often. Even women younger than he called him: 'Little one!' My aunt, sitting next to him, leaned her cheek down against his forehead and said, carefully pronouncing each syllable in a tone somewhere between crying and screaming, 'Why did you decide to leave me? Why have you gone away? Everyone here loved you! Everyone!. . . . You're beautiful, beautiful as yesterday when you were sleeping. Only you're cold, my son, cold as marble!'

From time to time, Uncle Carlo, sitting a little way off, sent through the room a gaze that was pale, thin, and bright, like the light of an old lantern. The day was growing longer. The room started to fill with people I didn't know. The women whispered words into ears. Little by little, what they said in each other's ears became very important, and by comparison the dead man himself, lying in the middle of the room, became as small as a little boy found on the street, looking around as the crowd, forgetting about him, discusses some general proposals for ways of helping home-less children. Finally, someone walked over to my aunt and begged her to get up. My aunt immediately threw herself on her father's cadaver, sticking her fingernails into his black suit. She screamed and refused to let go of her grip. I got up and left the room and took refuge in a parlor, where, during my boyhood, I used to sleep at night, breathing in smells of cloth roses, velvet headboards, and portraits. It was Holy Thursday, the day when a group of people roams through the streets of Pachino carrying a trumpet and a drum, rep-resenting the drama of the Madonna crying out her Son's name through the streets of Jerusalem. When the group arrives outside the door, a rapid drum roll can be heard, followed by a sad and deep sound from the trumpet. For an hour at least I had been hearing that double call, from neighborhood to neighborhood, making its way toward us. Then I stopped hearing it. And then, suddenly, as I was sitting in the parlor, that precipitous drum roll that sends the knick-knacks on the table trembling and the old, faded portraits vibrating. And the clear voice of the trumpet. My chest tightened and it felt like my ankles had been hit by a blow from an ax. When they called me from the street, I could barely stand up. Somehow or other, I made it outside. Pachino was whiter than ever, and on its dusty, sun-bathed streets the dark dresses of the procession stood out like hawks. With one hand on the coffin, carried on our arms, I arrived inside the church. The organ was already playing, and the little girls kneeling in the pews were singing with their silver voices. Soon the voice of the priest was added to the chants. It was then that I heard my own name, pronounced in Latin in a loud voice, and always followed by the words, 'through the endless ages.' This served to make it clear to me, as clear as one plus one, that my grandfather and my boyhood had gone forever.

On the way back from the cemetery, in the midst of a little group that was already talking about other things, we came into the piazza and as I glanced up at the façade of the church I saw it as a blackboard where, when I had turned my back to go down to the cemetery, someone had erased, with the sweep of a sponge, the words that my grandfather and my own boyhood had written there. I felt that same painful impression, of words erased and an empty blackboard, in front of the little round windows that I used to look out on, for hours on end, from my grandfather's doorway, standing erect on the little step where the shutter swung open and closed with a creaking sound and that on moonlit nights was half silver and half black.

I left, on my own, the next afternoon. As usual, the sun was bright and the wind carried the constant sounds, piercing and cold, of the blacksmith's hammer. The large coach that takes travelers on the hour's journey from the piazza in Pachino to the train station in Noto was already covered with dust before it left. I boarded behind an old woman and sat down between two baskets, one of which had a rabbit's foot sticking out of it and the other an apple. I turned to look out the window and saw, framed tightly at the end of a narrow street, the sea of Marzamemi; the sea that I had seen shimmering endlessly in the afternoons of my childhood and that now was as dim as a switched-off lamp at the end of a party.

A few minutes later, a hunter got on and sat next to me. The coach started off, the town vanished on both sides and the mountains of Noto loomed in the distance.

An old man, who was sitting in front of me, turned slowly and, pointing at the sky, asked the hunter,

'Good hunting?'

'Nothing!' the other replied. 'Didn't see so much as a wing this year. . . .'

Yes, my boyhood was really over. My boyhood was dead. One night, a little boy, standing erect in front of the mirror, I had played the most useless and desperate of games, trying to see the expression that my face took on when I closed my eyes. Now, my boyhood was finished, the handsome gentleman with the gray goatee had vanished from the earth. I knew very well that a man doesn't die all at once, but age by age. And I knew that the ages of a man are two: boyhood and maturity. That year, not even a wing had been seen in the sky, and my first age had died. But I still had another age left. I still had time to be honest, to be truthful, and above all to be simple. But a part of my life had ended; one of my eyes had closed forever.

ELIO VITTORINI

From

CONVERSATIONS
IN SICILY (1941)

Translated by Alane Salierno Mason

X

'HOW ABOUT THAT, I'm at my mother's,' I thought when I got off the bus, at the foot of the long flight of steps that led to the highest reaches of my mother's town.

The name of the town was inscribed on a wall just as it appeared on the cards I sent every year to my mother, and everything else, this flight of steps between old houses, the mountains all around, the clumps of snow on the roofs, was there before my eyes just as I suddenly remembered having seen it, once or twice, during my childhood. And it seemed to make some difference to me to be there, and I was glad to have come, not to have stayed in Siracusa, not to have taken the train back again to Northern Italy, not to have finished my journey yet. That was the most important thing: not to have finished my journey yet, maybe even to have just started out. This way, at least, I felt something, as I looked at the long flight of steps and the houses and the church domes high up, the overhangs of houses and rock, and the roofs in the ravine below, the smoke from a chimney, the clumps of snow, the straw, and the little crowd of Sicilian children barefoot on the crust of ice on the ground, around the cast-iron fountain in the sun.

'How about that, I'm at my mother's,' I thought again, and it was as if I had arrived there spontaneously, just as spontaneously as one finds oneself in a certain place in memory – or even more fantastical, as if I had begun travel-ing in the fourth dimension. It seemed there was nothing, only a dream, a spiritual intermission, between being in Siracusa and being there in my mother's town; it seemed I had arrived there just by resolving to go, through a motion of memory, not of my body; and thus the morning of being there, the cold of the mountain, and the pleasure of it; and I didn't even regret not being there the night before, in time for my mother's name-day, as if this light were not that of December 9th but still that of December 8th, or of a day in a fourth dimension.

I knew my mother lived in the highest part of town, I remembered climbing these steps as a child, when I came to visit my grandparents, and I began to climb. There were faggots of wood on the steps in front of some of the houses, and I continued up, and every once in a while there was a hem of snow round the steps, and in the cold, in the morning sun (by now it was almost noon), I finally arrived at the top, overlooking the vast mountain town and the ravines mottled with snow. There was no one around, only barefoot children, their feet ulcered with chilblains, and I made my way between the houses high up round the dome of the big Mother Church, which I also recognized, as ancient as I remembered it.

I made my way holding the greeting card on which was written the name of the street and the number of the house where my mother lived, and I was able to find my way very easily, guided by the greeting card like a postman, and guided a bit by memory, too. I also asked, because I wanted to, at some little grocery stores I saw, filled with sacks and barrels. And so I came to visit Mrs. Concezione Ferrauto, my mother, looking for her as if I were a postman, with the greeting card in my hand and her name, Concezione Ferrauto, on my lips. The house was the last one on its street, astride a little garden, with a short flight of steps outside.

I went up them in the sun, looking once more at the address on the card, and I was at my mother's, I knew the doorway and it did make some difference to me to be there, it was all the more fully a journey in the fourth dimension.

I pushed open the door and entered the house and from another room a voice said, 'Who is it?' And I recognized that voice, after fifteen years of not remembering it; it was the same voice I now recalled from fifteen years before, high and clear, and I remembered the childhood sound of my mother talking from another room.

'Signora Concezione,' I said.

XI

THE LADY OF the house appeared, tall and white-haired, and I recognized my mother perfectly, a tall woman with nearly blond chestnut-brown hair, and a sharp chin, sharp nose, dark eyes. She had a red shawl over her shoulders to keep herself warm.

I laughed. 'Happy name-day,' I said.

'Oh, it's Silvestro,' my mother said, and came close.

I gave her a kiss on the cheek. She kissed me on the cheek and said, 'But what the devil brings you here?'

'How did you recognize me?' I said.

My mother laughed. 'I'm asking myself the same thing,' she said. The room smelled of roasting herring, and my mother added, 'Let's go into the kitchen . . , I have herring on the fire.'

We went into the next room where the sun struck the dark iron bedstead, and from there into the little kitchen where the sun struck everything. On the ground, beneath a wooden platform, a copper brazier was lit. The herring was roasting over it, smoking, and my mother bent over to turn it. 'You'll taste how good it is,' she said.

'I will,' I said, and breathed in the smell of herring, and it made a difference to me, I liked it, it brought back the smell of the meals of my childhood. 'I can't imagine anything better,' I said, and asked, 'Did we have it when I was a boy?'

'Oh yes,' my mother said. 'Herring in the winter and peppers in the summer. That's what we always had. Don't you remember?'

'And fava beans with thistles,' I said, remembering.

'Yes,' my mother said. 'Fava beans with thistles. You loved fava beans with thistles.'

'Oh,' I said. 'I loved them?'

And my mother: 'You'd always want a second helping . . . And the same thing with lentils done with artichoke, sun-dried tomatoes, and lard . . .'

'And a sprig of rosemary, yes?' I said.

And my mother: 'Yes . . . And a sprig of rosemary.'

And I: 'I always wanted a second helping of that, too?'

And my mother: 'Oh yes! You were like Esau . . . You would have given away your birthright for a second plate of lentils . . . I can still see you when you came home from school, at three or four in the afternoon, on the train . . .'

'That's right,' I said, 'on the freight train, in the baggage compartment . . . First me by myself, then me and Felice, then me, Felice and Liborio . . .'

'All of you so sweet,' my mother said. 'With your heads thick with hair, your little faces black, your hands always black . . . And right away you'd ask: are there lentils today, mamma?'

'We were living in those plate-layers' houses then,' I said. 'We'd get off the train at the station, at San Cataledo, at

Serradifalco, at Acquaviva, all those places we lived, and we had to walk a mile or two to get home.'

And my mother: 'Yes, sometimes three. When the train passed, I knew you were on the way, along the tracks, and I'd heat up the lentils, roast the herring, and then I'd hear you shout, "Land! Land!" '

' "Land"? Why "land"?' I asked.

'Yes, "land"! It was some game you played,' my mother said. 'And then once, in Racalmuto, the plate-layer's house was up an incline and the train had to slow down, and you'd worked out how to jump off the train while it was moving so you could get off in front of the house. And I had a black fear you'd end up under the wheels, so I'd wait outside for you with a cane . . .'

'And you'd spank us?'

And my mother: 'Oh yes! Don't you remember? I could've broken your legs with that cane. I even made you go without dinner, sometimes.'

She got up again, holding the herring by the tail to examine it on one side, then the other; and as I smelled the herring I saw that her face had lost nothing of the young face it had once been, as I was remembering it now, but age had added something to it. This was my mother: the memory of her fifteen years earlier, twenty years earlier, young and terrifying, the cane in her hand as she waited for us to jump off the freight train; that memory, plus all the time that had passed since then, the something-more of the present. In short, she was twice real. She examined the herring on one side then the other, holding it up, and even the herring was both a memory and the something-more of the present – the sun, the cold, the copper brazier in the middle of the kitchen, the existence in my mind of that place in the world where I found myself, everything had this quality of being

101

twice real; and maybe this was why it made a difference to me to be there, to be on a journey, because of everything that was twice real, even the journey down from Messina, and the oranges on the ferry, and the Big Lombard on the train, and Whiskers and Without Whiskers, and the malarial green, and Siracusa – in all, Sicily itself, everything twice real, and on a journey in the fourth dimension.

XII

THE HERRING WAS filleted, put on a plate, sprinkled with oil, and my mother and I sat at the table. In the kitchen, that is; with the sun shining through the window behind my mother's shoulders wrapped in the red shawl and her very light chestnut-brown hair. The table was against the wall, and my mother and I sat across from each other, with the brazier beneath the table, and on top of it the plate of herring almost overflowing with olive oil. And my mother tossed me a napkin, reached over with a plate and a fork, and pulled from the breadbox a large half-eaten loaf of bread.

'Do you mind if I don't put out a tablecloth?' she asked.

'Of course not,' I said.

And she: 'I can't do the wash every day . . . I'm old now.'

But when I was a child we always ate without a tablecloth, except for Sundays and holidays, and I remembered my mother always saying she couldn't wash every day. I began to eat the herring with bread, and asked: 'There's no soup?'

My mother looked at me and said, 'Who knew you were coming?'

And I looked at her, and said: 'But I mean for you. You don't make soup for yourself?'

'You mean for me?' my mother said. 'I've hardly ever

eaten soup in my life. I made it for you and your father, but for me, this is what I always ate: herring in the winter, roasted peppers in the summer, lots of oil, lots of bread . . .'

'Always?'

'Always. Why not?' my mother said. 'Olives, too, of course, and sometimes pork chops, or sausage, when we had a pig . . .'

'We had a pig?' I asked.

'Don't you remember?' my mother said. 'Some years we kept a pig and raised it on prickly pears, then we butchered it . . .'

Then I remembered the countryside around a plate-layer's house with the railway track, and the prickly pears, and the snorts of a pig. We were well-off in those plate-layers' houses, I thought. We had all the countryside to run around in, without having to farm it, without farmers around, only an occasional sheep and the sulphur miners who came by on their way back from the sulphur mines at night, when we were already in bed. We were well-off, I thought, and asked: 'Didn't we also have chickens?'

My mother said yes, of course, we did have a few, and I said: 'We made mustard . . .'

And my mother: 'We made all kinds of things . . . sun-dried tomatoes . . . prickly pear biscuits.'

'We were well-off,' I said, and I believed it, thinking of the tomatoes drying in the sun on summer afternoons without a living soul in the whole countryside. It was dry country, the color of sulphur, and I remembered the great buzzing of summer and the welling up of silence, and I thought once again that we were well-off. 'We were well-off,' I said. 'We had wire screens.'

'They were malarial places, for the most part,' my mother said.

'That mighty malaria!' I said.

And my mother: 'Mighty is right!'

And I: 'With the cicadas!' And I thought of the forest of cicadas there on the metal screens in the windows that looked out onto the veranda, in that loneliness of sunlight, and I said: 'I thought malaria meant the cicadas!'

My mother laughed. 'Maybe that's why you caught so many of them?'

'I caught them?' I asked. 'But it was their singing I thought was malaria, not them . . . I'd catch them?'

'Oh yes!' my mother said. 'Twenty, thirty at a time.'

And I: 'I must've caught them thinking they were crickets.' And I asked: 'What did I do with them?'

My mother laughed again. 'I think you ate them,' she said.

'I ate them?' I exclaimed.

'Yes,' my mother said. 'You and your brothers.'

She laughed and I was disconcerted. 'How could that be?'

And my mother said: 'Maybe you were hungry.'

And I: 'We were hungry?'

And my mother: 'Maybe so.'

'But we were well-off, in our house!' I protested.

My mother looked at me. 'Yes,' she said. 'Your father got paid at the end of every month, and so for ten days we were well-off, we were the envy of all the farmers and sulphur miners . . . But when the first ten days were up, we were in the same boat as them. We ate snails.'

'Snails?' I said.

'Yes, and wild chicory,' my mother said.

And I said: 'The others ate only snails?'

And my mother: 'Yes, poor people ate only snails, most of the time. And we were poor the last twenty days of every month.'

And I: 'We ate snails for twenty days?'

And my mother: 'Snails and wild chicory.'

I thought about it, smiled, and said: 'But I bet they were pretty good, anyway.'

And my mother: 'Delicious. You can cook them so many ways.'

And I: 'What do you mean, so many ways?'

And my mother: 'Just boiled, for example. Or with garlic and tomato. Or breaded and fried.'

And I: 'What a thought! Breaded and fried? In the shell?'

And my mother: 'Of course! You eat them by sucking them out of the shell . . . Don't you remember?'

And I: 'I remember, I remember . . . Seems to me sucking the shell is the best part.'

And my mother: 'Hours can go by, just sucking . . .'

XIII

FOR TWO OR three minutes we sat in silence, eating the herring, then my mother began to talk again, telling me a few ways to cook snails. So I could teach my wife, she said. But my wife didn't cook snails, I told her. And my mother wanted to know what my wife usually cooked, and I told her she usually made something boiled.

'Boiled? Boiled what?' my mother exclaimed.

'Boiled meat,' I said.

'Meat? What kind of meat?' my mother exclaimed

'Beef,' I said.

My mother looked at me with disgust. She asked me how it tasted. And I told her that it didn't have any particular taste, that we ate pasta in the broth.

'And the meat?' my mother asked me.

And I told her, truthfully, that there usually wasn't any meat after we ate the broth. I explained it all: the carrots, the celery, the piece of bone we called meat; explaining everything accurately so she would understand that in Northern Italy we were much better off than in Sicily, at least nowadays, in the city at least, and that we ate more or less like Christians.

My mother was still looking at me with disgust.

'Oh!' she exclaimed. 'Every day, that's what you eat?'

And I said: 'Yes! Not just Sundays! When one is working and earning money, at least!'

My mother was disconcerted. 'Every day! And don't you get bored?' she said.

'Don't you get bored with herring?' I said.

'But herring is tasty,' my mother said. And she began to tell me how much herring she thought she had eaten in her life, and how, in her capacity for eating herring and more herring, she was like her father, my grandfather.

'I think herring has something good for the brain,' she said. 'It gives you a good complexion, too.' And she pointed out all the good she thought herring did for various human organs and functions; maybe it was really thanks to herring, she declared, that my grandfather was a great man.

'He was a great man, Grandpa?' I asked. I vaguely remembered having grown up, in my most distant child-hood, under a shadow; it must have been the shadow of the greatness of my grandfather. I asked: 'He was a great man, Grandpa?'

'Oh yes! You didn't know that?' my mother said.

I said yes, I knew, but I wanted to know what he had done that was great, and my mother shouted that he was great in every way. He had brought into the world daughters who were tall and beautiful, all daughters, she shouted, and had built this house where she now lived, without even being a mason, with his own hands.

'He was a great man,' she said. 'He could work eighteen hours a day, and he was a great socialist, a great hunter and great on horseback in the procession on Saint Joseph's Day.'

'He rode in the procession on Saint Joseph's Day?' I said.

'Oh yes! He was a great horseman, better than anyone else in this town, or in Piazza Armerina,' my mother said. 'How could they have had a cavalcade without him?'

And I said: 'But he was a socialist?'

And my mother: 'He was a socialist . . . He didn't know how to read or write, but he understood politics and he was a socialist . . .'

And I: 'But how could he ride behind Saint Joseph if he was a socialist? Socialists don't believe in Saint Joseph.'

'What a beast you are!' my mother said then. 'Your grandfather wasn't just a socialist like all the others. He was a great man. He could believe in Saint Joseph and still be a socialist. He could hold a thousand things in his head at the same time. And he was a socialist because he understood politics . . . But he could believe in Saint Joseph. He never said anything against Saint Joseph.'

'But the priests, I imagine, must have thought there was a contradiction,' I said.

And my mother: 'And what did he care about priests?'

And I: 'But the procession was the business of priests!'

'You really are an idiot!' my mother exclaimed. 'It was a procession of horses and men on horses. It was a cavalcade.' She got up and went to the window, and I understood that I was meant to follow her there. 'You see,' she said. The window overlooked the slope of roofs and then the ravines, the stream, and the woods in the winter sun, and the mountain with its rockface mottled with snow. 'You see,' my mother said. And I looked more closely, at those roofs with smokeless chimneys, and the stream, the carob woods, the spots of snow; more closely, that is, seeing them twice real, and my mother said:

'The procession started from there, across from us, and went towards that telegraph pole . . . There's a little church you can't see from here, on that mountain, but they would light it up inside and outside and it would look like a star. The cavalcade left from the church, with lanterns and bells, and went down the mountain. It was always at night, of course. We could see the lights and I knew my father was there at the head, a great horseman, with everyone waiting in the piazza down below or on the bridge. And the cavalcade entered the woods, we couldn't see the lanterns any more, we could only hear the bells. It went on for a long time and then the cavalcade appeared on the bridge, with all the noise of the bells, and the lanterns, and him at the head as if he felt like a king . . .'

'I think I remember,' I said, and in fact it seemed I'd at least dreamed something similar, the ringing bells of horses and a great star in front of the mountain, in the heart of the night, but my mother said: 'Nonsense! You were just three the only time you saw it.'

And I looked again at that Sicily outside, then at my mother all wrapped up in her shawl, from her light-haired head to her feet, and I saw she was wearing men's shoes, my father's old plate-layer's shoes, ankle high and maybe with studs, like the ones I remembered she always had the habit of wearing in the house, so as to be more comfortable, or to feel herself in some sense rooted in a man, and a bit of a man herself, a rib of man.

GIUSEPPE TOMASI
DI LAMPEDUSA

THE SIREN (1957)

Translated by Stephen Twilley

LATE IN THE autumn of 1938 I came down with a severe case of misanthropy. I was living in Turin at the time, and my local girl no. 1, rifling my pockets in search of a spare fifty-lire note as I slept, had also discovered a short letter from girl no. 2. Spelling mistakes notwithstanding, it left no room for doubt concerning the nature of our relations.

My waking was both immediate and violent. Outbursts of angry dialect echoed through my modest lodgings on Via Peyron, and an attempt to scratch my eyes out was averted only by the slight twist I administered to the dear girl's left wrist. This entirely justified act of self-defence put an end to the row, but also to the romance. The girl dressed hurriedly, stuffing powder puff, lipstick, and a little handkerchief into her bag along with the fifty-lire note, 'cause of so great a calamity,' thrice flung a colorful local alternative to 'Swine!' in my face, and left. Never had she been so adorable as in those fifteen minutes of fury. I watched from the window as she emerged and moved away into the morning mist: tall, slender, adorned with regained elegance.

I never saw her again, just as I never saw a black cashmere sweater that had cost me a small fortune and possessed the woeful merit of being cut to suit a woman just as well as a man. All she left were two of those so-called invisible hair-pins on the bed.

That same afternoon I had an appointment with no. 2 in a patisserie in Piazza Carlo Felice. At the little round table in the western corner of the second room – 'our' table – I saw not the chestnut tresses of the girl whom I now desired more than ever but the sly face of Tonino, her twelve-year-old brother. He'd just gulped down some hot chocolate with a double portion of whipped cream. With typical Turinese urbanity, he stood as I approached.

'Sir,' he said, 'Pinotta will not be coming; she asked me to give you this note. Good day, sir.'

He went out, taking with him the two brioches left on his plate. The ivory-colored card announced that I was summarily dismissed on account of my infamy and 'southern dishonesty.' Clearly, no. 1 had tracked down and provoked no. 2, and I had fallen between two stools.

In twelve hours I had lost two usefully complementary girls plus a sweater to which I was rather attached; I also had to pick up the bill for that infernal Tonino. I'd been made a fool of, humiliated in my very Sicilian self-regard; and I decided to abandon for a time the world and its pomps.

There was no better place for this period of retreat than the café on Via Po where, lonely as a dog, I now went at every free moment, and always in the evening after my work at the newspaper. It was a sort of Hades filled with the wan shades of lieutenant colonels, magistrates and retired professors. These vain apparitions played draughts or dominoes, submerged in a light that was dimmed during the day by the clouds and the arcade outside, during the evenings by the enormous green shades on the chandeliers. They never raised their voices, afraid that any immoderate sound might upset the fragile fabric of their presence. It was, in short, a most satisfactory Limbo.

Being a creature of habit, I always sat at the same little corner table, one carefully designed to provide maximum discomfort to the customer. On my left two spectral senior officers played trictrac with two phantoms from the appeals court; their military and judicial dice slipped tonelessly from a leather cup. On my right sat an elderly man wrapped in an old overcoat with a worn astrakhan collar. He read foreign magazines one after another, smoked Tuscan cigars, and frequently spat. Every so often he would close his magazine and appear to be pursuing some memory in the spirals of smoke; then he would go back to reading and spitting. His hands were as ugly as could be, gnarled and ruddy, with fingernails that were cut straight across and not always clean. Once, however, when he came across a photograph in a magazine of an archaic Greek statue, the kind with widespread eyes and an ambiguous smile, I was surprised to see his disfigured fingertips caress the image with positively regal delicacy. When he realized that I'd seen him, he grunted with displeasure and ordered a second espresso.

Our relations would have remained on this plane of latent hostility if not for a happy accident. Usually I left the office with five or six daily papers, including, on one occasion, the *Giornale di Sicilia*. Those were the years when the Fascist Ministry of Popular Culture, or MinCulPop, was at its most virulent, and every newspaper was just like all the others; that edition of the Palermo daily was as banal as ever, indistinguishable from a paper published in Milan or Rome, if not by its greater share of typographical errors. My reading of it was accordingly brief, and I soon set it aside on the table. I had already begun to contemplate another product of MinCulPop's vigilance when my neighbor addressed me: 'Pardon me, sir, would you mind if I glanced at this *Giornale di Sicilia* of yours? I'm Sicilian, and it's been twenty years since I came across a newspaper from my part of the world.' His voice was as cultivated as any I'd ever heard, the accent impeccable; his grey eyes regarded me with profound indifference.

'Be my guest. I'm Sicilian myself, you know. If you like, I can easily bring the paper every evening.'

'Thank you, but that won't be necessary; my curiosity is a purely physical one. If Sicily remains as it was in my time, I imagine nothing good ever happens there. Nothing has for the past three thousand years.'

He glanced through the paper, folded it, and gave it back to me, then plunged into reading a pamphlet. When he stood to go, it was clear that he hoped to slip out unnoticed, but I rose to introduce myself; he quietly muttered his name, which I failed to catch, yet neglected to extend his hand. At the threshold of the café, however, he turned, doffed his hat, and loudly shouted, 'Farewell, fellow countryman.' He disappeared down the arcade, leaving me speechless while the shades at their games grumbled disapprovingly.

I performed the magical rites necessary to conjure a waiter; pointing at the empty table, I asked him, 'Who was that gentleman?'

'That,' he replied, 'is Senator Rosario La Ciura.'

The name said a great deal even to an ignorant journalist. It belonged to one of the five or six Italians with an indisputable international reputation – to the most illustrious Hellenist of our time, in fact. I understood the thick magazines and the caressing of the illustration, the unsociability and hidden refinement, too.

In the newspaper offices the following day I searched through that peculiar drawer of the obituary file containing the 'advancers.' The 'La Ciura' card was there, for once tolerably well drafted. I read how the great man had been born into an impoverished petit bourgeois family in Aci Castello (Catania), and that thanks to an astonishing aptitude for ancient Greek, and by dint of scholarships and scholarly publications, he had at the age of twenty-seven attained the chair of Greek literature at the University of Pavia. Subsequently he had moved to the University of Turin, where he remained until retirement. He had taught at Oxford and Tübingen and travelled extensively, for not only had he been a senator since before the Fascists came to power and a member of the Lincean Academy; he had also received honorary degrees from Yale, Harvard, New Delhi and Tokyo, as well as, of course, from the most prestigious European universities from Uppsala to Salamanca. His lengthy list of publications included many that were considered fundamental, especially those on Ionic dialects; suffice to say that he had been commissioned to edit the Hesiod volume in the Bibliotheca Teubneriana, the first foreigner so honored, to which he had added an introduction in Latin of unsurpassed scientific rigor and profundity. Finally, the greatest honor of all, he was *not* a member of the Fascist Royal Academy of Italy. What had always set him apart from other exceedingly erudite colleagues was a vital, almost carnal sense of classical antiquity, a quality on display in a collection of essays written in Italian, *Men and Gods*, which had been recognized as a work not only of great erudition but of authentic poetry. He was, in short, 'an honor to a nation and a beacon to the world,' as the card concluded. He was seventy-five years old and lived decorously but far from lavishly on his pension and senator's benefits. He was a bachelor.

There's no use denying that we Italians – original sons (or fathers) of the Renaissance – look on the Great Humanist as superior to all other human beings. The possibility of finding myself in daily proximity to the highest representative of such subtle, almost magical, and poorly remunerated wisdom was both flattering and disturbing. I experienced the same sensations that a young American would on meeting Mr. Gillette: fear, respect, a certain not ignoble envy.

That evening I descended into Limbo in quite a different spirit than that of the previous days. The senator was already at his spot and responded to my reverential greeting with a faint grumble. When, however, he'd finished reading an article and jotted down a few things in a small notebook, he turned toward me and, in a strangely musical voice, said, 'Fellow countryman, from the manner in which you greeted me I gather that one of these phantoms has told you who I am. Forget it, and, if you haven't already done so, forget the aorist tense you studied in secondary school. Instead tell me your name, because your introduction yesterday evening was the usual mumbled mess and I, unlike you, do not have the option of learning who you are from others. Because it's clear that no one here knows you.'

He spoke with insolent detachment. To him I was apparently something less than a cockroach, more like a dust mote whirling aimlessly in a sunbeam. And yet the calm voice, precise speech and use of the familiar *tu* radiated the serenity of a Platonic dialogue.

'My name is Paolo Corbera. I was born in Palermo, where I also took my law degree. Now I work here for *La Stampa*. To reassure you, Senator, let me add that on my exit exams I earned a "5 plus" out of 10 in Greek, and I suspect that the "plus" was only added to make sure I received my diploma.'

He gave a half smile. 'Thank you for telling me this. So much the better. I detest speaking with people who think they know what they in fact do not, like my colleagues at the university. In the end they are familiar only with the external forms of Greek, its eccentricities and deformities. The living spirit of this language, foolishly called "dead," has not been revealed to them. *Nothing* has been revealed to them, for that matter. They are poor wretches, after all: how could they perceive this spirit without ever having had the opportunity to hear Greek?'

Pride is fine, sure, it's better than false modesty, but it seemed to me the senator was going too far. I even wondered whether the years might have succeeded in softening somewhat his exceptional mind. Those poor things, his colleagues, had had just as much opportunity to hear ancient Greek as he had – that is, none.

He went on: 'Paolo, you're lucky to bear the name of the one apostle who had a bit of culture and a smattering of reading under his belt. Though Jerome would have been better. The other names you Christians carry around are truly contemptible. The names of slaves.'

I was disappointed again. He really seemed like nothing more than a typical anticlerical academic with a pinch of Fascist Nietzscheism thrown in. Could it be?

His voice rose and fell appealingly as he continued to speak, with the ardor, perhaps, of someone who had passed a great deal of time in silence. 'Corbera . . . Is that not one of the great names of Sicily, or am I mistaken? I remember that my father paid the annual rent for our house in Aci Castello to the administrator of a House of Corbera di Palina, or Salina, I can't recall which. He'd always joke and say that if there was one thing that was certain in this world, it was that those few lire weren't going to end up in the pockets of the "demesne," as he called it. But are you one of those Corberas, or just a descendant of some peasant who took his master's name?'

I confessed that I really was a Corbera di Salina, the sole surviving specimen, in fact. All the opulence, all the sins, all the uncollected rents, all the unpaid debts, all the political opportunism of the Leopard were concentrated in me alone. Paradoxically, the senator seemed pleased.

'That's fine, just fine. I have a great deal of respect for the old families. Their memory is . . . minuscule, of course, but still it's greater than the others'. It's as much of physical immortality as your sort can hope for. Think about getting married soon, Corbera, seeing as how your sort haven't found any better way to survive than scattering your seed in the strangest places.'

He was definitely trying my patience. 'Your sort.' Who was that? The whole contemptible herd that was not fortunate enough to be Senator La Ciura? Who'd attained physical immortality? You'd never know it from looking at his wrinkled face, his sagging flesh . . .

'Corbera di Salina,' he continued, undeterred. 'You don't mind if I call you *tu*, as I do with my students in their fleeting youth?'

I professed to be not only honored but delighted, and I was. Moving beyond questions of names and protocol, we now spoke of Sicily. It had been twenty years since he'd set foot on the island, and the last time he'd been 'down there,' as he called it in the Piedmontese manner, he'd stayed a mere five days, in Syracuse, to talk to Paolo Orsi about the alternating choruses in classical theatre.

'I remember they wanted to take me in a car from Catania to Syracuse; I accepted only when I learned that at Augusta the road passes far from the sea, whereas the train follows the coastline. Tell me about our island. It's a beautiful place, even if it is inhabited by donkeys. The gods once sojourned there – and perhaps in some endless Augusts they return. But don't on any account speak to me about those four modern temples of yours, not that that's anything you'd understand, I'm sure.'

So we spoke about eternal Sicily, the Sicily of the natural world; about the scent of rosemary on the Nebrodi Mountains and the taste of Melilli honey; about the swaying cornfields seen from Etna on a windy day in May, some secluded spots near Syracuse, and the fragrant gusts from the citrus plantations known to sweep down on Palermo during sunset in June. We spoke of those magic summer nights, looking out over the gulf of Castellammare, when the stars are mirrored in the sleeping sea, and how, lying on your back among the mastic trees, your spirit is lost in the whirling heavens, while the body braces itself, fearing the approach of demons.

The senator had scarcely visited the island for fifty years, and yet his memory of certain minute details was remarkably precise. 'Sicily's sea is the most vividly colored, the most romantic of any I have ever seen; it's the only thing you won't manage to ruin, at least away from the cities. Do the trattorias by the sea still serve spiny urchins, split in half?'

I assured him that they did, though adding that few people ate them now for fear of typhus.

'And yet they are the most beautiful thing you have down there, bloody and cartilaginous, the very image of the female sex, fragrant with salt and seaweed. Typhus, typhus! They're dangerous as all gifts from the sea are; the sea offers death as well as immortality. In Syracuse I demanded that Orsi order them immediately. What flavor! How divine in appearance! My most beautiful memory of the last fifty years!'

I was confused and fascinated: a man of such stature indulging in almost obscene metaphors, displaying an infantile appetite for the altogether mediocre pleasure of eating sea urchins!

Our conversation stretched out, and on leaving he insisted on paying for my espresso, not without a display of his peculiar coarseness ('Everyone knows kids from good families are always broke'). We parted friends, if you disregard the fifty-year difference between our ages and the thousands of light years separating our cultures.

We proceeded to see each other every evening; even as my rage against humanity began to wane, I made it my duty never to fail to meet the senator in the underworld of Via Po. Not that we chatted much; he continued to read and take notes and only addressed me occasionally, but when he spoke it was always a melodious flow of pride and insolence, sprinkled with disparate allusions and strands of impenetrable poetry. He continued to spit as well, and eventually I observed that he did so only while he read. I believe that he also developed a certain affection for me, but I didn't delude myself. If there was affection it wasn't anything like what one of 'our sort' (to adopt the senator's term) might feel for a human being; instead it was similar to what an elderly spinster might feel for her pet goldfinch, whose vacuousness and lack of understanding she is well aware of, but whose existence allows her to express aloud regrets in which the creature plays no part; and yet, if the pet were not there, she would suffer a distinct malaise. In fact, I began to notice that when I arrived late the old man's eyes, haughty as ever, were fixed on the entrance.

It took roughly a month for us to pass from topical observations – always highly original but impersonal on his part – to more indelicate subjects, which are after all the only ones that distinguish conversations between friends from those between mere acquaintances. I was the one who took the initiative. His spitting bothered me – it had also bothered the guardians of Hades, who finally brought a very shiny brass spittoon to his spot – such that one evening I dared to inquire why he didn't seek a cure for his chronic catarrh. I asked the question without thinking and immediately regretted risking it, expecting the senatorial ire to bring the stucco work on the ceiling raining down on my head. Instead his richly toned voice replied calmly, 'But my dear Corbera, I have no catarrh. You who observe so carefully should have noticed that I never cough before spitting. My spitting is not a sign of sickness but of mental health: I spit out of disgust for the rubbish I happen to be reading. If you took the trouble to examine that contrivance' – (and he gestured at the spittoon) – 'you would realize that it contains hardly any saliva and no trace of mucus. My spitting is symbolic and highly cultural; if you don't like it, go back to your native drawing rooms, where people don't spit only because they can't be bothered to be nauseated by anything.'

His extraordinary insolence was mitigated solely by his distant gaze; I nevertheless felt the desire to stand up and walk out on him then and there. Fortunately I had the time to reflect that the fault lay in my rashness. I stayed, and the impassive senator immediately passed to counterattack. 'And you then, why patronize this Erebus full of shades and, as you say, catarrh sufferers, this locus of failed lives? In Turin there's no shortage of those creatures your sort finds so desirable. A trip to the Castello hotel in Rivoli, or to the baths in Moncalieri and your squalid aspiration would soon be fulfilled.'

I began to laugh at hearing such a cultured mouth offer such precise information about the Turinese demimonde. 'But how do you come to know about such places, Senator?'

'I know them, Corbera, I know them. Anyone spending time with politicians or members of the Academic Senate learns this, and nothing more. You will, however, do me the favor of being convinced that the sordid pleasures of your sort have never been stuff for Rosario La Ciura.' One could sense that it was true: in the senator's bearing and in his words there was the unmistakable sign of a sexual reserve (as one said in 1938) that had nothing to do with age.

'The truth is, Senator, it was precisely my search for some temporary refuge from the world that first brought me here. I'd had trouble with two of just the sort of women you've so rightfully condemned.'

His response was immediate and pitiless. 'Betrayed, eh, Corbera? Or was it disease?'

'No, nothing like that. Worse: desertion.' And I told him about the ridiculous events of two months earlier. I spoke of them in a light, facetious manner; the ulcer on my self-regard had closed, and anyone but that damned Hellenist would have teased me or possibly even sympathized. But the fearful old man did neither; instead he was indignant.

'This is what happens, Corbera, when wretched and diseased beings couple. What's more, I'd say the same to those two little trollops with respect to you, if I had the revolting misfortune to meet them.'

'Diseased, Senator? Both of them were in wonderful shape; you should have seen how they ate when we dined at Gli Specchi. And as for wretched, no, not at all: each was a magnificent figure of a young woman, and elegant as well.'

The senator hissingly spat his scorn. 'Diseased, I said, and made no mistake. In fifty, sixty years, perhaps much sooner, they will die; so they are already now diseased. And wretched as well. Some elegance they've got, composed of trinkets, stolen sweaters and sweet talk picked up at the movies. Some generosity too, fishing for greasy banknotes in their lover's pockets rather than presenting him, as others do, with pink pearls and branches of coral. This is what happens when one goes in for those little monstrosities with painted faces. And were you all not disgusted – they as much as you, you as much as they – to kiss and cuddle your future carcasses between evil-smelling sheets?'

I replied stupidly, 'But Senator, the sheets were always perfectly clean!'

He fumed. 'What do the sheets have to do with it? The inevitable cadaver stink came from you. I repeat, how can you consent to carouse with people of their kind, of your kind?'

I, who already had my eyes on an enchanting sometime seamstress, took offense. 'It's not as if one can sleep with nothing but Most Serene Highnesses!'

'Who said anything about Most Serene Highnesses? They're bound for the charnel house like the rest. But this isn't something you'd understand, young man, and I was wrong to mention it. It is fated that you and your girlfriends will wade ever further into the noxious swamps of your foul pleasures. There are very few who know better.' Gazing up at the ceiling, he began to smile; a ravished expression spread over his face; then he shook my hand and left.

We didn't see each other for three days; on the fourth I received a telephone call in the editorial office. 'Is this Signor Corbera? My name is Bettina Carmagnola, I'm Senator La Ciura's housekeeper. He asks me to tell you that he has had a bad cold, and that now he is better and wishes to see you tonight after dinner. Come to 18 Via Bertola at nine, second floor.' The call, abruptly interrupted, became unappealable.

The building at 18 Via Bertola was a dilapidated old struc ture, but the senator's apartment was large and – thanks, I suppose, to the diligence of Bettina – well maintained. In the entrance hall began the parade of books, of those modest-looking, economically bound volumes found in all living libraries; there were thousands of them in the three rooms I crossed. In the fourth sat the senator, wrapped in a very ample camel-hair dressing gown that was smoother and softer than any I'd ever seen. I learned later that the fabric wasn't camel at all but was made from the precious wool of a Peruvian animal, and that the gown was a gift from the Academic Senate of Lima. The senator refrained from rising when I entered but welcomed me with considerable warmth. He was better, completely fine, in fact, and planned to be back in circulation as soon as the bitter cold spell that had descended on Turin in those days had passed. He offered me some resinous Cypriot wine, a gift from the Italian Institute of Athens; some atrocious pink *lokums* from the Archaeological Mission of Ankara; and some more sensible Turinese sweets purchased by the provident Bettina. He was in such good humor that he gave two full-mouth smiles and even went so far as to apologize for his outbursts in Hades.

'I know, Corbera, I know. I was excessive in my words, however restrained – believe me – in my concepts. Don't give it another thought.'

I really didn't think about it; indeed I was full of respect for the old man, whom I suspected of being tremendously unhappy notwithstanding his triumphant career. He devoured the revolting *lokums*.

'Sweets, Corbera, ought to be sweet and nothing but. If they have another flavor they are like perverted kisses.' He gave large crumbs to Aeacus, a stocky boxer that had entered the room at some point. 'This creature, Corbera, for those capable of appreciating him, more closely resembles the Immortals, despite his ugliness, than your little temptresses.' He refused to show me his library. 'It's all classics, stuff that wouldn't interest someone like you, a moral failure in Greek.' But he did lead me around the room we were in, which was his study. There were few books, among which I noted the theatre of Tirso de Molina, Fouqué's *Undine*, Giraudoux's play of the same name, and, to my surprise, the works of H. G. Wells; but in compensation, on the walls, were enormous life-size photographs of archaic Greek statues, and not the typical photographs that any of us could procure for ourselves but stupendous reproductions, clearly requested with authority and sent with devotion by museums around the world. They were all there, the magnificent creatures: the Louvre's *Horseman*, the *Seated Goddess* from Taranto that is in Berlin, the *Warrior* from Delphi, one of the *Korai of the Acropolis*, the *Apollo of Piombino*, the *Lapith Woman* and the *Phoebus* from Olympia, the famous *Charioteer* . . . The room shone with their ecstatic and at the same time ironic smiles, gloried in the calm arrogance of their bearing. 'You see, Corbera, perhaps these, if one is so fortunate; the local "maidens," no.' Above the fireplace, ancient amphorae and craters: Odysseus tied to the mast of his boat, the Sirens casting themselves down onto the rocks in expiation for having let their prey escape. 'Lies, Corbera, the lies of petit bourgeois poets. No one escapes, and even if someone did, the Sirens would never destroy themselves for so little. In any case, how could they die?'

On an end table stood a faded old photograph, simply framed, of a young man around twenty, almost nude, his curly hair disheveled, with a bold expression and features of rare beauty. Perplexed, I stopped myself for a moment. I thought I understood. Not at all. 'And this, countryman, this was and is, and *will be*,' he stressed, 'Rosario La Ciura.'

The broken-down senator in a dressing gown had been a young god.

Our conversation then turned to other matters. Before I left he showed me a letter in French from the rector of the University of Coimbra inviting him to be a guest of honor at a Greek studies conference in Portugal in May. 'I'm very pleased. I'll go aboard the *Rex* in Genoa along with the French, Swiss and German participants. Like Odysseus I'll plug my ears in order not to hear the drivel of those moral cripples, and there'll be beautiful days of sailing: the sun, the blue sky, the smell of the sea.'

On my way out we again passed the shelf containing the works of Wells, and I ventured to show my surprise at seeing them there. 'You're right, Corbera, they're ghastly. There's one novella there that, were I to reread it, would make me spit nonstop for a month; and even you, salon lapdog that you are, you would be appalled.'

Following my visit our relations became decidedly cordial – on my part at least. I went to great lengths to have some exceptionally fresh sea urchins brought in from Genoa. When I learned that they would arrive the following day I procured some Etna wine and farmer's bread and nervously invited the senator to visit me in my tiny apartment. To my great relief he very happily accepted. I picked him up in my Fiat 508 and dragged him all the way to Via Peyron, which is something of a backwater. In the car he displayed some fear and no confidence whatsoever in my driving skills. 'I know you now, Corbera; if we're unlucky enough to encounter one of your abortions in a frock, you're liable to turn your head and send us both smashing into the corner of a building.' We met no skirted monstrosity worthy of note and arrived safely.

For the first time since I met him I saw the senator laugh – when we entered my bedroom. 'So then, Corbera, this is the theater of your vile exploits.' He examined my few books. 'Fine, fine. Perhaps you're less ignorant than you seem. This one here,' he added as he picked up a volume of Shakespeare, 'this one here understood something. "A sea-change into something rich and strange."* "What potions have I drunk of Siren tears?" '†

When the good Signora Carmagnola entered the drawing room carrying the tray of sea urchins, lemons, and the rest, the senator was ecstatic. 'This was your idea? How did you know they are the thing I long for more than any other?'

'You can safely enjoy them, Senator; this morning they were still in the Ligurian Sea.'

'Yes, of course, your sort are always the same, slaves to your decadence, to your putrescence; your long, asinine ears always straining to make out the shuffling steps of Death. Poor devils! Thank you, Corbera, you've been a good famulus. It's a shame they're not from the sea down there, these urchins, that they haven't been steeped in our algae; their spines have surely never drawn a drop of divine blood. You've done what was possible, certainly, but these urchins, having dozed on the cold reefs of Nervi or Arenzano, they're almost *boreal*.' It was clear that he was one of those Sicilians for whom the Ligurian Riviera – considered a tropical region by the Milanese – may as well be Iceland. The urchins, split in half, revealed their wounded, blood-red, strangely compartmentalized flesh. I'd never paid attention before now, but after the senator's bizarre comparisons they really did seem like cross sections of who knows what delicate female organs. He consumed them avidly but without cheer, with a meditative, almost sorrowful air. He didn't want to squeeze any lemon over them.

'Your sort, always combining flavors! Sea urchins have to taste also like lemon, sugar also like chocolate, love also like

* William Shakespeare, *The Tempest*, act 1, scene 2.
† William Shakespeare, *The Sonnets*, 119.

127

paradise!' When he finished he took a sip of wine and closed his eyes. After a bit I noticed, slipping from beneath his shriveled eyelids, two tears. He stood up and walked to the window, where he furtively dried his eyes. Then he turned. 'Have you ever been to Augusta yourself, Corbera?' I'd spent three months there as a recruit; during off-duty hours two or three of us would take a boat out on the transparent waters and explore the gulfs. After my answer he was silent; then, in an irritated voice: 'And did you grunts ever arrive as far as the inland gulf past Punta Izzo, behind the hill overlooking the saltworks?'

'We certainly did, it's the most beautiful spot in Sicily, yet to be discovered, thankfully, by the Dopolavoro crowds.* The coast is wild there, right, Senator? It's completely deserted, and you can't see a single house; the sea is the color of peacocks; and behind it all, beyond the shifting waves, rises Mount Etna. From no other spot is it so beautiful – calm, powerful, truly divine. It's a place where you can see the island in one of its eternal aspects, as it was before it so foolishly turned its back on its vocation, which was to serve as pasture for the Cattle of the Sun.'

The senator was silent. Then: 'You're a good kid, Corbera; if you weren't so ignorant, something might have been made of you.' He came toward me and kissed my forehead. 'Now bring round your jalopy. I want to go home.'

In the weeks that followed we continued to see each other regularly. Now we also took late-night walks, generally down Via Po and across the martial expanse of Piazza Vittorio; we went to gaze at the rushing river and the Turin hills, elements

* The Opera Nazionale Dopolavoro (National Recreational Club) was the Italian Fascist leisure and recreational organization.

that introduced a drop of fantasy into the geometrical rigor of the city. Then began the spring, that affecting season of threatened youth; the first lilacs sprouted on the banks, and the most impetuous of the young couples without a place to retreat to braved the dampness of the grass. 'Down there the sun already blazes, the algae blooms, the fish appear at the surface of the water on moonlit nights and flashes of bodies can be made out between the lines of luminous foam. We stand here before this insipid, lifeless current of water, before these big ugly buildings that look like soldiers or monks all in a line, and we hear the sobs of these dying creatures coupling.' It cheered him, however, to think about the impending voyage to Lisbon, not far off now. 'It will be pleasant. You ought to come along as well. A shame that it's not open to those deficient in Greek; with me at least you can speak Italian, but if Zuckmayer or Van der Voos found out you didn't know the optative of every irregular verb, you'd be done for. This even though you may be more in touch with Greek reality than they are; not through cultivation, clearly, but through animal instinct.'

Two days prior to his departure for Genoa he told me that he would not be returning to the café the following day, but that he would expect me at his house at nine that evening.

The protocol was identical to the last time: the images of the gods of three thousand years ago radiated youth as a stove radiates heat; the faded photograph of the young god of fifty years ago seemed dismayed at watching his own metamorphosis into a white-haired old man sunk in an armchair.

When the Cypriot wine had been drunk the senator called Bettina and told her she could go to bed. 'I will see Signor Corbera out myself when he goes.' Then: 'Believe me, Corbera, if I've asked you here this evening at the risk of upsetting any Rivoli fornication plans you might have had, it's because I need you. I leave tomorrow, and when you go away at my age you never know if it won't be necessary to stay away forever, especially when you go by sea. Please know that I genuinely care for you: your ingenuousness touches me, your unconcealed carnal intrigues amuse me, and it seems to me that, as is sometimes the case with the best kind of Sicilians, you have managed to achieve a synthesis of the senses and reason. Therefore you deserve not to be left empty-handed, without hearing me explain the reason behind some of my eccentricities, of some sentences I've spoken in your presence that will certainly have appeared to you worthy of a madman.'

I protested weakly: 'I haven't understood many of the things you've said, but I've always attributed my incomprehension to the inadequacy of my own mind, never to an aberration of yours.'

'Don't worry, Corbera, it doesn't matter. All of us old people seem crazy to you young people, and often in fact the opposite is true. To explain myself, however, I'll have to tell you about my adventure, an uncommon one. It happened when I was "that young gentleman there,"' and he pointed at his photograph. 'I have to go back to 1887, a time that will seem prehistoric to you but is not for me.'

He moved from his place behind the desk and came to sit down beside me on the same couch. 'Pardon me, but from now on I'll have to speak in a low voice. Important words cannot be bellowed; the "cry of love" or hate is to be found only in melodrama or among the most uncultivated people, which comes to the same thing in the end. In 1887, then, I was twenty-four years old; I looked like the person in that photograph. I already had my degree in ancient literature and had published two articles on Ionic dialects that had caused a certain stir in my university; and for the previous year I'd been preparing for a competition for a post at the University of Pavia. Also, I had never known a woman. As a matter of fact, I have never known women either before or after that year.' I was sure that my face had remained stonily impassive, but I was deceived. 'Your eyelash fluttering is very ill-mannered, Corbera. What I say is the truth – the truth and a boast. I know that we Catanesi are held to be capable of impregnating our own nannies, and that may even be true. Not in my case, however. When one passes one's days and nights with goddesses and demigoddesses, as I did during that period, there remains little desire to climb the stairs of the brothels of San Berillo. At the time I was also held back by religious scruples. Corbera, you really should learn to control your eyelashes; they betray you constantly. Yes, I said religious scruples. I also said "at the time." Now I no longer have them; but they were worthless in any case.

'You, young Corbera, who probably obtained your position at the newspaper thanks to a note from some Party official, you don't know what it is to prepare for a competition for a university chair of Greek literature. For two years you slog away, to the limits of sanity. I already knew the language fairly well, fortunately, as well as I know it now; and I don't say so just for the sake of it, you know . . . But the rest: the Alexandrine and Byzantine variants of the texts; the passages cited, always poorly, from Latin authors; the countless connections between literature and mythology, history, philosophy, science! I repeat, it's enough to drive you mad. So I studied like a dog, and also gave lessons to students who'd flunked the subject, to pay the rent on my place in the city. You could say I subsisted on nothing but black olives and coffee. On top of all this came the disastrous summer of 1887, one of those truly infernal summers that we have every so often down there. At night Etna vomited back the fire of the sun that it stored up fifteen hours a day; if you touched the railing of a balcony at noon you'd have to run to the emergency room; volcanic paving stones seemed on the point of returning to their liquid state; and almost every day the sirocco swatted you in the face with sticky bats' wings. I was on the verge of collapse when a friend came to my aid. He found me wandering the streets, exhausted, muttering Greek verses I no longer understood. My appearance troubled him. "Look, Rosario, if you stay here you'll go mad, and then so much for the competition. Myself, I'm off to Switzerland" – the fellow had money – "but in Augusta I've got a three-room cabin twenty yards from the sea, far from the village. Pack a bag, take your books and go stay there for the rest of the summer. Come by my place in an hour and I'll give you the key. Just wait till you see, it's something else. Ask for the Carobene place at the station, everyone knows it. But you're really got to leave – tonight."

'I followed his advice and left that same evening. On awaking the next morning, rather than the toilet pipes across the courtyard that used to greet me at dawn, I found before me a pure expanse of sea, and beyond it a no longer pitiless Etna, wrapped in the morning mist. The spot was completely deserted, as you said it still is now, and of a singular beauty. The little house's dilapidated rooms contained just the sofa on which I'd slept, a table, and three chairs; the kitchen, a few earthenware pots and an old lamp. Behind the house were a fig tree and a well. Paradise. I went into the village and tracked down the farmer of the small Carobene estate, and worked out that every few days he would bring me some bread, pasta, vegetables and kerosene. Olive oil I had, from the supply my poor mother had sent me in Catania. I rented

132

a dinghy that the fisherman brought round that afternoon along with a wicker fish basket and a few hooks. I'd decided to stay there for at least two months.

'Carobene was right: it really was something else. The heat was violent in Augusta too, but, no longer reflected back by walls, it produced not dreadful prostration but a sort of submissive euphoria; the sun, shedding its executioner's grimace, was content to be a smiling if brutal giver of energy, and also a sorcerer setting mobile diamonds in the sea's slightest ripple. Study ceased to be toil: gently rocked by the boat in which I spent hours on end, each book seemed no longer an obstacle to be overcome but rather a key offering me passage into a world, a world I already had before my eyes in one of its most enchanting aspects. I often happened to recite the verses of poets aloud, and thus the names of those gods, which most people have forgotten or never knew, again skimmed the surface of the sea that would have once, at their mere mention, risen up in turmoil or subsided into dead calm.

'My isolation was absolute, interrupted only by visits from the farmer who brought me my few provisions every three or four days. He would only stay for five minutes; seeing me so exhilarated and disheveled, he must have thought me dangerously close to madness. And in truth, the sun, the seclusion, the nights passed beneath the wheeling stars, the silence, the scant nourishment, the study of remote subjects wove around me a spell that predisposed me to marvels.

'This came to pass on the morning of 5 August, at six o'clock. I hadn't been up for long before I was in the boat; a few strokes of the oars took me away from the pebbled shore. I'd stopped at the base of a large rock whose shadow might protect me from a sun that was already climbing, swollen with dazzling fury and turning the whiteness of the auroral sea gold and blue. As I declaimed I sensed that the side of the boat, to my right and behind me, had abruptly been lowered, as if someone had grabbed on to climb up. I turned and saw her: the smooth face of a sixteen-year-old emerged from the sea; two small hands gripped the gunwale. The adolescent smiled, a slight displacement of her pale lips that revealed small, sharp white teeth, like dogs'. This, however, was not a smile like those to be seen among your sort, always debased with an accessory expression of benevolence or irony, of compassion, cruelty or whatever the case may be; it expressed nothing but itself: an almost bestial delight in existing, a joy almost divine. This smile was the first of her charms that would affect me, revealing paradises of forgotten serenity. From her disordered hair, which was the color of the sun, seawater dripped into her exceedingly open green eyes, over features of infantile purity.

'Our suspicious reason, howsoever predisposed, loses its bearings in the face of the marvelous, and when it perceives it, tries to rely on the memory of banal phenomena. Like anyone else would have, I supposed that I'd met a swimmer. Moving cautiously, I pulled myself up to her level, leaned toward her and held out my hands to help her aboard. Instead she rose with astonishing strength straight out of the water to her waist, encircled my neck with her arms, wrapping me in a never before experienced perfume and allowed herself to be pulled into the boat. Her body below the groin, below the buttocks, was that of a fish, covered with tiny pearly blue scales and ending in a forked tail that slapped gently against the bottom of the boat. She was a Siren.

'She lay back, resting her head on interlaced fingers, displaying with serene immodesty the delicate little hairs of her armpits, her splayed breasts, her perfect stomach. She exuded what I have clumsily referred to as a perfume, a magical smell of the sea, of decidedly youthful sensuality. We were in the shade but twenty yards from us the seashore reveled in the sun and quivered with pleasure. My near-complete nudity ill concealed my own emotion.

'She spoke and thus was I overwhelmed, after her smile and smell, by the third and greatest of her charms: her voice. It was a bit guttural, husky, resounding with countless harmonics; behind the words could be discerned the sluggish undertow of summer seas, the whisper of receding beach foam, the wind passing over lunar tides. The song of the Sirens, Corbera, does not exist; the music that cannot be escaped is their voice alone.

'She spoke Greek and I struggled to understand her. "I heard you speaking to yourself in a language similar to my own. I like you: take me. I am Lighea, daughter of Calliope. Don't believe the stories about us. We don't kill anyone, we only love."

'I bent over her as I rowed, staring into her smiling eyes. When we reached the shore I took her aromatic body into my arms and we passed from the blazing sun into the deep shade; there she poured into my mouth such sensual pleasure that it is to your terrestrial kisses as wine is to insipid water.'

The senator narrated his adventure in a low voice. I who in my heart had always set my own varied experiences with women against those he regarded as mediocre, and had derived from this a foolish sense of reduced distance, was humiliated: in matters of love as well, I saw myself sunk to unfathomable depths. Never for a moment did I suspect he was lying to me, and had anyone else been there, even the most sceptical of witnesses, he too would have perceived the certainty of truth in the old man's tone.

'So began those three weeks. I have no right, nor would it be merciful to you, to go into details. Suffice to say that in those embraces I enjoyed the highest form of spiritual pleasure along with the greatest physical gratification, devoid of any social resonance, the same that our solitary mountain shepherds experience when they couple with their goats. If the comparison repels you, it's because you're not capable of performing the necessary transposition from the bestial to the superhuman plane – planes that were, in this case, superimposed.

'Think about how much Balzac dared not express in "Une Passion dans le désert." From her immortal limbs flowed such life force that any loss of energy was immediately compensated, increased, in fact. In those days, Corbera, I loved as much as a hundred of your Don Juans put together, over their entire lives. And what love! Sheltered from conventions and crimes, the rancor of commendatori and the triviality of Leporellos, far from the claims of the heart, the lying sighs, the phony melting weakness that inevitably mark your sort's wretched kisses. To be honest, a Leporello did disturb us the first day, and it was the only time: around ten I heard the sound of the farmer's boots on the path that leads down to the sea; just in time, with the farmer at the door, I managed to throw a sheet over the uncommon body of Lighea. Her uncovered head, throat, and arms led our Leporello to believe this was some commonplace affair and hence commanded his sudden respect. His stay was shorter than usual. As he went he winked his left eye, and with his right thumb and index finger at the corner of his mouth made the motion of curling an imaginary mustache; and he returned up the path.

'I spoke of our having spent twenty days together. However, I wouldn't want you to imagine that during those three weeks she and I lived, as they say, "conjugally," sharing our bed, meals and occupations. Lighea's absences were quite frequent. Without any advance notice she would dive into the sea and disappear, sometimes for many hours. When she returned, almost always first thing in the morning, either she found me in the boat or, if I was still in the cabin, wriggled up the pebbled shore till she was half out of the water, on her back and pushing with her arms, calling to be helped up the slope. "Sasà," she would call, because I'd told her this was the diminutive form of my name. In this maneuver made awkward by the same part of her body that granted her agility in the sea, she gave the pitiable impression of a wounded animal, an impression immediately obliterated by the smile in her eyes.

'She ate nothing that was not alive. I often saw her rise out of the sea, delicate torso sparkling in the sun, teeth tearing into a still-quivering silver fish, blood running down her chin; after a few bites the mangled hake or bream would be tossed over her shoulder and sink into the water, staining it red, while she shouted in childish delight and ran her tongue over her teeth. Once I gave her some wine. Drinking from a glass was impossible for her, so I was obliged to pour some into her small and slightly greenish hand; she lapped up the liquid as dogs do, her eyes registering surprise at the unfamiliar flavor. She said it was good but afterward always refused it. From time to time she came to shore with hands full of oysters or mussels, and while I struggled to open the shells with a knife, she crushed them with a stone and sucked down the throbbing mollusk along with bits of shell that did not trouble her in the least.

'I told you before, Corbera: she was a beast and at the same time an Immortal, and it's a shame that we cannot continuously express this synthesis in speaking, the way she does, with absolute simplicity, in her own body. Not only did she display in the carnal act a cheerfulness and a delicacy altogether contrary to wretched animal lust, but her speech was of a powerful immediacy, the likes of which I have only ever found in a few great poets. Not for nothing was she the daughter of Calliope: oblivious to all cultures, ignorant of all wisdom, disdainful of any moral constraint whatsoever, she was nevertheless part of the source of all culture, of all knowledge, of all ethics, and she knew how to express this primitive superiority of hers in terms of rugged beauty. "I am everything because I am only the stream of life, free of accident. I am immortal because all deaths converge in me, from that of the hake just now to that of Zeus; gathered in me they once again become life, not individual and particular but belonging to nature and thus free." Then she said, "You are young and handsome. You should follow me into the sea now and escape sorrows and old age. You would come to my home beneath enormous mountains of motionless dark water, where all is silent calm so innate that those who possess it no longer even perceive it. I have loved you, and so remember: when you are tired, when you can truly bear it no longer, all you have to do is lean out over the sea and call me. I will always be there, because I am everywhere, and your dream of sleep will be fulfilled."

'She told me about her life below the sea, about bearded Tritons and glaucous caverns, but she said that these too were vain appearances and that the truth lay much deeper indeed, in the blind, mute palace of formless, eternal waters, without sparkle, without murmurs.

'Once she told me she would be away for some time, until the evening of the following day. "I must travel far, to where I know I will find a gift for you."

'In fact she returned with a stupendous branch of deep red coral encrusted with shells and algae. For a long while I kept it in a drawer and every night I would kiss the spots where I recalled the Indifferent, that is the Beneficent, one had placed her fingers. Then one day my housekeeper, Maria – Bettina's predecessor – stole it to give to one of her pimps. I later found it in a Ponte Vecchio jeweler's shop, deconsecrated, cleaned up and smoothed to the point of being virtually unrecognizable. I bought it back and that same night threw it into the Arno: it had passed through too many profane hands.

'She also spoke to me of the many human lovers she'd had during her thousand-year adolescence: fishermen and sailors – Greeks, Sicilians, Arabs, Capresi – including survivors of shipwrecks clinging to sodden debris, to whom she'd appeared in a flash of lightning during a storm to transform their last gasp into pleasure. "They all accepted my invitation and came to see me, some immediately, others after having lived what to them seemed a long time. Only one failed to show. He was a big beautiful young man with red hair and exceptionally white skin; I joined myself to him on a beach far away, where our sea flows into the great Ocean. He smelled of something stronger than the wine you gave me the other day. I believe that he failed to show not, surely, because he was happy, but because when we met he was so drunk as not to understand anything anymore. I must have seemed like one of his usual fisherwomen."

'Those weeks of high summer flew by as rapidly as a single morning; when they'd passed I realized that in fact I had lived centuries. That lascivious girl, that cruel little beast, had also been the wisest of Mothers; with her mere presence she'd uprooted faiths, dispelled metaphysics; with her fragile, often bloodstained fingers she'd shown me the path toward true eternal peace, and also toward an asceticism based not on sacrifice but on the impossibility of accepting other, inferior pleasures. I will certainly not be the second man to fail to heed her call, will not refuse this sort of pagan Grace that has been granted me.

'In accordance with its own violence, that summer was short. Not long after August 20 the first clouds timidly gathered; a few isolated blood-warm drops of rain fell. The nights brought to the distant horizon slow mute flashes of lightning, deduced one from the other like the cogitations of a god. Mornings the dove-gray sea suffered for its hidden restlessness; evenings it rippled without any perceptible breeze, in gradations from smoke gray to steel gray to pearl gray, all extremely soft colors and more affectionate than the splendor before. Faraway shreds of fog skimmed the water; on the coasts of Greece, perhaps, it was already raining. The color of Lighea's mood also changed, from radiance to gray affection. She was silent more often; spent hours stretched out on a rock, staring at the no longer motionless horizon; spent less time away. "I want to stay here longer with you; if I were to take to the open sea now my marine companions would keep me there. Do you hear them? They're calling me." At times I truly did seem to hear a different, lower note among the seagull calls, to make out flashes of movement from rock to rock. "They're blowing their conches, calling Lighea to the festival of the storm."

'This set upon us at dawn on the twenty-sixth day. From our rock we saw the approaching wind as it battered distant waters; closer by, sluggish leaden waves swelled ever larger. Soon the gusts arrived, whistling in our ears, bending the withered rosemary bushes. The sea churned below us and the first white-capped surge advanced. "Farewell, Sasà. You won't forget." The billow broke upon the rock; the Siren dove into the iridescent spray. I never saw her come down; she seemed to dissolve into the foam.'

* * *

The senator left the next morning; I went to the station to see him off. He was surly and cutting as usual, but, when the train began to move, his fingers reached through the window to graze my head.

The next day at dawn a telephone call came into the newspaper from Genoa: during the night Senator La Ciura had fallen into the sea from the deck of the *Rex* as it sailed toward Napoli; though lifeboats had been deployed immediately, the body was not found.

A week later came the reading of his will: to Bettina went the bank account and furniture; the library was donated to the University of Catania; in a recently added codicil I was named legatee of both the Greek crater with the Siren figures and the large photograph of the Acropolis kore.

I had the two objects sent to my house in Palermo. Then came the war and while I was stuck in Marmarica with a pint of water a day, the 'Liberators' destroyed my house. When I returned I found the photograph had been cut into strips and used by the looters for torches. The crater had been smashed to bits; the largest piece showed the feet of Odysseus tied to the mast of his ship. I still have it today. The books had been stored underground by the university, but, for lack of money for shelves, there they slowly rot.

LEONARDO SCIASCIA

THE WINE-DARK
SEA (1973)

Translated by Avril Bardoni

THE TRAIN THAT leaves Rome throughout the summer at 20.50 – '*diretto per Reggio Calabria e Sicilia*' announces a female voice over the loudspeakers, evoking for the stream of passengers making for the train clutching hold-alls and suitcases tied up with string, a vision of the face of a woman just past the first flush of youth floating in the evening sky among the overhead lines of the Termini station – boasts a single first-class carriage Rome–Agrigento, an enormous privilege granted at the request of three or four Deputies from western Sicily who ensure its perpetuation. Actually, of all the through trains to the south, this is the least crowded. In second class it is rare not to be able to find a seat, while in first class, especially in the Agrigento carriage, it is quite possible, by simply turning off the lights, drawing the curtains and distributing one's luggage around the seats, to have a compartment all to oneself at least as far as Naples, and, with a degree of circumspection, all the way to Salerno. After Salerno you can prepare to sleep in comfort, in a singlet perhaps or even going the whole hog and donning pyjamas, for no one will enter your particular compartment in search of a seat. Such convenience as regards the seating has to be weighed, however, against the inconvenience of the relative slowness of the journey compared to the express, which leaves two hours earlier and arrives at Agrigento, the end of the line, with at least a seven-hour advantage over the through train. For this reason, most Sicilians opt for the express.

But when Bianchi, a civil engineer travelling to Sicily for the first time – to Gela, to be precise, and on business – found that he would have to travel by rail as all the flights were booked up, he was advised to take the *diretto*, to travel in the Rome–Agrigento carriage and to make a reservation or he might have to stand for a whole night in the corridor. This was bad advice from first to last, particularly concerning the reservation, since in a reserved compartment there are invariably as many travellers as there are seats while in an unreserved one you may well have the whole compartment to yourself. Thanks to this advice, Bianchi inevitably found himself committed to an uncomfortable journey, sharing a compartment with five other people, three adults and two children. The adults were extremely talkative, the children – both boys – lively and undisciplined.

Of the three adults, two were the parents of the unruly children; the third, attached to the family by ties of family, friendship or casual acquaintance, was a girl of about twenty-three, rather colourless at first sight and clad in a severely simple dress of black edged with white. The children never left her alone, the elder boy leaning against her as if he was too sleepy to move, his younger brother repeatedly scrambling up to put his arms round her neck and pull her hair and then scrambling down again to sit on the floor. The bigger one was called Lulu, the smaller one Nene – diminutives, Bianchi learned shortly before the train reached Formia, for Luigi and Emanuele. But before they reached Formia, he knew practically everything about the four members of the family and the girl travelling with them. They came from Nisima in the province of Agrigento, a large rural community with plenty of land and wealthy proprietors; the air was fresh; the local government was social-communist; it was the home town of a notable member of the fascist regime; it had no railway station; it did have an ancient castle. Husband and wife both taught at the elementary school, as did the girl too, though not yet as a permanent member of staff. The family had come to Rome to attend the wedding of the signora's brother (Ministry of Defence, Group A; a power to be reckoned with in the Pensions Department) to a girl from Rome, a nice girl from a very good family (father in the Ministry of Education, Group A); the bride had a degree in literature and taught in a private school; a lovely girl, tall, fair-haired. They had been married that very day, in the church of San Lorenzo in Lucina, a beautiful church, not to be compared with the church of Sant'Ignazio, but very nice. Witnesses from Group A. The girl, entrusted to their care on the return journey by her brother (in the Ministry of Justice, Group A), had however been holidaying in Rome; she had just recovered from a serious illness and was wearing the black dress edged with white in fulfilment of a vow made to San Calogero, patron saint of Nisima and author of many miracles. The signora wondered why, in the whole of Rome, a city of churches, not one single church was dedicated to San Calogero. 'It doesn't seem possible,' she said. 'Not one church, not even an altar. And he was a great saint.'

At the mention of San Calogero the husband gave a small, sceptical smile. The girl confided that, as a child, she had been afraid of San Calogero with his black face, black beard and black cape, and that it had been her mother, rather than she herself, who had made the vow; not that that made any difference: for yet another month (and this was already the sixth) she was committed to wearing the black dress edged with white.

'At the height of summer, with the sun melting the very stones,' said the husband.

'That's what a vow's all about,' said his wife with a touch of

147

asperity. 'A vow that involves no discomfort is no vow at all.'

'Isn't it enough that everyone in Rome was turning round to stare at me?' asked the girl.

'No, that's not enough. Mortification and suffering; it takes both to release oneself from such an obligation.'

A flicker of scorn showed in the girl's face. Bianchi suddenly saw her in quite a different light. Beneath the drab dress she had beautiful breasts and a shapely body. And her eyes were large and luminous.

'I'm releasing my feet,' said the younger child, undoing his shoes and kicking. One shoe stayed on his foot, the other hit Bianchi on the chest.

'Nene!' shouted the parents in tones of warning and reproof. They apologized to Bianchi who, returning the shoe, said, 'Nothing to worry about: children will be children . . .' It was, indeed, nothing to worry about compared to what was in store for the unsuspecting Bianchi from the combined efforts of Nene and Lulu during the long journey, particularly when they really got into their stride between Naples and Canicattì.

'All this nonsense about vows!' exclaimed the husband, reviving the subject while replacing his son's shoe. 'Antiquated rubbish stemming from ignorance and superstition . . .'

'But you took the *Scala Santa* seriously enough,' retorted his wife sharply.

'What has that got to do with it?' said the man, parrying a blow that had evidently found its mark.

'Everything. Let's ask this gentleman what he thinks about that,' pursued the woman relentlessly. Bianchi attempted, with a faint smile and a timid hand-gesture, to indicate his unwillingness to be drawn into the argument.

'Oh but you must,' said the woman. 'You must tell him whether he's consistent or not when he observes all the ritual of the *Scala Santa* and then ridicules vows made to the saints.'

'Please do,' urged the man, hoping against hope for moral support.

'What is this ritual of the *Scala Santa*?' Bianchi asked, playing for time.

'Don't you know?' marvelled the woman.

'I've got a vague idea, but I can't remember precisely . . .' said Bianchi.

'A vague idea, you can't remember . . . Forgive me, but are you a Catholic or not?'

'Why yes, I'm a Catholic, but . . .'

'He thinks the same as I do,' broke in the husband triumphantly.

'You went up the *Scala Santa*,' his wife repeated, crushing him yet again.

'Only to keep you company,' ventured the man.

'I want something to eat!' shouted Nene. 'I want some mortadella, I want a banana.'

'And I want an orange squash,' said Lulu.

'You're not having any mortadella; it brings you out in a rash,' said his mother, pointing to some little red spots on Nene's arm.

'Mortadella, or I'll do the same as Don Pietro's donkey,' said Nene, with an expression that promised the immediate translation of words into action.

'What does Don Pietro's donkey do?' asked the girl, amused because she obviously knew already.

Nene slid off his seat to give a practical demonstration.

'For heaven's sake!' cried his parents, grabbing hold of him. They explained to Bianchi that Don Pietro's donkey had a habit of lying on his back and waving all four feet furiously in the air. Nene was capable of giving a perfect imitation.

They gave him some mortadella.

'Orange squash,' whined Lulu, 'orange squash, orange squash . . .'.

Everyone, including Bianchi, promised him orange squash when they got to Naples. To get what he wanted, Lulu's policy was to whine while Nene's was to use threats and blackmail. Bianchi preferred Nene's direct, no-nonsense approach: Lulu's whining grated unbearably on his nerves.

Kissed and cuddled by his parents, Lulu quietened down. The interlude had been providential: the tricky subject of the *Scala Santa* had been dropped.

'I see you're not married,' the woman declared after a rapid glance at Bianchi's left hand.

'People with a head on their shoulders stay single,' joked her husband.

'True, seeing that you did the opposite,' she retorted.

'On the contrary,' said Bianchi, 'I think that people with a head on their shoulders tend to get married sooner or later. With me it will be later rather than sooner, but I shall marry.'

'You see?' said the woman reprovingly to her husband. 'There speaks a person with sense.'

'I was only teasing . . . Seriously, however, speaking generally and objectively, I would say that marriage is a mistake. Speaking for myself, personally I have no reason to regret it. My wife (and I'm not saying this merely because she is present, I really mean it) is an angel . . .' – here his wife lowered her head to conceal the sudden flush of pleasure – '. . . and then there are these two little cherubs . . .'. He stroked Nene's head, just beside him, and the child responded by rubbing his face, shiny with grease from the mortadella, all over the front of the raw silk dress shirt that his father had had no time to change since his brother-in-law's wedding.

'Your shirt!' cried the woman. Too late: the shirt was now patterned with greasy hieroglyphics.

'My pet,' said the father, 'you have ruined Papa's shirt.'

'I want some more mortadella,' said Nene.

'Mention mortadella once more, and the marshal of the carabinieri will come and arrest you,' threatened his father.

'I won't mention it; I'll eat it,' said Nene, skirting skilfully round the veto.

'He's as sharp as a razor,' said his father proudly.

'I want some,' persisted Nene.

'No, no and again no,' said his father.

'As soon as we get home,' said Nene, 'I shall tell Aunt Teresina that you were saying nasty things about her to Uncle Toto.'

'Did we say anything nasty about her?' said his mother, placing her hand on her heart and looking anxious.

'You and Papa. You were telling Uncle Toto that she's stingy, that she never washes, that she's spiteful . . .' The child's memory was formidable.

'I'll give him the mortadella,' said his father.

'By all means,' agreed his mother, 'and when he comes out in a prickly rash all over, he can go and get Aunt Teresina to scratch it for him.'

'I shall scratch myself against the wall,' said Nene, snatching the mortadella triumphantly from his father.

During the apprehensive silence that now descended like a pall upon Nene's parents, Bianchi's imagination conjured up a picture of Aunt Teresina's face, sharp and shifty-eyed like a ferret. Finally, in order to ease the tension, he announced, 'Here we are in Naples already.' The lights of the city twinkled through the dark.

His words roused Lulu who had been leaning listlessly

against the girl, half asleep. He renewed his demand for orange squash.

As the train drew alongside the platform, Nene's curiosity was roused by the vendors' cries of '*Sfogliate, sfogliate!*' His father explained that *sfogliate* were sweetmeats made from puff pastry with a creamy filling and Nene, with enthusiasm and his habitual courtesy, demanded one. Bianchi treated Lulu to his orange squash and Nene to a *sfogliata*. Such generosity towards the children prompted a flood of gratitude from the parents and formal introductions: *professor* Miccichè, *ingeniere* Bianchi.

Nene, who had registered unutterable disgust at the first bite, now hurled his pastry away, much as one might hurl a bottle of champagne against the hull of a ship being launched, evidently aiming for his father's head and only just missing.

'You gutter-snipe!' cried his parents in unison.

'It's revolting,' said Nene. 'I want a *cannolo*.'

'A *cannolo*?' said his father. 'And where do you suppose I can find a *cannolo* here in Naples station?'

'I don't give a shit. I want a *cannolo*,' said Nene, revealing a proclivity for strong language unsuspected, until that moment, by the engineer.

The girl laughed. Miccichè and his wife were at their wits' end. They threatened the immediate arrival of the marshal with whip and chain and asked Bianchi to look out into the corridor to see if he was there, for, they said, Nene's lurid language would have summoned him without a doubt. Bianchi looked along the corridor and confirmed that he was indeed on his way.

'The marshal's a shit-head,' muttered Nene, frightened but determined not to be cowed.

Husband and wife began to argue about where and from

whom Nene had picked up his dreadful expressions. The club to which her husband took the boy every afternoon was, according to the mother, a positive den of foul language; and two men in particular, Calogero Mancuso and Luigi Finisterra, were directly responsible for the deterioration in Nene's language, being youths who had nothing better to do than amuse themselves by corrupting a child. 'You can't imagine,' she said, turning to Bianchi, 'the things they teach him: dreadful things, even about the saints, even about the Pope himself. Luckily they go in one ear and out the other.'

Nene's refutation was immediate – 'The Pope's a . . .' – but two hands, one of his mother's and one of his father's, shot out and clamped themselves firmly over his mouth, from which the scandalous definition, like water from a burst pipe roughly repaired, still trickled with a degree of audibility.

'You see?' said the signora to Bianchi. 'And I thought he had forgotten. That's the kind of thing they teach him.'

Of course, this would never have happened, according to the mother, if her husband had been paying attention to the child instead of being totally engrossed in his game of cards. Miccichè had a passion for *Quarantotto*.

But according to the father, the truth of the matter was quite different: it was not at the club, forum of elevated sentiments and chaste language, that Nene picked up his colourful expressions, but from the vulgar people who inhabited the courtyard below a balcony of their house, and the blame lay entirely with his wife for allowing the child to remain on this balcony for hours together.

Nene terminated the discussion succinctly: 'At the club.' Miccichè slumped, utterly confounded, but his wife, instead of gloating, changed the subject as the train drew out of Naples, recalling that they had come to the city on the second stage of their honeymoon, after Taormina.

It was now past midnight. Bianchi thought, 'There'll be no sleep here tonight,' and toyed with the idea of changing compartments; there were some, indeed, that were almost empty. But he was not actually sleepy, and the irritation that he had felt initially at finding himself burdened with such irrepressibly loquacious company – including those two exasperating children – had been succeeded first by amusement, and now, just as he was on the point of deciding to quit the compartment, by a vague emotion that was not truly affection but indeed rather like it. He had never had much to do with children and had always believed that he would dislike their company; he had always taken care, when travelling, to select a compartment where there were no children; yet Nene decidedly appealed to him. The girl appealed to him too, her every movement, her every word, making her seem more lively, more desirable. 'The fact is,' he mused, 'that a journey is like a representation of life, a synthesis of all its elements, contracted in space and time; rather like a play, indeed; and it re-creates, with a wealth of hidden artifice, all those elements, those influences and relationships which constitute our existence.' He decided to tell Miccichè that he was thinking of changing compartments. They would be able to relax more, he said, and the children would have a bit more space.

'I won't hear of it,' said the teacher. 'You must certainly not put yourself to any such inconvenience on our behalf. If anyone is to move, it should be us.'

There was an exchange of compliments and courtesies and the eventual decision was that none of them should move.

Lulu announced that he was sleepy; he wanted the lights turned out.

'I don't want it dark: I've got to see that the marshal doesn't get me,' said Nene, whose conscience was not entirely easy with regard to this officer of the law.

'Turn off the lights!' screamed Lulu. 'I want to go to sleep.'

Nene had immediate recourse to means that the marshal himself might have called 'physical persuasion': sliding from his seat, he launched himself upon his brother, and bit him in the leg. Lulu yelled and grabbed furiously at his brother's hair. The boys were separated by pinching Nene's nose to force him to open his teeth and prising open Lulu's fingers one by one. Nene received a light slap from his father and Lulu a mild scolding.

'Tell me, who is this marshal?' Bianchi asked Lulu with a smile.

'He's a shi . . .' Another rapid clamping of hands over Nene's mouth, again not entirely effective.

'You've made Baby Jesus cry. Every time you say naughty things, he cries,' said the mother.

'Where is Baby Jesus?' asked Nene.

'He's in heaven and here on earth too. He's everywhere.'

'I've never seen him,' said Nene frostily.

'You can't see him, but he's here all the same.'

'If I can't see him he isn't here.'

'Heathen!' said his mother.

'You'll go to hell,' commented Lulu.

'Marshals go to hell,' said Nene.

Everyone, including his mother, laughed.

'What a wicked little rascal you are!' said his father tenderly, caressing the child. He turned to Bianchi. 'Did you hear what he said? Have you ever known another child like him?' His eyes shone with pride.

Bianchi said 'Never' – and it was true.

'He's not a bad boy,' said the mother, 'only highly-strung.

And he's amazingly generous: as soon as he has something new, like a toy or a picture-book, he wants to give it away. He would give the house and everything in it to a needy person; the very sight of someone begging sends him completely mad: "Mama, let's give him a coat, a mattress, some plates . . ." He's convinced that poverty means not having plates and mattresses, and he's obsessed with the idea that beggars sleep on the floor and eat out of the cans that we throw away . . .'

'They sleep in front of the church,' said Nene, 'and eat out of tomato tins. I've seen them. And they die.'

'Of course they don't die,' said his father.

'They do die,' said Nene flatly. Then he added: 'But I'm going to be a beggar when I grow up, and then they won't die any more.'

'He wants to be a beggar!' scoffed Lulu. 'Idiot, I've told you a thousand times: people can be priests, or doctors when they grow up, but not beggars.'

'Is it true that you can't become a beggar?' Nene asked his father.

'Of course you can. Why ever not?' Miccichè replied hastily.

'See?' said Nene to Lulu. 'You're the idiot: you didn't know that.'

'And I shall be a marshal,' said Lulu, 'so that I can arrest you and all the other beggars.'

The blow was a severe one. Nene began to move.

'He's going to bite me!' yelled Lulu, raising his feet ready to repel an attack.

'I'm not going to bite you. I got up because I wanted to stretch my legs. Must I sit down the whole time?' said Nene in tones which oozed hypocrisy, as he sought the approval of the others. But a moment later he sat down again and became lost, to all appearances, in some melancholy reverie. Gradually, sleep overtook him.

The light was turned out, the windows lowered a few inches and the curtains closed. 'Let's hope that we can catch a little sleep,' said Miccichè, 'we've still got another fifteen hours' journey ahead. Goodnight.' They all said 'Goodnight', including Lulu who was already more asleep than awake. It was two o'clock.

Bianchi had the girl next to him; Lulu sat next to her on the other side. On the opposite side, Miccichè and his wife sat with Nene between them. Nene slept restlessly, troubled, perhaps, by the arrival on some dream-doorstep of the marshal, cracking his rawhide whip and rattling his handcuffs. One could not say that he was a beautiful child – Lulu was undoubtedly the better-looking – but he had an exceptional quality that opened up a dimension of thought, of feeling, of attachment that Bianchi had never before considered. As he watched the boy, he was conscious of an emotion that was almost overwhelming: here, it seemed, was an aspect of the meaning of life that had previously escaped him. The significance of his own life, of his work as an engineer, above all his work as an engineer, consisted definitively in the fact that Nene had lived four years to his own thirty-eight. 'One can have no faith in technology without faith in life: it would be futile to put satellites into orbit were it not for the existence of children of four, of children now being born, of children still to be born. Yet our society has begun to see children as a problem, as they already do in America where so much research in pedagogy and medicine is directed at the question of their freedom ... The point is that children are not a problem. Any society that views them as a problem separates itself from them, provokes a crisis of continuity. Lulu and Nene are not problems for

Miccichè and his wife, though they, as teachers, must have had to trot out all those American and Swiss theories for the benefit of the selection board . . . Apropos of the Swiss; that society of theirs, seemingly disinfected of all the germs of tragedy and history, has yet given rise to Max Frisch's Faber. Greek tragedy and the Zurich School of Engineering. And the bombshell bursts in the ancient land of Greece where fate is still alive and waiting, in ambush . . . Wait a moment: I was thinking about children; Faber doesn't come into that . . . Yes he does, but I'm not thinking lucidly enough to deal with it, I'm too sleepy . . . Ah yes, Greece, Sicily: perhaps there's a connection there . . . Classical education, ancient Greece popping up all the time . . . Yes, it's a fact that in Switzerland you only have to look at a child to see exactly what he will be like as an adult Swiss, while in Greece he is an individual, a man . . . And in Sicily too, I would think. These two children . . . Not much discipline in these places: no rules laid down, no techniques, no tradition of instilling discipline; only the bonds of affection; and both the Greeks and the Sicilians believe that there is no problem that cannot be solved by an appeal to the affections . . . Even the problem of death . . .' Waves of sleep washed gently over his mind.

He was woken by the heat. As she slept, the girl's head had fallen on to his chest; she slept deeply, hardly even breathing. A feeling of tenderness and inexplicable joy flooded through the engineer as he became conscious of the hair that nearly brushed his lips, the breast that pressed against the back of his hand. His body, which had been totally relaxed in sleep, now tensed.

All the others were asleep, Miccichè was snoring. They were now travelling through Calabria; every time the train stopped at a station snatches of dialect were audible in the sudden silence. One station was close to the sea and the sound of the water conjured up visions of human faces that came and went like faces in a film, 'faded' in and out upon the ebb and flow of the waves. Bianchi felt that he, too, was being penetrated and dissolved: he was experiencing, without consciously realizing it, a profound one-ness with nature, with love.

As the train moved off again, Bianchi heard Lulu stir; a few moments later he suddenly found the boy standing in front of him, regarding him with silent amazement and reproof. The child took the girl's face between his hands and, with a great effort, placed her head upright against the headrest. 'He's jealous,' thought the engineer. 'He's jealous because his attachment to the girl is like that of a lover; that's why he has been sitting so quietly, content to be beside her.' The girl awoke and realized what had happened. 'Forgive me,' she said to Bianchi, and then, to Lulu: 'Go back to sleep, pet, it's still dark; look, you can have my seat too, then you can stretch out and sleep comfortably.'

She settled him down in the larger space and stroked his head. Lulu said nothing; he regarded her with a mixture of resentment and pleading, racked, perhaps, by a pain to which he could give no name. The girl went out into the corridor.

Bianchi waited until Lulu was asleep before he followed her. She was standing at the end of the corridor with her cheek pressed against the window looking as if she were still lost in the world of dreams. Walking towards her, Bianchi said, 'He's gone back to sleep,' and then, after a long pause, 'He's jealous.'

'He is fond of me,' said the girl.

'He's very different from Nene: more reserved, more sensitive . . . Nene is an extraordinary child,' said the engineer.

'Nene's a holy terror. You haven't seen the half of it yet . . . He drives poor Lucia absolutely out of her wits.'

'Lucia? Is that the signora's name? I thought her husband called her something different.'

'He calls her Etta, short for Lucietta . . . My name is Gerlanda, but everyone calls me Dina, short for Gerlandina . . . No one in Sicily is ever called by their real name even if it's a pretty one.'

'Gerlanda is a very pretty name.'

'I don't like it, the sound's too heavy.'

'I've never heard it anywhere else in Italy.'

'It's only found in the province of Agrigento: San Gerlando is the patron saint of the city, its first bishop.'

'Was San Calogero also a bishop?'

'No, San Calogero was a hermit. There were seven brothers, according to the legend, all called Calogero: one lived in the area of Nisima. Seven handsome old men . . . Calogero means "handsome old man" in Greek. I don't know any Greek; do you?'

'I've studied it, but I couldn't claim to know much of it.'

'I should have liked to study, but my parents said that going to the *liceo* meant I would have to go on to university; and how, they asked, could one possibly let a girl go alone to a city like Palermo?'

'Are Sicilian families all like that?'

'Oh no, not all of them.'

'Is your family especially strict?'

'Not really: there are still a lot of people in Sicily who have a certain attitude towards life; they're suspicious . . .'

'What about?'

'They don't trust people in general, or themselves . . . And they're not entirely wrong . . . Before my illness I was less tolerant, more impatient. I wanted to apply for a post on the mainland, to get away . . . I see things differently now: life seems to have become more superficial, everyone seems prepared to cheat everyone else, without exception . . . I'm afraid I'm not explaining myself very well . . .'

'You explain yourself very well indeed.'

'When I was sitting in a café in Rome or Ostia, I was watching people streaming past and it struck me that there was a separateness about every individual, even those who were walking along in a group, arm in arm with their friends; they were like people taking part in a funeral procession, all thinking to themselves: "I'm all right; it was that other chap who died, it'll never happen to me" – as if they believed that everyone else would die, or even that the world itself would end, before anything could happen to them . . . Have you ever been in a funeral procession?'

'Occasionally.'

'I have, two or three times. You can understand, then, what I'm trying to say even if I'm expressing it in a rather muddled way: people seem to chase after happiness with that sort of attitude . . .'

'What you are saying is both true and profound.'

'My thoughts are probably just the ramblings of a convalescent. But don't you agree that life is becoming more superficial?'

'Not everywhere.'

'No, of course not everywhere. I believe that where I live, most people still take life very seriously . . . But on the surface things are drab and horrible . . . You're probably thinking that I'm drab, too, and old-fashioned, dressed like this . . .'

'No, no,' Bianchi protested, 'quite the contrary.'

'I do enjoy life. I like nice things, nice clothes . . . and I should like to wear lipstick and try smoking cigarettes.'

'You are the most enchanting girl I've ever met, even

in the dress you wear for your vow to San Calogero, even without lipstick.'

The girl lowered her eyes, began to trace letters on the window with her forefinger. 'What are you writing?' asked the engineer.

'What?'

'On the window, I mean. It looked as if you were writing something.'

'Oh, yes, my name. It's something I do automatically whenever I feel embarrassed.'

'You mustn't feel embarrassed when I say that you are a beautiful girl and that I enjoy talking to you. It's true.'

'Oh,' she said, clasping her hands as if to stop herself from writing on the window.

'It's probably not sensible to try to prolong an acquaintance such as ours beyond the limits of the journey, but I must admit that I should like to see you again.'

The head of *professor* Miccichè appeared in the corridor; poking out from between the curtains, it appeared to be severed from his body, and sleep and suspicion dripped from it like blood from the head of John the Baptist. 'Why did you two slip out?' he enquired with a hint of irritation.

The girl turned to Bianchi. 'I should like that too,' she said simply. Then, to allay her friend's anxiety, she returned to the compartment.

The train was pulling into Paola, and no sooner had the squeal of its brakes died away than the cries of '*fragole, fragole*' were heard – for which Miccichè was already prepared with six hundred lire clutched in his hand. He bought a tub of strawberries for each of them, Bianchi included.

The children woke and reached out for the strawberries almost before their eyes were open.

'You and your strawberries!' exclaimed his wife. 'Now you've woken the children.'

'No I didn't: the shouts woke them up,' Miccichè maintained.

'You got up from your seat even before we heard any shouts,' said his wife.

'I got up from my seat because . . .' He stopped in confusion then gave an almost imperceptible wink in the direction of Bianchi and the girl. There immediately surfaced in the signora's breast not the tutelary concern felt by her husband but the avowed vocation of every married woman to prod every unmarried one into wedlock, heightened in this particular case by the romance of a long train journey, a professional man from the prosperous north and a nice girl from her own home town.

Nene, who had hardly started his strawberries, announced 'I want some more.'

'You can have mine; I don't want any,' said his mother.

'Is that or is that not bad manners?' asked his father, seeking support from the company in general.

'He won't even finish his own tub. He talks off the top of his head like you do,' said the signora, intending a reproof to her husband for his little gaffe of a moment ago when he had interrupted himself.

'I'll eat mine and yours and then ten more, a hundred more tubs of strawberries,' said Nene.

'I'll eat a hundred tubs of strawberries!' mimicked Lulu.

'Two hundred, a thousand,' said Nene doggedly; but he was already struggling and a second later he held out the tub to his mother. 'I'll finish these later,' he said.

'Uh, uh, uh,' scoffed Lulu.

'Stop being such a pain in the arse,' countered Nene.

'That's not talking off the top of his head,' said Miccichè, reasserting himself after his wife's reproof. 'That's the language you can expect from a gutter-snipe . . . But I'll teach you; I'll pack you off to boarding-school, you'll see.'

'With the orphans?' Nene's curiosity was purely academic.

'Just so. With the orphans.'

'Unless you die, they won't take me. If you die, then I'll go.'

Miccichè turned this way and that in search of some 'lucky iron'. Clinging to the ashtray and thus protected, he turned to Bianchi as full of paternal pride as ever: 'What logic!' And to Nene he said, 'Don't fool yourself. They'd take you with your father still alive: a word in the ear of Father Ferraro would be quite enough.'

Accurately anticipating Nene's reaction, he leapt to his feet and towered threateningly over the child. 'Don't you dare say what you were going to about Father Ferraro, or I'll give you a thrashing that you'll remember for the next hundred years.'

'I won't say it: I'll think it,' said Nene, quite unruffled.

Miccichè passed his hand nervously over his face once or twice, then laughed. They all laughed. And while they were laughing the ticket inspector arrived; they showed their tickets and Miccichè enquired about arrival times. As soon as the inspector had gone, Nene said conversationally, 'I'm still thinking about Father Ferraro.'

'My God!' moaned Signora Miccichè. But her husband, Bianchi and the girl laughed until the tears ran down their faces.

They arrived at Villa San Giovanni having discussed Nene's liveliness from all possible angles and quelled a couple of sudden squabbles between the children. Strawberry-coloured smears on Bianchi's and Miccichè's shirts bore silent witness to the men's intervention in the role of peacemakers.

Once on the steamer, Miccichè, in great good spirits, suggested that they all go up on deck for a coffee.

'And what about the cases?' asked his wife.

'Ah yes, the cases . . .' said the teacher with a frown. And with the self-denigration beloved of all Sicilians, he explained to Bianchi that as they approached Sicily, it would be a wise precaution never to leave their luggage unattended: conditions here were very different from those in the north of Italy where, Miccichè fondly imagined, suitcases only moved, like dogs, at the behest of their legitimate owners.

Signora Miccichè, who had her own ulterior motives, suggested a solution: Bianchi and Dina should go for a coffee first, and when they came back – and they were to take all the time they wanted – she and her husband would go up with the children.

The protests of the children, who couldn't wait to go on deck, were firmly suppressed. Miccichè, to be sure, was not entirely easy about the plan, torn as he was between his duty to the girl's brother and his natural inclination to further a romance. But his wife's decision settled the matter.

Thus they found themselves alone, the girl and Bianchi, as the first rays of the sun turned the Straits of Messina into shining gold below them. They drank their coffee quickly and then sat in silence facing the compact, gleaming whiteness of Messina.

After their sleepless night, the brilliance of the morning sun upon the water seemed to dazzle their very thoughts. As the ship began to move, the girl said, 'Shall we go down? The children will be impatient to come on deck.'

The children were more than impatient: Lulu was grizzling and Nene was stretched in silent protest upon the floor.

Seeing Bianchi and the girl, Miccichè pointed scornfully

to his son. 'Look at that!' he exclaimed. 'Is it a boy or is it a dog?' But Nene was already up and away; his mother and Lulu followed him.

Miccichè was already out of the door when the thought that he was about to leave the girl alone with a man on an almost deserted ship pulled him up short. He returned, and more to ease his conscience than allay any anxiety, asked the girl if she would like to come with them. She said no, that she was tired.

'Professor Miccichè is uneasy,' said Bianchi.

'He wants to deliver me back home safe and sound,' said the girl, smiling.

'I hope he doesn't assume . . .' said the engineer. 'I hope you'll . . .' He floundered to a halt.

'Yes,' said the girl, blushing.

They were both silent and their silence made Miccichè wonder. Was the engineer so gentlemanly that he had dared to say nothing to the girl, or so *un*gentlemanly that he had made a pass at her and been rebuffed? His doubts were resolved by his wife, who, using the mute language of eyes and eyebrows, assured him that the idyll continued but that everything had been perfectly correct; you only had to look at their faces to know this.

Miccichè immediately felt easier, but it occurred to him that, if a romance was really afoot as his wife maintained that it was, then he had a moral obligation to discover more about the man with whom he was dealing. That he was an engineer, a bachelor (or so he claimed), aged about thirty-five, pleasant and seemingly of good character, this he knew already, but he must dig deeper. He asked 'Am I right in thinking that you come from somewhere near Venice?' (Miccichè had done an officer training course in Marostica and recognized the intonation.)

'Vicenza,' the engineer replied.

'A lovely city; very civilized place.'

'Vicenza, Vincenza, Vincenzina, Aunt Vincenzina,' chanted Lulu.

'Aunt Vincenzina's *panedispagna*,' said Nene, licking the remains of a bar of chocolate from his fingers.

'And you live in Vicenza?' Miccichè continued his interrogation.

'It's my legal residence, yes, but I only pay a fleeting visit now and then. My mother still lives there, and my brothers . . . I've spent a lot of time away from Italy – America, Iran . . . And now Sicily, at Gela.'

'Oil?'

'Oil.'

'Well tell me then, in confidence: is it true that there is oil in Gela, or not?' Miccichè asked, lowering his voice to a whisper.

'Certainly there is oil there.'

'Because there are rumours that it might be – how shall I put it? – a put-up job: that the quantity may be so small that the game's not worth the candle.'

'That's rubbish!' exclaimed the engineer.

'That's what I say. But sometimes – you know how it is – I get the feeling that they're trying to throw dust in our eyes . . . Don't misunderstand me: the man at the top is a genius, no question about it . . . Even if this Gela business were a swindle, it takes a genius to set up a swindle of that magnitude.'

'There's no swindle,' the engineer assured him.

'If you say so . . .' said the teacher, raising his hands in a gesture of surrender. And, dropping the subject of oil, he returned to that of more immediate interest, Bianchi himself.

'Are you staying long in Gela?'

'I expect so: if not in Gela itself, then in Sicily anyway. Troina, maybe, or Gagliano . . .'

'Do you like Sicily?'

'I think I shall like it very much. I've never been there before,' said Bianchi with a glance at the girl.

'How about that?' said Miccichè to his wife and the girl. 'He's been half-way round the world and has never been to Sicily! Jesus Christ, these people from the north are all the same!'

'But I've always meant to go to Sicily,' said Bianchi apologetically.

'Of course, of course! "The land of golden oranges that glow in foliage dark",' Miccichè quoted with bitter irony.

'It happens to everyone,' said his wife, defending Bianchi and at the same time hoping to take the edge off her husband's resentment. 'People put things off saying that they'll do them next year, and sometimes next year never comes, and they never even manage to see the places they've always longed to see, or, if they do, it's by pure chance. We ourselves, for instance, have never been to Piazza Armerina, yet my husband has been planning a visit ever since we were married.'

'It's quite true,' agreed her husband. 'It does happen. But whenever I meet someone as old as this gentleman . . . Forgive me, what is your age?' (Miccichè was not losing sight of his primary objective of gleaning every possible scrap of information about his travelling companion.)

'Thirty-eight.'

'That a man of thirty-eight should have never been to Sicily, well, I don't mean to be offensive, but that does tend to make me see red . . . Because what happens (I am of course speaking generally) is that strangers come along, knowing nothing about the place or the people but only seeing things in terms of their own so-called "boom" or economic miracle, and feel free to carve up our poor Sicily any way they please . . . So personally I don't give a fig for this "boom"; your "boom" is at Sicily's expense, you are frying us in our own fat . . . For pity's sake let's change the subject.'

Lulu and Nene had shouldered imaginary machine-guns and were firing salvoes of 'boom-boom-booms' at each other.

'He was a separatist,' said Signora Miccichè in order to explain her husband's heated words.

'Independent,' Miccichè corrected her. 'And I still am.'

'You have your oil now,' Bianchi said by way of consolation.

'Oil? Believe me, they'll soon grab it,' said Miccichè. 'Do you remember Musco in Martoglio's *San Giovanni*? He kept an oil lamp burning before an image of the saint until a neighbour came along and used the oil; so when the real devotees came to worship, the lamp was dry. And that's what will happen to our oil. One long pipe-line from Gela to Milan and they can just drain it off . . . The devotees, those who have the interests of Sicily at heart, will be left wringing their hands . . . I'd rather not talk about it.'

'But if this happens, either now or in the future, won't Sicilians, too, be to blame?'

'Certainly: it's a Sicilian failing to stand around and wait for the ripe fruit to fall off the tree straight into our mouths.'

'Then, forgive me, but if that's the case, I can't see what you would gain by becoming independent.'

'We're not all like that,' said the girl. 'The fact is, that we like to make others believe the worst about us, like people who imagine that they are suffering from every illness under the sun and find some relief in talking about it.'

'True enough,' said Miccichè, slightly abashed. But he

brightened up almost immediately at the sight of the sea off Taormina. 'What a sea!' he exclaimed. 'Where else would you see anything like this?'

'It looks like wine,' said Nene.

'Wine?' repeated his father, perplexed. 'What on earth's the matter with the child's eyesight? He doesn't seem to be able to tell one colour from another. Does the sea look wine-coloured to anybody else?'

'I don't know: it does seem to have some dark reddish streaks in it,' said the girl.

'I've either heard the expression before or I've read it somewhere: "A sea the colour of wine . . . dark as wine . . .",' mused Bianchi.

'Some poet may have written that maybe, but I've never seen any wine-coloured sea,' said Miccichè. And to Nene he explained: 'Look: just down here, by the rocks, the water is green. Further out it is blue, a deep blue.'

'To me it looks like wine,' said the child confidently.

'He's colour-blind,' pronounced Miccichè.

'He's nothing of the sort,' argued his wife. 'He's just obstinate.'

She too attempted to convince Nene that the sea was green and blue.

'It's wine,' said Nene.

'See how obstinate he is?' said his mother. 'He is now declaring that the sea actually is wine.'

'Just a moment,' said Miccichè, pulling his tie down from the luggage rack. It had green and black stripes. He showed it to the child, asking him 'What colour is this tie?'

'The colour of wine,' Nene replied decisively and with an impish grin. Miccichè threw the tie in the air.

'You may as well give up. He's just being obstinate,' said the signora.

'Perhaps he's colour-blind as well,' persisted Miccichè, but without conviction.

'Wine-dark sea: where have I heard that before?' Bianchi wondered. 'The sea is not the colour of wine; Miccichè's quite right. Very early in the morning, maybe, or even in the sunset, but not at this time of day. Yet the child has stumbled on to something. Perhaps it's the effect, almost like the effect of wine, which a sea like this produces. It isn't drunkenness, but it overpowers the senses, harks back to some ancient wisdom ... Eduardo De Filippo ought to recite the Dialogues of Plato – in Neapolitan ... But this is Sicily, and perhaps it's not the same.'

The railway line ran parallel to the most glorious sea that Bianchi had ever seen: at times the swaying of the train gave him the impression of being aboard an aircraft taking off, the landscape all tilted to one side along the flight path.

Miccichè, to whom the posing of alternatives seemed an habitual figure of speech, asked, 'Is that beautiful or is it not?' – gesturing towards the Aci coastline as if it were a painting he had just completed.

They all agreed that it was indeed beautiful – except Nene, who was totally absorbed in removing the safety pins that held in place the strips of linen that served as antimacassars.

'Is Nisima on the coast?' inquired Bianchi.

'Unfortunately not,' replied Miccichè regretfully. 'It's in the arid Sicilian hinterland ... Nevertheless, it has a beauty of its own, nothing as breathtaking as this, but the kind of beauty that grows on one, particularly in the form of nostalgia when one is away for a time ... Here the beauty is so obvious that it would dazzle even an idiot; it takes more time and more perception to appreciate the beauty of Nisima ... It's a different thing altogether.'

'Is there a local Mafia?' asked Bianchi.

'Mafia?' exclaimed Miccichè with the same incredulity he would have displayed had he been asked whether the inhabitants of Nisima had webbed feet. 'What Mafia? All nonsense!'

'Then what about this?' asked Bianchi, holding out his day-old newspaper and pointing to a headline that screamed across four columns: 'Mafia Says No to Dams'.

'Absolute nonsense,' retorted Miccichè again.

Bianchi mused: 'Here's an educated man, kind, courteous, a good father to his children; and he refuses to speak about the Mafia, is even surprised that one should mention it, as though to do so were to give undue importance to something trivial, a mere bagatelle. I'm beginning to understand something about the Mafia. Chilling.'

The train drew into Catania. 'Catania,' Miccichè announced. 'The end of the line for this locomotive; it stops here.'

'I'm getting out: I want a little walk,' said Nene.

'They're going to move the carriages on to another line now, so you'd better stay put,' said his father.

'I want a *granita*, a *granita* and some biscuits,' said Nene.

'Me too. I want a *granita* and some *brioches*,' said Lulu.

They had *granita*, biscuits and *brioches*.

'They call this stuff *granita*?' said Nene disgustedly, but only when he had drained (partly on to his clothes) the last mushy drop. 'Don Pasqualino makes real *granita*. As soon as we get to Nisima, I shall drink a bucketful!'

'This is better than Don Pasqualino's,' said Lulu for the sake of argument but without conviction.

'You don't know anything about it. This is made from water, lemon flavouring and sugar; Don Pasqualino uses real lemons and he puts egg-white in it too,' Nene explained knowledgeably.

'He knows it all,' said his mother. 'He's inquisitive about everything, always asking questions . . .'

'I'm not inquisitive. Aunt Teresina's inquisitive.'

'Now you're saying nasty things about her!' said his father triumphantly.

'You're always saying: She's so inquisitive, the old witch.'

Stung, Miccichè threatened the boy with a tremendous back-hander. Nene, totally unimpressed, explained for the benefit of the two non-family members of the party: 'Aunt Teresina is rich and she's going to leave all her land to us. But I don't give a . . .'

The slap came from his mother.

'Aunt Teresina's going to leave her land to me,' said Lulu.

'That's enough!' shouted his father.

'Aunt Teresina's got a wig. Aunt Teresina's got a squint . . .' chanted Nene.

'You ought to be ashamed of yourself!' said his mother.

'Aunt Teresina won't give you any more *ciambelle*,' said Lulu.

'*Ciambelle* covered in mould: it makes me feel sick just to think about them.' His masterly impression of vomiting earned him another slap.

To comfort him, the girl offered to take him for a walk along the corridor. Nene accepted, saying 'I'd be better off out of here, where you can't talk sensibly.'

But seconds later, he came rushing back alone, glancing over his shoulder as if he were being followed. He sat down and held an open newspaper in front of his face. The impression that he was reading it was spoiled by its being upside down. A marshal of the carabinieri loomed in the doorway, gigantic, corpulent and with an ugly, scowling face rendered even more ferocious by the heat and by the rivulets of sweat that coursed down it. Nene eyed him from behind the paper.

The marshal enquired if this were the right carriage for Agrigento, thanked them and went on down the train. Nene, lowering the paper, emerged from behind it like an actor taking a curtain-call; but he emerged to the jeers of Lulu and the laughter of the rest of them. Weeping with rage and mortification, he bit Lulu, chewed his knuckles and kicked his feet; then gradually, still sobbing, he fell asleep.

A discussion arose about the upbringing of children, and of a child like Nene in particular. The parents maintained that Nene was undisciplined, and for this they blamed themselves and also the Sicilian environment; on the mainland, they said, children were brought up better and were better behaved. Bianchi and the girl, on the other hand, maintained that although Nene's language left something to be desired and his reactions tended to be violent, he undoubtedly possessed a lively intelligence and a ready wit, and his nature was generous. Miccichè and his wife clung to their point of view, though with a certain archness, and finally allowed the full tide of their affection to flow over the sleeping child.

As the train travelled on through the sun-baked, deserted landscape, they were like figures in a nativity scene grouped around the slumbering child, with their honest affections, their faith in life. Surely all this friendship, all this love must endure beyond the chance encounter, the shared journey, thought Bianchi, believing that he had at last penetrated the very core of life, epitomized by the essential goodness of this Sicilian family. He could, he mused, prolong it for a lifetime with this quiet, serious girl of few words and profound feelings; he had to say something definite to her before they separated, even accompany her home, speak to her parents. But when Miccichè began to reach down the cases because they were about to arrive in Canicattì, he told himself he was no longer a child, that there was a time and a place for everything and that he would be able to spend his first free day on a brief visit to Nisima.

They began to say their farewells long before they arrived at the station, renewing them on the platform where the diesel for Campobella, Licata and Gela was already waiting. They were all much affected – except for Lulu, who did everything in his power to distract the girl. Nene invited the engineer to go with them to Nisima, promising him one of Don Pasqualino's *granitas* and an evening at the club. Bianchi, his eyes on the girl, promised Nene that he would come soon. The child hugged him. Miccichè gave him his card.

From the train, where he had taken a seat near the window, Bianchi watched them as, laden with luggage, they made their way to the exit.

'I shall go to Nisima this coming Sunday,' he decided.

But as the train moved off, all his emotion of sorrow and of love was immediately blotted out by sleep. Just before he drifted into unconsciousness he had a vision of the face of the man who had advised him to take this particular train, to travel in this particular carriage: the face wore a sadistic, satisfied expression. 'Lord, what a trip!'

VINCENZO CONSOLO

THE TREE OF THE
FOUR ORANGES

From

THE SMILE OF THE
UNKNOWN MARINER (1976)

Translated by Joseph Farrell

THE *SAN CRISTOFERO* made its way into the port through a crush of boats, caiques and skiffs, each with fishermen plying the oars, attending to ropes, sails, lamps, nets, working with tallow, tow, tar; it proceeded through shouts, yells, cries bawled out inside individual boats, from boat to boat, from boat to quay where women and children stood huddled together adding to the din and commotion. A further crowd gathered at the Saracen houses above the harbour; windows, balconies, verandas, terraces, roofs, walls, battlements, rounded and pointed arches, haphazard breeches in the wall giving a glimpse of curtains, clothes, dresses, table-cloths and handkerchiefs blowing in the wind.

Above the hubbub, above the noisy, rowdy mass below on the quay and in the houses, there loomed by contrast, in all its calm majesty, the pink, living stone of the Rock, with its ammunition store, temple of Diana, water tanks and castle on the summit. And above the row of low houses, against the backcloth of the Rock, stood the two imposing towers of the Cathedral, single- and mullion-windowed, topped by pyramidal cusps, both were so suffused with the same pink light as to seem engendered by the Rock, wrenched from it and given separate life by earthquake or by the conscious, thousand-year labours of storm, wind, freshwater rains or burning salt-water gales. The commotion concerned the huge catches landed in those days. There was no end of excited talk of kilo upon kilo of sardines, scombroids, horse-mackerel, anchovies, of blue fish in such profusion as to cause even the elders to wonder if those seas had ever before yielded up such bounty.

Excitement mounted, with quarrels between fleet and fleet, crew and crew, races to arrive first and secure the best place on the sixty steps. And there was rivalry, near warfare, between family and family. After the shouting was done and the washing pulled into the houses, windows were slammed furiously shut. The panes glinted in the sun as it set on the horizon over the headland at Santa Lucia, in the direction of Imera, Solunto, l'Aspra, Monte Pellegrino. It was November, almost Martinmas, and the whole coast was still a shimmer of fish scales, glimmering like the gold stones in the mosaics in the Cathedral ceiling, or between the angels' peacock wings in the vaults, between the vine leaves and the palms on the crossbeams, and in the flowing locks of Christ Pantocrator.

Calm was restored. Little by little the quay emptied.

'Giovanni, we're in Cefalu!' exclaimed the Lipari merchant on board the *San Cristofero*, as though awakening with a start from the spell cast over him by that riotous life-filled spectacle. He smiled and turned to the boy to receive from him too some sign of satisfaction. Instead, he found him depressed, in the grip of fear or ill-humour.

'Our fishermen in the Aeolian islands don't make such a racket. And everybody else manages to stay calm,' said Palamara, the young servant.

'But this is Sicily, Giovanni!' replied the merchant, putting his hand on the boy's shoulder. Giovanni looked at him, drew a deep breath and laughed uproariously.

'Come on. They're starting to disembark,' said the merchant. 'Let's go and get the chest.'

Giovanni looked down at the round, half-eaten roll in

his hand which, in the excitement of entering port, he had forgotten to finish. He leaned over the railing of the quarterdeck and tossed it into the sea. A shoal of grey mullets instantly went for it, creating foam and spray on the surface of the water.

As soon as the gangway was in place, Chinnici and Bajona were the first on board. Whatever the explanation, those two guardians of the law managed to be present in every street, courtyard, alleyway, square, doorway, incline and descent along the entire shoreline. At any hour, from first light till three or four o'clock in the night. Taciturn, surly and suspicious, Chinnici was noted for his permanently outstretched palm. Always the same, since the day he had first set foot in Cefalu two years previously. He would present himself at the grocer's with a list: pasta, tomato purée, goat's cheese, sheep's cheese, cream cheese, tuna, roe, herrings, stockfish . . . (you know how it is, wife and three children to support, each with an appetite that would shame a wolf). With his thumb and index finger he would dip his hand into a waistcoat pocket, draw out a silver piece, look the shopkeeper straight in the eye, put the coin under his nose. 'Well now? How are you off for change?' he would say. 'Your excellency enjoys a little joke,' came the usual reply. 'How could I ever change that? You can hand it in next time you pass by.' The same story with the butcher, the fishmonger, the baker, the waterseller, the greengrocer. He even took advantage of Ersilia, the old woman who had her regular place on the street where, depending on the season, she sold chicory, artichokes, asparagus, fennel, snails.

Bajona's little weakness – perhaps because he was a bachelor and a Neapolitan into the bargain – was for anything in a skirt. Crucilla, Francavilla, Marchifava, Giudecca and the whole of the slum area were the districts he preferred.

He would turn up at a certain hour, belly protruding and moustache neatly trimmed, white envelope in hand, knock at a door where the man of the house was a guest of the Vicaria prison or else of Favignana. 'Who is it?' 'It's Bajona, the law, open up. I've news from your husband.' Click click, and there he was inside.

They presented themselves to the captain shoulder to shoulder, the one, Chinnici, as dark as a crow, the other, Bajona, tall and as fair and red as a ripe peach.

'Cargo?'

'Liquid foam fire.'

'Talking bollocks, are we?'

'God forbid!'

'Well then?'

'Have a look for yourselves,' said the captain, pulling back the hatch. The two leaned forward, shading their eyes to see more clearly into the darkness. Bones? Salt? Flour? Manna? Snow? Or perhaps some of that dust from Cyprus for ladies' cheeks and hair?

Neither dared open his mouth.

'Can't see a fucking thing.' It was Bajona who spoke.

'Down below?' asked the captain.

'What do you mean? What are you saying?' said Bajona.

'You said . . .' began the captain.

'I said you can't see a thing . . .' said Bajona.

'Except something white . . .'

'A Virgin Mary!' interrupted the merchant, throwing open the side of the wooden chest Giovanni was cradling in his arms. In a niche, as though framed by the straw, there appeared the head of a woman, cut off at the base of the neck.

She was a beautiful woman, stately, well-nourished, her glance empty and distant, her neatly parted hair flowing back like the waves of the sea. On her head she wore a crown or hat in the form of a water vessel. The statue was of terracotta, slightly damaged, with one crack running across the left eye and another going from the bottom of the nose, cutting into the lip and ending on the chin. Other lesser cuts criss-crossed the forehead. Chinnici and Bajona stood transfixed staring in turn at the Madonna, at that man with the scoffing smile who had spoken, at the stolid, unmoving servant, at the group which had appeared on either side of them from nowhere.

'What Virgin Mary?' Bajona managed to stutter out.

'Kore,' rejoined the merchant.

'Saint Kore?' said Bajona.

'No. Just Kore,' said the merchant.

'Who are you? What do you want?' blurted Bajona.

'Nothing more than a passenger who wants to disembark. Let me introduce myself: Don Gaetano Profilo, thirty-three years old, native of Lipari, a merchant by trade. And this is my servant, Giovanni Palamara, seventeen years old, also a native of Lipari.' So saying, the merchant handed Bajona his papers. Bajona stared at them a moment, pretending to be able to read, then handed them over to Chinnici. Chinnici held them up under his nose, and with the aid of his index finger laboriously spelt out the words.

'Are you selling these Madonnas?' asked Bajona.

'No . . .' replied the merchant with a smile.

'Then what have you come to Cefalu to sell?'

'I am here to buy.'

'Buy what?'

'Tuna fish – pickled tuna, steaks, roe, heart, liver, entrails.'

'And this Madonna?'

'A present.'

'Who for?'

'For the Baron Mandralisca from the apothecary Carnevale, a friend of his who resides in Lipari.'

'What's he going to do with it? A Madonna head of the same clay as the vases they make – no offence intended – over at Santo Stefano Camastro, and all covered in cracks into the bargain . . . these nobles, they're weird folk,' pontificated Chinnici. The merchant, smiling at him, closed the chest.

'May we disembark?'

'All right,' said Bajona.

'All right,' said Chinnici.

The merchant, having said goodbye to the captain and the two policemen, set off with his servant, but stopped, turned back and said:

'The "liquid foam fire" the captain declared corresponds to pumice stone; and if in the future he talks of the "sweet tear of autumnal fluid", he means malvasia wine; and if he refers to "marine wall rosebuds", you can take it he's talking about capers.'

'Ah,' said Bajona.

'Ah,' said Chinnici.

'Our captain talks in metaphors, the language of people who live out their days going back and forth on the seas, like the Bedouins in the desert.'

'Ah,' said Bajona and Chinnici together.

The captain, none too pleased at this revelation, took out a piece of paper and handed it over.

Is it necessary to repeat that Bajona could not read and that it would have taken Chinnici a year to decipher the document?

So, entertaining a great respect for the reader and well aware that real time and narrative time are sometimes in conflict, we reproduce it here below.

In the name of God and in the hope of salvation, I have in this harbour of Sotto Il Monastero loaded the deck and hold of this ship, the San Cristofero, *against the account, and at the full liability of Signor Ferlazzo Onofrio. The Master, Bartolomeo Barbuto, is charged with transporting and delivering at the end of the voyage, in Cefalu, the below named and duly enumerated wares, in dry, whole and serviceable condition.*

The aforementioned Captain pledges on his safe arrival to consign the said goods to Signor Michelangelo Di Paola, at which time the hire fee will be duly paid as per contract.

As sole proof of completion of the contract, this document, and any other relevant papers, will be signed by the Captain, and in the event of his not being able to write, will be signed by some other competent third party. All other documents shall be deemed null and void.

Item: 1428 (one thousand four hundred and twenty eight) chests of pumice stone.

Item: 175 (one hundred and seventy five) gallons of malvasia wine.

Item: 7 (seven) barrels of prime quality, salted capers.

Leaving Chinnici to expend untold energy on his reading, we will follow our merchant and his young companion Palamara, wooden chest over one shoulder and his master's personal effects clutched with his other arm against his side, all muscle and high spirits, walking with the lithe nimbleness of a man with two goldfinches perched on one finger.

Having walked down the quay, they passed through the Maritime Gate, and set off up the road known as Fiume. Giovanni found himself exhilarated and engrossed by the spectacle of the teeming street-life of the city: gangs of boys running everywhere, dashing out from alleyways, from squares, from streets with names like Della Corte, Porto Salvo, Vetrani, from courtyards, leaping up from warehouse basements, cavorting down stairs that appeared suddenly in the walls and wound upwards, towards the heavens, to end nowhere; old men standing in the doorways busily repairing coops and nets; arrogant women, huge baskets brimful of dripping clothes balanced on their heads, hands pressed firmly against sides, making their way back from the mouth of the underground river, the Cefalino, near the Pirajno and Martino houses, where the stones and basins had been in use for centuries as washing-place and bath-house. The cadenced ring of countless hammers falling on fresh leather, as unseen cobblers laboured in their workshops, resounded even over the myriad conversations, voices, shouts and guffaws.

The merchant, as he had when watching the earlier quay-side spectacle from the decks of the *San Cristoforo*, looked everywhere, elated and smiling.

They passed the church of San Giorgio, the Orphanage, the church of Sant'Andrea, the monastery of the Hermit Fathers, and reached the corner of Strade Badia, a street as narrow and straight as a blade, running all the way from Strada Fiume to the square in front of the church. At the foot of the street the massive, soaring, left-hand bell tower of the Cathedral of the Most Holy Saviour (the Bishop's Tower, according to the experts) dominated the scene.

'Here we are,' said the merchant. 'Baron Mandralisca lives in this street.'

He asked a nun, encased in skirts, mantles and veils, standing in ecstasy in front of a tabernacle, where the palace was. Without raising her eyes from the naked, arrow-covered, bleeding body of Saint Sebastian, the nun pointed to a stoutly bolted door near by. The merchant lifted the cast-iron, lion-head door-knocker and delivered first a gentle blow on the door, then a series of blows which grew in volume and frequency. The women across the way stopped to stare at the two hapless foreign gentlemen and broke into a loud cackle. The merchant replied with a broad smile but did not ask for an explanation of the silence and deafness that reigned in that house. He came to a decision; he put his shoulder to the door, and it gave way like a damask curtain.

While the two were making their way up the stairs, a clatter of clogs announced the arrival of Rosario, the Baron's butler and manservant, red in the face, out of breath, shoes unlaced, striped apron pulled over his uniform.

'Jesus and Mary, Jesus and Mary!' he exclaimed as he came towards them. He came to a halt when he became aware that the two, quite unabashed, had no intention of stopping.

'Who are you? What do you want?'

The merchant, smiling, continued climbing the stairs, with Giovanni close behind. Rosario found himself almost face to face with them. Terrified, he stretched out his arms, which only had the effect of displaying his full girth.

'Stop! No further!' he intimated in a high-pitched, quivering voice. 'You can't go up there.'

'Announce me at once to Baron Mandralisca,' the merchant told him, placing an envelope in his hand.

'The Baron is resting . . . I mean, he's working . . . He's writing . . . and when he's writing, he doesn't want . . .'

'Just announce me,' the merchant interrupted him.

'Yes sir,' said Rosario. He turned and, with his legs slightly akimbo, clambered heavily up the stairs.

The merchant and Giovanni quickly reached the landing and waited in the entrance. Giovanni set down the suitcase, and then, more gingerly, the chest.

'Welcome to this house, sir,' said Mandralisca, appearing at the doorway of his study, dressed in silk house-coat and skullcap, quill pen between his fingers, peering at them over a pince-nez balanced uncertainly on the tip of his nose.

'Giovanni Interdonato,' replied the counterfeit merchant, with a deep bow.

'The deputy?'

'If your Excellency still believes that there is a deputation . . .'

'No, no, you know that I am referring to 1848 . . . we were colleagues, but I don't remember ever having met you in Parliament. Were you not in exile? In London, I seem to recall or in Paris.'

'I was and still am in Paris. Even now when you believe you see me here before you, in conversation with you,' added Interdonato in a low voice. 'I, sir, have the honour of being the merchant Gaetano Profilio from Lipari, charged with visiting your lordship by the apothecary Carnevale, who sends you this present,' – he pointed to the wooden chest on the floor – 'as a mark of respect and gratitude. For the rest, the card which preceded me should have explained clearly . . .'

'Yes, yes, I understand,' interrupted the Baron, smiling. He put the pen down on a shelf and came towards him, hands outstretched. They greeted each other with a warm handshake.

'Please, make yourself at home, come into my study,' said the Baron, putting his arm around the other's shoulder as though intending to push him forward. Interdonato turned to indicate his servant Palamara who, arms crossed on his chest and a smile fixed on his features, stood there enjoying the whole scene.

'Ah yes, Rosario will take care of him,' said the Baron, pulling a bell cord.

Rosario appeared immediately, elegant in his uniform but with a look of evident displeasure on his face.

'Your excellency . . .'

'Fix up that boy in your quarters and bring the gentleman's baggage to the Green Room which overlooks the terrace. Leave the chest where it is,' ordered Mandralisca.

He went into the study with Interdonato, closing the door behind him.

Such was the confusion and disorder induced by the relentless search for truth that the Baron's chamber could have been the studio of a Saint Jerome or Saint Augustine, or a cross between the cell of the learned Sicilian monk Fazello and the laboratory of Paracelsus. On all sides, lining the walls, stood cabinets filled with books old and new, with codices, with parchments all overflowing and cascading, individually or in random piles, on to the desk, the armchairs, the floor. On top of the cupboards there was an array of stuffed birds from Sicily, Malta and the Aeolian islands, perched in the most bizarre poses on stands or branches, some with one foot, others with both, all complete with staring glass eyes. Telescope and armillary sphere. Inside the display cabinets and cases, on the surface of tables and consoles, the greatest profusion of objects: marble heads, hands, feet and arms; terracotta pieces, obols, lanterns, tiny pyramids, spindles, masks, ancient pots and stone bowls, both intact and cracked; shells from snails and sea-creatures. In the few remaining spaces on the walls, diplomas and canvases. Facing the desk, in the space between the cabinets, hung Antonello's portrait of the Unknown Man; on the wall opposite, above the desk, pride of place was occupied by an enlarged and coloured copy, executed by the painter Bevelacqua to a commission from the Baron himself, of Passafiume's seventeenth-century map of Cefalu. The city was viewed from above, from the perspective of a hovering bird, with the walls shutting it off from the sea and the banners fluttering from the ramparts at the four gates. The little houses, all identical, all packed together like lambs in the pen formed by the semicircle of the walls sloping down to the sea and the Rock closing the city off from the rear, were cut into neat, square blocks by the transverse line of Strada Regale and the vertical lines of the streets that ran from the mountain down to the sea. Like huge protective shepherds, the Cathedral and the Bishop's Palace, the Dominican Convent, the Abbey of Saint Catherine, the Grand Hostelry loomed over the flock of the houses. In the gale-lashed harbour, galleys, feluccas and brigs tossed on the waves. A scroll with the legend CEPHALEDU SICILIAE URBS PLACENTISSIMA was deployed like an oriflamme or flying jib in undulating folds in the sky, and above it was the oval coat of arms, edged with coils and whorls, divided into two sections, of which the upper panel depicted King Ruggero offering to God his Saviour the model of the Cathedral and the lower panel displayed three grey mullets in a star formation, biting simultaneously into a loaf of bread.

For Interdonato, that coat of arms recalled the bread tossed into the water by Giovanni and immediately devoured by the grey mullets. His mind was filled with flashes of thought, images, fantasies. The three diverging tails or legs representing the coat of arms of Cefalu, and of all Sicily, but equally representing a universal coat of arms of this globe called Earth, a symbol of history since the emergence of humanity until the present: the struggle for bread, a bestial struggle where the strong prevail and the weak succumb . . . (*Qu'est-ce que la propriété?*) . . . But today is the vigil of the Great Reform: the mullet, *cefalo* in the Sicilian tongue . . . every mullet will be allotted an equal place and the loaf divided in equal parts, with no more killing, no more animal-like savagery. And *cefalo* like *Cefalù* means head, and head implies reason, mind, man . . . might it be that from this stretch of land . . .?

He smiled and took his eye off the map, saying to Mandralisca: 'Never seen such a display of science, not even in Paris in the home of Victor Hugo, the writer, nor in the residence of Proudhon, the philosopher.'

'Please, for goodness' sake . . .' the Baron warded off the compliment from a mixture of embarrassment and surprise at hearing such names. He moved the books off a chair to let his guest sit down.

'I am only now getting down to the work on the general terrestrial and fluvial malacology of Sicily which has been absorbing my energies for some time, and which, I may say, has left me thoroughly worn out,' explained Mandralisca, collapsing onto a seat behind the desk as though exhausted.

'And do you really believe, Mandralisca, that at this moment in history there are people out there waiting with baited breath to find out the private facts of life and the intimate details of the trails and shells of Sicilian slugs?'

'No, no, I'm not saying . . .' countered Mandralisca, slightly offended. 'It's just that I promised, was it fifteen years ago? when I published my monograph on the malacology of the Madonie mountains . . .'

'My dear Mandralisca, don't you realise what has been going on in those fifteen years? Aren't you aware of the times we are living through?'

'How dare you?' Mandralisca spluttered.

'Ah but I do dare, Baron, because you are no *crazy fool*, no *imbecile* or feeble minded buffoon, unlike the majority of Sicilian nobles or scholars. You are a man gifted with the capacity of mind and heart to understand. And you are one of the few who has never reneged.'

'So you, you . . .' Mandralisca made a futile effort to get the words out, opening his eyes wide behind the lenses of his pince-nez, switching his glance rapidly from Interdonato's face to the face above him, on Antonello's portrait. Those two faces, the one alive and the other in paint, were identical: the same olive colouring of the skin, the same sharp and searching eyes, the same pointed nose, and above all the same ironic, piercing smile.

'The mariner!' exclaimed Mandralisca.

'Yes, Baron, I was the mariner on the sailing ship which four years ago travelled from Lipari to Cefalù, via the port of Tindaro. And I knew perfectly well what you were hugging close to your breast, wrapped up in that waxed canvas.'

'How?'

'Catena.'

'Carnevale's daughter?'

'Yes sir.'

'A rather unconventional young lady.'

'Catena is my fiancée.'

'I beg your pardon.'

'No need. Her unconventionality consists in her having seen her fiancé, in person, on no more than five occasions, always fleetingly and always in hiding. And her ordeal was sharpened by the presence, an elusive and evanescent but also perpetual and enraging presence of this portrait by Antonello which, as you yourself pointed out, could not have been a better resemblance of me if I had been the sitter. The smile was the final straw. Now you see why one day Catena deliberately ripped the mouth, and why the apothecary her father sold it? The poor girl had the misfortune to fall in love with a revolutionary.'

'But what were you doing on that ship disguised as a sailor?'

'I was making my way from Paris, Baron, where I had been charged by the Executive Committee, by Landi, Friscia, Michele Amari, Carini and Milo Gugino, to keep in touch with Mazzini and the National Committee in London and with other groups of exiles scattered all over the world, in Marseilles, Genoa, Turin, Florence, Pisa, Livorno, Tunis and Malta, not to mention Alexandria and Constantinople. I was, and still am, a kind of clandestine ambassador, always on the move, assuming the role of mariner or merchant or of some other poor devil so as to keep one step ahead of the police or, even worse, of spies and informers. So, when I had the good fortune to meet up with you, I was on the way from Livorno to the Aeolian islands to spend a few moments with Catena. From Palermo I proceeded to Tunis . . .'

'And now, Interdonato?' asked Mandralisca, growing more amazed by the minute.

'Now, Baron, time is short, these are explosive days. We are on the very eve of the Great Event. We have reached an agreement to act under a neutral banner, as you may have read in the *Free Word*, all of us, Pisacane, Mordini, Pilo, Mazzini, Fabrizi, La Masa, Calvino, Errante . . .'

'What about La Farina?' asked Mandralisca timidly.

'That traitor, Cavour's lackey!' Interdonato exploded. 'Forgive me. My only regret is that he comes from Messina, like me . . . and like Antonello,' he added with a smile. He paused, folded his arms, drew himself up straight, looked at the Baron unflinchingly and spoke in a clear voice. 'Baron, this time I came deliberately to your house to ask three favours of you.'

'Name them,' said the Baron, opening his arms, half willing and half hesitant.

'First: to hold here, in a house which is free of all suspicion, a meeting with the brothers in this district. I want to meet the two Bottas, Guarnera, Bentivegna, Civello, Buonafede, Gugino . . .'

'Poor Spinuzza . . .'

'I know, I know that he has been in jail for three years . . . but not for much longer, I promise.'

'The second?'

'To receive from your lordship a letter of introduction for Landolina in Syracuse. From there I will set sail for Malta.'

'Finally?'

'To leave with you, for a brief period, the boy you saw just now in the entrance hall. He's not my servant but the son of Palamara, a rich merchant in Lipari, Catena Carnevale's cousin. It was she who gave him his education. He's only seventeen and he's already aflame with revolutionary ideas. In Lipari, they were liable to seize him at any moment and lock him up in a cell in the castle above the citadel.'

Mandralisca began to drum with his fingers on the surface of his desk, absentmindedly, lost in thought. Interdonato watched him in amusement.

'Agreed,' said Mandralisca, awakening from his reverie with a start, and looking Interdonato full in the face. 'I will do my best to meet your requests, but I have to confess that the first will be the most difficult. Don't consider me cowardly or inhospitable. You have no idea how this house swarms with gossiping, empty-headed busybodies and, even more worrying, with devoted admirers of the Bourbon king. Don't lay the blame at my door. You must be aware how hard it is in Sicily to steer clear of so-called friends. You can defend yourself for a certain time, but then out of sheer weariness you give way, you surrender . . . And these people turn up at your door at any hour of the day or night with the most banal of excuses, which they present as the most pressing, urgent of problems. The truth of the matter is that they are terrified of being on their own, they are weighed down by the panic of existence. They couldn't give a damn for anything or anybody apart from themselves, because their deepest conviction is that the blessed state in which they alone were born was due to the irreversible will of God. As you were coming in you saw how Rosario, doing violence to a naturally peaceable and pliant temperament, has transformed himself into my personal gendarme . . . at least during those hours when I must work . . . Rather – I was wondering if it would not be better to meet with you and the others in an outhouse on one of my estates, Campo di Musa, not too far from Cefalu?'

There was a knock at the door and the butler entered to announce that the Baroness and Signorina Anna were already dressed for dinner.

'We can talk further another time,' said the Baron rising to his feet. He told Rosario: 'Accompany the gentleman to his room.'

The steam was rising from the pasta with its sauce of sardines, pine nuts, fennel and raisins, encouraging Interdonato, fork in hand, eyes half closed, to open his nostrils and abandon himself, after enduring so much hardship, to the pleasures of delicious, homely scents.

Annetta Parisi e Pereira, the Baron's niece, looked furtively at their guest and laughed with that tinkling laugh of hers. The talk turned to Parisian sauces, to couscous and the spices of Tunis and Malta, to the colourless cuisine – nothing but raw or boiled beef with, as occasional touch of fantasy, a side plate of beans – of Turin.

'Peasants and bumpkins!' pontificated Annetta.

'And those wines of theirs!' added Mandralisca. 'Sad and lifeless, and as dull as the Turinese themselves.'

And they discussed fish: the cuttlefish, lobsters and squid of the Aeolian islands; the sardines, anchovies, horse mackerel from the seas around Palermo; the swordfish and saury pike from the Straits of Messina.

'Stuffed squid!' exclaimed Annetta, and immediately broke into a raucous guffaw such as was scarcely fitting for a young lady like her.

'Annetta!' her aunt called her to account.

'I'm sorry, very sorry,' said Annetta, trying to hold back her laughter. And she explained how when she was still living in the Aeolians that nickname had been attached (and it had been Catena who had invented it, Catena Carnevale herself) to a young lad who had been making eyes at her.

'Have you ever seen squid stuffed with breadcrumbs, eggs and cheese, drenched in its own ink? When you put it on the platter it's all firm and round, and shiny and smooth so that you think it's going to explode. That was just like Bartolo Cincotta. His father was a doctor. He had a squeaky little voice . . . The last I heard of him he was locked away in a seminary.'

'Some day he will make a fine bishop or even a cardinal,' smiled Interdonato.

'Oh that Catena . . . what an imagination she had!' said Annetta.

'She hasn't lost it, not at all,' said Interdonato. 'Quite the reverse. I believe it's now being given even freer rein.'

'In what way?'

'She's writing poetry.'

'Love poems, I bet.'

'Far from it. I would call them poems of hatred.'

'Hatred for whom?'

'For all that is perverted, unjust, inhuman in this world. She writes with special feeling about the pain and suffering of the fishermen, peasants, pumice-stone quarrymen of the Aeolians, about those sacred rights of theirs which have always been trampled on; she rails with the rage of the Furies against those who are responsible for the inequalities and afflictions . . .'

'Goodness!' exclaimed Annetta. 'Now that I think about it, I remember that she was always reading . . . or else embroidering.'

'She has certainly never stopped reading. I doubt if there is a single writer she is not familiar with. First she had a great passion for Italian writers, for Campanella, Bruno, Vico, Pagano, Filangieri . . . but now she's more drawn to the French, to Rousseau, Babeuf, Fourier, Proudhon as well as to Victor Hugo and Georges Sand. She never stops asking me to send her books from Paris. As for the embroidery, she says it helps relieve tension and at the same time it enables her to get to grips with what she has been reading.'

'Beccafichi!' shouted Rosalia, Rosario's wife, bursting into the dining room, serving dish in hand. Her dark, youthful, solid figure was the picture of joy and happiness.

'They must be eaten hot, piping hot,' she said, laying the stuffed sardines on the table.

'What's become of Giovanni, the young lad I entrusted to your care?' Mandralisca asked Rosalia.

'He was dying of starvation. Never seen a lad bolt his food so fast!' answered Rosalia, hands flailing in the air and coal-black eyes open wide.

'As fast as Rosario,' Mandralisca hazarded, with a smile.

'Oh, what's your Excellency saying? Rosario's got no appetite at all. He picks at everything. He suffers from acidity . . . nothing like Giovanni at all. This Giovanni's just a young lad . . . robust, good-looking, God bless him, he enjoys his food . . .'

'Come on, admit it. You're falling in love with him, Rosalia,' said Mandralisca, amused.

'Enrico!' his wife reproved him sternly.

'Mother of God, Excellency, what are you saying? He's just a boy, I could be his mother.'

'Rosalia, get back to the kitchen,' ordered the Baroness. Annetta burst into one of her full-throated laughs.

'Excuse me,' Interdonato said to Rosalia before she left. 'When the lad has finally finished eating, tell him, if the Baron and Baroness have no objection, to come in here.'

'Of course, of course,' said the Baron.

'As you wish,' said Rosalia graciously.

As they were about to proceed to the fruit and sorbets, they saw Giovanni Palamara emerge into the bright light of the dining-room, a smile on his face but eyes betraying embarrassment.

'Oh!' exclaimed Annetta. 'Good-looking as well! Rosalia got it right this time.'

Her aunt threw her a disapproving glance.

'Giovanni, what's this? Aren't you going to greet our hosts?' Interdonato asked him. Giovanni immediately bowed, but no one grasped what he murmured under his breath.

Annetta fired a barrage of questions at him, about his relatives and relatives' relatives, his friends and acquaintances, about the people of Lipari and Canneto, Santa Marina and Malfa di Salina, about all the towns in the seven islands of the tiny Aeolian archipelago. Giovanni replied in monosyllables, peevishly, intimidated by the familiarity assumed by that patrician Signorina.

'Giovanni,' said Interdonato when Annetta appeared to have finally run out of questions, 'if the Baron doesn't mind, would you go down to the entrance hall and bring up the chest. You are the only one who knows how to carry it.'

'At once,' said Giovanni, relieved at being able to free himself from the conversation with the young lady, and from the burden of having all eyes on him.

He returned with the chest, and placed it gently on the floor.

Interdonato rose to his feet, went over to the box, and with Giovanni's help drew out from the wood and straw an ancient terracotta Kore figure. He took it in both hands and placed it cautiously on a sideboard.

'Oh,' Mandralisca, the Baroness and their niece Annetta exclaimed simultaneously. Mandralisca began to tremble uncontrollably. Unable to remain seated, he rose to his feet, put his pince-nez in place and approached the Kore. He examined it in a state of ecstasy, his nose almost touching the top of the statue, running his eye over every segment, from head to neck, and then to the back where the wavy hair was gathered up in a chignon.

'Beautiful,' he exclaimed, 'beautiful beyond words. How can I thank the apothecary? Look,' he said, walking backwards but keeping his eyes fixed on the Kore, 'if I had to produce an image of the new Italy, Free and United, I would think of a statue like this . . .'

'Ah, too beautiful, Baron, too perfect . . . perhaps I should say too ideal,' said Interdonato. 'But there's another present, for Annetta from Catena.' Interdonato put his hand inside the hollow in the crown on the statue's head and pulled out a little embroidered silk table-cloth. He opened it out and presented it to Annetta. She received it with evident delight and spread it out on the table to examine it more closely. Curiosity got the better even of the Baroness Maria Francesca and she too approached the table. At first view, it appeared an odd piece of work, sewn fancifully and without discipline. The borders consisted of drawn threads, but the needlework at the centre was a riot of the most disparate stitches: the moss stitch was confused with the cross stitch, which slid into the feather stitch and merged with the chain stitch. And the colours! It passed instantly from the most subtle, delicate shades to the most gaudy greens and fiery reds. It looks, thought the Baroness, like a table-cloth sewn by a madwoman possessed by a fury, who deliberately set aside laws, numbers, measure and harmony so as to make it seem that reason had deserted her. Nevertheless it was clear that the intricate needlework at the centre represented a tree with a knotty, twisted trunk, topped by a single leafless branch on one side, while the other was adorned by a green triangular patch of foliage and by lesser, extravagant marks. Four red balls, intended to look like oranges, hung from the branches over towards the right, with some words embroidered around them, in a semicircle, written backwards.

'It seems to be an orange tree. But what do those words mean?' asked Annetta.

'From where you are looking at it, it is indeed an orange tree,' replied Interdonato, still enjoying himself. 'But if you turn it over . . .'

'But it's Italy!' exclaimed Annetta, looking at the table-cloth from the other side.

'Yes, it's Italy,' confirmed Interdonato. 'And the four oranges become the four volcanoes of the Kingdom of the Two Sicilies – Vesuvius, Etna, Stromboli and Vulcano. And it is from here, suggests Catena, from these mouths of fire which have lain so long suppressed, and above all from Sicily which contains three in such a small area, that the flames of revolution will burst forth and set all Italy alight.'

DACIA MARAINI

From

BAGHERIA (1993)

Translated by Dick Kitto and Elspeth Spottiswood

THE NAME BAGHERIA is thought to come from the Arabic *bab el gherib* meaning 'the gate of the wind'. Others, however, say that Bagheria derives from the word *baharia* which means 'the seashore'.

I prefer to think of it as 'the gate of the wind' because Bagheria has not much in the way of seashore even though the sea is only a kilometre away from the town. It was created, with its splendid architecture, as a country retreat for the nobility of Palermo during the eighteenth century. It has kept something of the atmosphere of a summer garden enriched by lemon groves and olive trees, poised between the hills, cooled by the salt winds coming from the direction of Capo Zafferano.

I try to imagine Bagheria as it was before the random development of the fifties, before the systematic destruction of its beauty; and earlier still, before the famine and the plagues when it was the favourite summer resort for the nobility of Palermo. In the distant past it had resembled the mother of antiquity, from whose womb the town and all around it were born. Writing one hundred years before Christ, the Greek historian Polybius spoke of great wooded expanses 'near Panormo' as the scene of a battle between the Carthaginians and republican Rome.

Between Mount Cannita, where the city of Kponia apparently arose as a place devoted to the cult of the goddess Athene, and the Cozzo Porcara, where the remains of a

Phoenician necropolis have been found, there was this 'small and pleasant valley', later called Bagheria. It is triangular in shape, with the rocky point of Capo Zafferano rising out of the sea like the prow of a ship. One side takes in the villages of Santa Flavia, Porticello and Sant'Elia: until after the war, the other side, wilder and lashed by the sea, encompassed only the village of Aspra, with fishing boats drawn up out of the water on the white sand. In the centre, lying between the hills, surrounded by a mass of olive and lemon trees, is Bagheria, lapped by the river Eleuterio, which today is reduced to a trickle. In the time of Polybius this river was navigable right down to the sea.

Holm oaks, cork oaks, ash, nut trees, figs and carobs, almonds, and fruiting cactuses were the most widespread plants and trees. And the eye could stretch from one side of the triangle to the other, between light and dark shades of green, imagining that a naked giant with one eye in the middle of his forehead might suddenly spring out of nowhere.

Today the view is horribly disfigured: trees, parks, gardens and ancient buildings have been hacked down to make way for houses and large tasteless mansions. Something still remains of the old greatness of Bagheria, but only in isolated fragments between the vestiges of abandoned villas, amidst the obscenity of new motorways that have forced a way right into the centre of the town, savagely destroying gardens, fountains, and everything that exists beneath one's feet.

My mother has told me that when she was a little girl there used to be a Carthusian monastery inside the Villa Butera. 'It was a monastery in miniature, with all the rooms and chapels of a real monastery. When you went in, you would be met by a lay brother carrying a jar of water. Then you'd go further down the corridor and you'd be able to look into the cells where monks with cassocks down to their feet were intent on praying or writing. They seemed absolutely real but they were made of wax filled with straw. In the middle of the prayer hall there was even a bear with a head that could move.

'The walls were decorated with paintings in the style of Velázquez. There was also an old manservant wearing slippers and draped in aprons, who was busily sweeping the paving stones in the courtyard. In one of the larger cells a supper party was displayed: Admiral Horatio Nelson and Queen Maria Carolina were being served by a black footman. There was a kitchen too, with a cook busily frying two eggs in a pan. In another room the Norman King Roger was perusing a manuscript. And at the end, in the dining-hall, was the Prince Branciforte, sitting at table and calmly talking with Louis XVI and the Bourbon Ferdinand the First. People used to come from everywhere to visit the Monastery of Bagheria. But do they come now?'

Today the monastery is no more. I have no idea who was responsible for its destruction. But Bagheria has such a poor opinion of itself that it does not attach any importance to its most valued memories.

It has always been thought that the Sicilians possess a certain darkness of character, a dry, sullen mentality springing from the earth which generates them. The frequent violence of their political behaviour can only stem from those inaccessible grey and rugged rocks, that hostile overpowering sea, that rough dry countryside, arid and deathly, from the great treeless fields of grain without any shelter from the sun. Out of ruined walls bristling with thorns emerges the agave plant, raising its beautiful head to the sky in a transparent spike of scented flowers only at the heart-rending moment of its death.

If you read the writers of antiquity you discover that it has not always been like this. Once there were luxuriant streams, woods of great leafy trees, hard-working people passing to and fro beneath their restful shade. They spoke a language that would be incomprehensible today, they ate bread cooked on stones and drank wine diluted with water and mixed with honey, and they laughed at heaven knows what, showing their white teeth and their dark eyes.

Under those leafy branches walked Phoenicians, and they tell me it was perhaps they who gave Bagheria its name from the Phoenician word *bayaria* meaning 'return': or so I am told. But it is difficult to be sure of the truth; etymology is frequently a mystery.

Under these branches Greeks and Romans also used to walk; and eventually fleet-footed Arabs with their long robes of embroidered cotton. The Arabs brought to Sicily the silkworm, the olive and the fruiting cactus. The Spaniards brought the cultivation of sweet oranges along with their horses and their warriors, and at the same time the Aragonese introduced the use of sugar cane.

As a child I used to go into the fields around the villa with a group of children from Bagheria to look for mulberries; our dresses would become stained with the juice and we would get a scolding from our mothers. But these soft, swelling berries that coloured your tongue blue and red were irresistible.

Today there are no more mulberries in Bagheria. They have all been cut down. But on the quay at Mondello along the coast from Palermo, it is still possible to find fruit stalls where for a few coins they will sell you a bag made of sugar paper with a handful of juicy mulberries inside.

The mulberry was also the tree that consoled me during the two years in the concentration camp at Nagoya. Every day the guards used to put us all into a queue and count us. But sometimes they used to forget us children, and I would take advantage of their oversight to squeeze through the barbed wire and run off to the peasants to work for a few hours, happy to be rewarded with an onion and a piece of *daikon*, a sort of radish that lay motionless on the plate, white and twisted like a small corpse, with a taste of putrid water which I hated. But it was better than being hungry.

Daikon also resembled ginseng which in its turn brings to mind a dwarf with thin legs and thread-like arms: like a little man or a new-born baby with very white soft limbs. But no one ever points out that mandrake was just the same. So much confused information lies embedded in the memory, and often we don't attempt to question it. Today I know that mandrake is a poisonous herb with white flowers, segmented leaves and large tuberous roots to which magical properties were once attributed.

In the fourteenth century, I believe it was called *mandragora*. Then, no one knows how, it was changed to *mandragola*. In Latin it was pronounced *mandragoram* and in Greek *mandragoras*. But there is also a suggestion that the word comes from the Persian *mardum-gia*, meaning 'plant of man'.

In the concentration camp I learned to understand the deep-rooted ironic relationship that exists between food and the magic of the imagination. It is starvation that makes the senses reel and fantasy dance. It is deprivation that is the origin of all desire and also of all the more or less secret distortions of our thinking.

Having to eat *daikon* was enough to make me cry. But I also knew it was the only fresh vegetable that ever arrived on our table and we had to make the best of it. I still remember how I used to sit miserable and paralysed and full of hatred in front of a small dish of boiled *daikon*, while tears welled up involuntarily and, sliding down my hollow cheeks, ended up in my lap. I saw *daikon* as evil, white and repugnant, even though it did me good. Its roots stirred my poor empty stomach with agonizing cramps. So I used to put off the moment when I forced them into my mouth. *Daikon* would stay there mutely on the plate and pretend to be dead. But far from it. It was still very much alive. Doesn't *daikon* make one think of *daimon*? A small demon with flesh that appears white and innocent, a faked innocence which was camouflaged in the plain earthenware dishes of the camp.

I was happiest when I was able to play among the peasants. I used to slip my small hands into the huge basket where the men had thrown mulberry leaves. I would pull them out, light and slightly downy, and spread them over the beds of little grubs. These small creatures were silkworms; they were blind and touchy and stayed shut inside their cocoons made of something very like a spider's web, which stuck to the fingers and gave out a faint smell of flour and cut grass.

Sometimes I would hold one in the palm of my hand before it had become imprisoned in its nest of opaque spittle. I remember the extraordinary softness of its tiny body, almost as if its flesh were made out of clouds. My hands are good at retaining the memory of anything they touch. They are small dry hands with the nails always cut very short, my little finger much smaller than the others. The veins stand out as if I used my hands a lot: indeed my fingers flit backwards and forwards on the keyboard of my electronic typewriter for hours on end. I have worked hard trying to learn how to balance the weight of my fingers on the keys. In order to use the little finger I had to bend my hands askew and push my wrists out. In the end I decided to give up and now I have abandoned using the little fingers and type only with the other eight.

The tepid floury softness of the silkworm, almost ready to disintegrate in my fingers – I found it again when for the first time in my life I held a penis in my hand. A family friend who, like the American Marine had done, took advantage of a moment when we were alone to unzip his trousers and put his penis in my hand. I looked at it with curiosity, not at all frightened. We were in Bagheria and I was ten years old. Since it was clear that he did not want to touch my body (which I would have found abhorrent), but only gently and trustingly to show me his, I was not upset. It was the first penis I had ever seen. How strange it is that the word *pene* (penis) should be so close to the word *pena* (pain). Who knows whether using the word penis is not also a way of insinuating that the bearer of a penis is also a bearer of pain? But maybe this is only a fluke of language.

Seeing a penis for the first time brought me some slight pain. I was only a child and he was imposing his grown-up body on me, even though there was no violence, and this man was a good friend of the family, a frequent visitor to the house.

Up till then I had only once caught a glimpse of my father's penis, but it was in repose and was not being offered to me. Indeed, he was shamed by my glance and immediately covered himself in embarrassment. And my dear father was never shameless. Throughout my childhood I gave him my love without its being returned. My love was a solitary love. I watched over him, his secret smells, over his every footprint, never to be retraced.

He was forever on his travels, forever far away. I transformed my longing into an intricate, airy architecture, into the mirage of a city and the desire to dream with open eyes. Whenever he came back from one of his journeys I took meticulous note of the smells he brought back with him, the smell of apples (why does the inside of haversacks always have that strong musty underlying smell of apples?), of dirty washing, of hair warmed by the sun, of crumpled books, dry bread, old shoes, withered flowers, tobacco, and tiger balsam against rheumatism.

The combined smell was not unpleasant, indeed it had a unique sweetness about it. It is a smell that today still makes my heart leap whenever I come across it in some corner of the house, in some old garment, in some shoulder bag cast to one side. It was the smell of a solitary man, impatient of all ties, of all responsibilities, who travelled ceaselessly from one continent to another; a pilgrim with Spartan tastes, used to sleeping on the ground, to living on almost nothing, abstemious and sober but capable of much eating and drinking if he were in good company on the top of a mountain or in an abandoned bathing-hut among the rocks beside the sea. Occasionally he would smoke a pipe, but I was not conscious of the smell of tobacco in his clothes – only once in a while in his 'rucksack', as it came to be called in the family. In the concentration camp he and the other men used to smoke rolled-up cherry leaves which tasted hot and bitter. But I liked the smell; it had a light flowery scent.

I loved my father so much, more than it is right to love a father, with a painful torment – as if I anticipated in my heart the distance that would later separate us, his old age that already seemed intolerable, an image of his death which would leave me inconsolable, but of which I saw the shadow between his delicate eyelashes, between his untamed thoughts, in the corners of his subtle delicate lips.

'What's this white stuff that's coming out of your body?' I asked the family friend who was bent over with a jerk of pleasure while his silkworm swelled between my hands and, after a quiver, began to grow smaller, leaving a white sticky fluid in my child's palm.

He smiled. He did not know what to say to me. Or perhaps he said something like 'you'll understand later, when you're grown-up'. For a moment I thought it was an illness, a purulent eruption, something secret and unnatural which threatened his health. I was so astounded by the sudden metamorphosis of the little worm that I thought 'he must have swallowed a piece of mushroom like Alice. Now he'll eat another piece and it will become big and strong again.' There was definitely something startling and unexpected in this growing and diminishing of flesh in a grown-up person. And I still did not know it was called a penis.

Then for days on end this friend of the family was not to be seen. And I thought with a mixture of repulsion and curiosity about the way his body had leaned forward, of that spurt of milk that had dirtied my hands, of the shameful expression on his face as it bent strangely above me but without touching me, as if his detached closeness demonstrated that he was separate from what he was doing.

His act of putting such a soft and defenceless worm into my hand I saw then as one of total trust, and it made me feel proud of myself. When I met him again, some time later, he seemed severe and he drew away from me. He told me off for being a precocious little girl, too nosy, given to forward behaviour. And he succeeded in convincing my mother, to such an extent that he induced her to throw away a sleeveless dress with a short skirt which I was very attached to, in order to make a longer one with pleats, which I hated.

Years later, during the seventies and eighties, I found myself with friends in one of the 'self-awareness' groups (as they were then called) that formed the backbone of the women's movement. We would meet for lunch or supper when we were free of our respective jobs, and we talked for hours on end, taking turns to analyse methodically our earliest experiences connected with the discovery of sex, love, the desire for children and so on. It was then I discovered that so-called sexual abuse of children by adults was very common and well known to all, or almost all, little girls. They often kept quiet about it for the rest of their lives, terrified by threats and intimidations from the men who had taken them into dark corners, always feeling guilty as if it was they who had stretched out their hands, conceived forbidden thoughts and provoked the uncertain desires of men, even though the reality was quite the opposite. And once it came to light, they had to struggle with incredulous mothers who were ready to lay all the blame on their daughters, instead of on fathers, lovers, cousins, brothers, and friends of the family.

Such is the trauma that most women just blot it out of their memory and it can take years of therapy to bring it into the open. After ten years of psychotherapy, a friend of mine found out how as a child she had been abused by her grandfather. But she had conveniently 'forgotten' it to keep the peace in the family and to avoid upsetting her mother.

It has been a relief and a source of mutual knowledge to learn that it is not a solitary, isolated experience, but underlying it there is a universal system with established techniques for keeping little girls silent and shut away inside their 'dirty' secrets, as if they were responsible for the precarious family happiness. We have initiated a shared discourse on the age-old violence of patriarchy and the men who have always considered it their right and destiny to possess and manipulate the women of their household.

PETER ROBB

A MARKET

From

MIDNIGHT IN SICILY (1996)

I WOKE WITH a start about an hour after midnight. The boat was still throbbing doggedly through the dark but I couldn't breathe. The roof of the cabin was a few inches above my face and there was no oxygen in the damp salty fug that was gathered there. The passengers on the other three bunks made no sound in the darkness. Maybe they were dead. I sweated, pressed and paralysed, buried alive. Deep regular breathing brought no calm. I scrambled down without the ladder, putting a foot on an unseen face. The dim corridor was hardly better. The fug was thick with ship's smell of engine oil and paint and stale brine. I found a companion-way up to a deck where I waited till dawn among the lifeboats, still oppressed by the visible and palpable marine haze but breathing. All the oxygen seemed leached from the air on this fine and starless night.

Summer hadn't yet broken. The voyage south brought back other unbearable summer nights in the Mezzogiorno. The canopy of that heavy, airless dead stillness was over us like a fallen tent. In the morning, back in the cabin, I saw someone had screwed shut the cabin's ventilation duct. Everybody seemed to have had a bad crossing. As we eased up to the dock in Palermo smartly dressed passengers were pressing like desperate refugees or immigrants at the place the gangplank would reach. I tried to imagine the place the arriving Greeks and Phoenicians called Panormus, *all port*, three thousand years ago. A wheelchair with a slavering lolling-headed idiot was shoved into this edgy ill-tempered crowd, ready to be first off. A cluster of nuns was poised for flight.

The yellow taxis lined up on the dock were all gone when I disembarked. After a coffee, several coffees, near the waterfront, I trudged up towards the centre of Palermo, past a showroom with half a dozen new red Ferraris on display. A little further on the carabinieri had set up a road block. There were carabinieri and soldiers, a lot of them, and fretful. The little hotel on via Maqueda, the hotel opposite the *art nouveau* kiosk, was abandoned. The windows on the first floor were shuttered or glassless, and the peeling wooden door on the street swung open on ruins. Retracing my steps, I found another place, in a third floor warren back towards the harbour, reached in a rattling metal cage. The room was above a coffee wholesaler's, and full of the smell of roasting coffee. Down the road soldiers in camouflage were standing guard with legs wide apart at the entrance to a building of no evident interest. One of them caught my oblique glance as I passed and slipped the safety catch on his machine gun. Seven thousand troops had arrived in Sicily from *the continent* in the summer of 1992. Three years later the troops were still there. In a certain view, Operation Sicilian Vespers was yet another foreign occupation, and an oddly named one, since it recalled the bloody thirteenth-century uprising by the locals against the occupying Angevins from France, when thousands were massacred in days.

The new place was even closer to where I was headed, which was the *panelleria*. A lot of the best things in Sicily have lasted since Arab days, and fried slices of chick pea flour must have been around since the ninth century. I've never seen *panelle* outside of Palermo, and hardly ever outside the Vucciria market. The *panelleria* was down in a side alley of the tiny market square, a small bare room on the street with a table for cutting out the small rectangles of chick pea dough and a vat of hot oil to fry them in. The *panelle* were a cheap and austere food, but they were surrounded by abundance.

> As in certain sweet and savoury dishes that contain everything, where the savoury merges into the sweet and the sweet into the savoury, dishes that seem to realize a hungry man's dream, so the most abundant and overflowing markets, the richest and most festive and the most baroque, are those of the poor countries where the spectre of hunger is always hovering . . . in Baghdad, Valencia or Palermo, a market is more than a market . . . it's a vision, a dream, a mirage.

The market the Sicilian writer Leonardo Sciascia had in mind here was the Vucciria. It'd been like a dream when I first wandered into it at the end of an earlier summer years and years ago. Whenever I went back to Palermo, the market was the first place I headed for. It was a way of getting my bearings. That first time, twenty-one years earlier, I'd arrived in Palermo mapless from Enna, in the high parched bleak centre of the island, the poorest province in Italy, and strayed through the ruins of the old city. The old city centre of Palermo had been gutted by bombs in 1943, in the months before the Allied armies invaded Sicily. A lot of its finest buildings, palazzi of the seventeenth and eighteenth centuries, the family homes of the Sicilian nobility, about a third of them, were destroyed.

Other European cities had been bombed in the forties, and many worse than Palermo. What was unique to Palermo was that the ruins of the old city were still ruins, thirty years, fifty years on. Staircases still led nowhere, sky shone out of the windows, clumps of weed lodged in the walls, wooden roof beams jutted towards the sky like the ribs of rotting carcasses. Slowly, even the parts that had survived were crumbling into rubble. There were more people living there in the early seventies, in the buildings that were still intact, or partly so, and it must've been a Monday because the washing was strung across the alleys like flags, whipping and billowing everywhere in the powerful sun. It was a very hot day. When I stepped into the Vucciria from a narrow crooked alley, it was a move from the wings on to a stage set in mid-show. The noon sun fell vertically on the tiny space and the stallkeepers had winched out brown canvas awnings. The piazzetta of the Vucciria market was so small and deep that on one side you climbed a flight of stone steps to leave, and when the awnings were out on all sides the sky was covered and everyone was inside a kind of circus tent. The sun beating on the reddish canvas filled the space with a warm diffused light, and the canvas trapped and intensified the odours of the food that was steeply massed on display. It was the belly of Palermo and the heart too. The visual centre of the close and brilliant and almost claustrophobic indoor outdoor theatre was the big fish. On the table were the black eye and the silver rapier and the tail's arc of a swordfish whose body had been mostly sliced away, and blocks of blood-red tuna.

The swordfish and tuna were flanked by many smaller fish, striped mackerel and fat sardines, and squid and prawns and octopus and cuttlefish. I don't remember seeing shellfish. I remember how the diffused red light of the market enhanced the translucent red of the big fishes' flesh and the silver glitter of the smaller ones' skins. The meat was bright red too, redder than usual in this hot muted light. The eye passed more rapidly over the rows of flayed kids' heads with melancholy deep black eyes. There were coils of pearly intestines. There was horse flesh and beef and pork and veal and skinny Mediterranean kids and lambs. There were pale yellow chooks strung up by their bright yellow feet, red crest downmost, and batteries of eggs. The fruit and vegetables were summer things with the sun in their colours. Purple and black eggplant, light green and dark green zucchini, red and yellow peppers, boxes of eggshaped San Marzano tomatoes. Spiked Indian figs with a spreading blush, grapes, black, purple, yellow and white, long yellow honeydew melons, round furrowed canteloupes, slashed wedges of watermelon in red, white and green and studded with big black seeds, yellow peaches and *percocche*, purple figs and green figs, little freckled apricots. There were sprigs of leaves around the fruit.

It may have been too early for the oranges, but the lemons were there. There may have been only one kind of fig. *On that day*. There was bread, cheeses, sacks of chick peas, lentils, white beans and nuts, ranks of bottled oil and tinned tomatoes, big open tins of salted anchovies and tuna in oil, blocks of dried tuna roe, there were wine shops and coffee bars. Fat produce from the north, hams and salami, parmesans and gorgonzolas, was harder to find. The *odori* were in an alley just off the piazza, a bravura massing of thyme and oregano and marjoram and rosemary in dusty drying clumps, chilli bushes uprooted with their leaves still green and the fruit fat, larger chillies dried a dark lacquered red and hanging like cords of horns against the evil eye, plaited ropes of garlic, papery white and tinged with purple, dried mud clinging to their root hairs, vats of olives, black and green, large and small, in brine and oil, spiced and not. The booth smelt like a hill in Sardinia at dawn in summer, a concentrate of fragrant Mediterranean scrub.

I list these things now because a lot of them were already

gone by 1995. The Vucciria in the summer of 1995 was a slowly fading and diminished place, and words in any case seemed inadequate to recall the lost plenty. What you once found in the Vucciria, and all the markets of the south, was the dense, scarred, irregular and deeply coloured fruit of backbreaking labour. The meaning of this produce was in how it looked, and that was beyond semantics. It might have been caught in an image. Taste, texture, what each thing might become when cooked and combined, these were also matters for the eye. Flavour was form and colour. Freshness translated into the gleam in a fish's eye, the sheen on an eggplant, the resilience of a leaf, the moistness of a speck of manure still clinging to an egg.

There was no shouting at the Vucciria. We weren't in Naples. People in Sicily moved with quiet purpose, and the cadence when you heard it was reproachful, not protesting. The silence of buyers and sellers, housewives and growers and labourers, is enhanced now by the dreamlike patina of memory and the underwater feel of that heaped earthly plenty, and the sea's too, glowing under canvas. And high above the narrow alleys, the faded cottons whipping against the blinding sun. Years after wandering into this *hungry man's dream*, I learnt that this massed harvest was at that very same time being fixed in an image, though not in Palermo and not from life. It was taking form in the summer of 1974 as a painter's dream in the far north of Italy, and in writing the following winter about the sweet and savoury markets of the Mediterranean, Leonardo Sciascia was describing not the market itself, but this painting of *The Vucciria*, this dream, by Sciascia's friend the famous Sicilian painter Renato Guttuso, on the occasion of the first showing in Palermo of the painting that would thereafter be the icon of Palermo, the city's ideal image of itself. In the way of images, it represented, that dream of Mediterranean plenty and a people who gathered and consumed it, something that was no longer real. The market and the old city it fed were dwindling and fading as Guttuso painted them from miles away. If I hadn't seen the market for myself that first summer day when I was hungry, I'd have doubted now whether it ever existed.

Guttuso's name prompted a further twenty-year leap back in time, to 1954. In England 1954 wasn't a specially good year, halfway down from coronation euphoria to the humiliation of Suez. But food rationing ended in 1954, and at the year's close Evelyn Waugh named Elizabeth David's *Italian Food* as one of the year's two books that had given him most pleasure. Elizabeth David was *stunned by the compliment*, coming as it did from *Mr Evelyn Waugh, a writer whose books have given me more pleasure than I have power to acknowledge*. She was particularly gratified because the book had given her a lot of trouble. *All that pasta. We've got enough stodge here already*, her English friends had said as she set off to garner material. First maddened by the preindustrial imprecision of Italian cooks, then stirred by a *fever to communicate*, finally returning home to be chilled by her publisher's indifference, she'd felt her two years' work was in vain. Then Renato Guttuso's promised illustrations, long awaited, started arriving one or two at a time from Rome.

> To have had for my book those magnificent drawings and the dazzling jacket picture ... I would have gone through the whole agony of writing it all over again.

What she liked was their unsentimentality. The cheap battered aluminium pans, the ravenous pasta eaters, the glistening fatty salami, the bunches of artichokes: everything was everyday, but by Guttuso invested with a quite dangerously blazing vitality, for this artist even the straw round the neck of a wine flask is unravelling itself in a manner positively threatening in its purpose and intensity.

Elizabeth David was as good a critic here of drawing as of cooking. Her book matched its illustrations. *Italian Food* was a great hymn to the intensity of everyday eating pleasures and a sustained denunciation of Englishness in food, a denunciation whose fury seemed to intensify in each new edition's revisions. Forty years after Elizabeth David's book appeared, its author was lately dead and *Italian Food* was still in print and still made an exhilarating read. The 1995 edition still included Elizabeth David's passionate praise of Guttuso, but the object of her praise was now gone. The new edition eliminated his illustrations. Only the brilliant lemons remained, in colour on the Penguin cover. The others had been replaced by plates from a sixteenth-century cooking manual. Another tiny step had been taken in Guttuso's progress towards oblivion. Twenty-something years ago he'd been at the height of his fame and painting *The Vucciria*.

That first blazing summer vision hadn't been my only sight of Palermo before 1995. There'd been other visits in between. The second was five years after the first, at the end of the seventies, a wet winter's fag end when I started seeing the shadows in Palermo. By then I'd been living in Naples for a couple of years, and Naples then was terminally decrepit but intact. The old capital of the Bourbon kingdom belonged to the people who lived in it. By virtue, it had to be said, largely of neglect. Naples was lived in, and densely, all through its centre. It was a city whose people possessed their streets, stayed out in them until the early morning. It was a city whose days and weeks and seasons were strongly marked for everyone by meal hours and holidays and the sea. If it were March 19, for instance, it was San Giuseppe and that meant *zeppole*, huge grooved shells of choux pastry baked or fried, flattened in the centre by a splodge of yellow pastrycook's cream and a fleck of bitter cherry conserve and dusted with icing sugar, would be on sale hot and fresh every few yards. It meant that the street where I lived, a main street of the business centre, would be given over, inexplicably, to an animal market, and full of goats, turtles, ducklings, goldfish, puppies, monkeys.

I returned to Palermo at the end of the seventies with a certain feel for the resources and shadings of city life in the Mezzogiorno, and by comparison with Naples Palermo was desolate. The streets were closed and shuttered outside business hours, and empty of pedestrians. I saw for the first time the extent of the ruination in the centre, the rubble, the abandon, the places you couldn't see if they were lived in or not. Rain sharpened the sour smell of rotting masonry. Life after dark was silent files of cars along the main arteries. What spooked most was the newer area, the smart part of town I hadn't seen before, stacked with rows and rows of big apartment blocks along the via della Libertà, in place of the *art nouveau* villas and the parks of the *belle époque*. In the sinister quiet of Palermo, I realized, there was a lot of money, as there wasn't in Naples. Ingenuously, I asked a couple of people about the mafia. I remember the polite, puzzled blink, the inquiring gaze and the slightly cocked head before my interlocutor vanished. *Mafia?*

That first summer day in the Vucciria, everything above market stall level had been hidden by the lowered canvas awnings. It wasn't until a wet and miserable evening of the second visit when the canopies were furled that I saw that the building on one side of the little space had a kind of open verandah at first floor level, from which you could look out over the marketplace. This was the Shanghai. It was an eating place reached through a poky door in a side alley and a narrow flight of stairs: you emerged into the kitchen space and thence to the verandah. The rudimentary and rather slovenly cooking there was done in an oven that was also out on the verandah. There was nothing Chinese about it except the name. I couldn't remember if the name came from a distant port of call in the proprietor's seafaring days. I ate that rainy, gusty night on stuffed squid, the only customer on the dimly lit verandah, while the proprietor, who was whitehaired, exuberant and a tad intrusive, read aloud from his collected poems, which were written out in an exercise book. He had a loud voice and it rang out from the verandah over the dark and empty market square.

By the summer of 1995, heroin was now one of the more important commodities traded in the neighbourhood of the Vucciria. A lot more people had moved out. There was bad heroin on the streets of Palermo and junkies were dying like flies. There were killings in the Vucciria and raids every few days. A crowd the day before had rounded on a police patrol and roughed them up. It was lunchtime on a sunny day when I got there and the tables on the Shanghai's verandah were taken by pink and grey couples from northern Europe. There was a TV crew from northern Italy. A couple of listless girls said their grandfather wasn't well. They knew nothing about the Shanghai's name. They said I'd have to ask him. They didn't know when he'd be back. *And his poetry?* I asked. Was he still writing poems? *He was too busy drinking wine most of the time*, the poet's granddaughter said acidly, swiping at the laminex with a greasy dishcloth, *to think about writing poems*. It was the *panelle* I was really after, in any case, and the Shanghai didn't have them. I went downstairs to the *panelleria* and filled my stomach.

The sack of Palermo sounded as remote as the Sicilian Vespers, but it happened in the fifties and sixties. Most of it happened in four years under two men. Salvo Lima and Vito Ciancimino were two who'd joined early and risen fast when conservative politicians formed the Christian Democrat party, *la Democrazia cristiana*, at the end of the war in Italy. From 1945 until everything fell apart in 1992, the Christian Democrats were never out of government. Outside Italy the DC had the overt and covert support of the United States, obsessed with stemming the communist tide, and inside Italy it had the support of a Vatican no less obsessed with routing communist atheism. The party's bedrock, though, was the Mezzogiorno and especially the *friends* in Sicily. People didn't talk about the mafia in Sicily but they talked a lot about friends. And through the postwar years the party's most powerful leader in Sicily was Salvo Lima, and Salvo Lima was more than a friend. He was a *made man*, a fully inducted member of Cosa Nostra, bound by a lifelong vow to serve the interests of the mafia. As the most powerful politician in Sicily he was one of the more important people in Italy.

Salvo Lima was elected mayor of Palermo in 1958, which was when the sack of Palermo began, and after four years in office moved on to greater things. He later became a deputy minister in Rome and a member of the European parliament. Vito Ciancimino was in charge of public works under Lima and later mayor of Palermo himself. Lima and Ciancimino were an interesting pair. Ciancimino was a barber's son from Corleone who kept his close-clipped Sicilian barber's moustache and his country uncouthness long after he moved to Palermo at the end of the war and into politics. In 1984 he was the first public figure to be arrested, tried and eventually convicted as a mafioso. Twelve million dollars' worth of Ciancimino's personal assets were confiscated at that time. Lima on the other hand was almost too powerful to embarrass. Beyond a certain threshold, power erases embarrassment. He was a white-maned and silk-suited grandee, and when Salvo Lima walked into a Palermo restaurant, silence fell and people came to kiss his hand. The two worked well together in the interests of the friends and the transformation of Palermo in four years was concrete evidence of this.

In four years of early teamwork, these two released 4,200 permits for new building in the city. Nearly three-quarters of these permits, over 3,000 of them, were given to five obscure figures, illiterate or retired, who were fronts for mafia interests. The old centre's buildings, many of them stupendous palazzi of the seventeenth and eighteenth centuries, were encouraged to decay and their poorer inhabitants to leave for cheap mafia-built blocks on the city's outskirts. Those with money were urged into the flashier blocks springing up over the ruins of splendid villas and parks along the more central artery of the via della Libertà. In the fifties, sixties and seventies, while the overall population of Palermo doubled, the old centre's population dropped by two thirds. By 1995 Lima and Ciancimino had both been removed from the scene. Their work remained. When you walked into the new parts of Palermo it was like walking into the mafia mind. The sightless concrete blocks had multiplied like cancer cells. The mafia mind was totalitarian and even on a summer day it chilled you. Italy for decades consumed more cement per capita than any other country in the world and in Sicily construction was in the hands of Cosa Nostra.

Construction, property development, real estate had once been the main business for mafia firms. Now they were where the drug money went to the laundry.

Lima and Ciancimino had more in common than mafia. They were both Andreotti men. Giulio Andreotti was a Roman who'd had the most stunning rise of all in the DC after the war. Andreotti was a clever, scrawny little hunchbacked figure with heavy-lensed spectacles, thick black hair and triangular ears projecting batlike from his head. He was a *sacristy rat* who'd emerged from a war spent in the Vatican and catholic student organizations to rise in the shadow of the party's founder to become a cabinet minister in 1947 when he was only twenty-eight. Although he'd been a member of pretty well every Italian government thereafter, Andreotti had never, in the fifties and sixties, been prime minister. His faction in the DC was too narrowly based. He lacked a wide electoral base and so he lacked clout in the party and if he stayed that way he would never head the government. It was natural that a figure so wholly consumed by the hunger for power as the tiny ascetic Andreotti should want to enlarge his electoral base and it was natural that he should look to Sicily to do it.

So when Salvo Lima was elected to parliament in Rome in 1968, massively, Andreotti did a deal with him. Before their alliance was formalized, Lima advised Andreotti to check him out first with the Italian parliament's antimafia commission, in whose report he was later to figure so largely. *I knew I was talked about*, he said later, *and didn't want to cause him problems. Giulio asked and told me*, it's OK. And so, for years and years, it was, although the parliamentary commission shortly afterwards identified Lima as a central element of the mafia power structure in Palermo. Lima's clout in Sicily secured Andreotti the first of his seven prime ministerships a little over three years later. Sicily, from then on, was Andreotti's power base. Lima was eleven years later elected, overwhelmingly again, to the European parliament, but he found little time to spend in Strasbourg. He was needed in Rome. He was needed in Sicily. Andreotti in those days was *the god Giulio* and Lima was Giulio Andreotti's proconsul in Sicily. He was for decades reckoned the most powerful man in Palermo.

It was as such that Salvo Lima spent the warm spring morning of March 12, 1992 in his claret-coloured villa near the beach at Mondello. Lima was receiving allies and clients in the drawing room, which had a valuable sketch by Renato Guttuso on the wall, a preliminary for his painting of *The Vucciria*, that celebration of the market and its neighbourhood that Lima as mayor had bled almost to death. The sketch hung next to a photo of Lima with the Kennedy brothers, Jack and Bobby and Teddy. Lima that morning was discussing prospects for the Italian elections. They were due within three weeks and looking good. After heading the last two consecutive governments, Giulio Andreotti had decided to go to the polls.

There was an engagingly personal logic behind Andreotti's decision to go to the people, into which the people entered not at all. An ugly corruption scandal had broken out in Milan the month before and a determined magistrate called Di Pietro was pursuing it. The thing could only get bigger and uglier for the governing parties. It was a good moment for Andreotti to leave the fray for higher things. President Cossiga was about to cut short his increasingly bizarre term as head of state, to everyone's relief. Repository of a great many demochristian secrets, the president had lately been given to bouts of redfaced public rage and the delivery of long and weirdly free-associating harangues that had his party colleagues on edge. They never knew what he was going to say next. Whether Cossiga was now jumping or being pushed, his retirement meant that the Italian prime ministership and the presidency were up for grabs at the same time. Bettino Craxi, the socialist who'd enjoyed two highly lucrative terms in office during the eighties, was anxious to try his hand as prime minister again. The highly public secret deal was that he could have it, the *quid pro quo* for the DC being Giulio Andreotti's final apotheosis as head of state. The president may have had less power day to day than the prime minister, but he made and unmade governments in a country that usually saw at least one new government a year. The Italian president had clout. This was the way things went in Italy and a normal margin of error in the popular vote would have changed nothing. A direct line to the president would be interesting, Lima doubtless thought.

At mid-morning he left with two of his visitors for the Palace Hotel, where an electoral dinner with Giulio Andreotti was scheduled twelve days hence. Andreotti himself was due to arrive the next day to launch the Sicilian campaign. Lima and friends had hardly moved off when a Honda 600 XL motorbike with electronic fuel injection, straddled by two helmeted youths, overtook their car. Shots were fired from the bike. The car braked and stopped abruptly, and the three dignitaries scrambled out. Lima shrieked, *They're coming back!* and struggled out of his green loden overcoat and ran. They were his last words. His glove-soft leather pumps weren't made for speed, and it was an awful long time since those soft thighs had run anywhere at all. The next thing the other two noticed, from their hiding place behind a garbage skip, was the Hon. Lima lying face down and dead. He'd been neatly shot in the skull from close behind, at a slight angle. The killers ignored the other two DC potentates crouching behind the dumpster, one of whom was a professor of philosophy whose appointment Lima had been arranging to the board of the state railways, and leisurely left. *The friends no longer had any respect for him*, it was later explained by Gioacchino Pennino, a Palermo doctor, man of honour and DC politician who became the first political *pentito*. In the indictment of the Cosa Nostra leadership for the killing, the prosecutors described Lima as having been *Cosa Nostra's ambassador to Rome*. This was not said immediately. *Salvo*, said a close colleague, choosing his words of tribute carefully so soon after the actual shooting and exploiting Latinate abstraction to the full, *was a man of synthesis*. He didn't say of what.

Lima's standing within the DC was nevertheless undeniably such that certain people felt they had to come to Palermo for his funeral, however much they hated doing it, given the questions people were suddenly asking about the government's relations with the mafia. The president of Italy, still the demochristian Cossiga, at first said this was clearly a mafia crime, nothing to do with the state and that *he* wouldn't be coming to pay his last respects. Something or someone later changed his mind, and he came. The secretary of the DC was there too. So was prime minister Andreotti, who'd perhaps had something to do with convincing the others to come. People were struck by the shrunken, terrorized and humiliated figure the prime minister cut when he came down for Lima's funeral. The minister of justice at that time, Claudio Martelli, remembered two years later how Andreotti looked after Lima's murder: *His face had an even waxier look than usual. He was terrified, either because he didn't understand, or maybe because he did.* Huddled in his heavy overcoat, Andreotti looked like an aged tortoise retracting into its shell. His nerves frayed by the media's constant linking of his own name with that of Cosa Nostra's latest hit victim, its most *distinguished corpse*, prime minister Andreotti snapped a few days later that it was *really absurd to divide even the dead into political factions*. The presidency was slipping from his grasp, the only thing he'd ever wanted and failed to get. He was made a Life Senator as a consolation prize, *for distinguished service to the Republic*. Not being president was anyhow no longer even the worst of it. Andreotti can't have failed to see that killing as a portent.

CALABRIA

NORMAN DOUGLAS

OLD MORANO

From

OLD CALABRIA (1915)

QUITE A FEATURE in the landscape of Morano is the costume of the women, with their home-dyed red skirts and ribbons of the same hue plaited into their hair. It is a beautiful and reposeful shade of red, between Pompeian and brick-colour, and the tint very closely resembles that of the cloth worn by the beduin (married) women of Tunisia. Maybe it was introduced by the Saracens. And it is they, I imagine, who imported that love of red peppers (a favourite dish with most Orientals) which is peculiar to these parts, where they eat them voraciously in every form, particularly in that of red sausages seasoned with these fiery condiments.

The whole country is full of Saracen memories. The name of Morano, they say, is derived from *moro*,* a Moor; and in its little piazza – an irregular and picturesque spot, shaded by a few grand old elms amid the sound of running waters – there is a sculptured head of a Moor inserted into the wall, commemorative, I was told, of some ancient anti-Saracen exploit. It is the escutcheon of the town. This Moor wears a

---

* This is all wrong, of course. And equally wrong is the derivation from *morus*, a mulberry – abundant as these trees are. And more wrong still, if possible, is that which is drawn from a saying of the mysterious Oenotrians – that useful tribe – who, wandering in search of home-steads across these regions and observing their beauty, are supposed to have remarked: *Hic moremur* – here let us stay! Morano (strange to say) is simply the Roman Muranum.

red fez, and his features are painted black (this is *de rigueur*, for 'Saracens'); he bears the legend *Vivit sub arbore morus*. Near at hand, too, lies the prosperous village Saracena, celebrated of old for its muscatel wines. They are made from the grape which the Saracens brought over from Maskat, and planted all over Sicily.

The men of Morano emigrate to America; two-thirds of the adult and adolescent male population are at this moment on the other side of the Atlantic. But the oldsters, with their peaked hats (capello pizzuto) shading gnarled and canny features, are well worth studying. At this summer season they leave the town at 3.30 a.m. to cultivate their fields, often far distant, returning at nightfall; and to observe these really wonderful types, which will soon be extinct, you must take up a stand on the Castrovillari road towards sunset and watch them riding home on their donkeys, or walking, after the labours of the day.

Poorly dressed, these peasants are none the less wealthy; the post office deposit of Morano is said to have two million francs to its credit, mostly the savings of these humble cultivators, who can discover an astonishing amount of money when it is a question, for example, of providing their daughters with a dowry. The bridal dress alone, a blaze of blue silk and lace and gold embroidery, costs between six hundred and a thousand francs. Altogether, Morano is a rich place, despite its sordid appearance; it is also celebrated as the birthplace of various learned men. The author of the 'Calascione Scordato', a famous Neapolitan poem of the seventeenth century, certainly lived here for some time and has been acclaimed as a son of Morano, though he distinctly speaks of Naples as his home. Among its elder literary glories is that Leonardo Tufarelli, who thus apostrophizes his birthplace:

'And to proceed – how many *letterati* and *virtuosi* have issued from you in divers times? Among whom – not to name all of them – there has been in our days Leopardo de l'Osso of happy memory, physician and most excellent philosopher, singular in every science, of whom I dare say that he attained to Pythagorean heights. How many are there to-day, versed in every faculty, in theology, in the two laws, and in medicine? How many historians, how many poets, grammarians, artists, actors?'

The modern writer Nicola Leoni is likewise a child of Morano; his voluminous 'Della Magna Grecia e delle Tre Calabrie' appeared in 1844–1846. He, too, devotes much space to the praises of his natal city, and to lamentations regarding the sad condition of Calabrian letters during those dark years.

'Closed for ever is the academy of Amantea! Closed for ever is the academy of Rossano! Rare are the lectures in the academy of Monteleone! Rare indeed the lectures in the academy of Catanzaro! Closed for ever is the public library of Monteleone! O ancient days! O wisdom of our fathers! Where shall I find you? . . .'

To live the intellectual life amid the ferociously squalid surroundings of Morano argues an enviable philosophic calm – a detachment bordering on insensibility. But perhaps we are too easily influenced by externals, in these degenerate times. Or things may have been better in days of old – who can tell? One always likes to think so, though the evidence usually points to the contrary

CORRADO ALVARO

From

REVOLT IN
ASPROMONTE (1930)

Translated by Frances Frenaye

IT IS NO EASY life, that of the shepherds of Aspromonte, in the dead of winter when swollen streams rush down to the sea and the earth seems to float on the water. The shepherds stay in huts built of mud and sticks and sleep beside the animals. They go about in long capes with triangular hoods over their shoulders such as might have been worn by an ancient Greek god setting out upon a winter pilgrimage. The torrential streams make a deafening noise and in the clearings, amid the white snow, big black tubs, set over wood fires, steam with boiling milk curdled by a greenish ferment and a handful of wild herbs. The men standing around in their black capes and black wool suits are the only living beings among the dark surrounding mountains and the stiffly frozen trees. But even in this icy cold the nuts are ripening under the oak bark for the future delight of rooting pigs.

The men toss thick slices of bread into the tubs and draw them out with long carved wooden spoons, dripping and gleaming with a whiteness that only bread dipped in milk can acquire. Wood-carving is one of the shepherds' diversions. They cut flowering hearts into the ribs of their sweethearts' stays and sculpture figures out of olive branches to decorate their wives' distaffs. With red-hot spits they make holes in their reed flutes. They crouch at the entrance to their huts, looking across the shining white snow and waiting for the day when they can go down to the plain and hang up their capes and flasks on a tree of the lowlands. The new moon will break the cycle of rains and they will go down to the village, where there are houses with solid walls, heavy with the talk and sighs of women. The village is warm and its houses are huddled together like the sheep in a sheepfold. On fair days the oxen climb up the steep, rocky path like the animals in a Christmas play; white and well-built as they are, they seem larger than the trees, almost like huge, prehistoric beasts. Every now and then news comes that an ox has fallen into a gully and the whole village, like a pack of hounds, waits for the quartered animal to be hung up on a pole in front of the butcher's shop on the square. The dogs sniff at its blood and the women buy up the meat at a low price.

Neither the sheep nor the oxen nor the black pigs belong to the shepherds. They are the property of the local gentry, who are waiting to send them to market and to the whiskered traders who come from the coast. Up in the lonely, wind-swept mountains the shepherd draws at the charred tobacco in his pipe, watches his son frisk about like a roebuck and listens to the songs of his younger companions, which are accompanied by the sound of water running under the ice, murmuring like women who have gone out to chop wood. Someone sitting on a knoll, as if he were at the top of the world, may blow into his bagpipe and then they all think of women and wine and houses with solid walls. They think of Sundays in the village below when they fill the narrow streets with their heavy sighs, and mules from their stalls and pigs from their pens sigh back to them in answer, when children call out shrilly like sparrows, when crippled old men stare out at the last ray of light and old women rest their swollen and weary bellies, and brides are like quiet doves. They think of the call they will pay at the house of a prosperous neigh-bor, where they will see a bottle of wine gleam in the miserly hands of their host and the wine itself pour into the glass, which they will empty at a single gulp except for the last few drops thrown on the ground. Here in the mountains, where they are condemned to drink nothing but milk, the memory of this wine runs through their veins like liquid fire.

Sometimes it happens that an ox or a silly sheep strays away from a neighboring flock and crosses their path. They know each individual animal as if it were a man and recognize its owner as we recognize a stranger. The animal approaches hesitatingly and the vigilant dogs are silent. Quietly and cautiously the shepherds capture the animal and kill it. One of them sticks a spit through its body, another turns the spit over the flame, a third, with a bunch of wild herbs, sprinkles it with grease while it hangs there with all the solemnity of a sacrificial victim. They have only water to drink and yet this is enough to intoxicate them. But such evenings come no more than once a year to break the hardships of the winter.

At last, with the arrival of spring, the women come to join them. Then the sons of man frisk alongside the lambs on the grass, and babies rock in cradles swung between branches where dormice and squirrels play. Later even the rocks are covered with green, and with the summer breezes more people come up into the mountains. Pilgrims to the various sanctuaries pass from one valley to another, making music and singing night and day. The wine seller builds his hut of sticks near a fountain, and at night, in order to light their way, the pilgrims set fire to dried branches of trees. Lovers circulate among the throng, looking for their beloved, and there is a hurly-burly of mad dogs, fugitives from justice, penitents, thieves, and drunkards who roll like stones down the mountainous slopes. At this season the mountains come alive and the sky is bright with fireworks sent up from the villages down by the sea, in order to indicate that there are the houses, there are the saints with their faces like those of peasants who have ceased their labors and stand now in the spacious silence of the churches.

On such a night as this misfortune came to the shepherd Argiro. It was the eve of a feast day and it was silent in the shepherd's hut. In a somber voice Argiro said to his son:

'Antonello, you must come with me down to the village. Do you think you can make it?'

'Yes, Father, I do.'

'It's six hours of walking.'

'I can walk that far.'

'Well, there's a full moon and the night is cool.'

'I'll make it,' said Antonello, 'I'm strong.'

The boy was very serious, endowed with a capacity for sharing other people's sorrows which gave him a docile and thoughtful air. He had just begun to wear a shepherd's rig, with a wide leather belt around his waist, and he was pleased with the prospect of showing himself for the first time in his new mohair jacket. He had been born in the mountains and had no conception of a house with solid walls as they called it. Now, hearing his father fumble with something in the hut, he jumped up and said:

'Can I help you, Father?'

There was no reply. In the low hut, which a man could only enter crawling, his father was packing his belongings: his sack, his flask, his heavy winter cape.

'Are we taking everything with us?'

'As God wills it, my boy.'

Antonello searched the edge of the mud walls and found his whistle and a packet of crumpled images of the saints.

'Will you pack these for me?' he asked.

His father put them in and this mark of respect for his things gave the boy satisfaction. The shepherd laid the

246

sack down just outside the door of the hut, sat down for a moment to wipe the sweat off his brow, then got up and swung it over one shoulder.

'Let us go,' he said.

Before leaving, he closed the crude wooden door and rolled a huge stone in front of it. The sea shimmered far to the west below them, untouched as yet by the shadows of evening. Between them and the sea rose a pointed peak, like an uplifted finger, and closer still lay the white ribbon of a mountain stream. Night was coming silently over the mountains, pushing back the long rays of the dying sun. On the plain below, the shadows lengthened.

'Can I carry the sack, Father?'

The father turned the sack over to his son. It hung on the end of a stick which gave a sensation of pleasurable pain to the boy's shoulder. Then he gave a last look at the hut. From the first rise of ground they both looked back at the gaunt tree bending over it, the stones clustered around like sleeping animals or pieces of furniture upon which they had sat so often. Their big white dog, aware without being told of their departure, followed them on their way.

On the other side of the ridge they saw the road that wound along the edge of the gully crowded with men and animals on a pilgrimage. '*Viva Maria!*' the pilgrims called out. The shepherd raised his hand and made a weak response. Antonello called back too, in a silvery voice, happy to have a chance to open his mouth. From the other side of the gully came a volley of gunshots. The pilgrims wound their way along in Indian file. Babies cried from baskets balanced on their mothers' heads, mules carrying men of property knocked stones off the path with their hoofs into the valley below, a well-dressed woman walked with bare feet, holding her shoes in her hand, in fulfillment of a vow. One peasant woman wore her long hair flowing down her back and a man carried on his head a candle as large as himself. Antonello gaped at these sights. Darkness came down upon the valley and it was filled with the noise of a waterfall on the brink of a mountain. The moon hung over the sea, beyond the mountains, like a sentinel. The shepherd and his son stopped near a mud hut and the man inside, standing behind a counter lined with bottles, near a keg of wine, stuck his head out and said:

'Hello there, Argiro, what's the matter?'

'Trouble, Fermo, very bad trouble.'

'And what might it be?'

'I've lost everything. The oxen I take care of for Signor Filippo Mezzatesta have fallen into a ravine. It means my ruin.'

'When did it happen?'

'Today, just after noon. A fine holy day this is for me!'

'And did you own a half share in the animals?'

'Yes, I was joint owner with Signor Filippo Mezzatesta. What would you say to buying them? The hides are good and the meat is as fresh as if they'd been butchered today. They didn't die of disease. With all the pilgrims passing by you'd be sure to make sales.'

'It's the meat of dead animals, whatever you say.'

'It's just as if it were freshly butchered, I tell you. You of all people shouldn't be squeamish on that score. We two know. . . .'

'Shall we go see them, then?'

'They're down this way in the Monaco gully.'

'Four animals, you said?'

'Yes, and one of them a young heifer, a perfect beauty and tender as milk.' Then the shepherd turned to his son. 'You wait here,' he said.

'And if anyone asks for me,' Fermo added, 'say I'll be back right away. Don't let anyone touch a thing.'

'Fermo, my life is ruined,' groaned Argiro.

The two men walked away. Antonello sat down in front of the store, called the dog and held him by the collar. But the dog got loose and ran after his master, leaving Antonello alone and afraid. He smelled the strange, new odor of wine and looked at the many-colored bottles standing in a row, which made the name of a local liqueur, 'Rosolio,' come into his mind. The pilgrims were thinning out, but along came a group singing and shooting into the air. Leading the way was a man with a bagpipe and another who beat first with his whole fist and then with five fingers on a drum. Others followed them, fulfilling a vow by dancing and knocking their behinds against one another at intervals, both men and women, without so much as a smile. The moon grew red and night fell like a cloak. The trees, most of them seared and marked by lightning, seemed to grow larger in the darkness. The group of players and dancers retreated into the distance. A barefooted girl passed right in front of Antonello and he saw a thread of blood running down one foot.

'Girl, you're bleeding,' he called out.

'I know it,' she said with a laugh.

Another band of pilgrims went by, carrying guns and lighted torches. One of them stopped at the foot of an oak tree split in two by lightning and held a resin torch to its branches. The whole tree crackled and burst into flame like a gigantic torch. Antonello called out in a loud voice: 'Fido!' and the dog appeared at the edge of the road with his perpetually astonished eyes. A shout went up from the pilgrims: 'There's the mad dog!' and a shot rang out in the air. The dog sprawled on the ground, looking around him as if he could speak and were asking why. Antonello, his teeth chattering, crouched at the entrance of the hut as the pilgrims passed laughing by. The boy reached out for the sack and put it under him without daring to look up.

Argiro and his son reached the village at dawn. As they climbed over the crest of the hill the sight of the houses huddled together like a flock of sheep met their eyes. The village had lain for centuries in this hollow and had fallen asleep there. Around it, in a radius of a few miles, other villages, perched on rocky crags, melted into the stone, taking on the stone's structure and color the way a butterfly assumes the likeness of the flower on which it has come to perch. The whole effect was that of a desolate landscape on the moon. Travelers, by horse or mule, making their way along the river beds through the valleys in a silence punctuated only by the hoofbeats of their mounts, had an air of cave dwellers about them. But pushing one's way along the stream between the spurs of the mountains, one can feel the valley becoming animated with a secret life of its own and hear the voices of its multitude of streams. Here are villages topped by a ribbon of smoke, scattered voices, indeterminate sounds, the soprano tone of the church bells. This is a life into which one must be initiated if one is to understand it, a country which one can love only if one has been born into it, full as it is, like its villages, of rocks and thorns.

The road that has been under construction for the last twenty years has come to the last piece of rock to be dynamited before it is put through to its destination, and now strangers penetrate this fastness previously known only to an occasional *carabinière* investigating a crime, or an itinerant merchant buying up old rags and hair that the peasant women have hidden in holes in the walls. Ragged boys ride, straddling a colt's back, along well-worn paths, and oxen drag tree trunks with ropes around them down from the mountain heights without the aid of a wagon. It is a fact that here the idea of the wheel does not exist. But that will not be for long. Just as mummies fall into dust when they come into contact with the air, so this ancient way of life is breaking up as it comes into touch with something new. We have here a disappearing civilization. Let us not weep over its eclipse, but, if we were born into it, let us store up in our memory as much of it as we can. The liberation of the Kingdom of the Two Sicilies superseded an order of things that had been established for centuries, and the redistribution of feudal property only increased some already swollen private fortunes. This village remained what it had been from time immemorial, a cluster of one-story rustic houses on earth foundations with fireplaces hewed out of natural rock – all built around one nobleman's palace, with its gates, stables, gardens, kitchens and servants. The common people's interests and struggles centered about this palace, near the church, for it was the focal point of all the wealth, all the good and evil of the village.

Antonello could see the palace, set on a rise of ground above the rest, with a colonnade bearing a loggia on top of it. He leaped along in his father's footsteps without displaying any surprise at the sight of the houses with solid walls. On some of the buildings the darting sun was reflected from something shiny like ice, which grew brighter and brighter until it was smooth and clear as water.

'Which is the house where we shall find Mother?' was all he asked.

But this humble house was not to be seen; it was lost among the multitude of its equals. Then the boy's eyes wandered back to the palace with the colonnade and he thought to himself: 'That must belong to the Mezzatestas.'

Cocks were crowing at one another and scattered women's cries broke the silence. The boy amused himself by poking with a stick at some turnip plants with flopping red flowers, parched by the midsummer heat. Everything seemed to him softer in the mountains. When they reached the first house of the village the earth suddenly seemed to shrink. A gust of hot air blew out of the open door as from the mouth of an animal. A woman sat on the doorstep combing her hair and dipping the comb into a bowl of water. Because of the holiday the village was deserted and lazy. The few living souls to be seen were sitting in the open spaces in front of their houses or on the outside stairs, tidying their children or cleaning vegetables for the next meal. Some girls with bare feet but wearing their best dresses had medals of the Virgin Mary on colored ribbons around their necks. Suddenly a train of mules came out of a narrow street, led by a dealer in hides with a red face.

'What's wrong, Argiro?' he asked. And the story of the four oxen which had fallen over the precipice spread rapidly from door to door.

When they came to their house they found Antonello's mother at the door.

'For the love of God, what is it?'

In a few words Argiro told her the whole story. From neighboring windows women hung out to hear and spread the news. One of them came to the house with a maliciously humble air and said:

'Oh, Betta, have you a pound or two of meat for me?'

No one answered, but from inside Argiro shouted:

'A cursed lot you are, waiting to fatten yourselves on my misfortune. You can't even hold back until my troubles are over before you start closing in. I've sold every bit of the meat and you'll be the last to eat it. When something happens to a man his neighbors fall on him like a pack of dogs. Lord have mercy on us!'

Antonello had sat down on a linen chest and was listening to these words as if they were a dirge. For the first time he felt himself to be mixed up in something unjust. Awareness of his own condition came to him all of a sudden and clearly; he felt like a fallen angel. He stared hard at the image of Saint Luke hung on the door. His father was sitting on the bed. His mother gave him four figs and a slice of bread.

'Eat, my boy,' she said.

He felt his mother's hands, as warm as if they were his own. The room was cool and shut off from the outside world, whence he could hear sounds and voices in a sort of rhythm like a steady fall of rain. With his bread clenched in his fist, Antonello fell asleep on the chest.

VITO TETI

CLOUDS AND BACK STREETS (2011)

Translated by Francesco Loriggio and
Damiano Pietropaolo

'HOW CAN YOU still stand to stay in the village?' Mara asked Vittorino in full voice, in the middle of a long speech, full of pleasantries and half lies, of skirmishes and carefully chosen words, as happens to people after the end of a love affair who continue to be on good terms and even see each other from time to time. In villages like this one, relationships, good or bad, never really end.

He looked at her carefully, but without any surprise. Sooner or later, the inevitable questions arrive, punctual like summer storms, or the feasts of the saints: 'When did you come?' 'How are you?' 'When will you leave?' He was lying down on the bed in his room. The sun's rays flooded that side of the house with great intensity. The village – thought Vittorio – always questions about the village – how can I continue living in this village, what's happening in the village, nothing but the village seems to exist for her, and every time she returns it's the same ball-breaking routine, what are people talking about, why did you do this or that, who died, how can you live here, the town is emptying out more and more.

'You should have stayed here if you didn't wish the village to become an empty shell, and instead of talking to us about the world, the places in which you live, you come back to talk only about the village.' Vittorio had wanted to offer this reply, but he simply said: 'The village doesn't exist.'

Mara fixed her black, fleeting eyes on him: She saw right

through him. She was still beautiful, the woman with whom he had had an intense and long romance. He'd forgotten how and when their story had started and still couldn't understand when or how it ended.

'You're right,' she said, after a long silence in which she searched for something intelligent to say, 'the village isn't the same. Everything has changed, everything is different, I can't say in what way; maybe it's due to the fact that we've changed, we've gone away, nothing is the same as before, but I can't seem to stay away . . .'

Vittorio cut short this ancient, monotonous litany that had become part of their ritualized summer meetings and which, after so many years since their story had ended, for no reason or many reasons, they still couldn't avoid. He had remained in the village, not sure whether through conscious choice or need, and this litany rang out to him like a declaration of war from which he could defend himself with all the artillery in his possession: irony, sarcasm, silence, indifference. He feigned an excessive sense of belonging to the village in order to put into difficulty, with such an unpredictable attack, all who thought they'd left the village behind them, simply because they'd moved to faraway places.

He was aware that he was making himself wretched, but it was the only way to create discomfort in all who had come looking for confirmation of their choices, and perhaps even of their failures. In the end, though, it felt like he was the one who'd gone away. Many who returned, though not all, seemed to be in the throes of torment, of being in prison.

'No,' she replied, looking a bit distant but with some affection, 'that's not what I meant to say . . . I'm sorry, I don't think I can make myself understood today.'

Mara stood up from the chair where she was sitting, approached the foot of the bed on which Vittorio had settled comfortably, and waited for him to continue the conversation. She urged him on with her gaze.

'It's not that the village isn't the same as before. I mean something different: It no longer exists for me and I no longer exist for the village. Don't worry, I understand very well your desire to find the village wherever you are, whatever you do, however, always. It's a drawback for all who have left. Those who've stayed have lost their village; those who left can never be free of it.'

As he listened to himself talk in this way, he felt he was bringing to the surface forgotten heartaches, ancient resentments, traces of old battles in a war that they'd both lost. He detected aggressiveness in Mara's questions, in her gaze, perhaps the distance that she had never accepted. Full of sadness and detachment he said pointedly: 'The village doesn't exist, it has never existed.'

Mara smiled, moved closer to the bed, stroked his hair; she hadn't forgotten Vittorio's weakness for burying himself in the present, and resorted to her ancient ways to bring him back to the surface. Vittorio sat quietly, looked out towards the sun caressing the crowns of villages in the distance: in a short while he would dive into the sea. He realized that he'd exceeded the limits of Mara's tolerance. He sensed that the woman from his past was about to lose her patience, to put an end to the conversation with some banality, and he forestalled her.

'Come closer,' he said, sitting down on the bed, resting one foot on the floor. 'I'll make room for you.' He felt the nearness of her, of the body that he loved so much.

He smiled, thinking: 'Even Mara doesn't exist.'

'Are you having fun playing the mysterious type or are you simply joking?' she asked.

Yeah, Vittorio thought to himself, when she doesn't

understand I have no escape: I'm either playing at being mysterious or I'm simply a dumb ass.

'No,' he said complacent, but with a hint of the sweetness of the good times, 'I don't want to give you the run around. Do you see the great show out there, with the setting sun? Soon it'll cut across the clouds, hide in them for a while; then it'll cross over the mountains on the horizon and fall into the sea.'

Mara listened, silent, tense. Vittorio went on: 'See the dense and blond clouds that surround it, that hide it and reveal it? I feel like I'm their driver. I'm on top of the clouds; I leave and return. When I'm in the village I hide in the clouds. The village is no longer there because I'm not there anymore; I know how to become invisible, and appear whenever I want.'

Mara looked at him, somewhat annoyed, which is what Vittorio had wanted. She became serious; she couldn't speak, as though she was remembering something or looking to be forgiven. Mara asked Vittorio to put on a record.

'Our first record,' she said, almost chanting the words.

He didn't reply, and turned his gaze towards the church steeple. He looked on the rooftops and the narrow streets, and thought for a moment about the blue and gray clouds in winter. Many afternoons, when he rose from his desk, he stared at them with intensity and anxiety as we do when we're waiting for the return of a loved one. They hung so low and were so close that he wanted to caress them with his hand, to gather them and put them in his pocket. Sometimes he wanted to secure them to the ground as when, as a boy, he played with the cards of soccer players. He was tempted to fill the empty, dark streets, the deserted alleys and the abandoned houses with clouds. Other times he would hold on to them, lift them onto the rooftops, and raise them up high as if intending to build tall skyscrapers like those in Manhattan.

The notes of Springsteen's 'New York City Serenade' reminded him of times gone by. He had first listened to it when he was a student in Rome, when only a handful of music lovers from overseas knew *The Boss*. He remembered, as though it had happened only yesterday, an evening at the home of his friend Salvatore, in the company of two girls he had met at the *Alessandrina* library where he studied in the afternoon.

That summer he returned to the village and brought back the LP, and he made everyone who came to visit listen to it, especially Mara, and just at the time when their story was coming to an end. Their lives were out of sync: He was in Rome, and she was still in the village. Now she would move to Bologna to study at the Faculty of Arts, Theatre and Music, while he would return to the village from where he would commute to Messina, where he'd been offered a term appointment to teach comparative literature at the University.

Vittorio listened in a daze to that sweet serenade of love to New York, to the stories that spoke of the innocence of youth, of their running wildly and aimlessly in the nights along Robert De Niro's and Martin Scorsese's *mean streets*. The 'Serenade to New York' turned into a sorrowful serenade of love to the village, a tale of the sadness and longing of the young, of their desire to escape. It had become the soundtrack of frayed landscapes coming apart at the seams, of empty and abandoned houses, of closed and desolate neighborhoods; a longing for life, just like the songs of leaving and separation had been for a generation of emigrants, who left dreaming to return only to end up building a new life far away from these lost and abandoned places.

Sometimes he thought that the world was becoming all the same, that, truly, the world had finally become a village, and the village, in spite of it all, a kind of world. That song accompanied the loneliness and the flights into the night of the youth in the Big Apple, but also the dreams of young people in a place whose inhabitants were fewer than those who lived in a single skyscraper of the American metropolis. When he traveled to New York or other cities, however, it became apparent to him that both those who stay and those who leave need to tell each other fables, and that the world isn't at all the same. The soul of the places where we live forms a part of our own soul. In the streets of New York he felt comfortable, serene, without a past and imagined that it was a place where he might be able to live. He stared at the faces of passers-by as if seeking his own happy double.

Mara walked over to Vittorio and fumbled for his hair. She rested her head on his shoulder, as if to say: 'Something remains, it's not all over.' They embraced as if to confirm that they hadn't disappeared, as had happened to the old village. Vittorio got up and went to the balcony, looking for the sun that had already set.

'Never mind, I beg you,' he said with the tone of someone who is returning from a mysterious world. 'It doesn't make much sense now. Don't let me stay in the village, don't imagine me in a place outside of time where nothing happens. We're no longer who we once were, and even they didn't fare so well together. I don't want to think any more, I want to go far away, to fly up, like a child on his wooden horse, over that tuft of white and purple clouds, chasing after the sun to catch up to it near the sea just before it hides in the water and darkness falls.'

BASILICATA

CARLO LEVI

From

CHRIST STOPPED AT EBOLI (1945)

Translated by Frances Frenaye

1

MANY YEARS HAVE gone by, years of war and of what
men call History. Buffeted here and there at random I have
not been able to return to my peasants as I promised when
I left them, and I do not know when, if ever, I can keep my
promise. But closed in one room, in a world apart, I am glad
to travel in my memory to that other world, hedged in by
custom and sorrow, cut off from History and the State, eternally patient, to that land without comfort, or solace, where
the peasant lives out his motionless civilization on barren
ground in remote poverty, and in the presence of death.

'We're not Christians,' they say. 'Christ stopped short of
here, at Eboli.' 'Christian' in their way of speaking means
'human being,' and this almost proverbial phrase that I have
so often heard them repeat may be no more than the expression of a hopeless feeling of inferiority. We're not Christians,
we're not human beings; we're not thought of as men but
simply as beasts, beasts of burden, or even less than beasts,
mere creatures of the wild. They at least live for better or
for worse, like angels or demons, in a world of their own,
while we have to submit to the world of Christians, beyond
the horizon, to carry its weight and to stand comparison
with it. But the phrase has a much deeper meaning and,
as is the way of symbols, this is the literal one. Christ did
stop at Eboli, where the road and the railway leave the coast
of Salerno and turn into the desolate reaches of Lucania.
Christ never came this far, nor did time, nor the individual

soul, nor hope, nor the relation of cause to effect, nor reason nor history. Christ never came; just as the Romans never came, content to garrison the highways without penetrating the mountains and forests, nor the Greeks, who flourished beside the Gulf of Taranto. None of the pioneers of Western civilization brought here his sense of the passage of time, his deification of the State or that ceaseless activity which feeds upon itself. No one has come to this land except as an enemy, a conqueror, or a visitor devoid of understanding. The seasons pass to-day over the toil of the peasants, just as they did three thousand years before Christ; no message, human or divine, has reached this stubborn poverty. We speak a different language, and here our tongue is incomprehensible. The greatest travelers have not gone beyond the limits of their own world; they have trodden the paths of their own souls, of good and evil, of morality and redemption. Christ descended into the underground hell of Hebrew moral principle in order to break down its doors in time and to seal them up into eternity. But to this shadowy land, that knows neither sin nor redemption from sin, where evil is not moral but is only the pain residing forever in earthly things, Christ did not come. Christ stopped at Eboli.

2

I ARRIVED AT Gagliano one August afternoon in a rattling little car. I was wearing handcuffs and I was escorted by two stalwart servants of the State with vertical red bands on their trousers, and expressionless faces. I arrived reluctantly and ready for the worst, because sudden orders had caused me to leave Grassano, where I had been living and where I had learned to know the region of Lucania. It had been hard at first. Grassano, like all the villages hereabouts, is a streak of white at the summit of a bare hill, a sort of miniature imaginary Jerusalem in the solitude of the desert. I liked to climb to the highest point of the village, to the wind-beaten church, where the eye can sweep over an endless expanse in every direction, identical in character all the way round the circle. It is like being on a sea of chalk, monotonous and without trees. There are other villages, white and far away on the tops of their hills, Irsina, Craco, Montalbano, Salandra, Pisticci, Grottole, Ferrandina the haunts and caves of the brigands; and beyond the reach of vision lies the sea, and Metaponto, and Taranto. I felt that I had come to understand the hidden virtues of this bare land and to love it; I had no mind to change. I am by nature sensitive to the pangs of separation and for this reason I was anything but well disposed towards the new village where I had to adapt myself to living. I looked forward, however, to the trip from one locality to the other and to the chance of seeing places I had heard so much about, and had pictured in fancy, beyond the mountains hemming in the Basento Valley. We went by the precipice where a year earlier the village band of Grassano, on the way back late at night from playing in the square at Accettura, had been lost. Ever since that night the dead band-players meet at midnight at the foot of the precipice to blow their horns, and shepherds skirt the neighborhood in holy terror. But we passed by in broad daylight; the sun was bright, a wind from Africa scorched the earth, and not a sound came from the wastes of clay below.

At San Mauro Forte, just a little higher up on the mountain, I saw on the outskirts of the village the poles where for years the heads of brigands were exposed to view, and then we entered the Accettura Forest, one of the few bits left of the wooded land that once included all of Lucania. The definition of *Lucus a non lucendo* really holds true to-day when Lucania, the woodland, is quite bare. To see trees again at last, and fresh undergrowth, and green grass, and to smell the leaves was for me like a visit to fairyland. This was the kingdom of the brigands, and the mere remote memory of them causes the traveler to cross it even to-day with a mixture of fear and curiosity. But the kingdom is a narrow one and we soon left it behind as we went up to Stigliano, where Mark, the ancient crow, has been for centuries in the village square, like a local god, spreading his black wings above the cobblestones. After Stigliano we went down into the valley of the Sauro River with its bed of white stones and an island, now renowned for Prince Colonna's fine olive trees, where a battalion of *bersaglieri* troops was wiped out when the brigands of Boryes marched on Potenza. Here, at a crossroads, we left the route to the Agri Valley and turned to the left on a recently built narrow road.

Farewell, Grassano; farewell, country seen from afar or in the imagination! We had crossed to the other side of the mountains and were leaping up to Gagliano, where only a short time before the wheel of no vehicle had ever come. At Gagliano the road ends. My impression was an unpleasant one. At first sight the village did not seem to be a village at all, but merely a group of scattered white houses, slightly pretentious in their poverty. It was not on the summit of a hill, like the others, but perched on a sort of jagged saddle rising among picturesque ravines; as I first saw it there was lacking the severe and terrible aspect typical of the settlements in these parts. There were a few trees and a spot of green by the way where we had come in, and this very softening of character was displeasing to me. I was accustomed by now to the bare and dramatic austerity of Grassano, to its creviced plaster walls and its mysterious and meditative silence. The country air apparently hanging over Gagliano seemed to me to strike a false note in this land which had nothing of the countryside about it. And then, perhaps out of vanity, it seemed to me inappropriate that the place where I was condemned to live should not appear shut in, but spread out and almost welcoming. A prisoner may find greater consolation in a cell with romantic, heavy iron bars than in one that superficially resembles a normal room. But my first impression was only in part correct.

I was unloaded from the car and turned over to the village clerk, a spare man, hard of hearing, with pointed black whiskers on a yellowish face, who wore a sportsman's jacket. When I had been presented to the mayor and to the sergeant of the *Carabinieri* police and had said goodbye to my guards, who were anxious to be on their way, I found myself alone in the middle of the road. It was then that I became aware that I had not properly seen the village upon my arrival because it wound its way like a worm on either side of the single street, which sloped abruptly down the narrow ridge between two ravines, then climbed up and down again between two other ravines, and came to an abrupt end. The countryside which I thought I had seen at the very beginning was no longer visible. At every turn there were steep slopes of white clay with houses hanging from them as if they were poised in the air, and all around there was still more white clay, with neither trees nor grass growing upon it, eroded into a pattern of holes and hillocks like a landscape on the moon. Almost all the houses appeared to teeter over the abyss, their walls cracked and an air of general fragility about them. Their doors were framed with black pennants, some new, others faded by sun and rain, so that the whole village looked as if it were in mourning or decked out for All Souls' Day. I found out later that it was customary to drape with these pennants the door of a house where someone had died and that they are left hanging until time and the weather fade them out altogether.

There are no shops, properly speaking, in the village, and no hotel. The clerk had directed me, until I should find lodgings of my own, to his widowed sister-in-law, who had a room for occasional visitors and would give me my meals as well. Her house was near the entrance to the village, only a few steps from the town hall. Before examining my new residence more carefully I entered the black-framed door of the widow's house, carrying my bags and followed by my dog Barone, and sat down in the kitchen.

The air was black with thousands of flies, and other thousands covered the walls; an old yellow dog was stretched out on the floor with an air of infinite boredom. The same boredom and a sort of disgust, born of the experience of injustice and horror, were reflected on the widow's pale face. She was a middle-aged woman, dressed not as a peasant but in the manner of the fairly well-to-do, with a black veil on her head. Her husband had come to a bad end three years before. A peasant witch-woman had drawn him into her toils by means of love potions, and he had become her lover. A child was born to them, and because at this point he wished to break off their sinful relationship she had given him poison. His illness was long and mysterious; the doctors found no name for it. Gradually his strength melted away; his face grew dark until the skin was the color of bronze and finally quite black; then, at last, he died. His widow was left with a ten-year-old son and very little money, and so she rented a room to strangers. Her position was midway between that of the peasants and that of the gentry; she displayed the poverty of the one class and the good manners of the other. The boy had been sent to a seminary in Potenza for his schooling. When I came, he was at home for a holiday, a silent, gentle, and obedient lad, already set apart by his religious education, with his head shaved and a gray school uniform buttoned up round his neck.

I had been only a short time in the widow's kitchen and had just begun to question her about the village when there was a knock at the door and a group of peasants asked timidly if they might come in. There were seven or eight of them, wearing black hats and with an unusual seriousness in their dark eyes.

'Are you the doctor that has just arrived?' they asked me. 'Come at once, there is someone in a bad way.'

They had learned of my arrival at the town hall and had heard that I was a doctor. I told them that I was a doctor, to be sure, but I had not practised for many years, that there must be a doctor on call in the village and that for this reason I must refuse them. They answered that there was no doctor and that their friend was dying.

'Is it possible that there's no doctor?'

'None.'

I was greatly embarrassed and uncertain whether, after so many years away from medicine, I could be useful. But how was I to resist their pleas? One of them, an old man with white hair, came close to me and took my hand as if to kiss it. I drew back and blushed with shame, as I was to do on many more occasions during the following year when other peasants made the same gesture. Was this an entreaty or a remnant of feudalism? I got up and followed them to where the sick man lay.

The house was near at hand. The patient was lying on a sort of stretcher near the door, completely dressed, with his hat and shoes on. The room was dark and in the shadows I could just make out the figures of weeping women. A small

273

crowd of men, women, and children followed me in from the street and stood in a circle around me. From their broken sentences I gathered that the man had just been brought back into the house after they had taken him fifteen miles on a donkey to Stigliano to see a doctor. There were doctors at Gagliano but they were not decent Christians, they said. The doctor at Stigliano had told him to go back and die in his own house. Here he was and I should try to save him. But there was nothing I could do, for he was very near the end. The hypodermics I had found at the widow's house were of no avail, although, in order to satisfy my conscience, I tried hopelessly to revive him. He had suffered an acute attack of malaria, the fever had soared above every limit, and his body could endure no more. With his face an earthy color he lay limp on the stretcher, breathing with difficulty, and unable to speak, surrounded by the wailing of his friends. In a little while he was dead. The onlookers made way for me and I went out alone to the square, where the view widens over ridges and valleys in the direction of Sant' Arcangelo. The sun was setting behind the mountains of Calabria and, as the shadows overtook them, the peasants, dwarfed by distance, scurried along paths cut through the clay toward their homes.

APULIA

NICOLA LAGIOIA

From

FEROCITY (2014)

Translated by Antony Shugaar

IN THE MUGGY, suffocating night, he went on telling the story of the crash.

'Completely fucked up. You're just doing your job but that day Christ on the Cross decides to turn a blind eye to you. When He abandons you, He abandons you. I'm just saying that already that morning, things had started off badly.'

He'd told the story in the spring, and even before that, when the old single-pipe steam heating system was still struggling to ward off the chill in the recreation center, so that he, Orazio Basile, fifty-six years old, a former truck driver and now disabled, was forced to sniffle constantly. He sat there hunched over in his seat, his crutches crossed against the poker machine, with a grim, disgusted look on his face. And his audience – men on unemployment, steelworkers with ravaged lungs – listened closely every time, though not a comma of the story ever changed.

The rec center was in the old section of Taranto – the *borgo antico* – a small bean-shaped island connected to the rest of the city by the spans of a swing bridge. Charming, unless you lived there. Buildings with fronts eroded by time and by neglect, empty courtyards overgrown with weeds. Outside the rec center's front door was a parking area where semitrailers were left overnight. Between one truck and the next you could see fishing boats bobbing in the water alongside the deserted wharf. Then huge red forked tongues of flame. The sea crisscrossed by reflections from the oil refinery.

'That fucking city.'

As Orazio said it, he widened his eyes. He spoke in dialect and he wasn't referring to Taranto. The others pricked up their ears even before he opened his mouth. Watching him over time, they'd learned that the metronome preceded the opening notes of the music – the trouser leg stitched shut at knee length was coming to life. The stump bounced up and down, increasingly rapid and edgy.

That morning a faint blue haze covered the fields between Incisa and Montevarchi. He'd been at the wheel for hours, driving his delivery van down the A1. His passenger just wouldn't stop talking. Orazio regretted having picked him up.

He'd left Taranto the previous afternoon and spent the night at a service area in Mugello, lulled to sleep by the reefer units on semitrailers packed with perishable food products. By 8.30 that morning he was on the outskirts of Genoa. He picked his way through the industrial park, down roads marked by implausible points of the compass. Electronics. Toys. Household Goods. One after another, he passed wholesale warehouses. Apparel. That's where he slowed down. He rummaged through his pockets for the crumpled sheet of paper. He'd been there once months ago, but still he was afraid he might get mixed up. When the letters of the sign matched what was written on the paper, he stopped.

He let the warehousemen unload the merchandise. Five hundred pairs of jeans made in Puglia and destined for retail outlets across Northwest Italy. While the men were unloading the clothing, the owner emerged through a glass door from a small office.

'Nice to see you again,' said the wholesaler with a smile.

The man was about sixty, and wore a pinstriped three-piece

suit that had seen better days, his choice of attire suggesting superstition more than stinginess. Business must have been thriving for years, as many years as it had taken to fray the jacket cuffs this badly.

'Let's go get a cup of coffee.'

The wholesaler acted like someone who was sure he'd neither stepped across the watershed that marks the mid-point of a lifespan, nor was running the risk of doing so in the future. It would take more than twelve hours of driving to get back to Taranto; every minute was precious. Orazio was trying to come up with an excuse when the man laid a hand on his shoulder. Orazio let himself be jollied along. That had been his first mistake.

When they got back from the café, he'd followed the owner into his office to get his signature on the bills of lading. Only then did he see the cell phone salesman. The young man was sitting at the desk, reading the paper.

'The son of a longtime friend,' said the owner.

The kid stood up and came over to introduce himself. Slim-fit suit, black shoes. Just as relaxed as the wholesaler was, that was how hard it was for the thirty-year-old to keep both feet flat on the floor for more than three seconds at a time. Without moving his head, Orazio looked out the window at the leaden sky outside. He was eager to get going. The same kind of impatience that, Saturday nights in Taranto at the rec center, drove him to get into an argument with someone after a glass or two.

'It's practically a miracle that he's alive,' said the wholesaler.

The previous afternoon the salesman had crashed his Alfa 159 outside of Savona. A curve taken too fast. He was looking for a ride home.

'He's Pugliese, too,' added the wholesaler.

Orazio snapped to. 'Where from?' he asked.

The kid told him. The wholesaler nodded with satisfaction. One crash leads to another, thought Orazio. He considered the fact that giving him a ride wouldn't take him out of his way. He could drop him off right after the toll barrier and then continue on to Taranto. Easier to say yes than to say no. And yet he could say no. The problem was the wholesaler: the bubble of bliss he was floating along in was a way of presuming – to the point of imposing – total understanding between Orazio and the salesman. Joviality capable of showing itself for what it really was – suspicion and arrogance – only if and when the bubble popped. But that hadn't happened, ensuring that the wholesaler chose, like the last time, not to have the items of clothing counted before having them stacked in the warehouse along with other identical garments. All jeans of the same brand. An attitude the truck driver had counted on for this second trip. And so he'd had to give the youngster a ride.

The second mistake had been to let him spew all that nonsense.

His passenger had behaved perfectly until they stopped for coffee at the Sestri autogrill. Which is to say that for the remaining 560 miles, he'd never once shut up.

'First there's the panorama of the Riviera di Ponente. You know what I'm talking about, I'm sure. Pine trees and citrus groves just steps from the sea. At that point, *wham!* and I'm sitting on the asphalt without even a scratch on me. Jesus Christ, you can't begin to imagine. I didn't really get what had happened myself. It was a brand new 159. Before that, I drove a VW Golf Variant.'

He burst out laughing for no reason. 'A Variant,' he said again.

The accelerated precision of someone who'll go on being

thirty well past the age of fifty. After all, he came from the regional capital. He spoke lightly of the danger he'd escaped . . . When His talon sweeps past, just grazing you and inflicting nothing worse than a scare, the thing to do is shut up and keep going.

Orazio continued to drive and pretended to ignore him. He was forced to acknowledge his undeniable existence, though, when, at Caianello, he wasn't able to pull into the gas station. That's where, if he hadn't had the salesman along, he'd have met the fence and handed over the forty pairs of jeans he'd pilfered from his freight.

He would have set aside part of that money and whatever else was left after rent. The cash would come in handy the next time he had an argument with someone at the rec center. Like other times before, he'd choose to leave the center rather than get into a fistfight. He'd drive through the outskirts of Taranto until the lights of the refinery illuminated the city limits ever more faintly. A swarm of sparks would carve out the darkness at the end of a dirt lane. Whores. He'd head straight for them, thanking his lucky stars for leaving out on the streets the women he didn't have at home.

Instead he'd had to keep going, which left the salesman free to take the initiative a little further down the road: 'What do you say we stop here for a piss? Let me buy you an espresso.'

They set out again after a brief break. Orazio was on edge. He kept brooding over the income he'd so recently missed out on. He totted up numbers in his head as he drove, as twilight erased Irpinia and a clear, metal-black evening in late April descended over the plains of Puglia.

As they approached Candela they saw the enormous pylons of wind turbines in rows across the fields in the moonlight. They suggested a landscape imprisoned for too long in the realm of the imagination. Cars instead of horses. Mechanical towers instead of windmills. After ten minutes, the wind turbines vanished, and the horizon flattened.

The kid should have gotten off at the South Bari toll plaza. But just before they got there he said: 'Now, please, let me repay you.'

He spoke of a restaurant in the center of town. From how he described it, a very fancy place. He reeled off dishes and brands of wine, and when he stopped he still hadn't finished – Orazio had nodded in agreement. His third mistake. It wasn't greed but exhaustion that had convinced him that, when the kid offered to treat him to dinner, the damage was going to be made whole, at least in part.

They pulled through the South Bari toll barrier and headed toward the coast.

Quídde paíse de mmerd'!

At this point in the story – when he referred in dialect to 'that fucking city' – Orazio was usually already standing up. He'd hoisted himself erect with one hand gripping the armrest of his chair while, with the other, he harpooned his crutches. The effort charged him with an angry energy that swept over the counter and the bottles behind the bar, as well as over his audience as they nodded, in the throes of indignation, well aware that their own city might be an endless list of disasters and infamies of every kind. But Bari was even worse.

Any mentally sane individual would feel dismay upon entering Taranto from the Ionian state highway. The tranquil promise of the seacoast shattered against the crusher towers of the cement plant, against the fractionating columns of the refinery, against the mills, against the mineral dumps of the gigantic industrial complex that clawed the city. Every so often a foreman would be carted off in an ambulance after a grinding machine spun out of control. A plant worker would find his forearm stripped bare to the bone by the explosion of a machine tool. The machinery was organized so that it hurt men according to a cost-benefit equation calibrated by other men in offices where they optimized the most unbridled perversions. The regional assemblies ratified them, and the courts acquitted them at the end of battles the local press fed on. Thus, Taranto was a city of blast furnaces. But Bari was a city of offices, courthouses, journalists, and sports clubs. In Taranto it was possible to link a urothelial cell carcinoma classified as 'highly improbable in an adolescent' to the presence of dioxin, used in ninety percent of Italy's entire national production. But in Bari, on Sunday afternoons, an elderly appeals court judge might sit comfortably on the living room sofa watching his granddaughter pretend to swing a hula hoop around her hips, dressed in a filthy pair of sneakers and nothing else. That episode had been recounted by a worker at the cement plant whose own daughter was working as a maid in the regional capital.

That's why he shouldn't have accepted the salesman's invitation. What did it matter if he'd gotten a home of his own out of the story? Four sparkly clean rooms in a building in the better part of Taranto.

In Bari, after dinner, he abandoned the salesman to his fate.

He had no time to enjoy the solitude because he immediately got lost. He made a left turn, then a right and then another right, and found himself right back under the blinking neon owl outside the eyeglasses store. He cursed as he swung the van around. An advertising panel scrolled vertically from a sunny ad for toothpaste to a velvety one for a clothing store. That was when Orazio thought about the jeans still hidden in the van.

After driving around aimlessly for half an hour, he pulled onto the bridge that connected the center of town to the residential area. Ten minutes later he saw the Ikea tower and felt relief. He realized that he was on the state highway facing the cement barrier that separated the traffic going in opposite directions.

The person he was all this time later made a tremendous effort to lift a crutch to shoulder height. Wild-eyed, he pointed to the dark space beyond the breakwater, as if to say that not even a Man who'd come walking over the waters could have warded off his accident. The mistakes had piled up in the empty primordial space where life stories are written before the events make them indelible and comprehensible.

He barreled down the deserted state highway, jamming on the accelerator. The roadway rose so that the vineyards stretched out as far as the eye could see. The moon was just a few days short of full and right now it gave the illusion that it could wax ad infinitum. He accelerated into the curve, altering the relationship between the passing seconds and the reflectors on the pavement. In the distance, beyond a second curve, he saw the inflatable man flailing wildly atop the roof of an auto repair shop. There was something ridiculous about the dance. Orazio furrowed his eyebrows without losing sight of the angle of the road: the absence of lights in the visible stretch corresponded to the lack of dangers in the blind spot. He would have been able to see a car with its parking lights out of order. But what happened was impossible to avoid.

A woman, or maybe she was a girl. She was walking in the exact center of the roadway, completely naked, and covered with blood.

He violently jerked the wheel to the right. That was a mistake, since the van immediately shot in the opposite direction. It went whizzing past the girl. It hit the guardrail. The van slid across the road until it smashed into the barrier on the opposite side. It tipped, flipped, and landed on its side, so that he could very clearly see the wall of metal coming back toward him.

He woke up again at Bari General Hospital, in a room with bare walls where an old man with a fractured femur kept moaning.

The first signs of a sunny morning entered through the window. Dazed by the pain medicine, Orazio reached his arm out toward the nightstand. He felt his other arm. He grabbed the bottle. The long drink of water refreshed him – his thoughts lined up in a bridge of light, but then collapsed, jumping back into line in a different order.

He'd had a crash, but he was alive. A nasty crash. He remembered the highway, even the salesman. The van must be a wreck. Then something. An opalescent marble glittered amidst the rough gears he was using to reconstruct what had happened. That was strange, because the gears were interlocking, while the marble floated in thin air. It gleamed again and disappeared. The girl. That had to be a ghost, an imaginary shape risen from the depths of consciousness. He felt an itch. The patient in the adjoining bed wouldn't stop whining. He scratched his face. He scratched his left hand with his right. Still, an itch. He jerked himself upright, into a sitting position. He felt a tug, reached his arm down toward his right leg.

Two nurses came running at the sound of his screaming.

The next morning, as he lay in bed with the stump of his leg draining, the head physician came to see him, accompanied by a nurse. From that point on, Orazio began to believe that the girl was real.

The doctor was an old man, tall and deathly pale, with wispy white hair. He leaned over him. He observed him longer than was necessary. He smiled. He re-assumed the chilly persona that must have fit him comfortably and spoke to the nurse. The stump needed to be washed with delicate soap, he told her. An antiperspirant would reduce excessive sweating, while the inflammations should be treated with lotions.

'A corticosteroid cream,' he specified in a voice that was a caress to the patient's ears, and an order to the nurse.

Public hospitals. Orazio knew those places. Once a cousin of his had had her appendix removed, and after the operation they'd left her in the hallway for five hours. The head physician was a nameplate on a door with no one ever behind it. However much the old man might look at him, from behind the protection of his summa cum laude degrees, Orazio recognized in his eyes a strange eagerness to please.

And so he lay motionless in the bed. He stared at the head physician so that the old man's eyes followed his as he shifted them toward the other bed.

'Isn't there a fucking thing you can do to make him shut up?'

Two hours later, he'd been moved. A single room with a private bathroom. Really, an oversized room overlooking the eucalyptus trees in the courtyard. Maybe an oversized records room, emptied out at the last second, to which had been added a bed, a bedside table, and a television stand. Each of which now emanated the dreary aura of objects out of place.

They got him settled in the bed, vanished for a few hours. In the afternoon, a nurse came in carrying a tray with coffee and grapefruit juice. He furrowed his brow and glared at her. He pushed aside the tray, freeing up his line of sight. 'What a pathetic excuse for a screen.' He asked them to replace the television set. The next day two attendants were carrying in a 32-inch set fresh from the mall.

When the head physician came by to see him again, Orazio asked to have the nurse stationed outside the door. His request was granted.

The next day, the head physician returned, escorted by two men in dark suits. Under the jacket of the first man he glimpsed a dangling hem that looked very much as if it, too, might belong to a labcoat. The second man was in his early fifties, and his hair was brylcreemed. Notable polka-dot tie, chunky-toothed smile. He introduced himself: 'I'm Engineer Ranieri.' They started talking. The first man felt called upon to lower the shades, thinning the light.

At this point, no one was bringing up blood alcohol levels. At the rec center, no one was making any more wisecracks about the possibility that the crash had been fatal mostly for his memory. Those jokes had been made at first. He'd tell the story and the others would shake their heads. One of them had gotten hold of a copy of the paper from the day when the news report should have been published. 'Well?' He slapped the counter with the rolled-up paper. There they are, the things that happened that day. An out-of-work man had set fire to himself outside the Apple Store on Corso Vittorio Emanuele. The daughter of a well-known builder and developer had killed herself by jumping off the top tier of a parking structure. There was also a car crash on a highway, but on the Autostrada Adriatica. No reports of a girl on State

Highway 100 at two in the morning – neither naked, nor dressed, nor blood-smeared, nothing at all.

'So, Ora', do you want to tell us what really happened?'

But a few weeks later, Orazio had moved house. From the one-bedroom apartment in the old part of the city he'd moved into an airy apartment overlooking Via d'Aquino. The only problem was that there was no elevator. Absurd as it seems, he only realized it the second time he tried to climb the stairs, hobbling up them on his crutches. He didn't like it one bit. Three months later, a team of construction workers was hard at work on the scaffolding that rose up the side of the apartment building.

To anyone not convinced by the stump of his leg, this was more than adequate.

But Orazio hadn't stopped thinking about the girl.

It was early May, his hospital stay was coming to an end. One after the other, they'd unhooked his tubes and lightened his dose of pharmaceuticals. They'd given him a pair of crutches.

After his conversation with the head physician, it had become clear to him that it had been no dream. From a simple ghost, he had transformed the girl into the cause of the accident. Only that meant he'd now placed her in a service role that likewise stripped her of significance. She became the cause of the crash just as a tree or an oil patch might have been, as if tree and oil patch were logical transitions capable of leading to the word 'amputation.'

Every now and then, curses echoed through the hall. That's when they called for the orthopedic surgeon.

It wasn't just the fact that he mentally perceived the presence of his leg. He caught himself actually *moving* the toes of his right foot, he felt an *itch* on his right ankle, and *pain* – piercing stabs between his kneecap and shinbone, or on the knee that was no longer there. He clenched his teeth and broke out in a cold sweat.

Then, one night, he tracked the girl down once and for all.

The hospital was shrouded in silence. The laments of the other patients didn't reach his room. Neither, for that matter, did the sounds of the voices of the staff on duty. He had fallen asleep watching TV. He'd awakened with a start to a commercial for a jeweler offering to buy gold at twenty-five euros a gram. Two young men were rummaging around in a corpse's mouth, and in the next scene they were handing over the gold teeth to the jeweler. He switched off the television set, and rolled over onto his side. He must have fallen asleep at the precise moment he felt the urge to go to the bathroom. He dragged himself out of bed with his mind elsewhere, convinced he'd be able to support himself on both legs. He collapsed face-first onto the floor.

Angry, discomfited, he felt the chill on his forehead.

He tried to get himself into a sitting position by lifting with both hands. His breathing was labored. The room was immersed in quiet. The shadow of the eucalyptus trees stretched across the ceiling so that the leafy branches turned into seaweed, coral branches tossing in the shifting currents. His eyes grew accustomed to the darkness. It seemed to him that the floor was swept by a faint luminescence – the catalysis of fireflies and sea anemones – the radiance of the early May nights that the absence of artificial light gradually revealed. But the light that was capable of leaving him open-mouthed was right in front of him.

Further on, beyond the wide-open bathroom door, the magnifying mirror fastened to the wall was flooded with the moon. Reduced by half up in the sky, it still appeared full in the concavity of the reflective surface – a silvery puddle that emerged from the past, at the bottom of which he seemed to find her again. The small opaque patch took form, drawing closer. Orazio realized once and for all that she was beautiful. He realized that she was in her death throes. He realized, with a shiver, that sheer will couldn't have kept anyone on their feet like that, which meant there had been something else making her place one foot in front of the other. Movement itself, more than that from which the movement physically derived. A quicksand, a dead swelling beneath the summer rain.

He understood, above all, that he'd swerved not to avoid her but to save himself, because everything about her was a magnet and an absence of will, the hypnotic call that, once followed, makes everything identical and perfect, so that we cease to exist.

CAMPANIA

CAMPANIA

JOHANN WOLFGANG VON GOETHE

From

ITALIAN JOURNEY
(1816–17)

Translated by W. H. Auden and Elizabeth Mayer

TODAY THE SKY is overcast and a sirocco is blowing – just the weather for writing letters.

Besides, I have seen quite enough people (and a mixed bag they are), beautiful horses and extraordinary fish.

I won't say another word about the beauties of the city and its situation, which have been described and praised so often. As they say here, '*Vedi Napoli e poi muori!* – See Naples and die!' One can't blame the Neapolitan for never wanting to leave his city, nor its poets for singing the praises of its situation in lofty hyperboles: it would still be wonderful even if a few more Vesuviuses were to rise in the neighbourhood.

I don't want even to think about Rome. By comparison with Naples's free and open situation, the capital of the world on the Tiber flats is like an old wretchedly placed monastery.

The sea and shipping make one aware of new possibilities. Yesterday the frigate for Palermo sailed before a strong tramontana, and her passage cannot have taken more than thirty-six hours.

With longing, I watched her spread sails as she passed between Capri and Cape Minerva and finally disappeared. If I were to watch a person I loved sail away in this fashion, I should pine away and die. Today a sirocco is blowing; if the wind increases, the waves near the harbour wall should be a merry sight. It being a Friday, the great coach drive of the nobility took place, when they show off their carriages and even more their horses. Nothing could be more graceful than these creatures. For the first time in my life, my heart went out to them.

Today I rambled through the city in my usual fashion, noting many points which I hope to describe more fully later, for now, unfortunately, I have not the time.

Everything one sees and hears gives evidence that this is a happy country which amply satisfies all the basic needs and breeds a people who are happy by nature, people who can wait without concern for tomorrow to bring them what they had today and for that reason lead a happy-go-lucky existence, content with momentary satisfaction and moderate pleasures, and taking pain and sorrow as they come with cheerful resignation. Here is an amazing illustration of this.

The morning was cold and damp, for it had been raining a little. I came to a square where the large paving stones seemed to me to have been swept unusually clean, and was surprised to see a number of ragamuffins squatting in a circle with their hands pressed to the flat stones as if they were warming them. At first I thought they were playing a game, but the serious expression on their faces suggested some more practical purpose for their behaviour. I racked my brains trying to guess what they were up to, but found no satisfactory explanation, so I had to ask someone why these little monkeys formed this circle and took up such a peculiar posture.

I was told that a blacksmith in the neighbourhood had been putting a tyre on a cartwheel. This is done as follows: the iron band is laid on the ground, shavings are piled on it in a circle and set alight to make the iron sufficiently malleable. When the shavings have burnt themselves out, the tyre is fitted on to the wheel, and the ashes are carefully swept up. The little street arabs take advantage of the fact that the paving stones are still hot and stay there till they have absorbed the last bit of warmth from them.

I could give you countless other examples of this capacity to get the most out of the least and make careful use of what would otherwise be wasted. This people displays the most ingenious resource, not in getting rich, but in living free from care.

20 March

The news that another emission of lava had just occurred, invisible to Naples since it was flowing towards Ottaiano, tempted me to make a third visit to Vesuvius. On reaching the foot of the mountain, I had hardly jumped down from my two-wheeled, one-horse vehicle before the two guides who had accompanied us the last time appeared on the scene and I hired them both.

When we reached the cone, the elder one stayed with our coats and provisions while the younger followed me. We bravely made our way towards the enormous cloud of steam which was issuing from a point halfway below the mouth of the cone. Having reached it, we descended carefully along its edge. The sky was clear and at last, through the turbulent clouds of steam, we saw the lava stream.

It was only about ten feet wide, but the manner in which it flowed down the very gentle slope was most surprising. The lava on both sides of the stream cools as it moves, forming a channel. The lava on its bottom also cools, so that this channel is constantly being raised. The stream keeps steadily throwing off to right and left the scoria floating on its surface. Gradually, two levels of considerable height are formed, between which the fiery stream continues to flow quietly like a mill brook. We walked along the foot of this embankment while the scoria kept steadily rolling down its sides. Occasionally there were gaps through which we could see the glowing mass from below. Further down, we were also able to observe it from above.

Because of the bright sunshine, the glow of the lava was dulled. Only a little smoke rose into the pure air. I felt a great desire to get near the place where the lava was issuing from the mountain. My guide assured me that this was safe, because the moment it comes forth, a flow forms a vaulted roof of cooled lava over itself, which he had often stood on. To have this experience, we again climbed up the mountain in order to approach the spot from the rear. Luckily, a gust of wind had cleared the air, though not entirely, for all around us puffs of hot vapour were emerging from thousands of fissures. By now we were actually standing on the lava crust, which lay twisted in coils like a soft mush, but it projected so far out that we could not see the lava gushing forth.

We tried to go half a dozen steps further, but the ground under our feet became hotter and hotter and a whirl of dense fumes darkened the sun and almost suffocated us. The guide who was walking in front turned back, grabbed me, and we stole away from the hellish cauldron.

After refreshing our eyes with the view and our throats with wine, we wandered about observing other features of this peak of hell which towers up in the middle of paradise. I inspected some more volcanic flues and saw that they were lined up to the rim with pendent, tapering formations of some stalactitic matter. Thanks to the irregular shape of the flues, some of these deposits were in easy reach, and with the help of our sticks and some hooked appliances we managed to break off some pieces. At the lava dealer's I had already seen similar ones, listed as true lavas, so I felt happy at having made a discovery. They were a volcanic soot, precipitated from the hot vapours; the condensed minerals they contained were clearly visible.

A magnificent sunset and evening lent their delight to the return journey. However, I could feel how confusing such a tremendous contrast must be. The Terrible beside the Beautiful, the Beautiful beside the Terrible, cancel one another out and produce a feeling of indifference. The Neapolitan would certainly be a different creature if he did not feel himself wedged between God and the Devil.

JOSEPH CONRAD

IL CONDE (1908)

A PATHETIC TALE

'*Vedi Napoli e poi muori.*'

The first time we got into conversation was in the National Museum in Naples, in the rooms on the ground floor containing the famous collection of bronzes from Herculaneum and Pompeii: that marvellous legacy of antique art whose delicate perfection has been preserved for us by the catastrophic fury of a volcano.

He addressed me first, over the celebrated Resting Hermes which we had been looking at side by side. He said the right things about that wholly admirable piece. Nothing profound. His taste was natural rather than cultivated. He had obviously seen many fine things in his life and appreciated them: but he had no jargon of a dilettante or the connoisseur. A hateful tribe. He spoke like a fairly intelligent man of the world, a perfectly unaffected gentleman.

We had known each other by sight for some few days past. Staying in the same hotel – good, but not extravagantly up to date – I had noticed him in the vestibule going in and out. I judged he was an old and valued client. The bow of the hotel-keeper was cordial in its deference, and he acknowledged it with familiar courtesy. For the servants he was Il Conde. There was some squabble over a man's parasol – yellow silk with white lining sort of thing – the waiters had discovered abandoned outside the dining-room door. Our gold-laced door-keeper recognized it and I heard him directing one of the lift boys to run after Il Conde with it. Perhaps he was the only Count staying in the hotel, or perhaps he had the distinction of being the Count par excellence, conferred upon him because of his tried fidelity to the house.

Having conversed at the Museo – (and by the by he had expressed his dislike of the busts and statues of Roman emperors in the gallery of marbles: their faces were too vigorous, too pronounced for him) – having conversed already in the morning I did not think I was intruding when in the evening, finding the dining-room very full, I proposed to share his little table. Judging by the quiet urbanity of his consent he did not think so either. His smile was very attractive.

He dined in an evening waistcoat and a 'smoking' (he called it so) with a black tie. All this of very good cut, not new – just as these things should be. He was, morning or evening, very correct in his dress. I have no doubt that his whole existence had been correct, well ordered and conventional, undisturbed by startling events. His white hair brushed upwards off a lofty forehead gave him the air of an idealist, of an imaginative man. His white moustache, heavy but carefully trimmed and arranged, was not unpleasantly tinted a golden yellow in the middle. The faint scent of some very good perfume, and of good cigars (that last an odour quite remarkable to come upon in Italy) reached me across the table. It was in his eyes that his age showed most. They were a little weary with creased eyelids. He must have been sixty or a couple of years more. And he was communicative. I would not go so far as to call it garrulous – but distinctly communicative.

He had tried various climates, of Abbazia, of the Riviera, of other places, too, he told me, but the only one which suited him was the climate of the Gulf of Naples. The ancient Romans, who, he pointed out to me, were men expert in the art of living, knew very well what they were doing when they built their villas on these shores, in Baiae, in Vico, in Capri. They came down to this seaside in search of health, bringing with them their trains of mimes and flute-players to amuse their leisure. He thought it extremely probable that the Romans of the higher classes were specially predisposed to painful rheumatic affections.

This was the only personal opinion I heard him express. It was based on no special erudition. He knew no more of the Romans than an average informed man of the world is expected to know. He argued from personal experience. He had suffered himself from a painful and dangerous rheumatic affection till he found relief in this particular spot of Southern Europe.

This was three years ago, and ever since he had taken up his quarters on the shores of the gulf, either in one of the hotels in Sorrento or hiring a small villa in Capri. He had a piano, a few books: picked up transient acquaintances of a day, week, or month in the stream of travellers from all Europe. One can imagine him going out for his walks in the streets and lanes, becoming known to beggars, shopkeepers, children, country people; talking amiably over the walls to the contadini – and coming back to his rooms or his villa to sit before the piano, with his white hair brushed up and his thick orderly moustache, 'to make a little music for myself'. And, of course, for a change there was Naples near by – life, movement, animation, opera. A little amusement, as he said, is necessary for health. Mimes and flute-players, in fact. Only unlike the magnates of ancient Rome, he had no affairs of the city to call him away from these moderate delights. He had no affairs at all. Probably he had never had any grave affairs to attend to in his life. It was a kindly existence, with its joys and sorrows regulated by the course of

Nature – marriages, births, deaths – ruled by the prescribed usages of good society and protected by the State.

He was a widower; but in the months of July and August he ventured to cross the Alps for six weeks on a visit to his married daughter. He told me her name. It was that of a very aristocratic family. She had a castle – in Bohemia, I think. This is as near as I ever came to ascertaining his nationality. His own name, strangely enough, he never mentioned. Perhaps he thought I had seen it on the published list. Truth to say, I never looked. At any rate, he was a good European – he spoke four languages to my certain knowledge – and a man of fortune. Not of great fortune evidently and appropriately. I imagine that to be extremely rich would have appeared to him improper, outré – too blatant altogether. And obviously, too, the fortune was not of his making. The making of a fortune cannot be achieved without some roughness. It is a matter of temperament. His nature was too kindly for strife. In the course of conversation he mentioned his estate quite by the way, in reference to that painful and alarming rheumatic affection. One year, staying incautiously beyond the Alps as late as the middle of September, he had been laid up for three months in that lonely country house with no one but his valet and the caretaking couple to attend to him. Because, as he expressed it, he 'kept no establishment there'. He had only gone for a couple of days to confer with his land agent. He promised himself never to be so imprudent in the future. The first weeks of September would find him on the shores of his beloved gulf.

Sometimes in travelling one comes upon such lonely men, whose only business is to wait for the unavoidable. Deaths and marriages have made a solitude round them, and one really cannot blame their endeavours to make the waiting as easy as possible. As he remarked to me, 'At my time of life freedom from physical pain is a very important matter.'

It must not be imagined that he was a wearisome hypochondriac. He was really much too well-bred to be a nuisance. He had an eye for the small weaknesses of humanity. But it was a good-natured eye. He made a restful, easy, pleasant companion for the hours between dinner and bedtime. We spent three evenings together, and then I had to leave Naples in a hurry to look after a friend who had fallen seriously ill in Taormina. Having nothing to do, Il Conde came to see me off at the station. I was somewhat upset, and his idleness was always ready to take a kindly form. He was by no means an indolent man.

He went along the train peering into the carriages for a good seat for me, and then remained talking cheerily from below. He declared he would miss me that evening very much and announced his intention of going after dinner to listen to the band in the public garden, the Villa Nazionale. He would amuse himself by hearing excellent music and looking at the best society. There would be a lot of people, as usual.

I seem to see him yet – his raised face with a friendly smile under the thick moustaches, and his kind, fatigued eyes. As the train began to move, he addressed me in two languages: first in French, saying, 'Bon voyage'; then, in his very good, somewhat emphatic English, encouragingly, because he could see my concern: 'All will – be – well – yet!'

My friend's illness having taken a decidedly favourable turn, I returned to Naples on the tenth day. I cannot say I had given much thought to Il Conde during my absence, but entering the dining-room I looked for him in his habitual place. I had an idea he might have gone back to Sorrento to his piano and his books and his fishing. He was great friends with all the boatmen, and fished a good deal with lines from a boat. But I made out his white head in the crowd of heads, and even from a distance noticed something unusual in his attitude. Instead of sitting erect, gazing all round with alert urbanity, he drooped over his plate. I stood opposite him for some time before he looked up, a little wildly, if such a strong word can be used in connection with his correct appearance.

'Ah, my dear sir! Is it you?' he greeted me. 'I hope all is well.'

He was very nice about my friend. Indeed, he was always nice, with the niceness of people whose hearts are genuinely humane. But this time it cost him an effort. His attempts at general conversation broke down into dullness. It occurred to me he might have been indisposed. But before I could frame the inquiry he muttered:

'You find me here very sad.'

'I am sorry for that,' I said. 'You haven't had bad news, I hope?'

It was very kind of me to take an interest. No. It was not that. No bad news, thank God. And he became very still as if holding his breath. Then, leaning forward a little, and in an odd tone of awed embarrassment, he took me into his confidence.

'The truth is that I have had a very – a very – how shall I say? – abominable adventure happen to me.'

The energy of the epithet was sufficiently startling in that man of moderate feelings and toned-down vocabulary. The word unpleasant I should have thought would have fitted amply the worst experience likely to befall a man of his stamp. And an adventure, too. Incredible! But it is in human nature to believe the worst; and I confess I eyed him stealthily, wondering what he had been up to. In a moment, however, my unworthy suspicions vanished. There was a fundamental refinement of nature about the man which made me dismiss all idea of some more or less disreputable scrape.

'It is very serious. Very serious.' He went on, nervously, 'I will tell you after dinner, if you will allow me.'

I expressed my perfect acquiescence by a little bow, nothing more. I wished him to understand that I was not likely to hold him to that offer, if he thought better of it later on. We talked of indifferent things, but with a sense of difficulty quite unlike our former easy, gossipy intercourse. The hand raising a piece of bread to his lips, I noticed, trembled slightly. This symptom, in regard to my reading of the man, was no less than startling.

In the smoking-room he did not hang back at all. Directly we had taken our usual seats he leaned sideways over the arm of his chair and looked straight into my eyes earnestly.

'You remember,' he began, 'that day you went away? I told you then I would go to the Villa Nazionale to hear some music in the evening.'

I remembered. His handsome old face, so fresh for his age, unmarked by any trying experience, appeared haggard for an instant. It was like the passing of a shadow. Returning his steadfast gaze, I took a sip of my black coffee. He was systematically minute in his narrative, simply in order, I think, not to let his excitement get the better of him.

After leaving the railway station, he had an ice, and read the paper in a cafe. Then he went back to the hotel, dressed for dinner, and dined with a good appetite. After dinner he lingered in the hall (there were chairs and tables there) smoking his cigar; talked to the little girl of the Primo Tenore of the San Carlo theatre, and exchanged a few words with that 'amiable lady', the wife of the Primo Tenore. There was no performance that evening, and these people were going to the Villa also. They went out of the hotel. Very well.

At the moment of following their example – it was half-past nine already – he remembered he had a rather large sum of money in his pocket-book. He entered, therefore, the office and deposited the greater part of it with the book-keeper of the hotel. This done, he took a carozella and drove to the seashore. He got out of the cab and entered the Villa on foot from the Largo di Vittoria end.

He stared at me very hard. And I understood then how really impressionable he was. Every small fact and event of that evening stood out in his memory as if endowed with mystic significance. If he did not mention to me the colour of the pony which drew the carozella, and the aspect of the man who drove, it was a mere oversight arising from his agitation, which he repressed manfully.

He had then entered the Villa Nazionale from the Largo di Vittoria end. The Villa Nazionale is a public pleasure-ground laid out in grass plots, bushes, and flower-beds between the houses of the Riviera di Chiaja and the waters of the bay. Alleys of trees, more or less parallel, stretch its whole length – which is considerable. On the Riviera di Chiaja side the electric tramcars run close to the railings. Between the garden and the sea is the fashionable drive, a broad road bordered by a low wall, beyond which the Mediterranean splashes with gentle murmurs when the weather is fine.

As life goes on late at night in Naples, the broad drive was all astir with a brilliant swarm of carriage lamps moving in pairs, some creeping slowly, others running rapidly under the thin, motionless line of electric lamps defining the shore. And a brilliant swarm of stars hung above the land humming with voices, piled up with houses, glittering with lights – and over the silent flat shadows of the sea.

The gardens themselves are not very well lit. Our friend went forward in the warm gloom, his eyes fixed upon a distant luminous region extending nearly across the whole width of the Villa, as if the air had glowed there with its own cold, bluish, and dazzling light. This magic spot, behind the black trunks of trees and masses of inky foliage, breathed out sweet sounds mingled with bursts of brassy roar, sudden clashes of metal, and grave, vibrating thuds.

As he walked on, all these noises combined together into a piece of elaborate music whose harmonious phrases came persuasively through a great disorderly murmur of voices and shuffling of feet on the gravel of that open space. An enormous crowd immersed in the electric light, as if in a bath of some radiant and tenuous fluid shed upon their heads by luminous globes, drifted in its hundreds round the band. Hundreds more sat on chairs in more or less concentric circles, receiving unflinchingly the great waves of sonority that ebbed out into the darkness. The Count penetrated the throng, drifted with it in tranquil enjoyment, listening and looking at the faces. All people of good society: mothers with their daughters, parents and children, young men and young women all talking, smiling, nodding to each other. Very many pretty faces, and very many pretty toilettes. There was, of course, a quantity of diverse types: showy old fellows with white moustaches, fat men, thin men, officers in uniform; but what predominated, he told me, was the South Italian type of young man, with a colourless, clear complexion, red lips, jet-black little moustache and liquid black eyes so wonderfully effective in leering or scowling.

Withdrawing from the throng, the Count shared a little table in front of the cafe with a young man of just such a type. Our friend had some lemonade. The young man was sitting moodily before an empty glass. He looked up once, and then looked down again. He also tilted his hat forward. Like this –

The Count made the gesture of a man pulling his hat down over his brow, and went on:

'I think to myself: he is sad; something is wrong with him; young men have their troubles. I take no notice of him, of course. I pay for my lemonade, and go away.'

Strolling about in the neighbourhood of the band, the Count thinks he saw twice that young man wandering alone in the crowd. Once their eyes met. It must have been the same young man, but there were so many there of that type that he could not be certain. Moreover, he was not very much concerned except in so far that he had been struck by the marked, peevish discontent of that face.

Presently, tired of the feeling of confinement one experiences in a crowd, the Count edged away from the band. An alley, very sombre by contrast, presented itself invitingly with its promise of solitude and coolness. He entered it, walking slowly on till the sound of the orchestra became distinctly deadened. Then he walked back and turned about once more. He did this several times before he noticed that there was somebody occupying one of the benches.

The spot being midway between two lamp-posts the light was faint.

The man lolled back in the corner of the seat, his legs stretched out, his arms folded and his head drooping on his breast. He never stirred, as though he had fallen asleep there, but when the Count passed by next time he had changed his attitude. He sat leaning forward. His elbows were propped on his knees, and his hands were rolling a cigarette. He never looked up from that occupation.

The Count continued his stroll away from the band. He returned slowly, he said. I can imagine him enjoying to the full, but with his usual tranquillity, the balminess of this southern night and the sounds of music softened delightfully by the distance.

Presently, he approached for the third time the man on the garden seat, still leaning forward with his elbows on his knees. It was a dejected pose. In the semi-obscurity of the alley his high shirt collar and his cuffs made small patches of vivid whiteness. The Count said that he had noticed him getting up brusquely as if to walk away, but almost before he was aware of it the man stood before him asking in a low, gentle tone whether the signore would have the kindness to oblige him with a light.

The Count answered this request by a polite 'Certainly,' and dropped his hands with the intention of exploring both pockets of his trousers for the matches.

'I dropped my hands,' he said, 'but I never put them in my pockets. I felt a pressure there –'

He put the tip of his finger on a spot close under his breastbone, the very spot of the human body where a Japanese gentleman begins the operations of the Harakiri, which is a form of suicide following upon dishonour, upon an intolerable outrage to the delicacy of one's feelings.

'I glance down,' the Count continued in an awestruck voice, 'and what do I see? A knife! A long knife –'

'You don't mean to say,' I exclaimed, amazed, 'that you have been held up like this in the Villa at half-past ten o'clock, within a stone's throw of a thousand people!'

He nodded several times, staring at me with all his might.

'The clarionet,' he declared, solemnly, 'was finishing his solo, and I assure you I could hear every note. Then the band crashed fortissimo, and that creature rolled its eyes and gnashed its teeth hissing at me with the greatest ferocity, "Be silent! No noise or –"'

I could not get over my astonishment.

'What sort of knife was it?' I asked, stupidly.

'A long blade. A stiletto – perhaps a kitchen knife. A long narrow blade. It gleamed. And his eyes gleamed. His white teeth, too. I could see them. He was very ferocious. I thought to myself: "If I hit him he will kill me." How could I fight with him? He had the knife and I had nothing. I am nearly seventy, you know, and that was a young man. I seemed even to recognize him. The moody young man of the cafe. The young man I met in the crowd. But I could not tell. There are so many like him in this country.'

The distress of that moment was reflected in his face. I should think that physically he must have been paralysed by surprise. His thoughts, however, remained extremely active. They ranged over every alarming possibility. The idea of setting up a vigorous shouting for help occurred to him, too. But he did nothing of the kind, and the reason why he refrained gave me a good opinion of his mental self-possession. He saw in a flash that nothing prevented the other from shouting, too.

'That young man might in an instant have thrown away his knife and pretended I was the aggressor. Why not? He might have said I attacked him. Why not? It was one incredible story against another! He might have said anything – bring some dishonouring charge against me – what do I know? By his dress he was no common robber. He seemed to belong to the better classes. What could I say? He was an Italian – I am a foreigner. Of course, I have my passport, and there is our consul – but to be arrested, dragged at night to the police office like a criminal!'

He shuddered. It was in his character to shrink from scandal, much more than from mere death. And certainly for many people this would have always remained – considering certain peculiarities of Neapolitan manners – a deucedly queer story. The Count was no fool. His belief in the respectable placidity of life having received this rude shock, he thought that now anything might happen. But also a notion came into his head that this young man was perhaps merely an infuriated lunatic.

This was for me the first hint of his attitude towards this adventure. In his exaggerated delicacy of sentiment he felt that nobody's self-esteem need be affected by what a madman may choose to do to one. It became apparent, however, that the Count was to be denied that consolation. He enlarged upon the abominably savage way in which that young man rolled his glistening eyes and gnashed his white teeth. The band was going now through a slow movement of solemn braying by all the trombones, with deliberately repeated bangs of the big drum.

'But what did you do?' I asked, greatly excited.

'Nothing,' answered the Count. 'I let my hands hang down very still. I told him quietly I did not intend making a noise. He snarled like a dog, then said in an ordinary voice:

' "Vostro portofolio."

'So I naturally,' continued the Count – and from this point acted the whole thing in pantomime. Holding me with his eyes, he went through all the motions of reaching into his inside breast pocket, taking out a pocketbook, and handing it over. But that young man, still bearing steadily on the knife, refused to touch it.

He directed the Count to take the money out himself, received it into his left hand, motioned the pocketbook to be returned to the pocket, all this being done to the sweet thrilling of flutes and clarionets sustained by the emotional drone of the hautboys. And the 'young man', as the Count called him, said: 'This seems very little.'

'It was, indeed, only 340 or 360 lire,' the Count pursued.

'I had left my money in the hotel, as you know. I told him this was all I had on me. He shook his head impatiently and said:

' "Vostro orologio." '

The Count gave me the dumb show of pulling out his watch, detaching it. But, as it happened, the valuable gold half-chronometer he possessed had been left at a watch-maker's for cleaning. He wore that evening (on a leather guard) the Waterbury fifty-franc thing he used to take with him on his fishing expeditions. Perceiving the nature of this booty, the well-dressed robber made a contemptuous click-ing sound with his tongue like this, 'Tse-Ah!' and waved it away hastily. Then, as the Count was returning the disdained object to his pocket, he demanded with a threateningly increased pressure of the knife on the epigastrium, by way of reminder:

' "Vostri anelli." '

'One of the rings,' went on the Count, 'was given me many years ago by my wife; the other is the signet ring of my father. I said, "No. That you shall not have!" '

Here the Count reproduced the gesture corresponding to that declaration by clapping one hand upon the other, and pressing both thus against his chest. It was touching in its resignation. 'That you shall not have,' he repeated, firmly, and closed his eyes, fully expecting – I don't know whether I am right in recording that such an unpleasant word had passed his lips – fully expecting to feel himself being – I really hesitate to say – being disembowelled by the push of the long, sharp blade resting murderously against the pit of his stomach – the very seat, in all human beings, of anguishing sensations.

Great waves of harmony went on flowing from the band. Suddenly the Count felt the nightmarish pressure removed from the sensitive spot. He opened his eyes. He was alone. He had heard nothing. It is probable that 'the young man' had departed, with light steps, some time before, but the sense of the horrid pressure had lingered even after the knife had gone. A feeling of weakness came over him. He had just time to stagger to the garden seat. He felt as though he had held his breath for a long time. He sat all in a heap, panting with the shock of the reaction.

The band was executing, with immense bravura, the complicated finale. It ended with a tremendous crash. He heard it unreal and remote, as if his ears had been stopped, and then the hard clapping of a thousand, more or less, pairs of hands, like a sudden hail-shower passing away. The profound silence which succeeded recalled him to himself.

A tramcar resembling a long glass box wherein people sat with their heads strongly lighted, ran along swiftly within sixty yards of the spot where he had been robbed. Then another rustled by, and yet another going the other way. The audience about the band had broken up, and were entering the alley in small conversing groups. The Count sat up straight and tried to think calmly of what had happened to him. The vileness of it took his breath away again. As far as I can make it out he was disgusted with himself. I do not mean to say with his behaviour. Indeed, if his pantomimic rendering of it for my information was to be trusted, it was simply perfect. No, it was not that. He was not ashamed. He was shocked at being the selected victim, not of robbery so much as of contempt. His tranquillity had been wantonly desecrated. His lifelong, kindly nicety of outlook had been defaced.

Nevertheless, at that stage, before the iron had time to sink deep, he was able to argue himself into comparative equanimity. As his agitation calmed down somewhat, he became aware that he was frightfully hungry. Yes, hungry. The sheer emotion had made him simply ravenous. He left the seat and, after walking for some time, found himself outside the gardens and before an arrested tramcar, without knowing very well how he came there. He got in as if in a dream, by a sort of instinct. Fortunately he found in his trouser pocket a copper to satisfy the conductor. Then the car stopped, and as everybody was getting out he got out, too. He recognized the Piazza San Ferdinando, but apparently it did not occur to him to take a cab and drive to the hotel. He remained in distress on the Piazza like a lost dog, thinking vaguely of the best way of getting something to eat at once.

Suddenly he remembered his twenty-franc piece. He explained to me that he had that piece of French gold for something like three years. He used to carry it about with him as a sort of reserve in case of accident. Anybody is liable to have his pocket picked – a quite different thing from a brazen and insulting robbery.

The monumental arch of the Galleria Umberto faced him at the top of a noble flight of stairs. He climbed these without loss of time, and directed his steps towards the Cafe Umberto. All the tables outside were occupied by a lot of people who were drinking. But as he wanted something to eat, he went inside into the cafe, which is divided into aisles by square pillars set all round with long looking-glasses. The Count sat down on a red plush bench against one of these pillars, waiting for his risotto. And his mind reverted to his abominable adventure.

He thought of the moody, well-dressed young man, with whom he had exchanged glances in the crowd around the bandstand, and who, he felt confident, was the robber. Would he recognize him again? Doubtless. But he did not want ever to see him again. The best thing was to forget this humiliating episode.

The Count looked round anxiously for the coming of his risotto, and, behold! to the left against the wall – there sat the young man. He was alone at a table, with a bottle of some sort of wine or syrup and a carafe of iced water before him. The smooth olive cheeks, the red lips, the little jet-black moustache turned up gallantly, the fine black eyes a little heavy and shaded by long eyelashes, that peculiar expression of cruel discontent to be seen only in the busts of some Roman emperors – it was he, no doubt at all. But that was a type. The Count looked away hastily. The young officer over there reading a paper was like that, too. Same type. Two young men farther away playing draughts also resembled –

The Count lowered his head with the fear in his heart of being everlastingly haunted by the vision of that young man. He began to eat his risotto. Presently he heard the young man on his left call the waiter in a bad-tempered tone.

At the call, not only his own waiter, but two other idle waiters belonging to a quite different row of tables, rushed towards him with obsequious alacrity, which is not the general characteristic of the waiters in the Cafe Umberto. The young man muttered something and one of the waiters walking rapidly to the nearest door called out into the Galleria: 'Pasquale! O! Pasquale!'

Everybody knows Pasquale, the shabby old fellow who, shuffling between the tables, offers for sale cigars, cigarettes, picture postcards, and matches to the clients of the cafe. He is in many respects an engaging scoundrel. The Count saw the grey-haired, unshaven ruffian enter the cafe, the glass case hanging from his neck by a leather strap, and, at a word from the waiter, make his shuffling way with a sudden spurt to the young man's table. The young man was in need of a cigar with which Pasquale served him fawningly. The old pedlar was going out when the Count, on a sudden impulse, beckoned to him.

Pasquale approached, the smile of deferential recognition combining oddly with the cynical searching expression of his eyes. Leaning his case on the table, he lifted the glass lid without a word. The Count took a box of cigarettes and urged by a fearful curiosity, asked as casually as he could –

'Tell me, Pasquale, who is that young signore sitting over there?'

The other bent over his box confidentially.

'That, Signor Conde,' he said, beginning to rearrange his wares busily and without looking up, 'that is a young Cavaliere of a very good family from Bari. He studies in the University here, and is the chief, capo, of an association of young men – of very nice young men.'

He paused, and then, with mingled discretion and pride of knowledge, murmured the explanatory word 'Camorra' and shut down the lid. 'A very powerful Camorra,' he breathed out. 'The professors themselves respect it greatly . . . una lira e cinquanti centesimi, Signor Conde.'

Our friend paid with the gold piece. While Pasquale was making up the change, he observed that the young man, of whom he had heard so much in a few words, was watching the transaction covertly. After the old vagabond had withdrawn with a bow, the Count settled with the waiter and sat still. A numbness, he told me, had come over him.

The young man paid, too, got up, and crossed over, apparently for the purpose of looking at himself in the mirror set in the pillar nearest to the Count's seat. He was dressed all in black with a dark green bow tie. The Count looked round, and was startled by meeting a vicious glance out of the corners of the other's eyes. The young Cavaliere from Bari (according to Pasquale; but Pasquale is, of course, an accomplished liar) went on arranging his tie, settling his hat before the glass, and meantime he spoke just loud enough to be heard by the Count. He spoke through his teeth with the most insulting venom of contempt and gazing straight into the mirror.

'Ah! So you had some gold on you – you old liar – you old birba – you furfante! But you are not done with me yet.'

The fiendishness of his expression vanished like lightning, and he lounged out of the cafe with a moody, impassive face.

The poor Count, after telling me this last episode, fell back trembling in his chair. His forehead broke into perspiration. There was a wanton insolence in the spirit of this outrage which appalled even me. What it was to the Count's delicacy I won't attempt to guess. I am sure that if he had been not too refined to do such a blatantly vulgar thing as dying from apoplexy in a cafe, he would have had a fatal stroke there and then. All irony apart, my difficulty was to keep him from seeing the full extent of my commiseration. He shrank from every excessive sentiment, and my commiseration was practically unbounded. It did not surprise me to hear that he had been in bed a week. He had got up to make his arrangements for leaving Southern Italy for good and all.

And the man was convinced that he could not live through a whole year in any other climate!

No argument of mine had any effect. It was not timidity, though he did say to me once: 'You do not know what a Camorra is, my dear sir. I am a marked man.' He was not afraid of what could be done to him. His delicate conception of his dignity was defiled by a degrading experience. He couldn't stand that. No Japanese gentleman, outraged in his exaggerated sense of honour, could have gone about his preparations for Harakiri with greater resolution. To go home really amounted to suicide for the poor Count.

There is a saying of Neapolitan patriotism, intended for the information of foreigners, I presume: 'See Naples and then die.' Vedi Napoli e poi muori. It is a saying of excessive vanity, and everything excessive was abhorrent to the nice moderation of the poor Count. Yet, as I was seeing him off at the railway station, I thought he was behaving with singular fidelity to its conceited spirit. Vedi Napoli! . . . He had seen it! He had seen it with startling thoroughness – and now he was going to his grave. He was going to it by the train de luxe of the International Sleeping Car Company, via Trieste and Vienna. As the four long, sombre coaches pulled out of the station I raised my hat with the solemn feeling of paying the last tribute of respect to a funeral cortege. Il Conde's profile, much aged already, glided away from me in stony immobility, behind the lighted pane of glass – Vedi Napoli e poi muori!

W. SOMERSET MAUGHAM

THE LOTUS
EATER (1935)

MOST PEOPLE, THE vast majority in fact, lead the lives that circumstances have thrust upon them, and though some repine, looking upon themselves as round pegs in square holes, and think that if things had been different they might have made a much better showing, the greater part accept their lot, if not with serenity, at all events with resignation. They are like tram-cars travelling for ever on the selfsame rails. They go backwards and forwards, backwards and forwards, inevitably, till they can go no longer and then are sold as scrap-iron. It is not often that you find a man who has boldly taken the course of his life into his own hands. When you do, it is worth while having a good look at him.

That was why I was curious to meet Thomas Wilson. It was an interesting and a bold thing he had done. Of course the end was not yet and until the experiment was concluded it was impossible to call it successful. But from what I had heard it seemed he must be an odd sort of fellow and I thought I should like to know him. I had been told he was reserved, but I had a notion that with patience and tact I could persuade him to confide in me. I wanted to hear the facts from his own lips. People exaggerate, they love to romanticize, and I was quite prepared to discover that his story was not nearly so singular as I had been led to believe.

And this impression was confirmed when at last I made his acquaintance. It was on the Piazza in Capri, where I was spending the month of August at a friend's villa, and a little before sunset, when most of the inhabitants, native and foreign, gather together to chat with their friends in the cool of the evening. There is a terrace that overlooks the Bay of Naples, and when the sun sinks slowly into the sea the island of Ischia is silhouetted against a blaze of splendour. It is one of the most lovely sights in the world. I was standing there with my friend and host watching it, when suddenly he said:

'Look, there's Wilson.'

'Where?'

'The man sitting on the parapet, with his back to us. He's got a blue shirt on.'

I saw an undistinguished back and a small head of grey hair, short and rather thin.

'I wish he'd turn round,' I said.

'He will presently.'

'Ask him to come and have a drink with us at Morgano's.'

'All right.'

The instant of overwhelming beauty had passed and the sun, like the top of an orange, was dipping into a wine-red sea. We turned round and leaning our backs against the parapet looked at the people who were sauntering to and fro. They were all talking their heads off and the cheerful noise was exhilarating. Then the church bell, rather cracked, but with a fine resonant note, began to ring. The Piazza at Capri, with its clock tower over the footpath that leads up from the harbour, with the church up a flight of steps, is a perfect setting for an opera by Donizetti, and you felt that the voluble crowd might at any moment break out into a rattling chorus. It was charming and unreal.

I was so intent on the scene that I had not noticed Wilson get off the parapet and come towards us. As he passed us my friend stopped him.

'Hullo, Wilson, I haven't seen you bathing the last few days.'

'I've been bathing on the other side for a change.'

My friend then introduced me. Wilson shook hands with me politely, but with indifference; a great many strangers come to Capri for a few days, or a few weeks, and I had no doubt he was constantly meeting people who came and went; and then my friend asked him to come along and have a drink with us.

'I was just going back to supper,' he said.

'Can't it wait?' I asked.

'I suppose it can,' he smiled.

Though his teeth were not very good his smile was attractive. It was gentle and kindly. He was dressed in a blue cotton shirt and a pair of grey trousers, much creased and none too clean, of a thin canvas, and on his feet he wore a pair of very old espadrilles. The get-up was picturesque, and very suitable to the place and the weather, but it did not at all go with his face. It was a lined, long face, deeply sunburned, thin-lipped, with small grey eyes rather close together and tight, neat features. The grey hair was carefully brushed. It was not a plain face, indeed in his youth Wilson might have been good-looking, but a prim one. He wore the blue shirt, open at the neck, and the grey canvas trousers, not as though they belonged to him, but as though, shipwrecked in his pyjamas, he had been fitted out with odd garments by compassionate strangers. Notwithstanding this careless attire he looked like the manager of a branch office in an insurance company, who should by rights be wearing a black coat with pepper-and-salt trousers, a white collar, and an unobjectionable tie. I could very well see myself going to him to claim the insurance money when I had lost a watch, and being rather disconcerted while I answered the questions he put to me by his obvious impression, for all his politeness, that people who made such claims were either fools or knaves.

Moving off, we strolled across the Piazza and down the street till we came to Morgano's. We sat in the garden. Around us people were talking in Russian, German, Italian, and English. We ordered drinks. Donna Lucia, the host's wife, waddled up and in her low, sweet voice passed the time of day with us. Though middle-aged now and portly, she had still traces of the wonderful beauty that thirty years before had driven artists to paint so many bad portraits of her. Her eyes, large and liquid, were the eyes of Hera and her smile was affectionate and gracious. We three gossiped for a while, for there is always a scandal of one sort or another in Capri to make a topic of conversation, but nothing was said of particular interest and in a little while Wilson got up and left us. Soon afterwards we strolled up to my friend's villa to dine. On the way he asked me what I had thought of Wilson.

'Nothing,' I said. 'I don't believe there's a word of truth in your story.'

'Why not?'

'He isn't the sort of man to do that sort of thing.'

'How does anyone know what anyone is capable of?'

'I should put him down as an absolutely normal man of business who's retired on a comfortable income from gilt-edged securities. I think your story's just the ordinary Capri tittle-tattle.'

'Have it your own way,' said my friend.

We were in the habit of bathing at a beach called the Baths of Tiberius. We took a fly down the road to a certain point and then wandered through lemon groves and vineyards, noisy with cicadas and heavy with the hot smell of the sun, till we came to the top of the cliff down which a steep winding path led to the sea. A day or two later, just before we got down my friend said:

'Oh, there's Wilson back again.'

We scrunched over the beach, the only drawback to the bathing-place being that it was shingle and not sand, and as we came along Wilson saw us and waved. He was standing up, a pipe in his mouth, and he wore nothing but a pair of trunks. His body was dark brown, thin, but not emaciated, and, considering his wrinkled face and grey hair, youthful. Hot from our walk, we undressed quickly and plunged at once into the water. Six feet from the shore it was thirty feet deep, but so clear that you could see the bottom. It was warm, yet invigorating.

When I got out Wilson was lying on his belly, with a towel under him, reading a book. I lit a cigarette and went and sat down beside him.

'Had a nice swim?' he asked.

He put his pipe inside his book to mark the place and closing it put it down on the pebbles beside him. He was evidently willing to talk.

'Lovely,' I said. 'It's the best bathing in the world.'

'Of course people think those were the Baths of Tiberius.' He waved his hand towards a shapeless mass of masonry that stood half in the water and half out. 'But that's all rot. It was just one of his villas, you know.'

I did. But it is just as well to let people tell you things when they want to. It disposes them kindly towards you if you suffer them to impart information. Wilson gave a chuckle.

'Funny old fellow, Tiberius. Pity they're saying now there's not a word of truth in all those stories about him.'

He began to tell me all about Tiberius. Well, I had read my Suetonius too and I had read histories of the Early Roman

Empire, so there was nothing very new to me in what he said. But I observed that he was not ill-read. I remarked on it.

'Oh, well, when I settled down here I was naturally interested, and I have plenty of time for reading. When you live in a place like this, with all its associations, it seems to make history so actual. You might almost be living in historical times yourself.'

I should remark here that this was in 1913. The world was an easy, comfortable place and no one could have imagined that anything might happen seriously to disturb the serenity of existence.

'How long have you been here?' I asked.

'Fifteen years.' He gave the blue and placid sea a glance, and a strangely tender smile hovered on his thin lips. 'I fell in love with the place at first sight. You've heard, I daresay, of the mythical German who came here on the Naples boat just for lunch and a look at the Blue Grotto and stayed forty years; well, I can't say I exactly did that, but it's come to the same thing in the end. Only it won't be forty years in my case. Twenty-five. Still, that's better than a poke in the eye with a sharp stick.'

I waited for him to go on. For what he had just said looked indeed as though there might be something after all in the singular story I had heard. But at that moment my friend came dripping out of the water very proud of himself because he had swum a mile, and the conversation turned to other things.

After that I met Wilson several times, either in the Piazza or on the beach. He was amiable and polite. He was always pleased to have a talk and I found out that he not only knew every inch of the island but also the adjacent mainland. He had read a great deal on all sorts of subjects, but his speciality was the history of Rome and on this he was very well informed. He seemed to have little imagination and to be of no more than average intelligence. He laughed a good deal, but with restraint, and his sense of humour was tickled by simple jokes. A commonplace man. I did not forget the odd remark he had made during the first short chat we had had by ourselves, but he never so much as approached the topic again. One day on our return from the beach, dismissing the cab at the Piazza, my friend and I told the driver to be ready to take us up to Anacapri at five. We were going to climb Monte Solaro, dine at a tavern we favoured, and walk down in the moonlight. For it was full moon and the views by night were lovely. Wilson was standing by while we gave the cabman instructions, for we had given him a lift to save him the hot dusty walk, and more from politeness than for any other reason I asked him if he would care to join us.

'It's my party,' I said.

'I'll come with pleasure,' he answered.

But when the time came to set out my friend was not feeling well, he thought he had stayed too long in the water, and would not face the long and tiring walk. So I went alone with Wilson. We climbed the mountain, admired the spacious view, and got back to the inn as night was falling, hot, hungry, and thirsty. We had ordered our dinner beforehand. The food was good, for Antonio was an excellent cook, and the wine came from his own vineyard. It was so light that you felt you could drink it like water and we finished the first bottle with our macaroni. By the time we had finished the second we felt that there was nothing much wrong with life. We sat in a little garden under a great vine laden with grapes. The air was exquisitely soft. The night was still and we were alone. The maid brought us *bel paese* cheese and a plate of figs. I ordered coffee and strega, which is the best liqueur they make in Italy. Wilson would not have a cigar, but lit his pipe.

'We've got plenty of time before we need start,' he said, 'the moon won't be over the hill for another hour.'

'Moon or no moon,' I said briskly, 'of course we've got plenty of time. That's one of the delights of Capri, that there's never any hurry.'

'Leisure,' he said. 'If people only knew! It's the most priceless thing a man can have and they're such fools they don't even know it's something to aim at. Work? They work for work's sake. They haven't got the brains to realize that the only object of work is to obtain leisure.'

Wine has the effect on some people of making them indulge in general reflections. These remarks were true, but no one could have claimed that they were original. I did not say anything, but struck a match to light my cigar.

'It was full moon the first time I came to Capri,' he went on reflectively. 'It might be the same moon as tonight.'

'It was, you know,' I smiled.

He grinned. The only light in the garden was what came from an oil lamp that hung over our heads. It had been scanty to eat by, but it was good now for confidences.

'I didn't mean that. I mean, it might be yesterday. Fifteen years it is, and when I look back it seems like a month. I'd never been to Italy before. I came for my summer holiday. I went to Naples by boat from Marseilles and I had a look round, Pompeii, you know, and Paestum and one or two places like that; then I came here for a week. I liked the look of the place right away, from the sea, I mean, as I watched it come closer and closer; and then when we got into the little boats from the steamer and landed at the quay, with all that crowd of jabbering people who wanted to take your luggage, and the hotel touts, and the tumbledown houses on the Marina and the walk up to the hotel, and dining on the terrace – well, it just got me. That's the truth. I didn't know if I was standing on my head or my heels. I'd never drunk Capri wine before, but I'd heard of it; I think I must have got a bit tight. I sat on that terrace after they'd all gone to bed and watched the moon over the sea, and there was Vesuvius with a great red plume of smoke rising up from it. Of course I know now that wine I drank was ink, Capri wine my eye, but I thought it all right then. But it wasn't the wine that made me drunk, it was the shape of the island and those jabbering people, the moon and the sea and the oleander in the hotel garden. I'd never seen an oleander before.'

It was a long speech and it had made him thirsty. He took up his glass, but it was empty. I asked him if he would have another strega.

'It's sickly stuff. Let's have a bottle of wine. That's sound, that is, pure juice of the grape and can't hurt anyone.'

I ordered more wine, and when it came filled the glasses. He took a long drink and after a sigh of pleasure went on.

'Next day I found my way to the bathing-place we go to. Not bad bathing, I thought. Then I wandered about the island. As luck would have it, there was a *festa* up at the Punta di Timberio and I ran straight into the middle of it. An image of the Virgin and priests, acolytes swinging censers, and a whole crowd of jolly, laughing, excited people, a lot of them all dressed up. I ran across an Englishman there and asked him what it was all about. "Oh, it's the feast of the Assumption," he said, "at least that's what the Catholic Church says it is, but that's just their hanky-panky. It's the festival of Venus. Pagan, you know. Aphrodite rising from the sea and all that." It gave me quite a funny feeling to hear him. It seemed to take one a long way back, if you know what I mean. After that I went down one night to have a look at the Faraglioni by moonlight. If the fates had wanted me to go on being a bank manager they oughtn't to have let me take that walk.'

'You were a bank manager, were you?' I asked.

I had been wrong about him, but not far wrong.

'Yes. I was manager of the Crawford Street branch of the York and City. It was convenient for me because I lived up Hendon way. I could get from door to door in thirty-seven minutes.'

He puffed at his pipe and relit it.

'That was my last night, that was. I'd got to be back at the bank on Monday morning. When I looked at those two great rocks sticking out of the water, with the moon above them, and all the little lights of the fishermen in their boats catching cuttlefish, all so peaceful and beautiful, I said to myself, well, after all, why should I go back? It wasn't as if I had anyone dependent on me. My wife had died of bronchial pneumonia four years before and the kid went to live with her grandmother, my wife's mother. She was an old fool, she didn't look after the kid properly and she got blood-poisoning, they amputated her leg, but they couldn't save her and she died, poor little thing.'

'How terrible,' I said.

'Yes, I was cut up at the time, though of course not so much as if the kid had been living with me, but I dare say it was a mercy. Not much chance for a girl with only one leg. I was sorry about my wife too. We got on very well together. Though I don't know if it would have continued. She was the sort of woman who was always bothering about what other people'd think. She didn't like travelling. Eastbourne was her idea of a holiday. D'you know, I'd never crossed the Channel till after her death.'

'But I suppose you've got other relations, haven't you?'

'None. I was an only child. My father had a brother, but he went to Australia before I was born. I don't think anyone could easily be more alone in the world than I am. There wasn't any reason I could see why I shouldn't do exactly what I wanted. I was thirty-four at that time.'

He had told me he had been on the island for fifteen years. That would make him forty-nine. Just about the age I should have given him.

'I'd been working since I was seventeen. All I had to look forward to was doing the same old thing day after day till I retired on my pension. I said to myself, is it worth it? What's wrong with chucking it all up and spending the rest of my life down here? It was the most beautiful place I'd ever seen. But I'd had a business training, I was cautious by nature. "No," I said, "I won't be carried away like this, I'll go tomorrow like I said I would and think it over. Perhaps when I get back to London I'll think quite differently." Damned fool, wasn't I? I lost a whole year that way.'

'You didn't change your mind, then?'

'You bet I didn't. All the time I was working I kept thinking of the bathing here and the vineyards and the walks over the hills and the moon and the sea, and the Piazza in the evening when everyone walks about for a bit of a chat after the day's work is over. There was only one thing that bothered me: I wasn't sure if I was justified in not working like everybody else did. Then I read a sort of history book, by a man called Marion Crawford it was, and there was a story about Sybaris and Crotona. There were two cities; and in Sybaris they just enjoyed life and had a good time, and in Crotona they were hardy and industrious and all that. And one day the men of Crotona came over and wiped Sybaris out, and then after a while a lot of other fellows came over from somewhere else and wiped Crotona out. Nothing remains of Sybaris, not a stone, and all that's left of Crotona is just one column. That settled the matter for me.'

'Oh?'

'It came to the same in the end, didn't it? And when you look back now, who were the mugs?'

I did not reply and he went on.

'The money was rather a bother. The bank didn't pension one off till after thirty years' service, but if you retired before that they gave you a gratuity. With that and what I'd got for the sale of my house and the little I'd managed to save, I just hadn't enough to buy an annuity to last the rest of my life. It would have been silly to sacrifice everything so as to lead a pleasant life and not have a sufficient income to make it pleasant. I wanted to have a little place of my own, a servant to look after me, enough to buy tobacco, decent food, books now and then, and something over for emergencies. I knew pretty well how much I needed. I found I had just enough to buy an annuity for twenty-five years.'

'You were thirty-five at the time?'

'Yes. It would carry me on till I was sixty. After all, no one can be certain of living longer than that, a lot of men die in their fifties, and by the time a man's sixty he's had the best of life.'

'On the other hand no one can be sure of dying at sixty,' I said.

'Well, I don't know. It depends on himself, doesn't it?'

'In your place I should have stayed on at the bank till I was entitled to my pension.'

'I should have been forty-seven then. I shouldn't have been too old to enjoy my life here, I'm older than that now and I enjoy it as much as I ever did, but I should have been too old to experience the particular pleasure of a young man. You know, you can have just as good a time at fifty as you can

338

at thirty, but it's not the same sort of good time. I wanted to live the perfect life while I still had the energy and the spirit to make the most of it. Twenty-five years seemed a long time to me, and twenty-five years of happiness seemed worth paying something pretty substantial for. I'd made up my mind to wait a year, and I waited a year. Then I sent in my resignation and as soon as they paid me my gratuity I bought the annuity and came on here.'

'An annuity for twenty-five years?'

'That's right.'

'Have you never regretted?'

'Never. I've had my money's worth already. And I've got ten years more. Don't you think after twenty-five years of perfect happiness one ought to be satisfied to call it a day?'

'Perhaps.'

He did not say in so many words what he would do then, but his intention was clear. It was pretty much the story my friend had told me, but it sounded different when I heard it from his own lips. I stole a glance at him. There was nothing about him that was not ordinary. No one, looking at that neat, prim face, could have thought him capable of an unconventional action. I did not blame him. It was his own life that he had arranged in this strange manner, and I did not see why he should not do what he liked with it. Still, I could not prevent the little shiver that ran down my spine.

'Getting chilly?' he smiled. 'We might as well start walking down. The moon'll be up by now.'

Before we parted Wilson asked me if I would like to go and see his house one day; and two or three days later, finding out where he lived, I strolled up to see him. It was a peasant's cottage, well away from the town, in a vineyard, with a view of the sea. By the side of the door grew a great oleander in full flower. There were only two small rooms, a tiny kitchen, and a lean-to in which firewood could be kept. The bedroom was furnished like a monk's cell, but the sitting-room, smelling agreeably of tobacco, was comfortable enough, with two large arm-chairs that he had brought from England, a large roll-top desk, a cottage piano, and crowded bookshelves. On the walls were framed engravings of pictures by G. F. Watts and Lord Leighton. Wilson told me that the house belonged to the owner of the vineyard who lived in another cottage higher up the hill, and his wife came in every day to do the rooms and the cooking. He had found the place on his first visit to Capri, and taking it on his return for good had been there ever since. Seeing the piano and music open on it, I asked him if he would play.

'I'm no good, you know, but I've always been fond of music and I get a lot of fun out of strumming.'

He sat down at the piano and played one of the movements from a Beethoven sonata. He did not play very well. I looked at his music, Schumann and Schubert, Beethoven, Bach, and Chopin. On the table on which he had his meals was a greasy pack of cards. I asked him if he played patience.

'A lot.'

From what I saw of him then and from what I heard from other people I made for myself what I think must have been a fairly accurate picture of the life he had led for the last fifteen years. It was certainly a very harmless one. He bathed; he walked a great deal, and he seemed never to lose his sense of the beauty of the island which he knew so intimately; he played the piano and he played patience; he read. When he was asked to a party he went and, though a trifle dull, was agreeable. He was not affronted if he was neglected. He liked people, but with an aloofness that prevented intimacy. He lived thriftily, but with sufficient comfort. He never owed a penny. I imagine he had never been a man whom sex had greatly troubled, and if in his younger days he had had now and then a passing affair with a visitor to the island whose head was turned by the atmosphere, his emotion, while it lasted, remained, I am pretty sure, well under his control. I think he was determined that nothing should interfere with his independence of spirit. His only passion was for the beauty of nature, and he sought felicity in the simple and natural things that life offers to everyone. You may say that it was a grossly selfish existence. It was. He was of no use to anybody, but on the other hand he did nobody any harm. His only object was his own happiness, and it looked as though he had attained it. Very few people know where to look for happiness; fewer still find it. I don't know whether he was a fool or a wise man. He was certainly a man who knew his own mind. The odd thing about him to me was that he was so immensely commonplace. I should never have given him a second thought but for what I knew, that on a certain day, ten years from then, unless a chance illness cut the thread before, he must deliberately take leave of the world he loved so well. I wondered whether it was the thought of this, never quite absent from his mind, that gave him the peculiar zest with which he enjoyed every moment of the day.

I should do him an injustice if I omitted to state that he was not at all in the habit of talking about himself. I think the friend I was staying with was the only person in whom he had confided. I believe he only told me the story because he suspected I already knew it, and on the evening on which he told it me he had drunk a good deal of wine.

My visit drew to a close and I left the island. The year after, war broke out. A number of things happened to me, so that the course of my life was greatly altered, and it was thirteen years before I went to Capri again. My friend had been back some time, but he was no longer so well off, and had moved into a house that had no room for me; so I was putting up at the hotel. He came to meet me at the boat and we dined together. During dinner I asked him where exactly his house was.

'You know it,' he answered. 'It's the little place Wilson had. I've built on a room, and made it quite nice.'

With so many other things to occupy my mind I had not given Wilson a thought for years; but now, with a little shock, I remembered. The ten years he had before him when I made his acquaintance must have elapsed long ago.

'Did he commit suicide as he said he would?'

'It's rather a grim story.'

Wilson's plan was all right. There was only one flaw in it and this, I suppose, he could not have foreseen. It had never occurred to him that after twenty-five years of complete happiness, in this quiet backwater, with nothing in the world to disturb his serenity, his character would gradually lose its strength. The will needs obstacles in order to exercise its power; when it is never thwarted, when no effort is needed to achieve one's desires, because one has placed one's desires only in the things that can be obtained by stretching out one's hand, the will grows impotent. If you walk on a level all the time the muscles you need to climb a mountain will atrophy. These observations are trite, but there they are. When Wilson's annuity expired he had no longer the resolution to make the end which was the price he had agreed to pay for that long period of happy tranquillity. I do not think, as far as I could gather, both from what my friend told me and afterwards from others, that he wanted courage. It was just that he couldn't make up his mind. He put it off from day to day.

He had lived on the island for so long and had always

settled his accounts so punctually that it was easy for him to get credit; never having borrowed money before, he found a number of people who were willing to lend him small sums when now he asked for them. He had paid his rent regularly for so many years that his landlord, whose wife Assunta still acted as his servant, was content to let things slide for several months. Everyone believed him when he said that a relative had died and that he was temporarily embarrassed because owing to legal formalities he could not for some time get the money that was due to him. He managed to hang on after this fashion for something over a year. Then he could get no more credit from the local tradesmen, and there was no one to lend him any more money. His landlord gave him notice to leave the house unless he paid up the arrears of rent before a certain date.

The day before this he went into his tiny bedroom, closed the door and the window, drew the curtain, and lit a brazier of charcoal. Next morning when Assunta came to make his breakfast she found him insensible but still alive. The room was draughty, and though he had done this and that to keep out the fresh air he had not done it very thoroughly. It almost looked as though at the last moment, and desperate though his situation was, he had suffered from a certain infirmity of purpose. Wilson was taken to the hospital, and though very ill, for some time he at last recovered. But as a result either of the charcoal poisoning or of the shock he was no longer in complete possession of his faculties. He was not insane, at all events not insane enough to be put in an asylum, but he was quite obviously no longer in his right mind.

'I went to see him,' said my friend. 'I tried to get him to talk, but he kept looking at me in a funny sort of way, as though he couldn't quite make out where he'd seen me before. He looked rather awful lying there in bed, with a week's growth of grey beard on his chin; but except for that funny look in his eyes he seemed quite normal.'

'What funny look in his eyes?'

'I don't know exactly how to describe it. Puzzled. It's an absurd comparison, but suppose you threw a stone up into the air and it didn't come down but just stayed there . . .'

'It would be rather bewildering,' I smiled.

'Well, that's the sort of look he had.'

It was difficult to know what to do with him. He had no money and no means of getting any. His effects were sold, but for too little to pay what he owed. He was English, and the Italian authorities did not wish to make themselves responsible for him. The British Consul in Naples had no funds to deal with the case. He could of course be sent back to England, but no one seemed to know what could be done with him when he got there. Then Assunta, the servant, said that he had been a good master and a good tenant, and as long as he had the money had paid his way; he could sleep in the woodshed in the cottage in which she and her husband lived, and he could share their meals. This was suggested to him. It was difficult to know whether he understood or not. When Assunta came to take him from the hospital he went with her without remark. He seemed to have no longer a will of his own. She had been keeping him now for two years.

'It's not very comfortable, you know,' said my friend. 'They've rigged him up a ramshackle bed and given him a couple of blankets, but there's no window, and it's icy cold in winter and like an oven in summer. And the food's pretty rough. You know how these peasants eat: macaroni on Sundays and meat once in a blue moon.'

'What does he do with himself all the time?'

'He wanders about the hills. I've tried to see him two or three times, but it's no good; when he sees you coming he runs like a hare. Assunta comes down to have a chat with me now and then and I give her a bit of money so that she can buy him tobacco, but God knows if he ever gets it.'

'Do they treat him all right?' I asked.

'I'm sure Assunta's kind enough. She treats him like a child. I'm afraid her husband's not very nice to him. He grudges the cost of his keep. I don't believe he's cruel or anything like that, but I think he's a bit sharp with him. He makes him fetch water and clean the cow-shed and that sort of thing.'

'It sounds pretty rotten,' I said.

'He brought it on himself. After all, he's only got what he deserved.'

'I think on the whole we all get what we deserve,' I said. 'But that doesn't prevent its being rather horrible.'

Two or three days later my friend and I were taking a walk. We were strolling along a narrow path through an olive grove.

'There's Wilson,' said my friend suddenly. 'Don't look, you'll only frighten him. Go straight on.'

I walked with my eyes on the path, but out of the corners of them I saw a man hiding behind an olive tree. He did not move as we approached, but I felt that he was watching us. As soon as we had passed I heard a scamper. Wilson, like a hunted animal, had made for safety. That was the last I ever saw of him.

He died last year. He had endured that life for six years. He was found one morning on the mountainside lying quite peacefully as though he had died in his sleep. From where he lay he had been able to see those two great rocks called the Faraglioni which stand out of the sea. It was full moon and he must have gone to see them by moonlight. Perhaps he died of the beauty of that sight.

CURZIO MALAPARTE

THE PLAGUE

From

THE SKIN (1949)

Translated by David Moore

NAPLES WAS IN the throes of the 'plague'. Every afternoon at five o'clock, after half an hour with the punching-ball and a hot shower in the gymnasium of the P.B.S. – Peninsular Base Section – Colonel Jack Hamilton and I would walk down in the direction of San Ferdinando, elbowing our way through the unruly mob which thronged Via Toledo from dawn until curfew time.

We were clean, tidy and well fed, Jack and I, as we made our way through the midst of the dreadful Neapolitan mob – squalid, dirty, starving, ragged, jostled and insulted in all the languages and dialects of the world by troops of soldiers belonging to the armies of liberation, which were drawn from all the races of the earth. The distinction of being the first among all the peoples of Europe to be liberated had fallen to the people of Naples; and in celebration of the winning of so well-deserved a prize my poor beloved Neapolitans, after three years of hunger, epidemics and savage air attacks, had accepted gracefully and patriotically the longed-for and coveted honour of playing the part of a conquered people, of singing, clapping, jumping for joy amid the ruins of their houses, unfurling foreign flags which until the day before had been the emblems of their foes, and throwing flowers from their windows on to the heads of the conquerors.

But in spite of the universal and genuine enthusiasm there was not a single man or woman in the whole of Naples who was conscious of having been defeated. I cannot say how this strange feeling had arisen in the people's breasts. It was an undoubted fact that Italy, and hence also Naples, had lost the war. It is certainly much harder to lose a war than to win it. While everyone is good at winning a war, not all are capable of losing one. But the loss of a war does not in itself entitle a people to regard itself as conquered. In their ancient wisdom, enriched by the doleful experience of many hundreds of years, and in their sincere modesty, my poor beloved Neapolitans did not presume to regard themselves as a conquered people. In this they undoubtedly revealed a grave lack of tact. But could the Allies claim to liberate peoples and at the same time compel them to regard themselves as conquered? They must be either free or conquered. It would be unjust to blame the people of Naples if they regarded themselves as neither free nor conquered.

As I walked beside Colonel Hamilton I felt incredibly ridiculous in my British uniform. The uniforms of the Italian Corps of Liberation were old British khaki uniforms, handed over by the British Command to Marshal Badoglio and – perhaps in an attempt to hide the bloodstains and bullet holes – dyed dark green, the colour of a lizard. They were, as a matter of fact, uniforms taken from the British soldiers who had fallen at El Alamein and Tobruk. In my tunic three holes made by machine-gun bullets were visible. My vest, shirt and underpants were stained with blood. Even my shoes had been taken from the body of a British soldier. The first time I had put them on I had felt something pricking the sole of my foot. I had thought at first that a tiny bone belonging to the dead man had remained stuck in the shoe. It was a nail. It would have been better, perhaps, if it really had been a bone from the dead man: it would have been much easier for me to remove it. It took me half an hour to find a pair of pliers and remove the nail. There was no gainsaying it: that stupid war had certainly ended well for us. It could not have ended better. Our amour propre as defeated soldiers was undamaged. Now we were fighting at the side of the Allies, trying to help them win their war after we had lost our own. Hence it was natural that we should be wearing the uniforms of the Allied soldiers whom we had killed.

When I at last succeeded in removing the nail and putting on my shoe I found that the Company of which I was to assume command had been assembled for some time past on the barrack square. The barracks consisted of an ancient monastery, which had been reduced by time and the air bombardments to a state of ruin. It was situated in the vicinity of La Torretta, behind Mergellina. The 'square' was a cloistered courtyard, bounded on three sides by a portico, which rested on slender columns of gray tufa, and on the fourth by a high yellow wall, dotted with specks of green mould and great slabs of marble, on which were carved long lists of names, surmounted by great black crosses. During some cholera epidemic of centuries before the monastery had been used as a hospital, and the names referred to those who had died of the disease. On the wall was written in large black letters: *Requiescant in pace*.

Colonel Palese had been anxious to introduce me to my soldiers himself in one of those simple ceremonies of which old military men are so fond. He was a tall, thin man, with completely white hair. He clasped my hand in silence and, sighing dolefully, smiled. The soldiers were nearly all very young. They had fought well against the Allies in Africa and Sicily, and for this reason the Allies had chosen them to form the first cadre of the Italian Corps of Liberation. Lined up before us in the middle of the courtyard, they eyed me with a fixed stare. They too were wearing uniforms taken from

British soldiers who had fallen at El Alamein and Tobruk, and their shoes were dead men's shoes. Their faces were pale and emaciated; their eyes, which were white and steady, consisted of a moist, opaque substance. They seemed to gaze at me without blinking.

Colonel Palese nodded his head, and the sergeant shouted: 'Company – 'shun!' The soldiers riveted their gaze upon me; it was sorrowful and intense, like the gaze of a dead cat. Their limbs became rigid and they sprang to attention. The hands that grasped their rifles were white and bloodless. The flabby skin hung from the tips of their fingers like a glove that is too big.

Colonel Palese began to speak. 'Here is your new commanding officer,' he said, and while he spoke I looked at those Italian soldiers with their uniforms that had been taken from British corpses, their bloodless hands, their pale lips and white eyes. Here and there on their chests, stomachs and legs were black spots of blood. Suddenly I realized to my horror that these soldiers were dead. They gave out a faint odour of musty cloth, rotten leather, and flesh that had been dried up by the sun. I looked at Colonel Palese, and he was dead too. The voice that proceeded from his lips was watery, cold, glutinous, like the horrible gurgling that issues from a dead man's mouth if you rest your hand on his stomach.

'Tell them to stand at ease,' said Colonel Palese to the sergeant when he had ended his brief address. 'Company, stand at – ease!' cried the sergeant. The soldiers flopped down on to their left heels in limp and weary attitudes and stared at me fixedly, with a softer, more distant look. 'And now,' said Colonel Palese, 'your new commanding officer will say a few words to you.' I opened my mouth and a horrible gurgling sound came out; my words were muffled, thick, flaccid. I said: 'We are the volunteers of Freedom, the soldiers of

352

the new Italy. It is our duty to fight the Germans, to drive them out of our homeland, to throw them back beyond our frontiers. The eyes of all Italians are fixed upon us. It is our duty once more to hoist the flag that has fallen in the mire, to set an example to all in the midst of so much shame, to show ourselves worthy of the present hour, of the task that our country entrusts to us.' When I had finished speaking Colonel Palese said to the soldiers: 'Now one of you will repeat what your commanding officer has said. I want to be sure you understand. You!' he said, pointing to a soldier. 'Repeat what your commanding officer said.'

The soldier looked at me; he was pale, he had the thin, bloodless lips of a dead man. Slowly, in a dreadful gurgling voice, he said: 'It is our duty to show ourselves worthy of the shame of Italy.'

Colonel Palese came up close to me. 'They understand,' he said in a low voice, and moved silently away. Under his left armpit was a black spot of blood which gradually spread over the material of his uniform. I watched that black spot of blood as it gradually spread, my eyes followed the old Italian colonel, with his uniform that had belonged to an Englishman now dead, I watched him slowly move away and heard the squeaking of his shoes, the shoes of a dead British soldier, and the name of Italy stank in my nostrils like a piece of rotten meat.

'This bastard people!' said Colonel Hamilton between his teeth, forcing his way through the crowd.

'Why do you say that, Jack?'

Having reached the top of the Augusteo we used to turn off each day into Via Santa Brigida, where the crowd was thinner, and pause a moment to regain our breath.

'This bastard people,' said Jack, straightening his uniform, which had been rumpled by the terrible pressure of the crowd.

'Don't say that, Jack.'

'Why not? This bastard, dirty people.'

'Hey, Jack! I am a bastard and a dirty Italian too. But I am proud of being a dirty Italian. It isn't our fault if we weren't born in America. I'm sure we'd be a bastard, dirty people even if we had been born in America. Don't you think so, Jack?'

'Don't worry, Malaparte,' said Jack. 'Don't take it to heart. Life is wonderful.'

'Yes, life is a splendid thing, Jack, I know. But don't say that.'

'Sorry,' said Jack, patting me on the shoulder. 'I didn't mean to offend you. It's a figure of speech. I like Italians. I like this bastard, dirty, wonderful people.'

'I know, Jack – I know you like this poor, unhappy, wonderful people. No people on earth has ever endured as much as the people of Naples. They have endured hunger and slavery for two thousand years, and they don't complain. They revile no one, they hate no one – not even their own misery. Christ was a Neapolitan.'

'Don't talk nonsense,' said Jack.

'It isn't nonsense. Christ was a Neapolitan.'

'What's the matter with you today, Malaparte?' said Jack, looking at me with his fine eyes.

'Nothing. What do you suppose is the matter with me?'

'You're in a black mood,' said Jack.

'Why should I be in a bad mood?'

'I know you, Malaparte. You're in a black mood today.'

'I am sad about Cassino, Jack.'

'To hell with Cassino.'

'I am sad, truly sad, about what is happening at Cassino.'

'To hell with you,' said Jack.

'It's really a shame that you're bringing such misery to Cassino.'

'Shut up, Malaparte.'

'Sorry. I didn't mean to offend you, Jack. I like Americans. I like the pure, the clean, the wonderful American people.'

'I know, Malaparte. I know you like Americans. But take it easy, Malaparte. Life is wonderful.'

'To hell with Cassino, Jack.'

'Oh, yes. To hell with Naples, Malaparte.'

There was a strange smell in the air. It was not the smell that comes down at eventide from the alleys of Toledo and from the Piazza delle Carrette and Santa Teresella degli Spagnoli. It was not the smell from the fried-fish shops, taverns and urinals nestling in the dark and fetid alleys of the *Quartieri* that stretch from Via Toledo up toward San Martino. It was not that nauseating, stuffy, glutinous smell, composed of a thousand effluvia, a thousand noisome exhalations – *mille délicates puanteurs*, as Jack put it – which at certain times of day pervades the city and emanates from the withered flowers that lie in heaps at the feet of the Madonnas in the chapels at the corners of the alleys. It was not the smell of the sirocco, which smacks of bad fish and of the cheese that is made from sheep's milk. It was not even that smell of cooked meat which towards evening spreads over Naples from the brothels – that smell in which Jean-Paul Sartre, walking one day along Via Toledo, *sombre comme une aisselle, pleine d'une ombre chaude vaguement obscène*, detected the *parenté immonde de l'amour et de la nourriture*. No, it was not that smell of cooked meat which broods over Naples toward sunset, when *la chair des femmes a l'air bouillie sous la crasse*. It was an extraordinarily pure, delicate smell, dry, light, unsubstantial – the smell of brine, the salt tang of the

355

night air, the smell of an ancient forest from the trees of which paper is made.

Parties of dishevelled, painted women, followed by crowds of Negro soldiers with pale hands, were parading up and down Via Toledo, cleaving the air above the thronged street with shrill cries of 'Hi, Joe! Hi, Joe!' At the entrances to the alleys loitered the public hairdressers, the *capere*. They formed long lines, and each stood behind a seat. On the seats, their eyes closed and their heads lolling against the backs or sunk upon their breasts, sat athletic Negroes with small round skulls and yellow shoes that shone like the feet of the gilded statues of the Angels in the church of Santa Chiara. Yelling and calling to one another with strange guttural cries, singing, or arguing at the top of their voices with their neighbours, who looked down from the windows and balconies as though from boxes at the theatre, the *capere* sank their combs into the Negroes' curly, woolly hair, drew them toward them with both hands, spat on the teeth to reduce the friction, poured rivers of brilliantine into the palms of their hands, and rubbed and smoothed the patients' wild locks like masseuses.

Bands of ragged boys knelt before their little wooden boxes, which were plastered with flakes of mother of pearl, sea shells and fragments of mirrors, and beat the lids with the backs of their brushes, crying 'Shoeshine! Shoeshine!' Meanwhile, with bony, eager hands, they grabbed the Negro soldiers by the edge of the trousers as they went past, swaying their hips. Groups of Moroccan soldiers squatted along the walls, enveloped in their dark robes, their faces riddled with pockmarks, their yellow deep-set eyes shining from dark, wrinkled sockets, inhaling through quivering nostrils the dry odor that permeated the dusty air.

Faded women, with livid faces and painted lips, their

emaciated cheeks plastered with rouge – a dreadful and piteous sight – loitered at the corners of the alleys, offering to the passers-by their sorry merchandise. This consisted of boys and girls of eight or ten, whom the soldiers – Moroccans, Indians, Algerians, Madagascans – caressed with their fingers, slipping their hands between the buttons of their short trousers or lifting their dresses. 'Two dollars the boys, three dollars the girls!' shouted the women.

'Tell me frankly – would you like a little girl at three dollars?' I said to Jack.

'Shut up, Malaparte.'

'After all, it's not much, three dollars for a little girl. Two pounds of lamb cost far more. I'm sure a little girl costs more in London or New York than here – isn't that so, Jack?'

'Tu me dégoûtes,' said Jack.

'Three dollars is barely three hundred lire. How much can a little girl of eight or ten weigh? Fifty pounds? Remember that on the black market two pounds of lamb cost five hundred and fifty lire, in other words five dollars and fifty cents.'

'Shut up!' cried Jack.

During the last few days the prices of girls and boys had dropped, and they were still falling. Whereas the prices of sugar, oil, flour, meat and bread had risen and were still on the increase, the price of human flesh was slumping from day to day. A girl between twenty and twenty-five years of age, who a week before was worth up to ten dollars, was now worth barely four dollars, bones included. This fall in the price of human flesh on the Neapolitan market may have been due to the fact that women were flocking to Naples from all parts of Southern Italy. During recent weeks the wholesalers had thrown on to the market a large consignment of Sicilian women. It was not all fresh meat, but the speculators knew that Negro soldiers have refined tastes, and prefer meat not to be too fresh. Yet Sicilian meat was not in great demand, and even the Negroes refused it in the end: Negroes don't like white women to be too dark. Every day there arrived in Naples, on carts drawn by wretched little donkeys or in Allied vehicles, but mostly on foot, parties of sturdily built, robust girls, nearly all of them peasants, attracted by the mirage of gold. They came from the Calabrias, the Apulias, the Basilicata and Molise. And so the price of human flesh on the Neapolitan market had been crashing, and it was feared that this might have a serious effect on the whole economy of the city. (Nothing of the kind had ever been seen in Naples before. It was certainly a disgrace, and the vast majority of the good people of Naples blushed with shame because of it. But why did it not bring a blush to the cheeks of the authorities, who were the masters of Naples?) In compensation, Negroes' flesh had risen in price, and this, luckily, was helping to reestablish a certain equilibrium on the market.

'What does Negroes' flesh cost today?' I asked Jack.

'Shut up,' he answered.

'Is it true that the flesh of a black American costs more than that of a white American?'

'Tu m'agaces,' answered Jack.

I certainly had no intention of offending him, nor of poking fun at him, nor even of being disrespectful to the American army – the loveliest, the kindest, the most respectable army in the world. What did it matter to me if the flesh of a black American cost more than that of a white American? I like Americans, whatever the colour of their skin, and I proved it a hundred times during the war. White or black, their souls are pure, much purer than ours. I like the Americans because they are good and sincere Christians; because they believe that Christ is always on the side of those who are in the right; because they believe that it is a sin to be in the wrong, that it is immoral to be in the wrong; because they believe that they alone are honourable men, and that all the nations of Europe are more or less dishonest; because they believe that a conquered nation is a nation of criminals, that defeat is a moral stigma, an expression of divine justice.

I like Americans for these reasons, and for many others that I have not mentioned. In that terrible autumn of 1943, which brought so much humiliation and grief to my fellow countrymen, the Americans' humanity and generosity, the pure and honest simplicity of their ideas and sentiments, and the genuineness of their behaviour, instilled in me the illusion that men hate evil, the hope that humanity would mend its ways, and the conviction that only goodness – the goodness and innocence of those splendid boys from across the Atlantic, who had landed in Europe to punish the wicked and reward the good – could redeem nations and individuals from their sins.

But of all my American friends the dearest was Staff Colonel Jack Hamilton. Jack was a man of thirty-eight – tall, thin, pale and elegant, with gentlemanly, almost European manners. On first acquaintance, perhaps, he seemed more European than American, but this was not the reason why I loved him; and I loved him like a brother. For gradually, as I got to know him intimately, he showed himself to be intensely and indisputably American. He had been born in South Carolina ('My nurse,' he used to say, 'was *une négresse par un démon secouée*'), but he was not merely what is known in America as a Southerner. Intellectually he was a man of culture and refinement, and at the same time there was about him an almost childlike simplicity and innocence. What I mean is that he was an American in the noblest sense of the word – one of the most admirable men I have ever met. He was a 'Christian gentleman'. How hard it is for me to express what I mean by the term 'Christian gentleman'! All who know and love the Americans will understand what I mean when I say that the American nation is a Christian nation, and that Jack was a Christian gentleman.

Educated at Woodberry Forest School and at the University of Virginia, Jack had devoted himself with equal enthusiasm to Latin, Greek and sport, putting himself with equal confidence in the hands of Horace, Virgil, Simonides and Xenophon and in those of the masseurs of the University gymnasiums. In 1928 he had been a sprinter in the American Olympic Track Team at Amsterdam, and he was prouder of his Olympic victories than of his academic honours. After 1929 he had spent some years in Paris as a representative of the United Press, and he was proud of his well-nigh perfect French. 'I learned French from the classics,' he used to say. 'My French tutors were La Fontaine and Madame Bonnet, the caretaker of the house in which I lived in Rue Vaugirard. Tu ne trouves pas que je parle comme les animaux de La Fontaine? It was he who taught me qu'un chien peut bien regarder un Évêque.'

'And you came to Europe,' I would say to him, 'to learn that? Un chien peut bien regarder un Évêque in America as well.'

'Oh non,' Jack would reply, 'en Amérique ce sont les Évêques qui peuvent regarder les chiens.'

Jack was also well acquainted with what he called *la banlieue de Paris*, in other words Europe. He had journeyed through Switzerland, Belgium, Germany and Sweden in the same spirit of humanism and with the same thirst for knowledge as the English undergraduates who, before Dr Arnold's reform, used to journey across Europe during their summer Grand Tour. After his travels Jack had returned to

America with the manuscripts of an essay on the spirit of European civilization and of a thesis on Descartes, which had earned him an appointment as Professor of Literature in a great American university. But academic laurels do not flourish on an athlete's brow as Olympic laurels do; and Jack could not get over the fact that a muscular strain in the knee prevented him from running again in the international contests for the honour of the Stars and Stripes. In an attempt to forget his misfortune Jack would repair to the changing-room of the University gymnasium and read his adored Virgil or his beloved Xenophon, surrounded by that odour of rubber, soaking towels, soap and linoleum which is peculiarly associated with classical culture in the universities of the Anglo-Saxon countries.

One morning I came upon him unawares in the changing-room – deserted at that hour – of the Peninsular Base Section's gymnasium, deeply engrossed in Pindar. He looked at me and smiled, colouring slightly. He asked me if I liked Pindar's poetry, adding that the Pindaric odes written in honour of the athletes who had triumphed at Olympia do not convey any idea of the long, hard drudgery of training, that those divine verses resound with the yells of the crowd and the triumphal applause, not with the hoarse whistling and the rasping sound that comes from the mouths of athletes when they make their last terrible effort. 'I know all about it,' he said, 'I know what the last twenty yards are. Pindar is not a modern poet. He is an English poet of the Victorian era.'

Although he preferred Horace and Virgil to all other poets because of their serene melancholy, Greek poetry and ancient Greece filled him with a sense of gratitude – not the gratitude of a scholar, but that of a son. He knew by heart whole books of the *Iliad*, and tears would come into his eyes when he declaimed, in Greek, the hexameters on the 'funeral Games in honour of Patroclus'. One day, as we sat on the bank of the Volturno, near the Bailey Bridge at Capua, waiting for the sergeant guarding the bridge to give us the signal to cross, we discussed Winckelmann and the concept of beauty among the ancient Hellenes. I remember Jack's telling me that the gloomy, funereal, mysterious imagery of ancient Greece, so raw and barbaric, or, as he put it, Gothic, appealed to him less than the joyful, harmonious, clear imagery of Hellenistic Greece, which was so young, vivacious and modern, and which he described as a French Greece, a Greece of the eighteenth century. And when I asked him what, in his opinion, was the American Greece, he replied with a laugh: 'The Greece of Xenophon'; and, still laughing, began to paint a remarkable and witty picture of Xenophon – 'a Virginia gentleman' – which was a disguised satire, in the style of Dr Johnson, of certain Hellenists of the Boston school.

Jack had an indulgent and mischievous contempt for the Hellenists of Boston. One morning I found him sitting under a tree, with a book on his knees, near a heavy battery facing Cassino. It was during the sad days of the Battle of Cassino. It was raining – for a fortnight it had been doing nothing but rain. Columns of trucks laden with American soldiers, sewn up in white sheets of coarse linen cloth, were going down in the direction of the little military cemeteries which were to be seen here and there beside the Via Appia and the Via Casilina. To keep the rain off the pages of his book – an eighteenth-century anthology of Greek poetry with a soft leather binding and gilt edges, presented to him by the worthy Gaspare Casella, the famous antiquarian bookseller of Naples and a friend of Anatole France – Jack was sitting with his body bent forward, covering the precious book with the edges of his mackintosh.

I remember his saying to me with a laugh that in Boston Simonides was not considered a great poet. And he added that Emerson, in his funeral panegyric of Thoreau, declared that 'his classic poem on *Smoke* suggests Simonides, but is better than any poem of Simonides'. He laughed heartily. 'Ah, ces gens de Boston! Tu vois ça? Thoreau, in the opinion of Boston, is greater than Simonides!' he said, and the rain entered his mouth, mingling with his words and his laughter.

His favourite American poet was Edgar Allan Poe. But sometimes, when he had drunk a whisky more than usual, he would confuse Horace's verses with Poe's, and be deeply astonished to find Annabel Lee and Lydia in the same Alcaic. Or he would confuse Madame de Sévigné's 'talking leaf' with one of La Fontaine's talking animals.

'It wasn't an animal,' I would say to him. 'It was a leaf – a leaf from a tree.'

And I would quote the relevant passage from the letter in which Madame de Sévigné wrote that she wished there was a talking leaf in the park of her castle, Les Rochers, in Brittany.

'Mais cela c'est absurde,' Jack would say. 'Une feuille qui parle! Un animal, ça se comprend, mais une feuille!'

'For the understanding of Europe,' I would say to him, 'Cartesian logic is useless. Europe is a mysterious place, full of inviolable secrets.'

'Ah, Europe! What an extraordinary place it is!' Jack would exclaim. 'I need Europe, to make me conscious of being an American.'

But Jack was not one of those *Américains de Paris* – they are found on every page of Hemingway's *The Sun Also Rises* – who round about 1925 used to frequent the Select in Montparnasse, who disdained Ford Madox Ford's tea parties and Sylvia Beach's bookshop, and who are said by Sinclair Lewis, alluding specifically to certain characters created by

Eleanor Green, to have been like the intellectual fugitives who frequented the Rive Gauche round about 1925, or like T. S. Eliot, Ezra Pound or Isadora Duncan – 'iridescent flies caught in the black web of an ancient and amoral European culture'. Nor was Jack one of those decadent transatlantic youths who formed the *Transition* clique. No, Jack was neither a *déraciné* nor a decadent. He was an American in love with Europe.

He had for Europe a respect compounded of love and admiration. But in spite of his culture and his affectionate familiarity with our virtues and our faults his attitude to Europe, like that of nearly all true Americans, was conditioned by a subtle species of 'inferiority complex', which manifested itself not, to be sure, in an inability to understand and forgive our misery and shame, but in a fear of understanding, a reluctance to understand which was due to a certain delicacy of feeling. In Jack this inferiority complex, this ingenuousness and wonderful delicacy of feeling, were perhaps more apparent than in many other Americans. Whenever, in a Neapolitan street, in a village near Capua or Caserta, or on the Cassino road, he happened to witness some distressing incident which typified our misery, our physical and moral humiliation, and our despair (the misery, humiliation and despair not only of Naples and Italy, but of all Europe), Jack would blush crimson.

Because of that way he had of blushing I loved Jack like a brother. Because of his wonderful delicacy of feeling, so profoundly and truly American, I was grateful to Jack, to all General Clark's G.I.s, and to all the men, women and children of America. (America – that luminous, remote horizon, that unattainable shore, that happy, forbidden country!) Sometimes, in an attempt to hide his delicacy of feeling, he would say, blushing crimson: 'This bastard, dirty people.' On such occasions I used to react to his wonderful sensitiveness with bitter and sarcastic words, accompanied by uneasy, malicious laughter, which I immediately regretted, and remembered with remorse all night long. He would perhaps have preferred it if I had started to cry: my tears would certainly have seemed to him more natural than my sarcasm, less cruel than my bitterness. But I too had something to hide. We too, in this miserable Europe of ours, are afraid and ashamed of our delicacy of feeling . . .

Jack and I, accompanied by Captain Jimmy Wren, of Cleveland, Ohio, used often to go and eat hot *taralli*, fresh from the oven, in a baker's shop situated on the Pendino di Santa Barbara, that long, gently sloping flight of steps which leads up from the Sedile di Porto in the direction of the Monastery of Santa Chiara.

The Pendino is a dismal alley. It owes its character not so much to its narrowness, carved out as it is between the high, mildewed walls of ancient, sordid houses, or to the eternal darkness that reigns within it even on sunny days, as to the strangeness of its inhabitants.

In point of fact, the Pendino di Santa Barbara is famous for the many female dwarfs who reside in it. They are so small that they barely come up to the knee of a man of average height. Repulsive and wrinkled, they are among the ugliest of their kind in the world. There are in Spain female dwarfs of great beauty, with well-proportioned limbs and features. And I have seen some in England who are truly exquisite, pink-skinned and fair-haired, like miniature Venuses. But the female dwarfs of the Pendino di Santa Barbara are frightful creatures. All of them, even the youngest, look like very old women, so wizened are their faces, so creased their foreheads, so thin and faded their dishevelled locks.

The most astounding thing about that noisome alley, with its horrible population of dwarf women, is the handsomeness of the men, who are tall and have very dark eyes and hair, leisurely, noble gestures, and clear, resonant voices. There are no male dwarfs to be seen on the Pendino di Santa Barbara, a fact which encourages the belief that they die in infancy or that their abbreviated limbs are a monstrous legacy inherited only by the women.

These dwarf women spend the whole day sitting on the doorsteps of the *bassi* or squatting on tiny stools at the entrances to their lairs, croaking to one another in froglike voices. Their shortness of stature seems prodigious against the background of the furniture that fills their dark caverns – chests of drawers, vast cupboards, beds that look like giants' couches. To reach the furniture the dwarf women climb on chairs and benches; they hoist themselves up with their arms, making use of the ends of the high iron beds. And anyone climbing the steps of the Pendino di Santa Barbara for the first time feels like Gulliver in the Kingdom of Lilliput, or a servant at the Court of Madrid among Velázquez's dwarfs. The foreheads of these female dwarfs are scored with the same deep wrinkles as furrow the foreheads of the horrible old women portrayed by Goya. Nor should this Spanish analogy be thought arbitrary, for the district is Hispanic in character and still alive with memories of the long years when Naples was subject to Castilian domination. There is an air of old Spain about the streets, alleys, houses and mansions, the strong, sweet smells, the guttural voices, the long, musical laments that echo from balcony to balcony, and the raucous strains of the gramophones that issue from the depths of the dark caverns.

Taralli are little rings of sweet pastry; and the bakery halfway up the steps of the Pendino, from which at all hours of the day there emanates the appetizing smell of fresh, crisp *taralli*, is famous throughout Naples. When the baker thrusts his long wooden shovel into the red-hot mouth of the oven the dwarf women run up, stretching out their little hands, which are as dark and wrinkled as the hands of monkeys. Uttering loud cries in their raucous little voices they seize the dainty *taralli*, all hot and steaming, hobble rapidly to different parts of the alley, and deposit the *taralli* on shining brass trays. Then they sit on the doorsteps of their hovels with the trays on their knees and wait for customers, singing '*Oh li taralli! oh li taralli belli cauri!*' The smell of the *taralli* spreads all through the Pendino di Santa Barbara, and the dwarf women, squatting on their doorsteps, croak and laugh among themselves. And one, a young one perhaps, sings at a little window high up, and looks like a great spider poking its hairy head out of a crack in the wall.

Bald, toothless dwarf women go up and down the slimy stairway, supporting themselves with sticks or crutches, reeling along on their little short legs, lifting their knees up to their chins in order to mount the steps, or drag themselves along on all fours, whimpering and slobbering. They look like the little monsters in the paintings of Breughel or Bosch, and one day Jack and I saw one of them sitting on the threshold of a cavern with a sick dog in her arms. As it lay on her lap, in her tiny arms, it seemed a gigantic animal, a monstrous wild beast. Up came a companion of hers, and the two of them seized the sick dog, the one by the hind legs, the other by the head, and with great difficulty carried it into the hovel. It seemed as if they were carrying a wounded dinosaur. The voices that ascend from the depths of the caverns are shrill and guttural, and the wails of the dreadful children, who are tiny and wrinkled, like old dolls, resemble the mewling of a dying kitten. If you enter one of these hovels you see, in

367

the fetid half-light, those giant cockroaches with enormous heads dragging themselves across the floor, and you have to take care not to crush them beneath the soles of your shoes.

Occasionally we saw some of these dwarf women climbing the steps of the Pendino in the company of gigantic American soldiers, white or coloured, with moist, shining eyes. Tugging them along by the trouser legs they would push them into their lairs. (The white soldiers, thank God, were always drunk.) I shuddered when I visualized the strange unions of those enormous men and those little monsters, on those high, vast beds.

And I would say to Jimmy Wren: 'I am glad to see that those little dwarfs and your handsome soldiers like each other. Aren't you glad too, Jimmy?'

'Of course I'm glad too,' Jimmy would answer, furiously chewing his gum.

'Do you think they'll get married?' I would say.

'Why not?' Jimmy would answer.

'Jimmy is a nice guy,' Jack would say, 'but you mustn't provoke him. He flares up easily.'

'I'm a nice guy too,' I would say, 'and I'm glad to think that you have come from America to improve the Italian race. But for you those poor dwarfs would have remained spinsters. By ourselves, we poor Italians couldn't have done anything about it. It's a lucky thing that you people have come from America to marry our dwarf women.'

'You will certainly be invited to the wedding breakfast,' Jack would say. 'Tu pourras prononcer un discours magnifique.'

'Oui, Jack, un discours magnifique. But don't you think, Jimmy,' I would say, 'that the Allied military authorities ought to encourage marriages between these dwarf women and your handsome soldiers? It would be an excellent thing if your soldiers married those little dwarfs. As a race you are too tall. America needs to come down to our level, don't you think so, Jimmy?'

'Yes, I think so,' Jimmy would answer, giving me a side-long glance.

'You are too tall,' I would say, 'too handsome. It's immoral that the world should contain a race of men who are so tall, so handsome and so healthy. I should like all the American soldiers to get married to those little dwarfs. Those "Italian brides" would score a tremendous hit in America. American civilization needs shorter legs.'

'To hell with you,' Jimmy would say, spitting on the ground.

'Il va te caresser la figure, si tu insistes,' Jack would say.

'Yes, I know. Jimmy is a nice guy,' I would say, laughing to myself.

It made me feel sick at heart to laugh in that way. But I should have been happy, truly happy, if all the American soldiers had one day gone back to America arm in arm with all the little dwarf women of Naples, Italy and Europe.

The 'plague' had broken out in Naples on October 1, 1943 – the very day on which the Allied armies had entered that ill-starred city as liberators. October 1, 1943, is a memorable date in the history of Naples, both because it marks the beginning of the liberation of Italy and Europe from the anguish, shame and sufferings of war and slavery, and because it exactly coincided with the outbreak of the terrible plague which gradually spread from the unhappy city all over Italy and all over Europe.

The appalling suspicion that the fearful disease had been brought to Naples by the liberators themselves was certainly unjust; but it became a certainty in the minds of the people when they perceived, with a mixture of amazement and superstitious terror, that the Allied soldiers remained strangely immune from the contagion. Pink-faced, calm and smiling, they moved about in the midst of the plague-stricken mob without contracting the loathsome disease, which gathered its harvest of victims solely from among the civilian population, not only in Naples itself, but even in the country districts, spreading like a patch of oil into the territory liberated by the Allied armies as they laboriously drove the Germans northward.

But it was strictly forbidden, under threat of the severest penalties, to insinuate in public that the plague had been brought to Italy by the liberators. And it was dangerous to repeat the allegation in private, even in an undertone, since among the many loathsome effects of the plague the most loathsome was that it engendered in its victims a mad passion, a voluptuous avidity for delation. No sooner were they stricken with the disease than one and all began to inform against fathers, mothers, brothers, sons, husbands, lovers, relations and dearest friends – but never against themselves. Indeed, one of the most surprising and repulsive character-istics of this extraordinary plague was that it transformed the human conscience into a horrible, noisome ulcer.

The only remedy which the British and American military authorities had discovered for the disease was to forbid the Allied soldiers to enter the most seriously infected areas of the city. On every wall one read the legends 'Off Limits' and 'Out of Bounds', surmounted by the aulic emblem of the plague – a black circle within which were depicted two black bars in the form of a cross, similar to the pair of crossed shinbones that appears beneath a skull on the saddlecloth of a funeral carriage.

Within a short space of time the whole of Naples was

declared 'off limits' with the exception of a few streets in the centre of the city. But the areas most frequented by the liberators were in fact those which were 'off limits', i.e., the most infected and therefore forbidden areas, since it is in the nature of man, and especially of the soldiers of all ages and every army, to prefer forbidden things to those that are permitted. And so the contagion, whether it had been brought to Naples by the liberators, or whether the latter carried it from one part of the city to another, from the infected areas to the healthy, very soon reached a terrible pitch of violence, rendered abominable, almost diabolical, by its grotesque, obscene manifestations, which were suggestive of a macabre public celebration, a funereal kermis. Drunken soldiers danced with women who were almost or completely naked in the squares and streets, in the midst of the wreckage of the houses that had been destroyed in the air raids. There was a mad orgy of drinking, eating, gaiety, singing, laughing, prodigality and revelry, amid the frightful stench that emanated from the countless hundreds of corpses buried beneath the ruins.

This was a plague profoundly different from, but no less horrible than, the epidemics which from time to time devastated Europe during the Middle Ages. The extraordinary thing about this most modern of diseases was that it corrupted not the body but the soul. The limbs remained seemingly intact, but within the integument of the healthy flesh the soul festered and rotted. It was a kind of moral plague, against which it seemed that there was no defence. The first to be infected were the women, who in every nation constitute the weakest bulwark against vice, and an open door to every form of evil. And this seemed an amazing and most lamentable thing, inasmuch as during the years of slavery and war, right up to the day of the promised and eagerly awaited liberation, the women – not only in Naples, but throughout Italy and Europe – had proved, amid the universal wretchedness and misfortune, that they possessed greater dignity and greater strength of mind than the men. In Naples and in every other city of Europe the women had refused to give themselves to the Germans. Only the prostitutes had had relations with the enemy, and even they had not done so openly, but in secret, either to avoid having to endure the sharp revulsion of popular feeling or because they themselves considered that to have such relations was to be guilty of the most infamous crime that a woman could commit during those years.

And now, as a result of this loathsome plague, which first corrupted the feminine sense of honour and dignity, prostitution on the most appalling scale had brought shame to every hovel and every mansion. But why call it shame? Such was the baneful power of the contagion that self-prostitution had become a praiseworthy act, almost a proof of patriotism, and all, men and women, far from blushing at the thought of it, seemed to glory in their own and the universal degradation. True, many, whose sense of justice was warped by despair, almost made excuses for the plague, implying that the women used the disease as a pretext for becoming prostitutes, and that they sought in the plague the justification of their shame.

But a more intimate knowledge of the disease subsequently revealed that such a suspicion was malicious. For the first to despair of their lot were the women; and I myself have heard many bewailing and cursing this pitiless plague which drove them, with an irresistible violence their feeble virtue was powerless to withstand, to prostitute themselves like bitches. Such, alas, is the nature of women, who often seek to buy with tears forgiveness for their deeds of shame,

372

and pity too. But in this case one must perforce forgive them and have pity on them.

If such was the lot of the women, no less piteous and horrible was that of the men. No sooner were they infected than they lost all self-respect. They lent themselves to the most ignoble transactions and committed the most sordid acts of self-abasement; they dragged themselves on all fours through the mire, kissing the boots of their 'liberators' (who were disgusted by such extreme and unasked-for abjectness), not only to obtain pardon for the sufferings and humiliations which they had undergone during the years of slavery and war, but so that they might have the honour of being trampled underfoot by their new masters; they spat on their own country's flag and publicly sold their own wives, daughters and mothers. They did all this, they said, to save their country. Yet those who seemed on the surface to be immune from the disease fell sick of a nauseating malady which made them ashamed of being Italians and even of belonging to the human race. It must be admitted that they did all they could to be unworthy of the name of men. Few indeed were those who remained free from taint, their consciences seemingly impervious to the disease; and they went about in fear and trembling, despised by all, unwelcome witnesses of the universal shame.

The suspicion, which later became a conviction, that the plague had been brought to Europe by the liberators themselves had filled the people with profound and heartfelt grief. Although it is an ancient tradition that the vanquished hate their conquerors, the people of Naples did not hate the Allies. They had awaited them with longing, they had welcomed them with joy. Their thousand-year-long experience of wars and foreign invasions had taught them that it is the habit of conquerors to reduce those whom they have vanquished to slavery. Instead of slavery, the Allies had brought them freedom. And the people had immediately loved these magnificent soldiers – so young, so handsome, so well groomed – whose teeth were so white and whose lips were so red. In all those centuries of invasions, of wars won and lost, Europe had never seen such elegant, clean, courteous soldiers. Always they were newly shaven; their uniforms were impeccable; their ties were tied with meticulous care; their shirts were always spotless; their shoes were eternally new and shining; they had never a tear in their trousers or at their elbows, never a button missing. Such were these wonderful armies, born, like Venus, of the sea foam. They contained not a soldier who had a boil, a decayed tooth, even a pimple on his face. Never had Europe seen soldiers who were so free from infection, without the smallest microbe either in the folds of their skin or in the recesses of their consciences. And what hands they had – white, well looked after, always protected by immaculate shammy-leather gloves! But what touched the people of Naples most of all was the kindliness of their liberators, especially the Americans: their urbane nonchalance, their humanity, their innocent, cordial smiles – the smiles of honest, goodhearted, ingenuous, overgrown boys. If ever it was an honour to lose a war, it was certainly a great honour for the people of Naples, and for all the other conquered peoples of Europe, to have lost this one to soldiers who were so courteous, elegant and neatly dressed, so goodhearted and generous.

And yet everything that these magnificent soldiers touched was at once corrupted. No sooner did the luckless inhabitants of the liberated countries grasp the hands of their liberators than they began to fester and to stink. It was enough that an Allied soldier should lean out of his jeep to smile at a woman, to give her face a fleeting caress, and

374

the same woman, who until that moment had preserved her dignity and purity, would change into a prostitute. It was enough that a child should put into its mouth a candy offered to it by an American soldier, and its innocent soul would be corrupted.

The liberators themselves were terrified and deeply affected by this dire scourge. 'It is human to feel compassion for the afflicted,' writes Boccaccio in his introduction to the *Decameron*, with reference to the terrible plague which swept Florence in 1348. But the Allied soldiers, especially the Americans, faced with the pitiable spectacle of the plague of Naples, did not only feel compassion for the unhappy people of that city: they felt compassion for themselves as well. The reason was that for some time past the suspicion had been growing in their ingenuous and honest minds that the source of the terrible contagion was in their frank, timid smiles, in their eyes, so full of human sympathy, in their affectionate caresses. The source of the plague was in their compassion, in their very desire to help these unfortunate people, to alleviate their miseries, to succour them in the tremendous disaster that had overtaken them. The source of the disease was in the very hand which they stretched out in brotherhood to this conquered people.

Perhaps it was written that the freedom of Europe must be born not of liberation, but of the plague. Perhaps it was written that, just as liberation had been born of the sufferings of war and slavery, so freedom must be born of the new and terrible sufferings caused by the plague which liberation had brought with it. The price of freedom is high – far higher than that of slavery. And it is not paid in gold, nor in blood, nor in the most noble sacrifices, but in cowardice, in prostitution, in treachery, and in everything that is rotten in the human soul.

On that day too we crossed the threshold of the *foyer du soldat*, and Jack, going up to the French sergeant, asked him timidly, almost in confidence, 'si on avait vu par là le lieutenant Lyautey.'

'Oui, mon colonel, je l'ai vu tout à l'heure,' replied the sergeant with a smile. 'Attendez un instant, mon colonel, je vais voir s'il est toujours là.'

'Voilà un sergent bien aimable,' said Jack to me, flushing with pleasure. 'Les sergents français sont les plus aimables sergents du monde.'

'Je regrette, mon colonel,' said the sergeant, coming back after a few moments, 'le lieutenant Lyautey vient justement de partir.'

'Merci, vous êtes bien aimable,' said Jack. 'Au revoir, mon ami.'

'Au revoir, mon colonel,' replied the sergeant with a smile.

'Ah, qu'il fait bon d'entendre parler français,' said Jack as he went out of the Caffè Caflisch. His face had lit up with childish joy, and at such moments I felt that I really loved him. I was glad to like a better man than myself. I had always despised or felt bitter toward better men than myself, and this was the first time I had ever been glad to like such a man.

'Let's go and look at the sea, Malaparte.'

Crossing the Piazza Reale, we descended the Scesa del Gigante and leaned on the parapet at the bottom. 'C'est un des plus anciens parapets de l'Europe,' said Jack, who knew the whole of Rimbaud by heart.

The sun was setting, and little by little the sea was turning the colour of wine, which is the colour of the sea in Homer. But in the distance, between Sorrento and Capri, the water and the high rugged cliffs, the mountains and their shadows were slowly taking on a flame-bright coral hue, as if the coral reefs which cover the bottom of the gulf were slowly emerging from the depths of the sea, tinging the sky blood-red with their reflected glory, as of old. Far away the barrier of Sorrento, thick with orchards, rose from the sea like a hard slab of green marble, which the sun, as it sank below the farther horizon, smote with its weary, oblique rays, bringing out the warm, golden glory of the oranges and the cold, bluish glitter of the lemons.

Like an ancient bone, thin and worn smooth by wind and rain, Vesuvius rose, solitary and naked, into the vast cloudless sky. Little by little it began to glow with a pink, furtive light, as if the fires within its womb were showing through its hard, pallid lava crust, which shone like ivory: until the moon broke the edge of the crater like an eggshell and rose clear and ecstatic, marvellously remote, into the blue abyss of the evening. From the farthermost horizon, as if borne on the wind, the first shadows of the night climbed into the sky. And whether on account of the magical limpidity of the moonlight, or of the cold cruelty of that unreal, ghostly scene, the moment had in it a delicate, fleeting sadness, like a presage of a happy death.

Ragged boys, seated on the stone parapet which rose sheer from the sea, sang with their eyes turned to the sky, their heads tilted slightly on to their shoulders. Their faces were pale and thin, their eyes blinded by hunger. They sang as the blind sing, their faces uplifted, their eyes fixed upon the heavens. Human hunger has a wonderfully sweet, pure voice. There is nothing human about the voice of hunger. It is a voice that arises from a mysterious level of man's nature, wherein lie the roots of that profound sense of life which is life itself, our most secret, most intense life. The air was clear and sweet to the lips. A light breeze, redolent of salt and seaweed, blew from the sea. The mournful cry of the gulls rippled the golden reflection of the moon upon the waves, and far away, low on the horizon, the pallid ghost of Vesuvius sank little by little into the silver mist of the night. That cruel, inhuman scene, so insensible to the hunger and despair of men, was made purer and less real by the singing of the boys.

'There is no kindliness,' said Jack, 'no compassion in this marvellous Nature.'

'It is malignant,' I said. 'It hates us, it is our enemy. It hates men.'

'Elle aime nous voir souffrir,' said Jack in a low voice.

'It stares at us with cold eyes, full of frozen hatred and contempt.'

'Before it,' said Jack, 'I feel guilty, ashamed, miserable. It is not Christian. It hates men because they suffer.'

'It is jealous of men's sufferings,' I said.

I liked Jack because he alone, among all my American friends, felt guilty, ashamed and miserable before the cruel, inhuman beauty of that sky, that sea, those islands far away on the horizon. He alone realized that this Nature is not Christian, that it lies outside the frontiers of Christianity, and that this scene was not the face of Christ, but the image of a world without God, in which men are left alone to suffer without hope. He alone realized how much mystery there is in the story and the lives of the people of Naples, and how their story and their lives are so little dependent on the will of man. There were, among my American friends, many intelligent, cultured and sensitive young men; but they despised Naples, Italy and Europe, they despised us because they believed that we alone were responsible for our miseries and misfortunes, our acts of cowardice, our crimes, our perfidies, our infamies. They did not understand what mystery and inhumanity there is behind our miseries and

378

our misfortunes. Some said: 'You are not Christians: you are pagans.' And there was a hint of scorn in their voices as they uttered the word 'pagans'. I liked Jack because he alone realized that the word 'pagan' does not in itself reveal the deep-seated, historic, mysterious causes of our suffering, and that our miseries, our misfortunes, our infamies, our way of being miserable and happy, the very reasons for our greatness and our degradation, are outside the realm of Christian ethics.

Although he called himself Cartesian, affecting to put his trust wholly and always in reason and to believe that reason can probe and explain everything, his attitude to Naples, Italy and Europe was one of affection tempered both with respect and with suspicion. To him, as to all Americans, Naples had been an unexpected and distressing revelation. He had believed he was setting foot in a world dominated by reason and ruled by the human conscience; and he had found himself without warning in a mysterious country, where men and the circumstances that make up their lives seemed to be governed not by reason and conscience, but by obscure subterranean forces.

Jack had travelled all over Europe, but he had never been to Italy. He had landed at Salerno on September 9, 1943, from the deck of an L.S.T. – a landing barge – amid the din and smoke of the explosions and the hoarse cries of the soldiers as they hobbled rapidly across the sands of Paestum under the fire of German machine guns. In his ideal Cartesian Europe, the *alte Kontinent* of Goethe, governed by mind and reason, Italy was still the land of his beloved Virgil and Horace. It suggested to his imagination the placid green and blue panorama of his own Virginia, where he had completed his studies and spent the better part of his life, and where he had his home, his family and his books. In the Italy of his

379

heart the peristyles of the Georgian houses of Virginia and the marble columns of the Forum, Mount Vernon and the Palatine combined in his mind's eye to form a familiar scene, in which the brilliant green of the fields and woods blended with the brilliant white of the marble under a limpid blue sky like that which stretches in an arch above the Capitol.

When, at dawn on September 9, 1943, Jack had leapt from the deck of an L.S.T. on to the beach at Paestum, near Salerno, he had seen a wonderful vision rising before his eyes through the red cloud of dust thrown up by the caterpillars of the tanks, the explosions of the German grenades and the tumult of the men and machines hurrying up from the sea. On the edge of a plain thickly covered with myrtles and cypresses, to which the bare mountains of Cilento, so like the mountains of Latium, provide a background, he had seemed to see the columns of the Temple of Neptune. Ah, this was Italy, the Italy of Virgil, the Italy of Aeneas! And he had wept for joy, he had wept with religious emotion, throwing himself on his knees upon the sandy shore, as Aeneas had done when he landed from the Trojan trireme on the sandy beach at the mouth of the Tiber, opposite the mountains of Latium, with their sprinkling of castles and white temples set amid the deep green of the ancient Latin woods.

But the classical setting of the Doric columns of the temples of Paestum concealed from his eyes a secret, mysterious Italy. It concealed Naples, that terrible, wonderful prototype of an unknown Europe, situated outside the realm of Cartesian logic – that *other* Europe of whose existence he had until that day had only a vague suspicion, and whose mysteries and secrets, now that he was gradually probing them, filled him with a wondrous terror.

'Naples,' I told him, 'is the most mysterious city in Europe. It is the only city of the ancient world that has

380

not perished like Ilium, Nineveh and Babylon. It is the only city in the world that did not founder in the colossal shipwreck of ancient civilization. Naples is a Pompeii which was never buried. It is not a city: it is a world – the ancient, pre-Christian world – that has survived intact on the surface of the modern world. You could not have chosen a more dangerous place than Naples for a landing in Europe. Your tanks run the risk of being swallowed up in the black slime of antiquity, as in a quicksand. If you had landed in Belgium, Holland, Denmark, or even in France, your scientific spirit, your technical knowledge, your vast wealth of material resources might have given you victory not merely over the German army, but over the very spirit of Europe – that *other*, secret Europe of which Naples is the mysterious image, the naked ghost. But here in Naples your tanks, your guns, your machines provoke a smile. They are scrap iron. Jack, do you remember the words of the Neapolitan who, on the day you entered Naples, was watching your endless columns of tanks passing along Via Toledo? '*What beautiful rust*!' Here, your particular American brand of humanity stands revealed in all its nakedness – defenceless, dangerously vulnerable. You are only big boys, Jack. You cannot understand Naples, you will never understand Naples.'

'Je crois,' said Jack, 'que Naples n'est pas impénétrable à la raison. Je suis cartésien, hélas!'

'Do you think, then, that Cartesian logic can help you, for instance, to understand Hitler?'

'Why particularly Hitler?'

'Because Hitler too is an element in the mystery of Europe, because Hitler too belongs to that *other* Europe which Cartesian logic cannot penetrate. Do you think, then, that you can explain Hitler solely with the help of Descartes?'

'Je l'explique parfaitement,' replied Jack.

Then I told him that Heidelberg *Witz* which all the students in the German universities laughingly pass from one to the other. At a conference of German scientists held at Heidelberg, all present found themselves agreed after lengthy discussion in asserting that the world can be explained with the aid of reason alone. At the end of the discussion an old professor, who until that moment had remained silent, with a silk hat jammed down over his eyes, got up and said: 'You who explain everything – could you tell me how on earth this thing has appeared on my head tonight?' And, slowly removing the silk hat, he revealed a cigar, a genuine Havana, which was projecting from his bald cranium.

'Ah, ah, c'est merveilleux!' said Jack, laughing. 'Do you mean, then, that Hitler is a Havana cigar?'

'No, I mean that Hitler is *like* that Havana cigar.'

'C'est merveilleux! un cigare!' said Jack; and he added, as though seized by a sudden inspiration, 'Have a drink, Malaparte.' But he corrected himself, and said in French: 'Allons boire quelque chose.'

The bar of the P.B.S. was crowded with officers who already had many glasses' start on us. We sat down in a corner and began to drink. Jack looked into his glass, and laughed; he banged his fist on his knee, and laughed; and every so often he exclaimed: 'C'est merveilleux! un cigare!' – until his eyes glazed over and he said to me, laughing – 'Tu crois vraiment qu'Hitler . . .'

'Mais oui, naturellement.'

Then we went in to supper, and sat down at the big table reserved for senior officers of the P.B.S. All the officers were in a merry mood, and they smiled at me sympathetically because I was 'the bastard Italian liaison officer, that bastard S.O.B'. At a certain point Jack began telling the story of the conference of German scientists at Heidelberg University, and all the senior officers of the P.B.S. looked at me in amazement, exclaiming: 'What? A cigar? Do you mean that Hitler is a cigar?'

'He means that Hitler is a Havana cigar,' said Jack, laughing.

And Colonel Brand, offering me a cigar across the table, said to me with a sympathetic smile: 'Do you like cigars? This is a genuine Havana.'

ANNA MARIA ORTESE

A PAIR OF
EYEGLASSES (1953)

Translated by Ann Goldstein and Jenny McPhee

'AS LONG AS there's the sun . . . the sun!' the voice of Don Peppino Quaglia crooned softly near the doorway of the low, dark, basement apartment. 'Leave it to God,' answered the humble and faintly cheerful voice of his wife, Rosa, from inside; she was in bed, moaning in pain from arthritis, complicated by heart disease, and, addressing her sister-in-law, who was in the bathroom, she added: 'You know what I'll do, Nunziata? Later I'll get up and take the clothes out of the water.'

'Do as you like, to me it seems real madness,' replied the curt, sad voice of Nunziata from that den. 'With the pain you have, one more day in bed wouldn't hurt you!' A silence. 'We've got to put out some more poison, I found a cockroach in my sleeve this morning.'

From the cot at the back of the room, which was really a cave, with a low vault of dangling spiderwebs, rose the small, calm voice of Eugenia:

'Mamma, today I'm putting on the eyeglasses.'

There was a kind of secret joy in the modest voice of the child, Don Peppino's third-born. (The first two, Carmela and Luisella, were with the nuns and would soon take the veil, having been persuaded that this life is a punishment; and the two little ones, Pasqualino and Teresella, were still snoring, as they slept feet to head, in their mother's bed.)

'Yes, and no doubt you'll break them right away,' the voice of her aunt, still irritated, insisted, from behind the door of the little room. She made everyone suffer for the disappointments of her life, first among them that she wasn't married and had to be subject, as she told it, to the charity of her sister-in-law, although she didn't fail to add that she dedicated this humiliation to God. She had something of her own set aside, however, and wasn't a bad person, since she had offered to have glasses made for Eugenia when at home they had realized that the child couldn't see. 'With what they cost! A grand total of a good eight thousand lire!' she added. Then they heard the water running in the basin. She was washing her face, squeezing her eyes, which were full of soap, and Eugenia gave up answering.

Besides, she was too, too pleased.

A week earlier, she had gone with her aunt to an optician on Via Roma. There, in that elegant shop, full of polished tables and with a marvelous green reflection pouring in through a blind, the doctor had measured her sight, making her read many times, through certain lenses that he kept changing, entire columns of letters of the alphabet, printed on a card, some as big as boxes, others as tiny as pins. 'This poor girl is almost blind,' he had said then, with a kind of pity, to her aunt, 'she should no longer be deprived of lenses.' And right away, while Eugenia, sitting on a stool, waited anxiously, he had placed over her eyes another pair of lenses, with a white metal frame, and had said: 'Now look into the street.' Eugenia stood up, her legs trembling with emotion, and was unable to suppress a little cry of joy. On the sidewalk, so many well-dressed people were passing, slightly smaller than normal but very distinct: ladies in silk dresses with pow- dered faces, young men with long hair and bright-colored sweaters, white-bearded old men with pink hands resting on silver-handled canes; and, in the middle of the street, some beautiful automobiles that looked like toys, their bodies painted red or teal, all shiny; green trolleys as big as houses, with their windows lowered, and behind the windows so many people in elegant clothes. Across the street, on the opposite sidewalk, were beautiful shops, with windows like mirrors, full of things so fine they elicited a kind of longing; some shop boys in black aprons were polishing the windows from the street. At a café with red and yellow tables, some golden-haired girls were sitting outside, legs crossed. They laughed and drank from big colored glasses. Above the café, because it was already spring, the balcony windows were open and embroidered curtains swayed, and behind the curtains were fragments of blue and gilded paintings, and heavy, sparkling chandeliers of gold and crystal, like baskets of artificial fruit. A marvel. Transported by all that splendor, she hadn't followed the conversation between the doctor and her aunt. Her aunt, in the brown dress she wore to Mass, and standing back from the glass counter with a timidity unnatural to her, now broached the question of the cost: 'Doctor, please, give us a good price . . . we're poor folk . . .' and when she heard 'eight thousand lire' she nearly fainted.

'Two lenses! What are you saying! Jesus Mary!'

'Look, ignorant people . . .' the doctor answered, replacing the other lenses after polishing them with the glove, 'don't calculate anything. And when you give the child two lenses, you'll be able to tell me if she sees better. She takes nine diopters on one side, and ten on the other, if you want to know . . . she's almost blind.'

While the doctor was writing the child's first and last name – 'Eugenia Quaglia, Vicolo della Cupa at Santa Maria in Portico' – Nunziata had gone over to Eugenia, who, standing in the doorway of the shop and holding up the glasses in her small, sweaty hands, was not at all tired of gazing through them: 'Look, look, my dear! See what your consolation costs! Eight thousand lire, did you hear? A grand total of a good eight thousand lire!' She was almost suffocating. Eugenia had turned all red, not so much because of the rebuke as because the young woman at the cash register was looking at her, while her aunt was making that observation, which declared the family's poverty. She took off the glasses.

'But how is it, so young and already so nearsighted?' the young woman had asked Nunziata, while she signed the receipt for the deposit. 'And so shabby, too!' she added.

'Young lady, in our house we all have good eyes, this is a misfortune that came upon us . . . along with the rest. God rubs salt in the wound.'

'Come back in eight days,' the doctor had said. 'I'll have them for you.'

Leaving, Eugenia had tripped on the step.

'Thank you, Aunt Nunzia,' she had said after a while. 'I'm always rude to you. I talk back to you, and you are so kind, buying me eyeglasses.'

Her voice trembled.

'My child, it's better not to see the world than to see it,' Nunziata had answered with sudden melancholy.

Eugenia hadn't answered her that time, either. Aunt Nunzia was often so strange, she wept and shouted for no good reason, she said so many bad words, and yet she went to Mass regularly, she was a good Christian, and when it came to helping someone in trouble she always volunteered, wholeheartedly. One didn't have to watch over her.

Since that day, Eugenia had lived in a kind of rapture, waiting for the blessed glasses that would allow her to see all people and things in their tiny details. Until then, she had been wrapped in a fog: the room where she lived, the courtyard always full of hanging laundry, the alley overflowing with colors and cries, everything for her was covered by a thin veil: she knew well only the faces of her family, especially her mother and her siblings, because often she slept with them, and sometimes she woke at night and, in the light of the oil lamp, looked at them. Her mother slept with her mouth open, her broken yellow teeth visible; her brother and sister, Pasqualino and Teresella, were always dirty and snot-nosed and covered with boils: when they slept, they made a strange noise, as if they had wild animals inside them. Sometimes Eugenia surprised herself by staring at them, without understanding, however, what she was thinking. She had a confused feeling that beyond that room always full of wet laundry, with broken chairs and a stinking toilet, there was light, sounds, beautiful things, and in that moment when she had put on the glasses she had had a true revelation: the world outside was beautiful, very beautiful.

'Marchesa, my respects.'

That was the voice of her father. Covered by a ragged shirt, his back, which until that moment had been framed by the doorway of the basement apartment, could no longer be seen. The voice of the marchesa, a placid and indifferent voice, now said:

'You must do me a favor, Don Peppino.'

'At your service . . . your wish is my command.'

Silently, Eugenia slid out of bed, put on her dress, and, still barefoot, went to the door. The pure and marvelous early morning sun, entering the ugly courtyard through a crack between the buildings, greeted her, lit up her little old lady's face, her stubbly, disheveled hair, her rough, hard little hands, with their long, dirty nails. Oh, if only at that moment she could have had the eyeglasses! The marchesa was there, in her black silk dress with its white lace neckpiece. Her imposing yet benign appearance enchanted Eugenia, along with her bejeweled white hands; but she couldn't see her face very well – it was a whitish oval patch. Above it, some purple feathers quivered.

'Listen, you have to redo the child's mattress. Can you come up around ten-thirty?'

'With all my heart, but I'm only available in the afternoon, Signora Marchesa.'

'No, Don Peppino, it has to be this morning. In the afternoon people are coming. Set yourself up on the terrace and work. Don't play hard to get . . . do me this favor . . . Now it's time for Mass. At ten-thirty, call me.'

And without waiting for an answer, she left, astutely avoiding a trickle of yellow water that was dripping down from a terrace and had made a puddle on the ground.

'Papa,' said Eugenia, following her father, as he went back inside, 'how good the marchesa is! She treats you like a gentleman. God should reward her for it.'

'A good Christian, that one is,' Don Peppino answered, with a meaning completely different from what might have been understood. With the excuse that she was the owner of the house, the Marchesa D'Avanzo constantly had the people in the courtyard serving her: to Don Peppino, she gave a wretched sum for the mattresses; and Rosa was always available for the big sheets; even if her bones were burning she had to get up to serve the marchesa. It's true that the marchesa had placed her daughters in the convent, and so had saved two souls from the dangers of this world, which for the poor are many, but for that basement space, where everyone was sick, she collected three thousand lire, not one less. 'The heart is there, it's the money that's lacking,' she loved to repeat, with a certain imperturbability. 'Today, dear Don Peppino, you are the nobility, who have no worries . . . Thank . . . thank Providence, which has put you in such a condition . . . which wanted to save you.' Donna Rosa had a kind of adoration for the marchesa, for her religious sentiments; when they saw each other, they always talked about the afterlife. The marchesa didn't much believe in it, but she didn't say so, and urged that mother of the family to be patient and to hope.

From the bed, Donna Rosa asked, a little worried: 'Did you talk to her?'

'She wants me to redo the mattress for her grandson,' said Don Peppino, in annoyance. He brought out the hot plate to warm up some coffee, a gift of the nuns, and went back inside to fetch water in a small pot. 'I won't do it for less than five hundred,' he said.

'It's a fair price.'

'And then who will go and pick up Eugenia's glasses?' Aunt Nunzia asked, coming out of the bathroom. Over her nightgown, she wore a torn skirt, and on her feet slippers. Her bony shoulders emerged from the nightgown, gray as stones. She was drying her face with a napkin. 'I can't go, and Rosa is ill.'

Without anyone noticing, Eugenia's large, almost blind eyes filled with tears. Now maybe another day would pass without her eyeglasses. She went up to her mother's bed, and in a pitiful manner, flung her arms and forehead on the blanket. Donna Rosa stretched out a hand to caress her.

'I'll go, Nunzia, don't get worked up . . . In fact, going out will do me good.'

'Mamma . . .'

Eugenia kissed her hand.

Around eight there was a great commotion in the courtyard. At that moment Rosa had come out of the doorway: a tall, lanky figure, in a short, stained black coat, without shoulder pads, that exposed her legs, like wooden sticks. Under her arm, she carried a shopping bag for the bread she would buy on her way home from the optician. Don Peppino was pushing the water out of the middle of the courtyard with a long-handled broom, a vain task because the tub was continually leaking, like an open vein. In it were the clothes of two families: the Greborio sisters, on the second floor, and the wife of Cavaliere Amodio, who had given birth two days earlier. The Greborios' servant, Lina Tarallo, was beating the carpets on a balcony, making a terrible ruckus. The dust, mixed with garbage, descended gradually like a cloud on those poor people, but no one paid attention. Sharp screams and cries of complaint could be heard from the basement where Aunt Nunzia was calling on all the saints as witnesses to confirm that she was unfortunate, and the cause of all this was Pasqualino, who wept and shouted like a condemned man because he wanted to go with his mamma. 'Look at him, this scoundrel,' cried Aunt Nunzia. '*Madonna bella*, do me a favor, let me die, but immediately, if you're there, since in this life only thieves and whores thrive.' Teresella, born the year the king went away and so younger than her brother, was sitting in the doorway, smiling, and every so often she licked a crust of bread she had found under a chair.

Eugenia was sitting on the step of another basement room, where Mariuccia the porter lived, looking at a section of a children's comic, with lots of bright-colored figures, which had fallen from the fourth floor. She held it right up to her face, because otherwise she couldn't read the words. There was a small blue river in a vast meadow and a red boat going ... going ... who knows where. It was written in proper Italian, and so she didn't understand much, but every so often, for no reason, she laughed.

'So, today you put on your glasses?' said Mariuccia, looking out from behind her. Everyone in the courtyard knew, partly because Eugenia hadn't resisted the temptation to talk about it, and partly because Aunt Nunzia had found it necessary to let it be understood that in that family she was spending her own . . . and well, in short . . .

'Your aunt got them for you, eh?' Mariuccia added, smiling good-humoredly. She was a small woman, almost a dwarf, with a face like a man's, covered with whiskers. At the moment she was combing her long black hair, which came to her knees: one of the few things that attested to her being a woman. She was combing it slowly, smiling with her sly but kind little mouse eyes.

'Mamma went to get them on Via Roma,' said Eugenia with a look of gratitude. 'We paid a grand total of a good eight thousand lire, you know? Really . . . my aunt is . . .' she was about to add 'truly a good person,' when Aunt Nunzia, looking out of the basement room, called angrily: 'Eugenia!'

'Here I am, Aunt!' and she scampered away like a dog.

Behind their aunt, Pasqualino, all red-faced and bewildered, with a terrible expression somewhere between disdain and surprise, was waiting.

'Go and buy two candies for three lire each, from Don Vincenzo at the tobacco store. Come back immediately!'

'Yes, Aunt.'

She clutched the money in her fist, paying no more attention to the comic, and hurried out of the courtyard.

By a true miracle she avoided a towering vegetable cart drawn by two horses, which was coming toward her right outside the main entrance. The carter, with his whip unsheathed, seemed to be singing, and from his mouth came these words: 'Lovely . . . Fresh,' drawn out and full of sweetness, like a love song. When the cart was behind her, Eugenia, raising her protruding eyes, basked in that warm blue glow that was the sky, and heard the great hubbub all around her, without, however, seeing it clearly. Carts, one behind the other, big trucks with Americans dressed in yellow hanging out the windows, bicycles that seemed to be tumbling over. High up, all the balconies were cluttered with flower crates, and over the railings, like flags or saddle blankets, hung yellow and red quilts, ragged blue children's clothes, sheets, pillows, and mattresses exposed to the air, while at the end of the alley ropes uncoiled, lowering baskets to pick up the vegetables or fish offered by peddlers. Although the sun touched only the highest balconies (the street a crack in the disorderly mass of buildings) and the rest was only shadow and garbage, one could sense, behind it, the enormous celebration of spring. And even Eugenia, so small and pale, bound like a mouse to the mud of her courtyard, began to breathe rapidly, as if that air, that celebration, and all that blue suspended over the neighborhood of the poor were also hers. The yellow basket of the Amodios' maid, Rosaria Buonincontri, grazed her as she went into the tobacco shop. Rosaria was a fat woman in black, with white legs and a flushed, placid face.

'Tell your mamma if she can come upstairs a moment today, Signora Amodio needs her to deliver a message.'

Eugenia recognized her by her voice. 'She's not here now. She went to Via Roma to get my glasses.'

'I should wear them, too, but my boyfriend doesn't want me to.'

Eugenia didn't grasp the meaning of that prohibition. She answered only, ingenuously: 'They cost a great amount; you have to take very good care of them.'

They entered Don Vincenzo's hole-in-the-wall together.

There was a crowd. Eugenia kept being pushed back. 'Go on . . . you really are blind,' observed the Amodios' maid, with a kind smile.

'But now Aunt Nunzia's gotten you some eyeglasses,' Don Vincenzo, who had heard her, broke in, winking, with an air of teasing comprehension. He, too, wore glasses.

'At your age,' he said, handing her the candies, 'I could see like a cat, I could thread needles at night, my grandmother always wanted me nearby . . . but now I'm old.'

Eugenia nodded vaguely. 'My friends . . . none of them have lenses,' she said. Then, turning to the servant Rosaria, but speaking also for Don Vincenzo's benefit: 'Just me . . . Nine diopters on one side and ten on the other . . . I am almost blind!' she said emphatically, sweetly.

'See how lucky you are,' said Don Vincenzo, smiling, and to Rosaria: 'How much salt?'

'Poor child!' the Amodios' maid commented as Eugenia left, happily. 'It's the dampness that's ruined her. In that building it rains on us. Now Donna Rosa's bones ache. Give me a kilo of coarse salt and a packet of fine . . .'

'There you are.'

'What a morning, eh, today, Don Vincenzo? It seems like summer already.'

Walking more slowly than she had on the way there, Eugenia, without even realizing it, began to unwrap one of the two candies, and then put it in her mouth. It tasted of lemon. 'I'll tell Aunt Nunzia that I lost it on the way,' she proposed to herself. She was happy, it didn't matter to her if her aunt, good as she was, got angry. She felt someone take her hand, and recognized Luigino.

'You are really blind!' the boy said laughing. 'And the glasses?'

'Mamma went to Via Roma to get them.'

'I didn't go to school; it's a beautiful day, why don't we take a little walk?'

'You're crazy! Today I have to be good.'

Luigino looked at her and laughed, with his mouth like a money box, stretching to his ears, contemptuous.

'What a rat's nest.'

Instinctively Eugenia brought a hand to her hair.

'I can't see well, and Mamma doesn't have time,' she answered meekly.

'What are the glasses like? With gold frames?' Luigino asked.

'All gold!' Eugenia answered, lying. 'Bright and shiny!'

'Old women wear glasses,' said Luigino.

'Also ladies, I saw them on Via Roma.'

'Those are dark glasses, for sunbathing,' Luigino insisted.

'You're just jealous. They cost eight thousand lire.'

'When you have them, let me see them,' said Luigino. 'I want to see if the frame really is gold. You're such a liar,' and he went off on his own business, whistling.

Reentering the courtyard, Eugenia wondered anxiously if her glasses would or wouldn't have a gold frame. In the negative case, what could she say to Luigino to convince him that they were a thing of value? But what a beautiful day! Maybe Mamma was about to return with the glasses wrapped in a package. Soon she would have them on her face. She would have . . . A frenzy of blows fell on her head. A real fury. She seemed to collapse; in vain she defended herself with her hands. It was Aunt Nunzia, of course, furious because of her delay, and behind Aunt Nunzia was Pasqualino, like a madman, because he didn't believe her story about the candies. 'Bloodsucker! You ugly little blind girl! And I who gave my life for this ingratitude . . . You'll

398

come to a bad end! Eight thousand lire no less. They bleed me dry, these scoundrels.'

She let her hands fall, only to burst into a great lament. 'Our Lady of Sorrows, holy Jesus, by the wounds in your ribs let me die!'

Eugenia wept, too, in torrents.

'Aunt, forgive me. Aunt . . .'

'Uh . . . uh . . . uh . . .' said Pasqualino, his mouth wide open.

'Poor child,' said Donna Mariuccia, coming over to Eugenia, who didn't know where to hide her face, now streaked with red and tears at her aunt's rage. 'She didn't do it on purpose, Nunzia, calm down,' and to Eugenia: 'Where've you got the candies?'

Eugenia answered softly, hopelessly, holding out one in her dirty hand: 'I ate the other. I was hungry.'

Before her aunt could move again, to attack the child, the voice of the marchesa could be heard, from the fourth floor, where there was sun, calling softly, placidly, sweetly:

'Nunziata!'

Aunt Nunzia looked up, her face pained as that of the Madonna of the Seven Sorrows, which was at the head of her bed.

'Today is the first Friday of the month. Dedicate it to God.'

'Marchesa, how good you are! These kids make me commit so many sins, I'm losing my mind, I . . .' And she collapsed her face between her paw like hands, the hands of a worker, with brown, scaly skin.

'Is your brother not there?'

'Poor Aunt, she got you the eyeglasses, and that's how you thank her,' said Mariuccia meanwhile to Eugenia, who was trembling.

'Yes, signora, here I am,' answered Don Peppino, who until that moment had been half hidden behind the door of the basement room, waving a paper in front of the stove where the beans for lunch were cooking.

'Can you come up?'

'My wife went to get the eyeglasses for Eugenia. I'm watching the beans. Would you wait, if you don't mind.'

'Then send up the child. I have a dress for Nunziata. I want to give it to her.'

'May God reward you . . . very grateful,' answered Don Peppino, with a sigh of consolation, because that was the only thing that could calm his sister. But looking at Nunziata, he realized that she wasn't at all cheered up. She continued to weep desperately, and that weeping had so stunned Pasqualino that the child had become quiet as if by magic, and was now licking the snot that dripped from his nose, with a small, sweet smile.

'Did you hear? Go up to the Signora Marchesa, she has a dress to give you,' said Don Peppino to his daughter.

Eugenia was looking at something in the void, with her eyes that couldn't see: they were staring, fixed and large. She winced, and got up immediately, obedient.

'Say to her: "May God reward you," and stay outside the door.'

'Yes, Papa.'

'Believe me, Mariuccia,' said Aunt Nunzia, when Eugenia had gone off, 'I love that little creature, and afterward I'm sorry, as God is my witness, for scolding her. But I feel all the blood go to my head, believe me, when I have to fight with the kids. Youth is gone, as you see,' and she touched her hollow cheeks. 'Sometimes I feel like a madwoman.'

'On the other hand, they have to vent, too,' Donna Mariuccia answered. 'They're innocent souls. They need time to weep. When I look at them, and think how they'll become just like us.' She went to get a broom and swept a cabbage leaf out of the doorway. 'I wonder what God is doing.'

'It's new, brand-new! You hardly wore it!' said Eugenia, sticking her nose in the green dress lying on the sofa in the kitchen, while the marchesa went looking for an old newspaper to wrap it in.

The marchesa thought that the child really couldn't see, because otherwise she would have realized that the dress was very old and full of patches (it had belonged to her dead sister), but she refrained from commenting. Only after a moment, as she was coming in with the newspaper, she asked:

'And the eyeglasses your aunt got you? Are they new?'

'With gold frames. They cost eight thousand lire,' Eugenia answered all in one breath, becoming emotional again at the thought of the honor she had received, 'because I'm almost blind,' she added simply.

'In my opinion,' said the marchesa, carefully wrapping the dress in the newspaper, and then reopening the package because a sleeve was sticking out, 'your aunt could have saved her money. I saw some very good eyeglasses in a shop near the Church of the Ascension, for only two thousand lire.'

Eugenia blushed fiery red. She understood that the marchesa was displeased. 'Each to his own position in life. We all must know our limitations,' she had heard her say this many times, talking to Donna Rosa, when she brought her the washed clothes, and stayed to complain of her poverty.

'Maybe they weren't good enough. I have nine diopters,' she replied timidly.

The marchesa arched an eyebrow, but luckily Eugenia didn't see it.

'They were good, I'm telling you,' the Marchesa said obstinately, in a slightly harsher voice. Then she was sorry. 'My dear,' she said more gently, 'I'm saying this because I know the troubles you have in your household. With that difference of six thousand lire, you could buy bread for ten days, you could buy . . . What's the use to you of seeing better? Given what's around you!' A silence. 'To read, maybe, but do you read?'

'No, signora.'

'But sometimes I've seen you with your nose in a book. A liar as well, my dear. That is no good.'

Eugenia didn't answer again. She felt truly desperate, staring at the dress with her nearly white eyes.

'Is it silk?' she asked stupidly.

The marchesa looked at her, reflecting.

'You don't deserve it, but I want to give you a little gift,' she said suddenly, and headed toward a white wooden wardrobe. At that moment the telephone, which was in the hall, began to ring, and instead of opening the wardrobe the marchesa went to answer it. Eugenia, oppressed by those words, hadn't even heard the old woman's consoling allusion, and as soon as she was alone she began to look around as far as her poor eyes allowed her. How many fine, beautiful things! Like the store on Via Roma! And there, right in front of her, an open balcony with a lot of small pots of flowers.

She went out onto the balcony. How much air, how much blue! The apartment buildings seemed to be covered by a blue veil, and below was the alley, like a ravine, with so many ants coming and going . . . like her relatives. What were they doing? Where were they going? They went in and out of their holes, carrying big crumbs of bread, they were doing this now, had done it yesterday, would do it tomorrow, forever, forever. So many holes, so many ants. And around them, almost invisible in the great light, the world made by God, with the wind, the sun, and out there the purifying sea, so vast . . . She was standing there, her chin planted on the iron railing, suddenly thoughtful, with an expression of sorrow, of bewilderment, that made her look ugly. She heard the sound of the marchesa's voice, calm, pious. In her hand, in her smooth ivory hand, the marchesa was holding a small book covered in black paper with gilt letters.

'It's the thoughts of the saints, my dear. The youth of today don't read anything, and so the world has changed course. Take it, I'm giving it to you. But you must promise to read a little every evening, now that you've got your glasses.'

'Yes, signora,' said Eugenia, in a hurry, blushing again because the marchesa had found her on the balcony, and she took the book. Signora D'Avanzo regarded her with satisfaction.

'God wished to save you, my dear!' she said, going to get the package with the dress and placing it in her hands. 'You're not pretty, anything but, and you already appear to be an old lady. God favors you, because looking like that you won't have opportunities for evil. He wants you to be holy, like your sisters!'

Although the words didn't really wound her, because she had long been unconsciously prepared for a life without joy, Eugenia was nevertheless disturbed by them. And it seemed to her, if only for a moment, that the sun no longer shone as before, and even the thought of the eyeglasses ceased to cheer her. She looked vaguely, with her nearly dead eyes, at a point on the sea, where the Posillipo peninsula extended like a faded green lizard. 'Tell Papa,' the marchesa continued, meanwhile, 'that we won't do anything about the child's mattress today. My cousin telephoned, and I'll be in Posillipo all day.'

'I was there once, too . . .' Eugenia began, reviving at that name and looking, spellbound, in that direction.

'Yes? Is that so?' Signora D'Avanzo was indifferent, the name of that place meant nothing special to her. In her magisterial fashion, she accompanied the child, who was still looking toward that luminous point, to the door, closing it slowly behind her.

As Eugenia came down the last step and out into the courtyard, the shadow that had been darkening her forehead for a while disappeared, and her mouth opened in a joyful laugh, because she had seen her mother arriving. It wasn't hard to recognize that worn, familiar figure. She threw the dress on a chair and ran toward her.

'Mamma! The eyeglasses!'

'Gently, my dear, you'll knock me over!'

Immediately, a small crowd formed. Donna Mariuccia, Don Peppino, one of the Greborios, who had stopped to rest on a chair before starting up the stairs, the Amodios' maid, who was just then returning, and, of course, Pasqualino and Teresella, who wanted to see, too, and yelled, holding out their hands. Nunziata, for her part, was observing the dress that she had taken out of the newspaper, with a disappointed expression.

'Look, Mariuccia, it's an old rag . . . all worn out under the arms!' she said, approaching the group. But who was paying attention to her? At that moment, Donna Rosa was extracting from a pocket in her dress the eyeglass case, and with infinite care opened it. On Donna Rosa's long red hand, a kind of very shiny insect with two giant eyes and two curving antennae glittered in a pale ray of sun amid those poor people, full of admiration.

'Eight thousand lire ... a thing like that!' said Donna Rosa, gazing at the eyeglasses religiously, and yet with a kind of rebuke.

Then, in silence, she placed them on Eugenia's face, as the child ecstatically held out her hands, and carefully arranged the two antennae behind her ears. 'Now can you see?' Donna Rosa asked with great emotion.

Gripping the eyeglasses with her hands, as if in fear that they would be taken away from her, her eyes half closed and her mouth half open in a rapt smile, Eugenia took two steps backward, and stumbled on a chair.

'Good luck!' said the Amodios' maid.

'Good luck!' said the Greborio sister.

'She looks like a schoolteacher, doesn't she?' Don Peppino observed with satisfaction.

'Not even a thank you!' said Aunt Nunzia, looking bitterly at the dress. 'With all that, good luck!'

'She's afraid, my little girl!' murmured Donna Rosa, heading toward the door of the basement room to put down her things. 'She's put on the eyeglasses for the first time!' she said, looking up at the first-floor balcony, where the other Greborio sister was looking out.

'I see everything very tiny,' said Eugenia, in a strange voice, as if she were speaking from under a chair. 'Black, very black.'

'Of course: the lenses are double. But do you see clearly?' asked Don Peppino. 'That's the important thing. She's put on the glasses for the first time,' he, too, said, addressing Cavaliere Amodio, who was passing by, holding an open newspaper.

'I'm warning you,' the cavaliere said to Mariuccia, after staring at Eugenia for a moment, as if she were merely a cat, 'that stairway hasn't been swept. I found some fish bones in front of the door!' And he went on, bent over, almost enfolded in his newspaper, reading an article about a proposal for a new pension law that interested him.

Eugenia, still holding on to the eyeglasses with her hands, went to the entrance to the courtyard to look outside into Vicolo della Cupa. Her legs were trembling, her head was spinning, and she no longer felt any joy. With her white lips she wished to smile, but that smile became a moronic grimace. Suddenly the balconies began to multiply, two thousand, a hundred thousand; the carts piled with vegetables were falling on her; the voices filling the air, the cries, the lashes, struck her head as if she were ill; she turned, swaying, toward the courtyard, and that terrible impression intensified. The courtyard was like a sticky funnel, with the narrow end toward the sky, its leprous walls crowded with derelict balconies; the arches of the basement dwellings black, with the lights bright in a circle around Our Lady of Sorrows; the pavement white with soapy water; the cabbage leaves, the scraps of paper, the garbage and, in the middle of the courtyard, that group of ragged, deformed souls, faces pocked by poverty and resignation, who looked at her lovingly. They began to writhe, to become mixed up, to grow larger. They all came toward her, in the two bewitched circles of the eyeglasses. It was Mariuccia who first realized that the child was sick, and she tore off the glasses, because Eugenia, doubled over and moaning, was throwing up.

'They've gone to her stomach!' cried Mariuccia, holding her forehead. 'Bring a coffee bean, Nunziata!'

'A grand total of a good eight thousand lire!' cried Aunt Nunzia, her eyes popping out of her head, running into the basement room to get a coffee bean from a can in the cupboard; and she held up the new eyeglasses, as if to ask God for an explanation. 'And now they're wrong, too!'

'It's always like that, the first time,' said the Amodios' maid to Donna Rosa calmly. 'You mustn't be shocked; little by little one gets used to them.'

'It's nothing, child, nothing, don't be scared!' But Donna Rosa felt her heart constrict at the thought of how unlucky they were.

Aunt Nunzia returned with the coffee bean, still crying: 'A grand total of a good eight thousand lire!' while Eugenia, pale as death, tried in vain to throw up, because she had nothing left inside her. Her bulging eyes were almost crossed with suffering, and her old lady's face was bathed in tears, as if stupefied. She leaned on her mother and trembled.

'Mamma, where are we?'

'We're in the courtyard, my child,' said Donna Rosa patiently; and the fine smile, between pity and wonder, that illuminated her eyes, suddenly lit up the faces of all those wretched people.

'She's half-blind!'

'She's a half-wit, she is!'

'Leave her alone, poor child, she's dazed,' said Donna Mariuccia, and her face was grim with pity, as she went back into the basement apartment that seemed to her darker than usual.

Only Aunt Nunzia was wringing her hands:

'A grand total of a good eight thousand lire!'

ELSA MORANTE

From

ARTURO'S
ISLAND (1957)

Translated by Ann Goldstein

CHAPTER I

KING AND STAR OF THE SKY

. . . Paradise
lofty and chaotic . . .
— SANDRO PENNA, *POESIE*

King and Star of the Sky

ONE OF MY first glories was my name. I had learned early (*he*, it seems to me, was the first to inform me) that Arturo – Arcturus – is a star: the swiftest and brightest light in the constellation of Boötes, the Herdsman, in the northern sky! And that this name was also borne by a king in ancient times, the commander of a band of faithful followers: all heroes, like the king himself, and treated by the king as equals, as brothers.

Unfortunately, I later discovered that that famous Arthur, King of Britain, was not a true story, only a legend; and so I abandoned him for other, more historical kings (in my opinion legends were childish). Still, another reason was enough in itself for me to give a noble value to the name Arturo: and that is, that it was my mother, I learned, who, although I think ignorant of the aristocratic symbolism, decided on that name. Who was herself simply an illiterate young woman but for me more than a sovereign.

In reality, I knew almost nothing about her, for she wasn't even eighteen when she died, at the moment that I, her only child, was born. And the sole image of her I ever knew was a portrait on a postcard. A faded, ordinary, almost ghostlike figure, but the object of fantastic adoration for my entire childhood.

The poor itinerant photographer to whom we owe this unique image portrayed her in the first months of her pregnancy. You can tell from her body, even amid the folds of the loose-fitting dress, that she's pregnant; and she holds her little hands clasped in front of her, as if to hide herself, in a timid, modest pose. She's very serious, and in her black eyes you can read not only submissiveness, which is usual in most of our girls and young village brides, but a stunned and slightly fearful questioning. As if, among the common illusions of maternity, she already suspected that her destiny would be death and eternal ignorance.

The Island

ALL THE ISLANDS of our archipelago, here in the Bay of Naples, are beautiful.

For the most part, the land is of volcanic origin, and, especially near the ancient craters, thousands of flowers grow wild: I've never seen anything like it on the mainland. In spring, the hills are covered with broom: traveling on the sea in the month of June you recognize its wild, caressing odor as soon as you approach our harbors.

Up in the hills in the countryside, my island has solitary narrow roads enclosed between ancient walls, behind which orchards and vineyards extend, like imperial gardens. It has several beaches with pale, fine sand, and other, smaller shores, covered with pebbles and shells, hidden amid high cliffs. In those towering rocks, which loom over the water, seagulls and turtledoves make their nests, and you can hear their voices, especially in the early morning, sometimes lamenting, sometimes gay. There, on quiet days, the sea is gentle and cool, and lies on the shore like dew. Ah, I wouldn't ask to be a seagull or a dolphin; I'd be content to be a scorpion fish, the ugliest fish in the sea, just to be down there, playing in that water.

Around the port, the streets are all sunless alleys, lined with plain, centuries-old houses, which, although painted in beautiful pink or grayish shell colors, look severe and melancholy. On the sills of the small windows, which are almost as narrow as loopholes, you sometimes see a carnation growing in a tin can, or a little cage that seems fit for a cricket but holds a captured turtledove. The shops are as deep and dark as brigands' dens. In the café at the port, there's a coal stove on which the owner boils Turkish coffee, in a deep blue enameled coffeepot. She's been a widow for many years, and always wears the black of mourning, the black shawl, the black earrings. A photograph of the deceased, on the wall beside the cash register, is festooned with dusty leaves.

The innkeeper, in his tavern, which is opposite the monument of Christ the Fisherman, is raising an owl, chained to a plank high up against the wall. The owl has delicate black and gray feathers, an elegant tuft on his head, blue eyelids, and big eyes of a red-gold color, circled with black; he always has a bleeding wing, because he constantly pecks at it with his beak. If you stretch out a hand to give him a little tickle on the chest, he bends his small head toward you, with an expression of wonder.

When evening descends, he starts to struggle, tries to take

off, and falls back, and sometimes ends up hanging head down, flapping on his chain.

In the church at the port, the oldest on the island, there are some wax saints, less than three palms high, locked in glass cases. They have skirts of real lace, yellowed, faded cloaks of brocatelle, real hair, and from their wrists hang tiny rosaries of real pearls. On their small fingers, which have a deathly pallor, the nails are sketched with a threadlike red line.

Those elegant pleasure boats and cruise ships that in greater and greater numbers crowd the other ports of the archipelago hardly ever dock at ours; here you'll see some barges or merchant ships, besides the fishing boats of the islanders. For many hours of the day the square at the port seems almost deserted; on the left, near the statue of Christ the Fisherman, a single carriage for hire awaits the arrival of the regularly scheduled steamers, which stop here for a few minutes and disembark three or four passengers alto-gether, mostly people from the island. Never, not even in summer, do our solitary beaches experience the commotion of the bathers from Naples and other cities, and all parts of the world, who throng the beaches of the surrounding areas. And if a stranger happens to get off at Procida, he marvels at not finding here that open and happy life, of celebrations and conversations on the street, of song and the strains of guitars or mandolins, for which the region of Naples is known throughout the world. The Procidans are surly, taciturn. All the doors are closed, almost no one looks out the window, every family lives within its four walls and doesn't mingle with the others. Friendship, among us, isn't welcomed. And the arrival of a stranger arouses not curiosity but, rather, distrust. If he asks questions, they are answered reluctantly, because the people of my island don't like their privacy spied on.

They are a small dark race, with elongated black eyes, like Orientals. And they so closely resemble one another you might say they're all related. The women, following ancient custom, live cloistered like nuns. Many of them still wear their hair coiled, shawls over their heads, long dresses, and, in winter, clogs over thick black cotton stockings; in summer some go barefoot. When they pass barefoot, rapid and noiseless, avoiding encounters, they might be feral cats or weasels.

They never go to the beach; for women it's a sin to swim in the sea, and a sin even to watch others swimming.

In books, the houses of ancient feudal cities, grouped together or scattered through the valley and across the hillsides, all in sight of the castle that dominates them from the highest peak, are often compared to a flock around the shepherd. Thus, too, on Procida, the houses – from those densely crowded at the port, to the ones spread out on the hills, and the isolated country farmhouses – appear, from a distance, exactly like a herd scattered at the foot of the castle. This castle rises on the highest hill (which among the other, smaller hills is like a mountain); and, enlarged by structures superimposed and added over the centuries, has acquired the mass of a gigantic citadel. To passing ships, especially at night, all that appears of Procida is this dark mass, which makes our island seem like a fortress in the middle of the sea.

For around two hundred years, the castle has been used as a penitentiary: one of the biggest, I believe, in the whole country. For many people who live far away the name of my island means the name of a prison.

On the western side, which faces the sea, my house is in sight of the castle, but at a distance of several hundred meters as the crow flies, and over numerous small inlets from which, at night, the fishermen set out in their boats with lanterns lighted. At that distance you can't distinguish the bars on the windows, or the circuit of the guards around the walls; so that, especially in winter, when the air is misty and the moving clouds pass in front of it, the penitentiary might seem the kind of abandoned castle you find in many old cities. A fantastic ruin, inhabited only by snakes, owls, and swallows.

The Story of Romeo the Amalfitano

MY HOUSE RISES alone at the top of a steep hill, in the middle of an uncultivated terrain scattered with lava pebbles. The façade looks toward the town, and on that side the hill is buttressed by an old wall made of pieces of rock; here lives the deep blue lizard (which is found nowhere else, nowhere else in the world). On the right, a stairway of stones and earth descends toward the level ground where vehicles can go.

Behind the house there is a broad open space, beyond which the land becomes steep and impassable. And by means of a long rockslide you reach a small, triangular, black-sand beach. No path leads to this beach; but, if you're barefoot, it's easy to descend precipitously amid the rocks. At the bottom a single boat was moored: it was mine, and was called *Torpedo Boat of the Antilles*.

My house isn't far from a small, almost urban square (boasting, among other things, a marble monument) or from the densely built dwellings of the town. But in my memory it has become an isolated place, and its solitude makes an enormous space around it. There it sits, malign and marvelous, like a golden spider that has woven its iridescent web over the whole island.

It's a two-story palazzo, plus the cellar and the attic (in

Procida houses that have around twenty rooms, which in Naples might seem small, are called palazzi), and, as with most of the inhabited area of Procida, which is very old, it was built at least three centuries ago.

It's a pale pink color, square, rough, and constructed without elegance; it would look like a large farmhouse if not for the majestic central entrance and the Baroque-style grilles that protect all the windows on the outside. The façade's only ornaments are two iron balconies, suspended on either side of the entrance, in front of two blind windows. These balconies, and also the grilles, were once painted white, but now they're all stained and corroded by rust.

A smaller door is cut into one panel of the central entrance door, and this is the way we usually go in: the two panels are, instead, never opened, and the enormous locks that bolt them from the inside have been eaten by rust and are unusable. Through the small door you enter a long, windowless hall, paved with slate, at the end of which, in the style of Procida's grand houses, a gate opens to an internal garden. This gate is guarded by two statues of very faded painted terra-cotta, portraying two hooded figures, which could be either monks or Saracens, you can't tell. And, beyond the gate, the garden, enclosed by the walls of the house like a courtyard, appears a triumph of wild greenery.

There, under the beautiful carob tree, my dog Immacolatella is buried.

From the roof of the house, one can see the full shape of the island, which resembles a dolphin, its small inlets, the penitentiary, and not far away, on the sea, the bluish purple form of the island of Ischia. The silvery shadows of more distant islands. And, at night, the firmament, where Boötes the Herdsman walks, with his star Arturo.

From the day it was built, for more than two centuries,

the house was a monastery; this fact is common among us, and there's nothing romantic about it. Procida was always a place of poor fishermen and farmers, and its rare grand buildings were all, inevitably, either convents, or churches, or fortresses, or prisons.

Later, those religious men moved elsewhere, and the house ceased to belong to the Church. For a certain period, during and after the wars of the past century, it housed regiments of soldiers; then it was abandoned and uninhabited for a long time; and finally, about half a century ago, it was bought by a private citizen, a wealthy shipping agent from Amalfi, who, passing through Procida, made it his home, and lived there in idleness for thirty years.

He transformed part of the interior, especially the upper floor, where he knocked down the dividing walls between numerous cells of the former monastery and covered the walls with wallpaper. Even in my time, although the house was run-down and in constant disrepair, it preserved the arrangement and the furnishings as he had left them. The furniture, which had been collected by a picturesque but ignorant imagination from the small antique and secondhand dealers of Naples, gave the rooms a certain romantic-country aspect. Entering, you had the illusion of a past of grandmothers and great-grandmothers, of ancient female secrets.

And yet from the time those walls were erected until the year our family arrived, they had never seen a woman.

When, a little more than twenty years ago, my paternal grandfather, Antonio Gerace, who had emigrated from Procida, returned with a modest fortune from America, the Amalfitano, who by then was an old man, still lived in the ancient palazzo. In old age, he had become blind; and it was said that this was a punishment from Santa Lucia, because he hated women. He had hated them since youth, to the point that he wouldn't receive even his own sisters, and when the Sisters of the Consolation came to beg he left them outside the door. For that reason, he had never married; and he was never seen in church, or in the shops, where women are more readily encountered.

He wasn't hostile to society; in fact, he had quite a splendid character, and often gave banquets, and even masked parties, and on such occasions he proved to be generous to the point of madness, so that he had become a legend on the island. However, no woman was admitted to his entertainments; and the girls of Procida, envious of their boyfriends and brothers who took part in those mysterious evenings, spitefully nicknamed the Amalfitano's abode the Casa dei Guaglioni, or Boys' House (*guaglione*, in Neapolitan dialect, means boy or youth).

My grandfather Antonio, disembarking in his homeland after some decades of absence, did not think that destiny had reserved the Casa dei Guaglioni for his family. He scarcely recalled the Amalfitano, with whom he had never had a friendly relationship; and that old monastery-barracks among the thorns and prickly pears did not in the least resemble the dwelling he had dreamed of for himself during his exile. He bought a house in the country, with a farm, in the southern part of the island, and went to live there, alone with his tenant farmers, being a bachelor with no close relatives.

Actually, there existed on the earth one close relative of Antonio Gerace, whom he had never seen. This was a son, born during his early life as an emigrant, from a relationship with a young German schoolteacher, whom he soon abandoned. For several years after the abandonment (the emigrant had moved to America following a short stint in

Germany), the girl-mother had continued to write to him, begging him for material help, because she found herself without work, and seeking to move him with marvelous descriptions of the child. But the emigrant was himself so wretched at the time that he stopped answering the letters, until the young woman, discouraged, stopped writing. And when, returning to Procida aged and without heirs, Antonio tried to find her, he learned that she had died, leaving the child, now around sixteen, in Germany.

Antonio Gerace then summoned that son to Procida, to finally give him his own name and his own inheritance. And so he who was to become my father disembarked on the island of Procida, dressed in rags like a gypsy (I learned later).

He must have had a hard life. And his childish heart must have been nourished on rancor not only toward his unknown father but also toward all the other innocent Procidans. Maybe, too, by some act or behavior, they affronted his irascible pride from the start, and forever. Certainly, on the island, his indifferent and offensive manner made him universally hated. With his father, who tried to win his affection, the boy was aloof to the point of cruelty.

The only person on the island he saw was the Amalfitano. It was some time since the latter had given entertainments or parties, and he lived isolated in his blindness, surly and proud, refusing to receive those who sought him out and pushing away with his stick those who approached him on the street. His tall, melancholy figure had become detested by everyone.

His house opened again to only one person: the son of Antonio Gerace, who formed such a close friendship with him that he spent every day in his company, as if the Amalfitano, and not Antonio Gerace, were his real father. And the Amalfitano devoted to him an exclusive and tyrannical affection: it seemed that he couldn't live a day without him. If the son was late in his daily visit, the Amalfitano went out to meet him, sitting at the end of the street to wait. And, unable to see if he was finally coming, in his blind man's anxiety he would every so often call out his name, in a hoarse voice that seemed already to come from the grave. If passersby answered that Gerace's son wasn't there, he would throw some coins and banknotes on the ground, haphazardly and with contempt, so that, thus paid, they would go and summon him. And if they returned later to say that they hadn't found him at home, he had them search the entire island, even unleashing his dogs in the hunt. In his life now there was nothing else: either being with his only friend or waiting for him. Two years later, when he died, he left him the house on Procida.

Not long afterward, Antonio Gerace died: and the son, who some months earlier had married an orphan from Massa, moved to the Amalfitano's house with his young, pregnant bride. He was then about nineteen, and the wife not yet eighteen. It was the first time, in almost three centuries since the palazzo was built, that a woman had lived within its walls.

The farmers remained in my grandfather's house and on his land, and are still tenants there today.

NORMAN LEWIS

From

NAPLES '44 (1978)

October 25

IT IS ASTONISHING to witness the struggles of this city so shattered, so starved, so deprived of all those things that justify a city's existence, to adapt itself to a collapse into conditions which must resemble life in the Dark Ages. People camp out like Bedouins in deserts of brick. There is little food, little water, no salt, no soap. A lot of Neapolitans have lost their possessions, including most of their clothing, in the bombings, and I have seen some strange combinations of garments about the streets, including a man in an old dinner-jacket, knickerbockers and army boots, and several women in lacy confections that might have been made up from curtains. There are no cars but carts by the hundred, and a few antique coaches such as barouches and phaetons drawn by lean horses. Today at Posilippo I stopped to watch the methodical dismemberment of a stranded German half-track by a number of youths who were streaming away from it like leaf-cutter ants, carrying pieces of metal of all shapes and sizes. Fifty yards away a well-dressed lady with a feather in her hat squatted to milk a goat. At the water's edge below, two fishermen had roped together several doors salvaged from the ruins, piled their gear on these and were about to go fishing. Inexplicably no boats are allowed out, but nothing is said in the proclamation about rafts. Everyone improvises and adapts.

Tonight I dined for the first time in a civilian house at

the invitation of a Signora Gentile recently released by a member of the section from the Filangieri gaol, where with a number of other women she had been imprisoned by the partisans on vague charges of collaboration. Here the mood was one of escapism, even of nostalgic frivolity. Our friends had made a huge effort to cast out of mind the unpleasantness of the immediate past. Several beautiful women were present – one in a blouse made from a Union Jack; all the old-style airs and graces banished by Mussolini were back again. The men kissed the ladies' hands, called each other 'egregious sir', and everybody used the polite form of address *lei* instead of the Fascists' forthright Roman *voi*.

We ate wurst, sipped schnapps, drank wine from glasses of the right shape and colour, somebody strummed a mandolin, and we talked about Naples and its traditions – the city that had ignored and finally overcome all its conquerors, dedicated entirely and everlastingly to the sweet things of life. Other wars were mentioned in passing, but this one was not. Neither were politics, Mussolini, food shortages or the rumoured outbreak of typhus.

All too soon the pleasant unreality of the evening was over, brought to an end by the curfew. As we were about to leave our hostess drew me aside and, showing a little hesitancy, said she had a favour to ask. She had a German soldier, she said, buried in her garden, and wondered what could be done about it. The story was that about two days before our arrival, when the partisans and the Germans were fighting on the streets, a German chased by armed Italians had knocked on the door and asked her to shelter him in the house. This she had felt unable to do, and next day, finding the soldier's body lying in the road outside, she had dragged it into the garden, taken a spade and buried it. What she was hoping now was that someone could be found to help in the task of digging this corpse up and smuggling it away, because it occurred to her that one day – perhaps even in years to come – she might want to sell the house, and she could imagine an embarrassing situation arising if the buyer happened to find a body in the garden. I told her that I could inform whatever authority it was that dealt with this kind of thing and leave it to them. She seemed disappointed, and said she wanted the thing done discreetly, and perhaps it would be better to leave things as they were. A mysterious business.

October 28

Neapolitans take their sex lives very seriously indeed. A woman called Lola, whom I met at the dinner-party given by Signora Gentile, arrived at HQ with some denunciation which went into the wastepaper basket as soon as her back was turned. She then asked if I could help her. It turned out she had taken a lover who is a captain in the RASC, but as he speaks no single word of Italian, communication can only be carried on by signs, and this gives rise to misunderstanding. Would I agree to interpret for them and settle certain basic matters?

Captain Frazer turned out to be a tall and handsome man some years Lola's junior. Having his hands on military supplies, he could keep her happy with unlimited quantities of our white bread, which for Neapolitans in general – who have been deprived of decent bread for two years – has come to symbolise all the luxury and the abundance of peace. She was also much impressed by his appearance. The Captain was a striking figure. His greatcoat had been specially made for him and it was the most handsome coat I had ever seen. His hat was pushed up in front and straightened with some kind of stiffener. This, although Frazer worked at a desk, made him look like an officer in a crack German SS formation. She wanted to know all about his marital status and he hers, and they lied to each other to their hearts' content while I kept a straight face and interpreted.

She asked me to mention to him in as tactful a way as possible that comment had been caused among her neighbours because he never called on her during the day. Conjugal visits at midday are *de rigueur* in Naples. This I explained, and Frazer promised to do better.

When the meeting was over we went off for a drink, and he confided to me that something was worrying him too. On inspecting her buttocks he had found them covered with hundreds of pinpoint marks, some clearly very small scars. What could they be? I put his mind at rest. These were the marks left by *iniezione reconstituenti*: injections which are given in many of the pharmacies of Naples and which many middle-class women receive daily to keep their sexual powers at their peak. Frequently the needle is not too clean, hence the scars.

She had made him understand by gestures one could only shudderingly imagine that her late husband although half-starved, and even when in the early stages of tuberculosis from which he died – never failed to have intercourse with her less than six times a night. She also had a habit, which terrified Frazer, of keeping an eye on the bedside clock while he performed. I recommended him to drink – as the locals did – marsala with the yolks of eggs stirred into it, and to wear a medal of San Rocco, patron of *coitus reservatus*, which could be had in any religious-supplies shop.

This seemed the moment, as Lola had offered her services as an informant, to check on her background in the dossiers section on the top floor of the Questura. It appeared from her *fasciolo* that since the death of her husband she had been

428

the mistress of a Fascist hierarch, and there were sardonic references in typical police style to other episodes of her love-life. It seemed extraordinary to me that a Fascist leading light could do nothing to shield his private life from invasion by the police.

November 1

The miserable news is that Counter-Intelligence funds are to be reduced to 400 lire – £1 per week per section member. The meanness impelling this decision leaves us stunned. Most of us have up to a dozen contacts prepared to devote their time to our interests, and this wretched sum – paid in occupation money which costs nothing to print – is all that is available to compensate them. This announcement followed closely on the heels of the tidings that other ranks would be paid an extra nine shillings per head to spend on Christmas festivities. What a peasant army this is!

Actually, although our paymasters have no way of knowing it, the money won't make any difference. The most dedicated informant, like the most devoted lover, rises above thoughts of monetary inducement to give what he has to give. What would make our task easier and give us a better conscience would be to offer these people who work for us, not money, but a little food. In large units – particularly American ones – it seems easy enough to smuggle rations out, and most soldiers who are invited into Italian homes find some way of taking the occasional tin of provisions with them. In a unit like ours of only thirteen men, rationing is absolutely cut and dried, and there are no extras to go astray. If anything happens to be left over at the end of a meal, our two servants see to it that no trace of it remains after they clear away. In this way, wherever we go, we go empty-handed.

Lattarullo called with a long whispered recital of new enormities on the part of the operators of the black market. He mentioned that the special Squadra Nucleo, organised by our vigilant Questore to act as a spearhead in the fight against corruption, had just been able to resolve a little problem for one of Naples's leading surgeons – who was already well known to us. It seemed that the doctor had managed to acquire a Fiat Mille Cinque-Cento, which turned out to have been stolen. In the ordinary way the regular Pubblica Sicurezza would have dealt with this predicament at a cost to the doctor of about 50,000 lire. As it is, he had the new Squadra to deal with, and has had to pay heavily for their incorruptibility – in fact 200,000 lire.

Lattarullo looked even weaker with hunger today than usual, and swayed from the waist, eyes closed, even when sitting down. After our chat I decided to take him for a meal to one of the side-street restaurants that have opened in the past few days.

We walked out together and faced this city which is literally tumbling about our ears. Everywhere there were piles of masonry, brought down by the air-raids, to be negotiated. Every few yards Lattarullo had to stop to gather breath and strength. When we tried to take a short cut through a familiar *vico* we found it freshly blocked by the collapse of tenements and filled with rubble to a depth of twenty feet. There was a terrible stench of shattered drains and possibly something worse, and the Middle Ages had returned to display all their deformities, their diseases, and their desperate trickeries. Hunchbacks are considered lucky, so they were everywhere, scuttling underfoot, and a buyer of the lottery tickets they offered for sale touched or stroked their humps as he made his purchase. A great collection of idiots and cretins included children propped against walls nodding their big heads. A

430

legless little bundle had been balanced behind a saucer into which a few lire notes and a sweet had been thrown. In a matter of two hundred yards, I was approached three times by child-pimps, and Lattarullo, appropriately enough, was offered a cut-price coffin. The only food shops open were bakers, but they sold no bread – only sugary sweets: *torrone* and marzipan, all made with sugar stolen from the Allies, and fetching 30 lire for a tiny cube. We were stopped at a bottleneck caused by a collapsed building in the Vico Chiatamone where a sanitary post had been set up, and here every passer-by was sprayed with a white powder against the typhus.

We found the restaurant and took our seats among the middle-class patrons, who kept their overcoats on against the cold. All the coats were made from our stolen blankets. A choking deodorant disinfectant burning in a brazier set everybody coughing, but failed to cloak the smell of sewers seeping up through the flagstones.

The ritual in this restaurant is for a waiter to appear and pass through the tables carrying on a dish what Lattarullo calls 'the show-fish', for the customers to inspect with murmurs of admiration. This had a good-looking head, but the body had already been cut up in portions and was therefore unidentifiable. As usual, there was a trick in it. Lattarullo insisted on examining the fish and pointed out to me that the body didn't match the head, and from its triangular backbone evidently belonged to the dogfish family, which most people avoided eating if they could. The other recommended item on the menu was veal, Milanese style, very white but dry-looking, which the waiter, under pressure, admitted to being horse. We settled for macaroni.

No attempt was made to isolate the customers from the street. Ragged, hawk-eyed boys – the celebrated *scugnizzi* of Naples – wandered among the tables ready to dive on any crust that appeared to be overlooked, or to snatch up leftovers before they could be thrown to the cats. Once again I couldn't help noticing the intelligence – almost the intellectuality – of their expressions. No attempt was made to chase them away. They were simply treated as nonexistent. The customers had withdrawn from the world while they communed with their food. An extraordinary cripple was dragged in, balancing face downwards on a trolley, only a few inches from the ground, arms and legs thrust out in spider fashion. Nobody took his eyes off his food for one second to glance down at him. This youth could not use his hands. One of the *scugnizzi* hunted down a piece of bread for him, turned his head sideways to stuff it between his teeth, and he was dragged out.

Suddenly five or six little girls between the ages of nine and twelve appeared in the doorway. They wore hideous straight black uniforms buttoned under their chins, and black boots and stockings, and their hair had been shorn short, prison-style. They were all weeping, and as they clung to each other and groped their way towards us, bumping into chairs and tables, I realised they were all blind. Tragedy and despair had been thrust upon us, and would not be shut out. I expected the indifferent diners to push back their plates, to get up and hold out their arms, but nobody moved. Forkfuls of food were thrust into open mouths, the rattle of conversation continued, nobody saw the tears.

Lattarullo explained that these little girls were from an orphanage on the Vomero, where he had heard – and he made a face – conditions were very bad. They had been brought down here, he found out, on a half-day's outing by an attendant who seemed unable or unwilling to stop them from being lured away by the smell of food.

The experience changed my outlook. Until now I had clung to the comforting belief that human beings eventually come to terms with pain and sorrow. Now I understood I was wrong, and like Paul I suffered a conversion – but to pessimism. These little girls, any one of whom could be my daughter, came into the restaurant weeping, and they were weeping when they were led away. I knew that, condemned to everlasting darkness, hunger and loss, they would weep on incessantly. They would never recover from their pain, and I would never recover from the memory of it.

ELENA FERRANTE

From

MY BRILLIANT
FRIEND (2011)

Translated by Ann Goldstein

3.

LILA APPEARED IN my life in first grade and immediately impressed me because she was very bad. In that class we were all a little bad, but only when the teacher, Maestra Oliviero, couldn't see us. Lila, on the other hand, was always bad. Once she tore up some blotting paper into little pieces, dipped the pieces one by one in the inkwell, and then fished them out with her pen and threw them at us. I was hit twice in the hair and once on my white collar. The teacher yelled, as she knew how to do, in a voice like a needle, long and pointed, which terrorized us, and ordered her to go and stand behind the blackboard in punishment. Lila didn't obey and didn't even seem frightened; she just kept throwing around pieces of inky paper. So Maestra Oliviero, a heavy woman who seemed very old to us, though she couldn't have been much over forty, came down from the desk, threatening her. The teacher stumbled, it wasn't clear on what, lost her balance, and fell, striking her face against the corner of a desk. She lay on the floor as if dead.

What happened right afterward I don't remember, I remember only the dark bundle of the teacher's motionless body, and Lila staring at her with a serious expression.

I have in my mind so many incidents of this type. We lived in a world in which children and adults were often wounded, blood flowed from the wounds, they festered, and sometimes people died. One of the daughters of Signora

Assunta, the fruit and vegetable seller, had stepped on a nail and died of tetanus. Signora Spagnuolo's youngest child had died of croup. A cousin of mine, at the age of twenty, had gone one morning to move some rubble and that night was dead, crushed, the blood pouring out of his ears and mouth. My mother's father had been killed when he fell from a scaffolding at a building site. The father of Signor Peluso was missing an arm, the lathe had caught him unawares. The sister of Giuseppina, Signor Peluso's wife, had died of tuberculosis at twenty-two. The oldest son of Don Achille – I had never seen him, and yet I seemed to remember him – had gone to war and died twice: drowned in the Pacific Ocean, then eaten by sharks. The entire Melchiorre family had died clinging to each other, screaming with fear, in a bombardment. Old Signorina Clorinda had died inhaling gas instead of air. Giannino, who was in fourth grade when we were in first, had died one day because he had come across a bomb and touched it. Luigina, with whom we had played in the courtyard, or maybe not, she was only a name, had died of typhus. Our world was like that, full of words that killed: croup, tetanus, typhus, gas, war, lathe, rubble, work, bombardment, bomb, tuberculosis, infection. With these words and those years I bring back the many fears that accompanied me all my life.

You could also die of things that seemed normal. You could die, for example, if you were sweating and then drank cold water from the tap without first bathing your wrists: you'd break out in red spots, you'd start coughing, and be unable to breathe. You could die if you ate black cherries and didn't spit out the pits. You could die if you chewed American gum and inadvertently swallowed it. You could die if you banged your temple. The temple, in particular, was a fragile place, we were all careful about it. Being hit with a stone could do it, and throwing stones was the norm. When we left school a gang of boys from the countryside, led by a kid called Enzo or Enzuccio, who was one of the children of Assunta the fruit and vegetable seller, began to throw rocks at us. They were angry because we were smarter than them. When the rocks came at us we ran away, except Lila, who kept walking at her regular pace and sometimes even stopped. She was very good at studying the trajectory of the stones and dodging them with an easy move that today I would call elegant. She had an older brother and maybe she had learned from him, I don't know, I also had brothers, but they were younger than me and from them I had learned nothing. Still, when I realized that she had stayed behind, I stopped to wait for her, even though I was scared.

Already then there was something that kept me from abandoning her. I didn't know her well; we had never spoken to each other, although we were constantly competing, in class and outside it. But in a confused way I felt that if I ran away with the others I would leave with her something of mine that she would never give back.

At first I stayed hidden, around a corner, and leaned out to see if Lila was coming. Then, since she wouldn't budge, I forced myself to rejoin her; I handed her stones, and even threw some myself. But I did it without conviction: I did many things in my life without conviction; I always felt slightly detached from my own actions. Lila, on the other hand, had, from a young age – I can't say now precisely if it was so at six or seven, or when we went together up the stairs that led to Don Achille's and were eight, almost nine – the characteristic of absolute determination. Whether she was gripping the tricolor shaft of the pen or a stone or the handrail on the dark stairs, she communicated the idea that whatever came next – thrust the pen with a precise motion into the wood of the desk, dispense inky bullets, strike the boys from the countryside, climb the stairs to Don Achille's door – she would do without hesitation.

The gang came from the railroad embankment, stocking up on rocks from the trackbed. Enzo, the leader, was a dangerous child, with very short blond hair and pale eyes; he was at least three years older than us, and had repeated a year. He threw small, sharp-edged rocks with great accuracy, and Lila waited for his throws to demonstrate how she evaded them, making him still angrier, and responded with throws that were just as dangerous. Once we hit him in the right calf, and I say we because I had handed Lila a flat stone with jagged edges. The stone slid over Enzo's skin like a razor, leaving a red stain that immediately gushed blood. The child looked at his wounded leg. I have him before my eyes: between thumb and index finger he held the rock that he was about to throw, his arm was raised to throw it, and yet he stopped, bewildered. The boys under his command also looked incredulously at the blood. Lila, however, manifested not the least satisfaction in the outcome of the throw and bent over to pick up another stone. I grabbed her by the arm; it was the first contact between us, an abrupt frightened contact. I felt that the gang would get more ferocious and I wanted to retreat. But there wasn't time. Enzo, in spite of his bleeding calf, came out of his stupor and threw the rock in his hand. I was still holding on to Lila when the rock hit her in the head and knocked her away from me. A second later she was lying on the sidewalk with a gash in her forehead.

4.

Blood. In general it came from wounds only after horrible curses and disgusting obscenities had been exchanged. That was the standard procedure. My father, though he seemed to me a good man, hurled continuous insults and threats if someone didn't deserve, as he said, to be on the face of the earth. He especially had it in for Don Achille. He always had something to accuse him of, and sometimes I put my hands over my ears in order not to be too disturbed by his brutal words. When he spoke of him to my mother he called him 'your cousin' but my mother denied that blood tie (there was a very distant relationship) and added to the insults. Their anger frightened me, I was frightened above all by the thought that Don Achille might have ears so sensitive that he could hear insults even from far away. I was afraid that he might come and murder them.

The sworn enemy of Don Achille, however, was not my father but Signor Peluso, a very good carpenter who was always broke, because he gambled away everything he earned in the back room of the Bar Solara. Peluso was the father of our classmate Carmela, of Pasquale, who was older, and of two others, children poorer than us, with whom Lila and I sometimes played, and who in school and outside always tried to steal our things, a pen, an eraser, the *cotognata*, so that they went home covered with bruises because we'd hit them.

The times we saw him, Signor Peluso seemed to us the image of despair. On the one hand he lost everything gambling and on the other he was criticized in public because he was no longer able to feed his family. For obscure reasons he attributed his ruin to Don Achille. He charged him with having taken by stealth, as if his shadowy body were a magnet, all the tools for his carpentry work, which made the shop useless. He accused him of having taken the shop itself, and transforming it into a grocery store. For years I imagined the pliers, the saw, the tongs, the hammer, the vise, and thousands and thousands of nails sucked up like a swarm of metal into the matter that made up Don Achille. For years I saw his body – a coarse body, heavy with a mixture of materials – emitting in a swarm salami, provolone, mortadella, lard, and prosciutto.

These things had happened in the dark ages. Don Achille had supposedly revealed himself in all his monstrous nature before we were born. *Before.* Lila often used that formulation. But she didn't seem to care as much about what had happened before us – events that were in general obscure, and about which the adults either were silent or spoke with great reticence – as about the fact that there really had been a before. It was this which at the time left her puzzled and occasionally even made her nervous. When we became friends she spoke so much of that absurd thing – *before us* – that she ended up passing on her nervousness to me. It was the long, very long, period when we didn't exist, that period when Don Achille had showed himself to everyone for what he was: an evil being of uncertain animal-mineral physiognomy, who – it seemed – sucked blood from others while never losing any himself, maybe it wasn't even possible to scratch him.

We were in second grade, perhaps, and still hadn't spoken to each other, when the rumor spread that right in front of the Church of the Holy Family, right after Mass, Signor Peluso had started screaming furiously at Don Achille. Don Achille had left his older son Stefano, his daughter Pinuccia, Alfonso, who was our age, and his wife, and, appearing for a moment in his most hair-raising form, had hurled himself at Peluso, picked him up, thrown him against a tree in the public gardens, and left him there, barely conscious, with blood coming out of innumerable wounds in his head and everywhere, and the poor man able to say merely: help.

5

I feel no nostalgia for our childhood: it was full of violence. Every sort of thing happened, at home and outside, every day, but I don't recall having ever thought that the life we had there was particularly bad. Life was like that, that's all, we grew up with the duty to make it difficult for others before they made it difficult for us. Of course, I would have liked the nice manners that the teacher and the priest preached, but I felt that those ways were not suited to our neighborhood, even if you were a girl. The women fought among themselves more than the men, they pulled each other's hair, they hurt each other. To cause pain was a disease. As a child I imagined tiny, almost invisible animals that arrived in the neighborhood at night, they came from the ponds, from the abandoned train cars beyond the embankment, from the stinking grasses called *fetienti*, from the frogs, the salamanders, the flies, the rocks, the dust, and entered the water and the food and the air, making our mothers, our grandmothers as angry as starving dogs. They were more severely infected than the men, because while men were always getting furious, they calmed down in the end; women, who appeared to be silent, acquiescent, when they were angry flew into a rage that had no end.

Lila was deeply affected by what had happened to Melina Cappuccio, a relative of her mother's. And I, too. Melina lived in the same building as my family, we on the second floor, she on the third. She was only a little over thirty and had six children, but to us she seemed an old woman. Her husband was the same age; he unloaded crates at the fruit and vegetable market. I recall him as short and broad, but handsome, with a proud face. One night he came out of the house as usual and died, perhaps murdered, perhaps of weariness. The funeral was very bitter; the whole

443

neighborhood went, including my parents, and Lila's parents. Then time passed and something happened to Melina. On the outside she remained the same, a gaunt woman with a large nose, her hair already gray, a shrill voice that at night called her children from the window, by name, the syllables drawn out by an angry despair: Aaa-daaa, Miii-chè. At first she was much helped by Donato Sarratore, who lived in the apartment right above hers, on the fourth and top floor. Donato was diligent in his attendance at the Church of the Holy Family and as a good Christian he did a lot for her, collecting money, used clothes, and shoes, settling Antonio, the oldest son, in the auto-repair shop of Gorresio, an acquaintance of his. Melina was so grateful that her gratitude became, in her desolate woman's heart, love, passion. It wasn't clear if Sarratore was ever aware of it. He was a friendly man but very serious – home, church, and job. He worked on a train crew for the state railroad, and had a decent salary on which he supported his wife, Lidia, and five children; the oldest was called Nino. When he wasn't traveling on the Naples–Paola route he devoted himself to fixing this or that in the house, he did the shopping, took the youngest child out in the carriage. These things were very unusual in the neighborhood. It occurred to no one that Donato was generous in that way to lighten the burdens of his wife. No: all the neighborhood men, my father in the lead, considered him a womanish man, even more so because he wrote poems and read them willingly to anyone. It didn't occur even to Melina. The widow preferred to think that, because of his gentle spirit, he was put upon by his wife, and so she decided to do battle against Lidia Sarratore to free him and let him join her permanently. The war that followed at first seemed funny; it was discussed in my house and elsewhere with malicious laughter. Lidia would hang out the sheets fresh from the laundry and Melina climbed up on the windowsill and dirtied them with a reed whose tip she had charred in the fire; Lidia passed under her windows and she spit on her head or emptied buckets of dirty water on her; Lidia made noise during the day walking above her, with her unruly children, and she banged the floor mop against the ceiling all night. Sarratore tried by every means to make peace, but he was too sensitive, too polite. As their vindictiveness increased, the two women began to insult each other if they met on the street or the stairs: harsh, fierce sounds. It was then that they began to frighten me. One of the many terrible scenes of my childhood begins with the shouts of Melina and Lidia, with the insults they hurl from the windows and then on the stairs; it continues with my mother rushing to our door, opening it, and looking out, followed by us children; and ends with the image, for me still unbearable, of the two neighbors rolling down the stairs, entwined, and Melina's head hitting the floor of the landing, a few inches from my shoes, like a white melon that has slipped from your hand.

It's hard to say why at the time we children took the part of Lidia Sarratore. Maybe because she had regular features and blond hair. Or because Donato was hers and we had understood that Melina wanted to take him away from her. Or because Melina's children were ragged and dirty, while Lidia's were washed, well groomed, and the oldest, Nino, who was a few years older than us, was handsome, and we liked him. Lila alone favored Melina, but she never explained why. She said only, once, that if Lidia Sarratore ended up murdered she deserved it, and I thought that it was partly because she was mean in her heart and partly because she and Melina were distant relatives.

One day we were coming home from school, four or five

girls. With us was Marisa Sarratore, who usually joined us not because we liked her but because we hoped that, through her, we might meet her older brother, that is to say Nino. It was she who first noticed Melina. The woman was walking slowly from one side of the *stradone*, the wide avenue that ran through the neighborhood, to the other, carrying a paper bag in one hand from which, with the other, she was taking something and eating it. Marisa pointed to her, calling her 'the whore,' without rancor, but because she was repeating the phrase that her mother used at home. Lila, although she was shorter and very thin, immediately slapped her so hard that she knocked her down: ruthless, as she usually was on occasions of violence, no yelling before or after, no word of warning, cold and determined, not even widening her eyes.

First I went to the aid of Marisa, who was crying, and helped her get up, then I turned to see what Lila was doing. She had left the sidewalk and was going toward Melina, crossing the street without paying attention to the passing trucks. I saw in her, in her posture more than in her face, something that disturbed me and is still hard to define, so for now I'll put it like this: she was moving, cutting across the street, a small, dark, nervous figure, she was acting with her usual determination, she was firm. Firm in what her mother's relative was doing, firm in the pain, firm in silence as a statue is firm. A follower. One with Melina, who was holding in her palm the dark soft soap she had just bought in Don Carlo's cellar, and with her other hand was taking some and eating it.

ACKNOWLEDGMENTS

CORRADO ALVARO: Chapters 1–2 from *Gente in Aspromonte*, Garzanti, Milan, 1930. *Revolt in Aspromonte*, translated by Frances Frenaye, 1962. The Estate of Frances Frenaye. VITALIANO BRANCATI: 'Il nonno' © Mondadori Libri S.p.A., Milano. Translation copyright © by Gregory Conti. Reprinted with permission. VINCENZO CONSOLO: From *Il sorriso dell'ignoto marinaio*, published by Giulio Einaudi editore (Turin, 1976). Reproduced with permission from the Italian Literary Agency. From *The Smile of the Unknown Mariner*, translated by Joseph Farrell, Carcanet Press, Manchester, 1994. NORMAN DOUGLAS: 'Old Morano' from *Old Calabria*. Reprinted with permission from The Society of Authors as the Literary Representative of the Estate of Norman Douglas. ELENA FERRANTE: Extract from *L'amica geniale*. Copyright © 2011 by Edizioni E/O. First Publication 2012 by Europa Editions. JOHANN WOLFGANG VON GOETHE: Extract from *Italian Journey* translated by W. H. Auden and Elizabeth Mayer. Curtis Brown UK. NICOLA LAGIOIA: From *La ferocia*. Copyright © 2014 by Giulio Einaudi editore s.p.a., Torino. First Publication 2017 by Europa Editions. GIUSEPPE TOMASI DI LAMPEDUSA: 'La Sirena' from *I Racconti*. Copyright © Giangiacomo Feltrinelli Editore, Milano, 1961, 1988. All rights reserved. First published by Giangiacomo Feltrinelli Editore in 1961. Reprinted with permission. Reprinted with the kind permission of Alma Books. Translation by Stephen Twilley from *The Professor and the Siren*, New York Review of Books, 2014. NYRB/The Wylie Agency. CARLO LEVI: From the Italian edition of *Cristo si è fermato a Eboli* by Carlo Levi in English language (taken from the officially translated version by Frances Frenaye). © 1945, 1963, 1975, 2010 and 2014 Giulio Einaudi editore s.p.a., Torino. *Christ Stopped at Eboli*, translation by Frances Frenaye, Farrar Straus & Giroux and Penguin Books. NORMAN LEWIS: Extract from *Naples '44*. The Estate of Norman Lewis. RCW Literary Agency. CURZIO MALAPARTE: *La Pelle* © 2010 Adelphi Edizioni S.p.A. Milano. (First published 1949.) Translation by David Moore, New York Review of Books. DACIA MARAINI: *Bagheria* © 1993, 1996 RCS Libri & Grandi Opere S.p.A., Milano; © 1997–2015 RCS Libri S.p.A., Milano; © 2016 Rizzoli Libri S.p.A. / BUR Rizzoli; © 2018 Mondadori Libri S.p.A. / BUR Rizzoli. Reprinted with permission. *Bagheria* by Dacia Maraini, Dick Kitto & Elspeth Spottiswood (trs), Peter Owen Publishers, UK. Reprinted

447